MW00974156

Advanc

"*Her: The Flame Tree* is a beautiful novel, rich with evocations of natural setting in coastal Vietnam; remembered action going back more than a hundred years, and characters both extraordinary and poignantly ordinary, developed by layer upon layer of stories.

The primary narrator, the Vietnamese-American Minh 'as a young writer looking for material,' follows the thread from a magazine article about a centenarian head eunuch (d. 1968) to his adopted daughter Miss Phượng. From her wavering memory, steadied by places and objects they visit, Minh elicits opening stories the old man told about his life that also evoke his perspective on the colorful ceremonies of a royal dynasty as it dissolved and his asexual love for an eventually high-ranking concubine Ân-Phi.

These lead into Miss Phượng's stories of her own life: her upbringing by her loving adoptive father as a Vietnamese-French orphan, not knowing her origins; the arrival of another young American in the late 1960s when she is a young woman, in search of the origins of his deceased lover, also Vietnamese-French; and his and Phượng's discovery of the girls' shared parenthood, as they fall into a love that's also for the dead twin.

The fairy-tale-like separation in infancy of twin girls and their reunification at least in story by a ruby phoenix pendant is grounded by this family of lives painfully conditioned before birth by the gender customs of a culture and the decades of colonial and post-colonial war around them. These also belong to the long-suppressed stories Minh presents so they might not be lost."

—Elizabeth Harris, judge and author of *Mayhem: Three Lives of a Woman*

"Early in Khanh Ha's latest novel *Her: The Flame Tree*, the author describes a book made of delicate leaves of gold. Such a volume would be ideal to record this shimmering and often tender tale of love, loss, and memory."

—Steve Evans, author of *The Marriage of True Minds*

Also by Khanh Ha

Novels

Flesh (2012)

The Demon Who Peddled Longing (2014)

Mrs. Rossi's Dream (2019)

Short Story Collections

A Mother's Tale & Stories (Winner of the C&R Press Fiction Award 2020)

All the Rivers Flow into the Sea & Stories (Winner of the EastOver Prize for Fiction 2021)

Her: The Flame Tree

Winner of the Gival Press Novel Award

Khanh Ha

Gival Press

Arlington, Virginia

Published by Gival Press, an imprint of Gival Press, LLC.

Gival Press, LLC
P. O. Box 3812
Arlington, VA 22203
www.givalpress.com

First edition
ISBN: 978-1-940724-45-4
eISBN: 978-1-940724-46-1
Library of Congress Control Number: 2023942544

Front cover art: © Natali22206
Back cover art: © Quang Bui Duc
Book Design by Ken Schellenberg

For my mother

and my sister H.L. Thuy

one

A black-and-white photograph fell out of the novel. April picked up the photograph and asked, "Who is she, Minh?"

I looked up from my desk. "Someone in the past, from Vietnam."

My wife turned the photograph over. There was nothing written on the back, I knew. "Your ex-girlfriend?"

"No, no, she's twice my age."

My wife, unconvinced, frowned. "She looks young and un-Vietnamese."

"She's half French, half Vietnamese." and,

"What's her name?"

"Phượng."

"*Foong?*"

"Yes. *Foong,*" I said, echoing her accent. "It means the flame tree in Vietnamese."

"Tell me about her."

So I told my beloved wife, a Virginia native, that one day, long ago, when I was a young writer looking for material in the Purple Forbidden City of Huế, I came upon an old Vietnamese magazine article written about a centenarian eunuch of the Imperial Court of Huế. He had died in 1968, two years before I was born. The writer had interviewed the eunuch's adopted daughter. At the end of the article was a small halftone photograph of her. The story had lodged deep in my brain. Months later I realized that it wasn't the story that was haunting me—it was the face in the photograph.

—o—

Phượng.

Dawn or dusk, you could see mottled-brown sandpipers running along the seashore, legs twinkling, looking for food. Twilight falling. I followed their tracks, like twiggy skeletons strewn across the marbled sand until they ended under the frothing waves. One delicate bird stood at the water's edge and gave out a cry.

I often think of Miss Phượng as that sandpiper standing at the edge of the sea, its cry lost in the sound of waves.

two

The sugarcane field was so still in the summer afternoon heat you could hear the rustle of leaves beneath the lull of cicadas.

"Take my hand," Miss Phượng said to me. "Let's get off the blacktop road. Take this dirt trail. It wasn't here—twenty some years ago, that night. Now, you see over there. Those huts in the middle of the field. Where they make syrup and block sugar. There was nothing there back then but sugarcane, this whole field."

Miss Phượng wore sepia cotton pants, the color of the dirt trail. Her short-sleeved shirt was so white its glare made you squint.

"Please tell me your name again. Minh? I hope you will forgive my failing memory. On a good day, I am myself. Let's stop here. Where you can still see the road. Here I found him. Jonathan Edward. He was young. Like you, Minh. I don't remember the year. Perhaps 1965. I was twenty-three. He came here, half the world away, like you. Could be this spot. I'm not sure. But it was here where I held him, sitting right here, cradling his head in my arms, while he died."

three

Miss Phượng met the last concubine of Emperor Tự-Đức when the woman was very old, in the final year of her long life. When the emperor died in 1883, she was only fifteen. She told Miss Phượng she was one hundred and twenty-three now. Small, birdlike, white hair parted in the middle, braided in two small plaits on the sides of her head.

She took Miss Phượng by the hand and led her into the cottage, which sat behind a bamboo hedge in the back of the mausoleum. She served tea from a tiny, blue-flowered pot the size of her hand. The nougats she offered were made of egg whites and brown sugar and chopped nuts. Brittle, they melted quickly in the mouth.

"I used to make them for the emperor," she told Miss Phượng. "A long time ago." Then regarding Miss Phượng, she nodded, "See the banyan out there?"

It dwarfed the cottage with its shade, like an immense pavilion. Miss Phượng traced its tortuous roots to the steps of the concubine's home.

"It was a little tree when I came," the old woman muttered.

"Yes," Miss Phượng said, "trees outlive us. My father had a magnolia planted outside the Trinh Minh Palace during his service as the grand eunuch for the imperial family. He would be three years older than you, Madam, if he still lived."

In the deceased emperor's personal room, the old concubine sat down on the carved rosewood bed. Hunched between the parted panels of the yellow mosquito net, she sat amidst her husband's belongings—the bed, its embroidered mat, the porcelain pillow, the tea, the rice liquor, the areca-nuts and betel leaves and a tiny pot of lime. They were here for him when he returned in spirit.

For one hundred and eight years she replenished them every morning so that when he arrived nothing was missing, nothing was stale. He could read his favorite books. He could write, as was his passion, in his annals, each page of which was a thin leaf of gold. He would find again his gold swords, jade shrubs, his chess men in green and white jade, chopsticks made of *kim-giao* white wood that turned black against any sort of poison. They were arranged there under glass.

Miss Phượng took the old woman's hand and led her out of her haunt, passing candle-lit nooks and corners and the eternally mildewed air of the sunless chambers.

—o—

Miss Phượng thought she heard a baby cry in her sleep. Waking, she opened the window. A breeze blew in across the dark backcourt beyond which lay the flagstone walkway under the shade of Indian almond trees. When was the last time she had heard a baby cry? This house had no nursery, no mother who lulled her child to sleep with her lullaby. But she could still hear it. She knew of superstitions. The indelible belief in animism. An unseen presence dwelling in an odd-looking rock by the roadside where people placed a bowl of rice grains and a stick of incense long gone cold.

She lit the oil lamp and sat down on a cane-backed chair. The smoky odor. The trembling shadows. What day is today? It must be an even day, for there is no electricity. But the helping girl, before leaving for the day, had made sure the oil lamp would be full of kerosene. The matchbox too was packed with ivory-yellow sticks. Out of a terra-cotta crock she picked a preserved persimmon, round, palm-sized, dusted white with flour to keep it dry. Its amber skin was like aged cognac. Hunger made her weak in the limbs. She ate, chewing slowly. She remembered the dark, sweet flavor. What is the name of this fruit? she asked herself.

In the lidded jar of china blue lay slivers of cinnamon bark. Rice paper, already cut into small round pieces the size of a centime, which sometimes had black sesame seeds in them and a fragrance. Her father, wearing his funny-looking eunuch hat with a mouse's tail on the back, had said to her, "Phượng, this is your favorite," as he turned the rice-paper snacks over the fire. Blistered and browned, she ate them and their wholesome aroma would linger on her fingertips.

four

"Chú ơi!"

Over me a haloed figure stood silhouetted against the sun's glare. A girl's face slowly came into focus. I pushed myself up, my back warmed by the stone well in the rising morning heat. Miss Phượng's helping girl looked down at me.

"Why're you sleeping out here?"

"A centipede crawled on my face last night."

The girl slowly sat down on her haunches. The briny air fanned my face.

"So, I turned on the light," I said. "No electricity. Used my Zippo and guess what I saw on the floor? Cockroaches. Bigger than my big toe."

"So? Every house has them, *chú*."

She called me *uncle*. I was only twenty-three. I couldn't tell her age though, for she had the thin body of a child and a woman's face. Her long-lashed eyes brooded. A small mouth that seldom smiled. When she did, a dimpled smile brightened her face. Sometimes she laughed. Fluty laughs. She wore her usual red kerchief around her head, saying, "Auntie Phượng made me wear it, so sand won't get in my hair. So I don't have to wash it every day." She wore her hair past her shoulders, sometimes in two plaits.

"Auntie's not feeling well," she said, "so you can't see her today, *chú*."

"She's not herself today? How could you tell?"

"She couldn't say my name."

"And what's your name?"

She said nothing. I looked at the long salmon burn on her left cheek. "How'd you get burned there?" I asked, pointing to my cheek.

She shook her head.

"Everyone has a name," I said, bringing my knees to my chest, and plugging a cigarette between my lips. She watched me click open my Zippo, her gaze following my hand. I blew the smoke upward. "You remember my name?"

"Yes, *chú*."

"Say it."

"Minh."

"What's yours?" I waited, blowing a series of small rings toward her. I saw her smile.

"That's pretty," she said, lifting her face to see where the rings went.

"You forgot your name? You not yourself today—like Auntie?"

"That's not funny. Auntie has a sickness, I don't."

I tapped the ash and saw it drift toward her. It clung to her peach-yellow blouse in gray specks.

"I'm sorry," I said. "Let me."

She shrank back. "Daddy smokes too," she said, flicking her gaze at me. "But he never takes the cigarettes out of his mouth. He has ashes all over his shirts. They burn holes in them."

I flicked open the Zippo then clicked it shut. "What does he do for a living?"

"He's a fisherman."

She held herself still, hands clutching the hem of her blouse to hold the scattered ashes. She looked up at me and grinned.

"What do I call you?"

"Does it matter?" she said.

"I don't even know how old you are."

"Do you have to know?"

"Sure, if you want to be my friend."

"I have friends. And we don't care how old we are. We never ask."

I rolled my eyes and took a last drag. "It's a different culture here, eh," I said.

"What're you saying? Aren't you Vietnamese too, *chú?*"

"Yeah, I am. But I left Vietnam when I was seven."

"You told Auntie you're from America?"

"I grew up over there."

"How come you speak Vietnamese so well?"

"Because my parents are Vietnamese," I said, grinning, and it seemed to irk her.

"Are you really from America?"

Now I stared at her as I lit another cigarette.

"Prove it," she said.

I was about to tell her to forget it, but then, with a sigh, I dug my driver's license out of my wallet. "Here."

She leaned forward, her eyebrows knitted.

"Can you read English?" I asked.

Her lips stopped moving. She flipped the plastic sleeve, stopped at the next one. Her head canted to one side. "Who is she?"

"My girlfriend."

"She's pretty. Her hair's not yellow though."

"She's a brunette."

"What's her name?"

"Do you have to know?"

She pushed away my hand. "You're mean," she said sharply. "I hate you."

I left her and went into the lodging house. When I came back out, holding a toothbrush, she was standing near a wooden table that sat under the eaves of the rear veranda. On the table was a brass pail. It was half-full with well water. A tin can floated in it. I dipped the water with the can, rinsed my mouth, gargling, and brushed my teeth. With the water left in the pail, I washed my hair.

"You don't have long hair like me. Why waste water?"

"I got sand in my hair," I said, combing its wet strands back with my fingers. "I was down on the beach last night. So windy. You should wash your hair every day too."

"Easy for you to say, *chú*. Clean water here is treasured like rice to every family."

"Where'd you get your water?"

"From a public well." She glanced toward the lodging house's well. "It has a pump like that one and it's always crowded there. I go there very early in the morning, but not this morning."

As I wiped my face with my hand, I could see a disturbed look in her eyes. Then she stamped her foot.

"What's wrong?" I said.

"You didn't ask me why I didn't go to the well this morning."

"Why didn't you go?"

She pointed at the empty pail. "Where'd you get the water from?"

"From that well. The landlord, he always leaves a pailful on the table. Every morning."

"You want another pail, *chú?*"

"Um, yes. I'm thinking of washing myself. It's getting hot."

"Try the pump. See if you can get any water."

Suddenly I laughed. At first she just looked at me, sullen. Then she laughed a small, clear laugh. I knew then why she didn't go to the public well.

"Guess I can't wash myself until we get the electricity back, eh? Such a shame they don't have a winch for the well. If you can't use the electric pump during the outage, you can haul water by hand with a crank. Next time bring a bucket and I'll get you water from the well here to take home. No waiting in line."

"Why are you so kind, *chú?*"

Her sourness piqued me. "Haven't you been around nice people?" The tone of my voice caused her to avert her eyes.

"You guessed wrong, *chú*. People here are nice. Daddy is nice, very nice."

"And Mom?"

She gave me a dark look. "Just Daddy," she said finally.

"What about Mom?"

Her eyelashes batted.

"Where is she?"

"Daddy said never talk about her. Said he doesn't know her."

The way she rushed the words kept me from asking further questions. I glanced at the empty pail. "Guess I'll be heading into town later on. At least they have electricity there."

"It'll be back on before evening, *chú*. Around here, nobody likes even days."

"Now I know. I'd better stock up water and wash myself on odd days then."

She unknotted her kerchief and knotted it again. It fluttered in the breeze coming in steadily now from the sea. "I must get going," she said, opening the safety pin on her blouse's front pocket. She took out a wad of money in rolled-up bills and counted them. Nodding, she stuffed them back into her pocket and fastened it with the pin. "I'm going to the market. You want anything there, *chú?*"

"Why're you so kind?"

"*Chú!*" She stomped her foot.

"Can you get me two packs of cigarettes?" I took out my wallet. "I wonder if..."

"They have the kind of cigarettes you smoke, *chú.*"

"How d'you know what kind I smoke?"

"I saw the pack."

I shook my head as I placed the money in her hand. "Do you cook?"

She didn't answer as she carefully added my bills to her bundle of cash. Her long, tapered fingers had dirt under the nails, some bitten down. I wondered what kind of help she provided Miss Phượng. Running errands. Cleaning the house, maybe. But cooking? She had a stick-thin body. A teenager, or perhaps a woman already. She was fastening the safety pin, smoothing the front of her blouse. I couldn't help noticing her small breasts.

"I cook, *chú.* Are you surprised? I cook for Daddy, for Auntie."

"You have time?"

"I make time stand still."

"Really?"

"When Daddy comes home from the sea, he's too tired. He's out to sea before sunrise, back at sunset. Well, you know how long each day is for a fisherman, *chú?*"

"I'm beginning to know."

"I help Auntie during the day. I take care of Daddy in the evening."

"Where is Mom?" I asked again.

"She's not with us."

The girl crossed the back court, passed the well and slipped down the dirt path overgrown with cogon grass so tall it hid her from view. She reappeared walking on the sand where patches of spider flowers bloomed yellow. Her figure grew smaller as she crossed the pumpkin patch, the pumpkins bright orange against the glare of white sand.

five

"The sight of red country figs always mesmerized me," Miss Phượng told me. We were standing in front of her house watching a bee crawl into a fig through a round opening at its tip. After a moment the bee's hind legs appeared as it backed out of the fig. With a twist it turned and flew off.

Miss Phượng watched the bee's flight. Long lashes shaded her eyes. Her curly hair shone in the sun as I looked at her face. Then she dropped her gaze.

Just as with her helping girl, I could not tell her age.

"Auntie," I said to her.

She looked up at me.

I opened my wallet and showed her a photocopied cutout of a black-and-white photograph.

"Me?" She smiled.

"When was this taken?"

She pursed her lips. Faint wrinkles around her mouth. "It could've been around the time my father passed away. How did you come to have it?"

I told her I clipped it from a magazine. She had no memory of what I'd told her before.

"What article?" she said. For a moment she gazed at the newspaper clipping. Then she made a hand motion for me to wait. She returned with a photograph framed in antique silver. "My father," she said.

He was a mammoth of a man, sitting solemnly on the edge of a black-wood divan, the long rear panel of his glossy green brocade robe swept under him, draping the divan. The seat was high, yet his feet were firmly on the floor. Next to him she stood like a little girl. His hair was white, thin on top and pulled into a chignon at the nape of his neck. His hands rested on his thighs; his nails curved like talons.

She said the photograph was taken in their old house. In his final years, a civilian after sixty-three years of serving the royal families, he had been sightless, blinded by cataracts.

She sat down on the rim of the rock basin in the center of the courtyard. A dragonfly lit on the water, causing a tiny ripple. She'd told me they had a rock basin like this one in the old house in which her father and she had lived. The rock basin on which she was sitting was built in his memory.

"That afternoon when I came back from school," she said, "I was crying. My father was sitting on the rim of the rock basin. He raised my chin with his finger and asked me why. The naughty kids at school, I told him. I told him that as I was peeling the sweet potato he'd packed for me, a girl in the class saw it, gathered other girls around me and sang:

The half-caste eats sweet potatoes, ho ho!
Without skin,
But when she eats dog meat she spares
No skin, no hair, heh heh!

"'You're half Vietnamese, half French,' my father said. He then held me in his arms. 'Let your teacher know they've offended you. Half-caste is a bad word.'

"I told him, 'You never speak of her. Did she die?' I could feel his hesitation. Then he said, 'Phượng, when I left the imperial palace, I wanted to have a child, so I went to an orphanage in Huế and found you among newborn babies.' In a soothing voice he explained about orphanages and why newborn babies were found there. Then he said, 'I don't know anything about your parents other than their nationality. But I am your father.'"

—o—

At times when she was herself, she could, at her leisure, repaint her past with ease. Places where she'd taken me would come back to life and the memories that haunted them, like a swath of sun-bleached fabric long forgotten, trembled with sounds and smells.

A week after I first met her, we took a trip to Upper Đinh-Xuân, the inland village that lay sixteen kilometers from the seaside. She grew up in Upper Đinh-Xuân with her foster father, a former grand eunuch of the Imperial Court of Huế. The villagers called him Sir Bộ because of the benefits awarded his own birth village in the deep south, by the Mekong River, when he was formally chosen by the Ministry of Rites.

To everyone who asked about her, her father told the same story, that he adopted her as a newborn from an orphanage in Huế. His neighbors adored the little girl whose dark brown hair was curly with a soft sheen. Many women loved to touch the little girl's nose. Then they laughed and giggled as they compared their own, short and flat, to hers. Pink and white bougainvillea dotted her village and a dirt path hemmed by hedges of bear's breeches led to her father's house. A flame tree stood outside the house. Year-round shade, as old as the earth. The loose foliage cast shifting light on the ground and in its broken shade the little girl would stop and pick up a flower cluster in scarlet. Her father named her for the flame tree's flowers. Phượng, a bright fire.

—o—

The summer heat often drove her and her father outside onto the steps of their house, where they'd sit sharing a bowl of rice. One such evening, when she was four, the air filled with the sawing of many locust wings. The sky was dark and bloated as the insects swarmed through the village. People ran out of their houses, some still holding rice bowls, some with toothpicks stuck in their teeth, some carrying todders astride their hips, all watching the sky. Phượng hid in the house, frightened by the sounds of their wings.

Night fell and the locusts still buzzed. They crashed against the window shutters like pebbles thrown by a boy, one after another. She couldn't sleep. Her father soothed her as the locusts detonated against the house.

That night she dreamed of a little girl standing by their pond. Drenched, she stood, looking at Phượng. The girl's eyes were beautiful in their tranquility. Long, curly lashes shading them. When Phượng woke, it was dawn. The air was quiet. She thought of the locusts, relieved they were finally gone, then thought of her dream. It shook her—it was so real.

She opened the door and went to the lotus pond with the girl's face still fresh in her mind. She stood in the exact spot where the girl had been, where old green moss coated the rim of the pond. In her pajamas, with dreams still clouding her eyes, she waited for something nameless. When she turned to look down into the pond, her foot slid on the moss, and she splashed into the water and sank.

All she saw then was her father, bright amid a long dark tunnel of water that made no sound. Breathless, she sensed that she had lost him forever. Just as everything collapsed in a black shroud, she felt a hand grab her.

After her father dried her, he sat her down and looked into her eyes, frowning.

"Phượng," he said soothingly, "what were you doing by the pond at this hour?"

"I wanted to see the girl."

"Little one, I didn't see anyone out there."

"I was scared last night. The girl came to be with me." Phượng glanced toward the pond. "She left to go to the water."

Her father nodded. "You saw her by the pond?"

"Yes."

"What did the little girl look like?"

Phượng pointed at her chest. "Like me. But it's not me. She's someone else."

He held her hands in his. "Dear, you were dreaming."

"I wasn't dreaming, father. I saw her."

He leaned down and touched his forehead to hers. "Don't ever go to the pond, unless I'm there with you."

—o—

People in the village knew her as the eunuch's daughter. She was different from the other children. She dwelled on the secret of her birth. As we spoke her eyes strained to piece together fragments of her childhood. Then she would mesmerize me as she pulled out memories, one by one, from the dark womb of her past. Time pinpointed. An early spring day in 1954. She was twelve.

—o—

That night, before bedtime, Bộ sat reading a newspaper he had picked up at the communal house. On the wall beside his bed hung a map of Vietnam. The valley of Đien Bien Phu, 282 kilometers west of Hanoi toward the Laotian border, was a tiny dot. The small valley in the fog and rain of the northwestern forest foreboded the imminent defeat of the surrounded French army. If the news was true, who would rule the country next? The nationalists were no match for the communists. If the communists won, would they pay his pension?

Phượng's voice startled him. "What're you looking at, father?"

"Nothing," Bộ said sharply, then softened his tone. "It's the fate of our country. Something that will affect our lives." He told her about the besieged French army.

"Our teacher talked about it today," she said. "He said the French were doomed."

"He's a Việt Minh sympathizer," Bộ said. He warned her not to talk negatively about the Việt Minh at school, because she could put him in jeopardy with the local government. "Did you write down what I told you about the emperor's dining protocol for your school assignment?"

"I don't need to. I remember what you told me."

At twelve, Phượng had an excellent memory. She was to deliver an oral discourse to the class on the emperor's dining protocol, a subject she chose with confidence, given her father's long tenure at court.

Bộ closed the curtains to his sleeping quarters and told her to get ready for bed. Phượng turned toward him. "You told me every Vietnamese name has a meaning. What does Đien Bien Phu mean?"

Bộ scratched his head. "It means seat-of-the-border district government. You want to be the best in everything, but the head can only hold so much information for one night. Keep your mind fresh and go to bed."

Phượng went into her bedroom. As Bộ dimmed the oil lamp, she came back to his bed. She stood in her shadow against the mosquito net.

"What is it?" Bộ said.

"How can the emperor eat thirty dishes by himself? Each meal? And three meals a day?"

Bộ parted the netting and closed the panels behind him. "Well, my dear, it may seem like a lot. But every condiment is a dish."

Phượng wasn't content with just facts. He had told her that the imperial kitchen had a staff of more than thirty, each in charge of a single dish. "Was he fat, father?"

"No. Despite the extravagant menus, he was a light eater."

"Who prepared his meals?"

"The Culinary Hall prepared the food. The food was stored in gilded-red lacquer containers and then a team of porters carrying parasols took the containers to the palace."

"Who served the emperor? You, father?"

Bộ was pleased by the question. "No, my dear, the emperor had his own attendants. Is that all?"

"Yes, that's all."

"You forgot the kind of rice they served him."

"I forgot about the rice." Phượng smiled. "What kind of rice was it?"

"Try to remember. It's still there in your mind."

—o—

The next day, when she came home in the afternoon, her father was sitting on the doorstep, drying his hair in the sun. Each time she saw his long hair she thought he looked like a wizened old woman with a huge man's body. He was reading parched, yellowed documents, and across his knees lay a long ivory bamboo tube, carved with flowers in red and yellow and lavender.

She knelt before him on the cement floor. The sunlight yellowed the paper scribbled with faded black letters. "What are you reading?"

"Documents from the court," he said, rubbing his eyes. He rolled up the opaque sheet and slid it carefully back into the bamboo tube. "I keep all the important documents in this tube. Documents about money and government pensions and the ownership of our house and property. You'll find it behind the altar. When I die, you'll know what to do."

She could smell the light, fresh scent of honey locust lingering in his washed hair.

"If you die," she said, "who will raise me?"

"I've thought about that. When that happens, you can move to the Temple of Guanyin and live there until you're an adult. The abbot will arrange for the sale of the house, or you can return to it when you are older. He will provide you with shelter and education on my behalf." Deftly her father twisted his hair into a knot. He never used a hairpin to hold his chignon in place. "Do you want to live in the temple if I die?"

"I know no one there."

"Sometimes one has to start all over again in life." Her father's voice was calm. "I hope you understand that."

"I'm not afraid. I know you'll protect me from the other world."

But what had he told her about the other world? When she said that, he cupped his large hands around hers, making them disappear. He said in his soul he didn't fear dying, but he feared the hardship his death would bring her. He gazed at the *phượng* flower in her hair and, after some musing, removed it. She saw tiny day-old wrinkles in its petals.

"Father, can a eunuch have children?"

"No, he can't."

"Why can't he?"

"Because eunuchs are males who were born without sexual organs."

"Is that why you couldn't have children?"

Her father grinned. "Did you do well with your presentation today?"

"Yes, but they laughed at me."

"Did you talk about the rice served to the emperor? Or did they laugh because you got it mixed up?"

"No. It came back to me. The town of An Cựu supplied the best quality rice grains. The imperial kitchen picked each grain and cooked the rice in a small clay pot made in the village of Phước Tích. The kitchen used a rice pot only once, one for every meal."

"But they laughed at you? Why?"

"Our teacher was very impressed with my presentation. He asked who helped me. I told him in front of the class that my father was the former grand eunuch of the court." She looked down at his gnarled hands. "At recess some of the kids yelled at me, 'Daughter of a eunuch? That's a miracle!' They said other things too."

"Let your teacher handle it," her father said. "Don't react to them. That only goads them into more harassment."

"They always come around, father. I was upset, but I didn't cry. Oh, you know something else? I thought how little I know about you." She sat down beside her father with her satchel between her knees. "That's all I've thought of today. I know so little about why you adopted me. Why?"

"I was old, and I never had a family of my own."

"Were you lonely?"

He put his arm around her.

"But why did you choose me?" she said. "Why not a pure Vietnamese baby?"

"Because . . . you looked like someone I once knew."

"Who?"

"Ân-Phi."

"The concubine?"

"Yes."

"How well did you know her?"

"I used to serve her. I was the grand eunuch for sixty-three years."

"What is a grand eunuch?"

"A grand eunuch is the head of the imperial servants."

"How long did you serve her, father?"

"Nearly twenty years."

"Was she as old as you when she died?"

"No, she died young, only in her thirties." Her father felt around in his cloth belt. "She gave me a gift once. I have it here."

She had a phoenix pendant in her hand. "When you're older, you can have it all the time if you wish."

She held it up before her eyes. "Beautiful," she said, her voice trailing.

"So was she, my dear. Beautiful to behold and in spirit."

"Why did she give it to you?"

"Because I tended to her during her years as a concubine."

"How did Ân-Phi become a concubine?"

"Her father offered her, his only daughter then at fifteen, to the next-to-last Nguyễn emperor. Not just anyone could do that. Her father, Sir Đông Các, was one of the four supreme mandarins of the Huế Court."

She asked what the concubines dressed like, and he told her: red, green, and blue. Silk, satin, and sometimes cotton. Never black or gold.

"And what about you, father? What color was your dress?"

"Green for the senior eunuchs and blue for the junior." He paused. His eyes had a faraway look. "Phượng," he said finally, "Do you know why the concubines were forbidden to wear black or gold?"

"Why?"

"Because gold was for the emperor and black is the death color."

"But Ân-Phi would have looked majestic in black."

He puckered his lips and thought for a moment before asking why.

"Because she must've had very beautiful skin, like me," she answered. "She had beautiful eyes too, like you."

"Why did you adore Ân-Phi, father? Did you love her like you love me?"

"I don't know. But if someone takes you away from me, I'd wither like a mummy."

"I want to be with you always. How did she die?"

"She went mad after she became a civilian. She used to give her jewels to the poor on the street in her insanity. No one knows how she died."

"Mad?" Phượng's eyes opened wide. "You didn't wither after she died, father, but you'd wither without me?"

He told her when Ân-Phi's death came so suddenly and without warning that he felt something like withering, a shock that left him numb. The numbness, he said, however hard, eased with time, which as Heaven intends, healed every mortal wound.

In his silence she caressed the flowers etched on the bamboo tube and said, "The people at the orphanage didn't tell you who gave me up?"

"They wouldn't do that. It's confidential."

"What about *your* family? Will I ever meet them?"

He told her where he came from—in the deep South, by the Mekong River—and how the anomaly of his sex made him a candidate for the palace. "The court sent for me when I was ten," he said. "Took weeks by sea, and many days by river." He told her that when he became the third-ranking palace eunuch, his father was exempted from labor tax for the rest of his life. He said his parents visited twice when he was still young. "The distance was so great back then and I wasn't allowed to return to my birthplace once I became a palace eunuch."

Hearing that, she rested her head against his side. "How awful to be alone, father," she said with a deep sigh.

He held her in his arms. She could feel him trembling.

—o—

She told me about the concubine, Ân-Phi. Her father routinely traveled to the village cemetery in Gia-Linh to pay homage to Ân-Phi. After the war there was no one to tend Ân-Phi's tomb. Men and women had followed one another to the "new world" in Cochinchina, where they found work on the French-owned rubber plantations; others headed for the coal mines in Tonkin. So her father took it upon himself to be the custodian. On those trips he carried Phượng on his back as they traveled by ferry to Gia-Linh. Every few months he bought white pebbles in jute bags to replace any around her tomb that went yellow. Other times he filled chinks in the masonry walls or on the headstone with mortar, and during rainy seasons he scooped muddy water from waterlogged holes dug by wild dogs and rodents and then refilled them.

During his many visits, she watched her father, solemn in his green brocade robe, walking around the tomb to inspect the weather-damaged stonewall. Bedded with white gravel, the tomb sat under tall, swaying cypresses. He wore his palace garb only once or twice a year, always with an ivory tablet hanging on his chest. Once she played with it and saw that its smooth surface was inscribed with Chinese characters. He said they told his name and rank during his tenure in the Imperial Court.

The incense he burned at the grave sent spirals of gray smoke drifting in the breeze. He placed a bundle of yellow bananas, a few mangoes and pomegranates on a dish beneath the incense holder, then stood in front of the headstone and bowed three times.

Phượng knelt by the headstone, reading the epitaph. She made out the words "Quỳnh Hương, Ân-Phi."

"Father, you never told me—what is a concubine?"

"A concubine is an emperor's wife, but she's not the queen. Our emperors used to have many wives."

Phượng examined the names on the headstone. At eight, she could read both French and Vietnamese, but some of the Vietnamese words on the headstone were beyond her grasp. "Is Quỳnh Hương her name?"

Her father squatted and dabbed her brow and cheeks with his handkerchief. "That was her name before she became a concubine," he said. "It means princess flower."

"So she was named after a flower like me?"

Her father smiled. "Yes. And then she became Ân-Phi. That was her concubine title." He folded the handkerchief away. "Every concubine had a title."

Phượng became familiar with the birds that nested in trees in the cemetery. On hot summer days she would hear cuckoos in the boxwood and bear's breeches, and her father told her he remembered the sounds back in the old days at the Palace Eunuch Hall, the lazy, throaty sounds that made one drowsy. A few times she spotted a family of crested mynas building their nest on a very tall tulip tree and, as she lay nestled in his lap, he told her how Canh, a young eunuch once under his care, used to tell him that mynas kept their dwellings out of human sight. Her father said Ân-Phi would be pleased to have such wondrous life around her. There were wagtails and starlings and kingfishers. As she watched them, each kind to its own special tree, her father recalled that Ân-Phi once told him that it was their instinct for safety made them do such a thing.

One day she saw a flock of parrots descending from the sky to perch on the poon trees around the concubine's tomb. It was noon and the earth around Ân-Phi's tomb—her father had bought the finest soil to build the foundation—was bright yellow in the sun. The sky was soon full of the rustling of wings as another flock of parrots came screeching to join the first. Soon the trees were full of them, red-beaked and black-beaked, crackling the air with their cries. In one deafening rush of wings, the birds swooped to the ground and started pecking at the yellow soil as if they were catching earthworms she could not see. But to her astonishment they were eating the yellow dirt, not insects, and devouring it with manic delight. Dust dulled their plumage, and soon one bird looked just like another. The white

pebbles were no longer white, but yellow, like the headstone and the surrounding walls.

Her father ran into the sea of birds, shooing them away with his conical
hat. In a loud whoosh, the parrots took to the air. Just as he threw his hat at
them, they descended to the ground again and resumed pecking at the yellow dirt. Soon so many were preening their plumage and eating in a frenzy
that the ground was a canvas of colors—blue, green and red, all dusted in
a yellow haze. Her father didn't know how to deter them. She yelled to him,
"Throw rocks at them, father!" But he shook his head firmly, said, "That'd
upset Ân-Phi. She'd share all that was hers with the world's creatures."

Her father felt guilty for failing to keep Ân-Phi's tomb sacrosanct. At
home, all night he pondered the parrots and their behavior. Why did the
birds ravage her tomb? Was Ân-Phi under some curse? Or was her spirit
trying to communicate with him through the parrots?

Soon father and daughter boarded a ferry to Gia-Linh to inspect the
damage. There were older people like her father on the ferry, and he struck
up a conversation with them about the birds at the tomb. An old man smoking a hand-rolled cigarette told him the yellow dirt was used to pack around
coffins for burial. He said there had to be something in the finest yellow
dirt the parrots needed to cure themselves of a certain disease, the same
way dogs chew certain leaves until they throw up to rid themselves of a
sickness.

Her father didn't know what to believe, but he thought of refilling the
ground with clay to buy peace of mind, and then on second thought decided
to use yellow dirt again to see if the birds would come back. Was it soil they
craved, or was it a sign he needed to heed? Her father made several trips to
the cemetery pushing a cart piled high with bags of the finest quality yellow
dirt. While she scampered after butterflies fluttering among the graves, he
filled the depressions around the tomb with yellow dirt. He finished late in
the afternoon. Dusty and tired, he sat under the cypress as he had before
and waited.

At sunset, she lay tired and resting across his lap. She saw the crested mynas returning to their nest on the tulip tree, but no parrots. At dusk
they went home but returned to Gia-Linh the following morning. He took a

seat beside Ân-Phi's tomb and watched the sky. No parrots, red-beaked nor black, returned.

—o—

Inside the house she took me to a room that had only a bamboo cot, a low table on which lay a teapot, two tiny blue-on-white teacups, a pair of fine long brushes, and a writing tablet in jade green. "My father's paraphernalia," she said, touching the teapot with her fingertips. Then she lifted a teacup in porcelain, small as a plum, its rim banded with gold. It had no handle. She raised the empty cup between thumb and forefinger, sipped, peering over its rim at me. "You know," she said, "I never overslept in those days when I was still working because my father never overslept. At dawn I'd wake to the bitter scent of tea in the air and find him sitting in the main room like a giant statue by the glimmer of dying coals. Once he joked, 'You'll oversleep the morning I die.' Then he told me the story of a butcher who lived by a pagoda. Every day before dawn, the monk in the pagoda chanted the morning sutra, and the butcher would wake and start his day by slaughtering a pig. One morning the monk was sick and skipped the sutra. The butcher overslept. When he woke and got ready to kill a sow, she was giving birth to a litter of ten."

"So did you oversleep?" I said. "After he died?"

She didn't answer. She sat down on the cot and ran her hand along its yellowed, smooth edge. It was a long cot, the kind rarely seen in Vietnam. "This is his cot," she said softly, as if her father were due back soon.

"You must've loved him very much, Auntie."

I realized it did not need to be said.

"My father," she said, "had known and touched many things in his life. Yet nothing made him feel more attached to this world than this cot."

I looked at her, at the bed's smooth bamboo, and felt the man's presence.

He was just a boy the first night he lay on this cot, trying to fall asleep in a strange place far from home. He was neither boy nor girl and his village saw his going as a benediction. Because of his service, the village was exempted from labor excises for several years. His father told him that he should be grateful to serve the emperor—the divine representative on earth, who maintained the harmonious balance between Earth and Heaven. Palace service would bring him that much closer to the divine. "Not many villages are blessed with a boy like you," his father said. "A boy born without the burden of sex; his thoughts are clean. That's why the Imperial Court of Huế values boys like you. Be proud, son, because you have brought blessings to our village."

But her father knew that being sexless was more burden than blessing.

The ten-year-old southern boy cried when the ferry pulled away from the landing, leaving his father a mere silhouette on the dock, and didn't stop until the boat reached Huế.

Later, much later, when he reached adulthood, he thought somebody's prescience gave him such a long cot. By then he stood six feet five inches tall, taller than all the Frenchmen who came to the Huế Imperial Court. But that first night in the Palace Eunuch Hall he slept on this long cot alone in a dark room and cried. An old eunuch came in and gave him a tubular pillow. The pillow, with its fresh smell of linen, bore an old scent from home.

—o—

In that age-old eunuch system, emperors came and emperors went. Her father served each one and in time witnessed the royal burial of each. He served each emperor's high-ranking concubines and saw them introduced at the age of fifteen to the emperor, watched them grow into womanhood, then old and feeble. His fellow eunuchs looked after the aged concubines in the Peaceful Hall outside the Purple Forbidden City until their last day. Some of the concubines, still in blossoming womanhood, were exiled to the emperor's necropolis when he died. There they lived out their lives tending his tomb.

One of the imperial concubines her father served came from Gia-Linh village. Her name was Quỳnh Hương. Her royal title was Ân-Phi and she was the second-ranking concubine of the nine rankings. When the emperor died in 1925, many people from the Gia-Linh village believed that, with her noble lineage, she would become the next queen mother. Because of Đông Các's stature in the imperial court, his daughter was made a third-ranking concubine and then elevated to second-ranking within three years.

By then the emperor had many wives, yet his bedmate was a male attendant. The emperor never touched Ân-Phi as one of his wives and she bore him no child. Frail with bone marrow cancer and often sick, he needed care even after defecation. A low-ranking eunuch would wipe him with a piece of gold silk, then another. His penis, small as a child's, could have qualified him to be a palace eunuch.

—o—

Among all the concubines, Miss Phượng told me, the aristocratic second-ranking Ân-Phi had impeccable manners and beauty, which suited her to be the next queen mother. But the emperor's will decreed that the only wife who had given him a son would be the next queen mother, even though she did not have the same pedigree. After the eight-year observation of the emperor's death, the coronation of the queen mother was to take place that year, 1933.

Miss Phượng said her father told her only once about the coronation of the queen mother.

—o—

On coronation day Bộ got up early.

Under the stone bridge the lotus pond mirrored a blue sky. A propitious day, according to the court astrologers, to crown the queen mother.

Bộ walked through courtyards under the shades of white-flowering poon and frangipani trees. Curving tile roofs, glazed yellow and blue, loomed into view behind green foliage, then disappeared from sight. Mourning doves cooed in the cloistered courts and flower gardens lay quiet, green in the sun. But, on this day of grandiose enthronement, he felt detached. He wondered how Ân-Phi felt.

The queen mother to be crowned did not have a respectable pedigree. The deceased emperor met her when he was still a prince who loved gambling. She conceived a child and implicated the prince in her pregnancy. The prince's mother, knowing her son's sexual incapacity, had her interrogated. They dug a shallow opening in the ground, made her lie facedown with her protruding belly secured in the aperture and beat her. Though she and her unborn baby survived the beating, the child's paternity was never revealed. The prince claimed the child was his. Without an heir, the French would never have enthroned him. He made the woman his queen.

Each night for the eight years following the emperor's death, Ân-Phi played the piano—some nights Schubert, some nights Mozart. Bộ gauged Ân-Phi's mood by the melody. On the evening before the coronation, Ân-Phi's music was blithe, rippling merrily. He admired her noble spirit. She was caring, natural and so humble he wondered how she had survived among the sharp tongues and mean spirits in the palace.

By midmorning of that day Bộ received news that the emperor's son, enthroned eight years before at age twelve, was on his way to the Palace of Diên Thọ, the new queen mother's residence. He hurried across the courtyard and entered the palace. The somber interior was cool in the summer, warm in the winter. He bowed to the queen mother. "Your Highness," he said, "it is time."

Ladies-in-waiting surrounded her, arranging the folds of her robe. The queen mother closed her eyes as one girl placed the crown—elaborately embroidered with nine phoenixes and filaments crusted with sparkling beads of ruby, pearls, and red corals falling from its sides—on her head. The crown transformed the queen mother from homely to elegant.

Bộ led the way across the reception hall. The queen mother minced in her golden knitted slippers with phoenixes on their tips, glittering with ruby dust. Even with two attendants on either side of her, she carried the weight of the imperial robe of magnificent richness like an octogenarian groping her way without a cane. How many weavers and dressmakers had touched the golden brocade?

Once on the throne behind a velvety curtain that hid her from view, she sat still in her golden brocade robe. Its front was stitched with an enormous Chinese character "Longevity." Beneath her robe she wore a handsewn gown of blood-red silk. The queen mother remained frozen, her face so sickly pale that her father felt not pity but empathy for the chosen. *Be yourself and be thankful to those who rendered their service to you.* With one final look at the queen mother-to-be and the female courtiers who stood at attention on either side of the throne, Bộ withdrew.

—o—

The French Resident—the representative of France and ruler of the country—and various dignitaries arrived, greeted by court ministers at the Palace Grand Gate. The hall hushed. The silence fell on the crowd of mandarins and royal families and soldiers. Floating music rose in the distance from the Grand Palace, drifting from open back doors. Slowly it drew nearer and nearer until one could hear the languid notes of a melancholy bar coming back and back again, its gentle sound altered by the melody of flutes and violins. The heralds pronounced the arrival of the emperor. Their voices echoed from the rear of the palace, relayed in succession from behind doors of long dark halls, on the open terraces, the winding corridors through which His Majesty must pass.

As the emperor sat down in the Main Hall, the French Resident proceeded across the floor of gleaming blue tiles until he came to stand in front of the throne on which the queen mother sat. His solemn voice echoing, the French Resident commenced the ceremony with a speech of good wishes. He recalled His Majesty's father's ascent to the throne, seventeen years earlier, reminiscing about that auspicious day in which he was honored to partake and expressing his deep gratitude to the Huế Court for recognizing his attention to His Majesty's father's service then and his diligence to the court now.

Looking at the queen mother's face, Bộ felt the woman's agony. She sat shrunken in her enormous ceremonious robe, her face flaxen, her small hands protruding from the long loose sleeves gripping the arms of her throne. Her soft black eyes darted from side to side as if she dared not make eye contact with her well-wisher. Her slightly thick lips in pale red rouge drooped at corners, and Bộ could tell tension had sapped the queen mother.

Now in his bright-yellow grand court robe, tied with a jade belt and a headdress carved with nine dragons vying for a pearl, the emperor came to kneel in front of his mother, folding his arms across his chest. In his monotonous Vietnamese, he offered his mother his best wishes and his accolade for the French recognition of her coronation. While he remained on his knees, a white-bearded mandarin translated the emperor's words into French.

Bộ dabbed his face with a folded handkerchief. Relieved, he let out a sigh as the melodrama was about to end for the queen mother. Bộ watched the Minister of Rites lead the royals to the enormous mat before the throne where they prostrated themselves, ten rows deep, rising and falling five times to the queen mother. Out in the sun-baked courtyard, imperial guards with yellow leggings ported long rifles with fixed bayonets, keeping order among rows of mandarins in flowered robes, who knelt on tiny mats, kow-towing in harmony with the prostrations inside.

Even from inside the hall, Bộ could hear the booming voice of the com-manding French officer shouting orders, and native imperial guards set off strings of firecrackers fluttering on bamboo poles from four corners of the courtyard. In the deafening noise, Bộ moved among servers in the hall, watching them serve iced champagne and cakes and sweetmeats. French guests peered up at the huge grand eunuch—here Miss Phượng paused with a gleam in her eyes, smiling at me, lifting her head to look up as if seeing her late father towering over her—who moved nimbly behind other eunuchs with high cheekbones, directing them to different spots in the hall.

By noon the ceremony was over. The royal orchestra played a farewell concerto and the high-pitched sounds of indigenous musical instruments rose clinking in the air.

As the emperor's entourage passed through the Palace Grand Gate, the Great Cannon fired three rounds. The ground shook. Bộ walked down the veranda, directing his staff to line everyone up according to rank and role. The human line shifted, merged, wrapped around the eastern and western verandas of the pavilion. Noon heat shimmered on the *yin-yang* tile roofs and white glare scorched the ground.

Ân-Phi stood under a huge pink parasol. The lady-in-waiting assigned to her was a new girl who had taken the place of Ân-Phi's old faithful atten-dant who had recently died. The wizened woman had spent three months to recover from her illness in Peaceful Hall across from the Palace Eunuch Hall. Then shortly after she returned to Ân-Phi's side, she died. They brought her body over the northwestern wall to be taken away for burial, and Ân-Phi and Bộ stood among her attendants watching the dead being hoisted with a winch and disappearing behind the high wall.

Now flashes of red, blue and yellow caught the eunuch's eyes. The queen mother, surrounded by ladies-in-waiting, was on her way back to her chamber.

Bộ shouted, "Kneel! Kowtow five times!"

The line dropped. Fabric rustled. "Rise!" Bộ roared.

The line rose: bearers of incense burners dressed in aqua blue, fan bearers in sea blue, and parasol bearers in royal blue. A sea of parasols shifted, bright, colorful. Huge fans flapped. Clouds of incense misted the sky, smelling of embalmed wood. After the queen mother passed by, Bộ surveyed the line of well-wishers. His gaze fell upon Ân-Phi. Had fate favored her, she would have been the object of all the accolades, all the prostrations.

At Ân-Phi's feet, her ruby earring caught Bộ's eyes. After the concubine gave him permission, he tenderly affixed the gem to her lobe.

"Ân-Phi," he said, "aren't you glad that it's over?"

"Bộ, I'm glad that it's over," Ân-Phi said, smiling. "So is the queen mother."

—o—

I often wondered if someone like her father, a born eunuch, could fall in love with a woman like Ân-Phi.

When I asked her such questions, Miss Phượng told me age never played itself into her father's life with Ân-Phi. His love for her was asexual. Miss Phượng was amazed at how time could not purge that delicate love, neither possessed nor possessing, and the only reason for its timelessness she knew was that it sprang in response to the concubine's transcendent beauty.

Miss Phượng passed to me this image. By a lotus pond stood the concubine watching the maids pluck the lotus seedpods, her hair draped over her shoulder in one long, black swath. Her body curved gracefully; one shoulder dipped slightly. Her eyelids drooped in a gentle curve, pensive and serene.

Then while I listened in silence, Miss Phượng slipped into a reverie. She relived his memories with a rare deliberate evocation of his first encounter with the concubine.

—o—

On the solemn day of her royal wedding, Ân-Phi arrived in a carriage drawn by four white horses outside the Trinh Minh Palace, home of the second- and third-ranking concubines. Bộ didn't see the concubine's face as she stepped down from the carriage holding a giant brocade fan in front of her. He stood beneath the portico observing the cortege escorting the new bride to the Throne Room where His Majesty was waiting. Two female courtiers, each holding a pink parasol, flanked her. Behind her, walking in pairs, trailed female porters carrying white-wicker snow geese, drooping willow twigs, long and fluttering, and lacquered coffers so black the white of the attendants' dresses hurt his eyes. Ân-Phi and her entourage followed the two female attendants, each with a Chinese lantern in her hand. As they entered the deep shadow of the portico, the lanterns glowed in brighter orange.

The eunuch gazed at the bride. Lively figures of dragon and phoenix hugging the moon were embroidered on her long vermillion robe, on her slippers. Each step her delicate feet took was accompanied by the tinkling music of her earrings and bracelets, encrusted with figures of nine phoenixes. As she drew near, he straightened his back then stood absolutely still. When he glimpsed her face, his heart stirred.

Ever since Ân-Phi's induction into the palace, Bộ tried never to lose sight of the concubine. He said, once, that to see her was to know what heaven meant by beauty.

—o—

On the afternoon after the wedding, Ân-Phi's tired feet brought her back to her reception chamber. She sat while a female attendant prepared tea. The girl went about her business as silently as a shadow, her feet seeming to glide, and she lifted and replaced objects with a light touch, as if the clink of porcelain on wood would shatter her lady's nerves.

When the attendant, her eyes downcast, brought tea on a red-lacquered tray, Ân-Phi inclined her head and the girl set the tray down soundlessly. Just as Ân-Phi was about to speak to her, the girl bowed and half-lifted her gaze. "We have an hour until lunch," she said. "Ân-Phi, please rest if you are tired." A warm whiff of incense came from her clothes as she bent to pick up a footstool and place it in front of the armchair. "Please rest your feet, Ân-Phi."

Gently she lifted the concubine's feet, still in jeweled slippers, onto the footstool. She served the bride a cup of chrysanthemum tea and as she put down the teapot, Ân-Phi spoke to her. "Thank you, Miss. You may now excuse yourself until I need you again. I'd like to have a moment for myself."

Ân-Phi looked around. The room was like a strange face peering at her, the solitary visitor. Yellow roses on the tea table drooped from a porcelain vase in a profusion of blooms, permeating the air with their scent, which clung to her skin, her clothes, her hair. The morning was spent, and the midday sun shone intensely through the stained-glass window, brushing shadows into the chamber corners like cobwebs.

A faint taste of wine from her toast with His Majesty lingered on her tongue. During the ceremony she had glimpsed the sickly sallow of his face, the receding chin, the birdlike fragility so effeminate that, enhanced by the sparkling gold crown and enormous diamond rings on his fingers, His Majesty resembled an aging dowager.

She sipped her tea, soothingly fragrant, but felt languor rather than comfort. She had no idea what the day would bring nor what the night might hold. A highly organized person always in charge of her life, she now felt lost in a labyrinth. Where would she find the map of her new life? Did she want to see it? At the thought exhaustion seized her, and when she woke later, she didn't know where she was until the bright light on the stained-glass window caught her eyes and the scent of roses made her wonder if she had been embalmed in her sleep.

A huge man in a shimmering green brocade robe standing beside her, like a tree, startled her. Hardly moving either head or lips, he said mildly, "Lady Ân-Phi, I am Bộ, the grand eunuch. I am honored to be at your service."

"Please be seated, Mr. Bộ." She motioned toward a rosewood armchair across the tea table.

"Please call me Bộ, and allow me to remain where I am in due respect to you, Ân-Phi."

She couldn't tell his age, though his hair, tightly woven and tucked under a black hat, looked pale gray. His large, deep eyes focused on space, never meeting hers. She asked why no one had told what was expected of her as the newly inducted concubine, save for a flurry of instructions before the ceremony.

Knitting his eyebrows, Bộ told her that he could not brief her on the protocol upon arrival because there was not enough time before the ceremony. In a soft, steady voice the eunuch explained what she could expect of her attendants—the tea must be served in a tiny cup while it was still hot; the rice must be served warm in a small bowl; and tea and rice must be refilled immediately the moment her attendants spotted them empty. Bộ paused and pointed to a pear-shaped silver bell hung by the door—whenever she wished to summon them, day or night, she should simply sound the bell.

"Why are they so passive in my attendance?" Ân-Phi asked.

Bộ tipped his head slightly as if to gauge her meaning. Though she understood their silence was part of royal protocol, she believed people should be allowed to behave more openly and reciprocally within reasonable bounds. She said the moment one became an automaton, the air everyone breathes and shares would be tainted and even flowers—she cast her glance at the abundant yellow roses—would wilt before their time.

Bộ clasped his large hands before him. The fingernails arched downward in opaque white. Then he said, "They are not to ask but rather to obey orders, Ân-Phi. The hundred-twenty-year-old protocol of the imperial court has been and shall be observed. Such is tradition. In light of your view, however, one can only surmise that protocol, being circumstantial at best, can be rewritten in favor of a certain monarchic rule, or, Heaven knows, the colonial rule. Only time will tell."

Then Bộ inquired about her well-being and explained the wedding ceremony to be followed with its arduous etiquette, the afternoon appointments with the queen and each of the royal concubines, and then the evening.

When the eunuch did not mention her wedding night, Ân-Phi asked calmly what arrangement he had in mind for her. He coughed a tiny cough and, with a quick glance toward her, said that His Majesty's health was everyone's concern for the time being, and therefore the nuptial night would have to be deferred—he paused with a nod—which was not unusual considering the monarch's ongoing illness.

Ân-Phi kept her composure at the news. Before she left home her mother had whispered to her, "When His Majesty heard your father's offer to betroth his daughter to him, he said, 'My palace is a monastery. It shall be your discretionary decision whether or not to turn your nubile daughter into a nun by bringing her here.'" Ân-Phi had locked this revelation in her heart.

After a sip of tea, Ân-Phi regarded the grand eunuch with equanimity and told him she expected to be briefed fully about her role as the third-ranking concubine. At her calm voice, Bộ bowed and said none of her attendants except him might brief her on the subject of protocol, which would come in due time. His mission was to be her chief attendant, that should she make any mistake regarding etiquette and decorum, the error would be his and his only because of his failure to prepare her. That said, he asked softly if she wished for anything. "A book," she said smiling.

When Bộ turned toward the door she thought he was leaving, but he stopped at the lectern and returned with a book. He placed it next to her tea, silently, as if noises were sins. Astounded, she looked at the title of the book, *Les Misérables*, and peered up at the eunuch, joy spreading across her face.

"Is it coincidence or serendipity that you picked this?" she said. "It's my favorite book."

"It *is* your book, Ân-Phi," Bộ said, stepping back.

During the nuptial ceremony he had asked her parents about her hobbies and then personally sorted through her book collection which, together with her other personal belongings, was being kept in a storage room pending one final examination of Ân-Phi's possessions to verify that everything was intact.

Bộ stood with his back to the lighted window, one hand cupping the other, and spoke of what she was perhaps expecting above all else. Her grand piano. It would arrive soon, he said, coming by ferry and then by cart.

Just before he left, Bộ bent over the tiny tea table, and tested the warmth of the teapot. Then, with a crisp motion he refilled her cup and bid her farewell. The mass of his body, softened by the fluttering panels of his robe, stirred the scent of chrysanthemum tea.

—o—

That night Ân-Phi couldn't sleep.

The gong of first watch sounded from the lookout tower. She listened to its echo, which trailed a soothing note. When it faded, she sucked the back of her hand. In the scent of her own flesh, the scent of her mother came to her. She sat up. Perhaps she could read as she did at home on wakeful nights. But her book was on the tea table in the reception chamber, and she didn't want to disturb the attendant who slept there.

She paced the room in the dark, hearing the tiny creaks the hardwood floor made under her bare feet, the fresh scent of her nightwear lingering in the air. Back and forth she paced, hoping the lump of homesickness would leave her throat and the weight on her chest would subside.

She heard a tap on the door and her attendant appeared holding an oil lamp in one hand and a long round pillow in the other. "Ân-Phi, since you can't sleep," the girl said, "perhaps you would like to see if this pillow would help."

A fragrance of grapefruit flowers came from the satin pillow as she took it from the attendant, who said the pillow came from Bộ, to be given to Lady Ân-Phi should she have a sleepless night.

So Bộ had also asked her parents about her favorite flower. In truth she loved many flowers, but as dazzling as roses were, their scent lacked the eternal captivation of the grapefruit blossom. That was a little secret she shared only with her mother.

She lay down, hugging the pillow. The scent hung frail in the chamber.

six

I stood in the narrow doorway of their small hut, watching Miss Phượng's helping girl clean her daddy's infected toe. He had passed out. "Drunk," she said. Every evening.

Twilight. The briny air was warm. Voices of the sea in the distance—the sound of crashing waves, the sibilant winds hissing through the dune grass, a sudden cry of a shore bird.

She rested his sore foot on a chair. I came in and looked at his swollen toe. She said she occasionally cut his thick toenails with a knife. He couldn't bend to cut them and one of the big toenails had become ingrown and infected.

I offered to cut them for her. Squinting, I held his foot up to the flickering oil lamp. "When do you see the doctor for him?"

"Doctor?" She frowned.

"I'm afraid so." I glanced at the bloodstains on the cuticle. "Wash the blood off and put something on it. Got iodine?"

She went to the back of the hut and then returned, balancing her footsteps, carrying in her hands a brass pan brimming with water. I washed his toes, then dried them with a towel. She dabbed his big toe with iodine. It dripped to the clay floor in bluish black drops. He was snoring, his torso bare, oxblood dark. I found myself staring at the lush tattoos splashed over his body—green sea serpents, fiery dragons, the fish, sea clouds floating, black giant birds flying.

She picked up a canvas bag and slung it over her shoulder. "I must fix Daddy's net."

Outside dusk was falling. Her red kerchief looked darker. "It took two days, two nights," she said, sauntering beside me, "when he let himself be tattooed with a lobster's claw's tip." That was before he married her mother. "It must've hurt very badly, *chú*. Bloody too. Then they colored his tattoos with a brush. Took a long time." Afterward, she said, he sat in the sun for two days. His skin turned red, then just a dull red. He washed the tattoos with warm rice liquor, believing their words that it would preserve the dyed images on his skin. That night, after two scorching days in the sun, he completed his initiation by drinking a large bowl of fermented lobster sauce.

"Which way to the wharf?" I asked.

"This way's shorter, *chú*."

"I never noticed the shrimp ponds around here."

"I don't like seeing them."

"Why?"

"I hate them."

"Because they pollute the water?"

Her lips crimped; she shook her head.

"Don't you care?" I said. "Those pesticides and chemical wastes from shrimp farms?"

"No." She threw me a mean sidelong glance. "I live here, *chú*, I know."

"But you don't care?"

"*Chú!*"

She must have also known that beyond the seaside, toward inland, shrimp farms had encroached the mangrove forests where fish and other marine life live and spawn, the forests for centuries protecting the inland from tidal waves, from wicked storms.

"Daddy said there're so many dead fish in the ocean now. Chemical wastes from those shrimp farms kill them." She paused then in a dead tone said, "Daddy will kill those shrimpers. He will."

Her face looked serious. "I hope not," I said, sighing.

Moral advice percolated in my head, but not a word left my mouth. I knew nothing about their lives here. Going down the foredune there was a tang of fish odor, a damp smell of kelp in the air. Fishing nets were piled up above the high-tide mark and beneath them lay the ocean litter of seaweed, soggy sticks, bits of crabs' claws. High tide was coming in, tinkling softly through the orphaned seashells studding the sand. I stopped when something scurried out from under the mass of wet nets. A rat. She followed its trail and said the bad rat was out looking for birds' eggs, those that nested above the high-tide line. A buoy clanged. A desolate sound guiding fisher-men ashore.

Her father's boat rested on the sand among others, its bow leaning down on a pair of wooden stakes. A net draped its length, spreading over the sand. Above the water the wharf shone bluish under the iron lanterns, and in their pale illuminations she inspected the net, hooking her fingers in the twines of the rips, her brow creased.

"Fresh tears?" I asked her.

She scratched her head, then said, "I hadn't had time to fix them," as she swung her bag down and dropped it on the sand.

"Anything I can do for you?"

"I can do this faster on my own. You'll get in my way if you help, *chú*."

I asked if it took long. She tilted back her head. "I wish you could fix a net just once and see how that'd do to your back after hours sitting on your knees."

"And how much did you get paid?"

She shook her head sadly, said, "*Chú*, different sizes different fees," then pointing at the worn-looking net, "that net is about the length of five arm stretches, I got fifteen thousand *đồng* to fix the rips and recrimp the leads."

"A dollar," I said.

"It isn't much where you come from, *chú*."

I said nothing, just looking at her headscarf, now a bruised red, the light blue of her short-sleeved blouse that hugged her scrawny body, the copper-tan of her skin, the long fingers that held the scissors as she snipped off the loose tag ends, cutting them off here and there all the way to the knots of each mesh. She did this quickly, cleanly.

I asked if she'd throw away the net damaged by a sizable hole. She put away the mending needle as if she didn't hear me, and then slowly she began removing the guiding twine that had been threaded through the meshes. Finally, she spoke without looking up. "You never throw away a net, *chú*. It's like throwing away our money."

"Okay then," I said. Annoyed by her quirky mood, I decided not to ask what she or her father would do with such a damaged net.

"Don't you want to know how I'd fix a large hole, *chú*?" She turned to me, her arms akimbo.

"Yes, I do."

"I'll patch it. It takes much longer to patch it." She saw my quizzical expression and shrugged. "It's hard for me to explain. You must see it, *chú*. Like you first trim the hole into a square or a rectangle. Then you cut out a patch from a scrap net, its edges must match the edges of the hole so when you lay the patch in, it fits. Then you can weave."

"How often did you have to do that?"

"Few times. Took a whole evening."

"Out here by yourself?"

"Yes, *chú*."

Something dark inside me made words sink back. Not pity, but helplessness. Had she, this child-woman, ever gone to school? Had she the time to rest? What did she dream when she slept?

"Would you like to go to school?" I asked before thinking it through.

"Yes, *chú*." Her quiet tone surprised me. "I hope someday I would be able to." She started looping the guiding twine around the mending needle and then tossed them into the bag. She spoke into the bag. "Auntie Phượng wanted to raise me and put me through school. But Daddy wouldn't allow that."

"I see. Well, he can't do much without you. . . ." *Useless ass!* I stopped before those words left my lips.

"Auntie loves me like her own daughter."

"But she doesn't have a daughter."

"No, *chú*. How could she? She never married!"

I chuckled. "Do you love her like you love your mom?"

The girl's eyes suddenly narrowed like a cat's eyes. "I don't love her," she said.

"Who?"

"Mom."

"And why's that?"

She picked up her bag and slung it over her shoulder.

We walked back up the dune, stepping over clumps of brown seaweed, our feet kicking up sand, sending sand fleas flitting across the sand. Then her voice came. "Mom ran off. She lives with a shrimper now."

seven

From behind a dune dense with filao trees, Miss Phượng's house looked toward the sea. The evening was windy, and the wind stripped filao cones from the trees and they fell like hail on her roof. In the lull, the sound of falling cones stayed with me.

Miss Phượng picked up on the veranda a cone the size of an acorn. "Do you have these in America?" She put the cone in my palm.

"I don't know," I said, rolling it with my fingers. It felt spiny with its woody sharp scales colored reddish brown like cockroaches.

"They make for prickly walking," she said.

I took the teacup and its saucer and stood as she lowered herself onto the glider. Then, feeling awkward, I perched on the railing. It was dim where she sat but the glow from the lamp inside shimmered over her face, which was white against her hair.

Miss Phượng never wore lipstick or mascara. She didn't need to, for, at her age, she still had the wholesomeness of a cold-climate fruit like a red apple. In a beige blouse and a moss-green skirt, she looked as fresh as the white cups of Queen Anne's lace that dotted America's roadsides.

"May I ask you a personal question?" I said.

"Yes, Minh."

"Are you French or Vietnamese in your soul?"

"I am both."

As I smiled, she said, "Jonathan once asked me something like that."

"Jonathan?" I said. "Oh, Jonathan Edward, who died in the cane field."

"He said to me, *Est-ce que vous êtes une française qui parle vietnamien, ou une vietnamienne qui parle français?* Because he spoke French very well. He could speak Vietnamese too, though not as well as French. *Je suis les deux,* I told him."

"So, which of your parents is French? What happened to your real parents?"

"I didn't know who they were. Even my foster father said he didn't know. For years. Would you like another cup?"

"If you don't mind, Auntie."

She went back inside. I gazed at the dune. The high wind had torn down the staked tomatoes and the ground was now scattered with fruit and leaves. A fruit bat might pick up the smell and eat the fallen tomatoes. She came out. I received my fresh cup of tea. "Thank you, Auntie."

She offered me a bar of chocolate.

"This is French chocolate," she said. "Not as sweet as American chocolate, that's my warning."

I didn't know how light it was until it melted in my mouth. She was right. I preferred the sweet Hershey chocolate. "It tastes . . . quite different," I said. The hot tea nearly scalded my tongue. Over the years, she told me, foreign journalists, writers mostly French had sought from her stories told by her father about life in the Purple Forbidden City. They came with gifts.

"Can I ask you another personal question?" I said.

"As long as it's not about French chocolate, which you might not like."

I smiled at her correct guess. "Did you find out who your real parents were?"

She came to the railing, standing a few feet from me and faced the sea. After a while she spoke.

"I had asked myself that question when I saw people worship their deceased parents on the altar. Who are my parents? Where did they come from? Then I stopped asking."

"Why's that, Auntie?"

She wrapped up what was left of her chocolate bar. "My foster father was a dignified civil servant. I was afraid . . ."

Suddenly I understood. I looked into her deep-set eyes. Those western eyes held my gaze briefly, then blinked. She was brought up by a respectable man. Dignity and decorum. I thought about the Indochina War, the French soldiers who raped or slept with native girls. There was a silence.

"You aren't afraid anymore to inquire about the truth?" I broke the silence.

"In my heart," she said, "I was dying to know who my natural parents were. But being abandoned at an orphanage, I didn't have the heart to know who that baby's parents were."

I drank my tea. "Auntie," I said, "Would it matter who you were supposed to be?"

"Who I am today," she said, smacking her lips, "isn't complete without knowing who I was supposed to be." Then holding up the pendant that always hung below her clavicle, she said, "This ruby phoenix has something to do with my birth. When my father gave it to me for keeps, he told me Ân-Phi gave it to him. When I was older, I learned that this ornament wasn't carved as a pendant. I believed that the gem had been cut into two equal halves, and one of its halves is with me."

She worked the chain off her neck and dropped the pendant in my hand. A piece of ruby, its back was flat and smooth-looking. She had worn it since childhood, and it wasn't until she was eighteen that she discovered that it wasn't meant to be worn as a pendant. On pendants, she explained, the animal carvings in gemstones were small and flat. Her phoenix was three-dimensional—the bird's long, ribbony plumes and crests, dancelike and real-looking with its tail feathers and wings. Its taut curved lines, its varying depths were difficult and rare achievements that only could have come from the hand of a master sculptor.

"It began with this pendant," she said once again palming the ruby. "But really it began with Jonathan Edward."

I leaned my head to one side staring at the stone's mellow shine. "Will you tell me more about this Jonathan Edward, Auntie?"

"Jonathan Edward," she repeated the name. Silence, then, "He was with the Agency for International Development. And his reason for studying Vietnamese was to help himself deal with South Vietnamese officials in developing a Vietnamese civil administration. He said, 'We want to win the people's hearts and minds and bring the boys home. But before that can happen, we have to earn the trust of the South Vietnamese officials. If they don't speak English, then we learn their language.'"

She smiled to herself then said, "I still feel the earnestness in his voice. He had a gentle, deep voice like you."

I smiled and asked, "So he was with the much-maligned AID pacification program."

"Yes. They must repeat the French pacification program in Vietnam. Except not fail. And you know what he said? He said it helps if you speak the language. The Vietnamese will treat you like a member of their family."

It caught me off balance. "Who told him that?"

"The Pentagon."

"Well," I said, shaking my head, "you might befriend a Vietnamese quicker if you speak to him in his mother tongue. But I don't know if he'd treat you like a member of his family."

"Me neither," she said.

I was so close to her I could feel the thumping of my heart as she told me of their first meeting.

—o—

They met on a late summer morning.

She was standing at the stove in her noodle shop. A young monk came in and asked her if she wouldn't mind to come out and meet someone. He led her out of the shop, and she looked at his companion, an American.

"She is his daughter," the monk spoke in English to his friend.

"*Chào cô,*" the American said.

She sensed his self-consciousness. "Hello," she said in her mother tongue. "Do you really speak Vietnamese?"

"Please, don't laugh, Miss. My Vietnamese is bad."

"Why are you looking for my father?"

"Mr. Bộ is your father, Miss?"

"Yes, he is."

She touched the moist rims under her eyes, for she'd been perspiring from the cooking heat and the sun.

"I need to see him," he said.

"What is this about?"

"This is Minh Tánh," he said, without taking his eyes off her, "my guide from the Guanyin Temple, and I'm Jonathan Edward."

Then in his hesitant Vietnamese he said he was looking for his lover's parents. Françoise was a Vietnamese-French girl, he said. It was here in the hamlet of Upper Đinh-Xuân in 1944 that she was found as a baby floating down a river. She had with her two photographs. They showed a thatch-roofed house with a lotus pond. He took a deep breath and said, "I just learned that your father lived in the house around that time."

She looked at the American, mesmerized by his tale. As she listened, something stirred in her. She thought of the little girl who had come to her in her childhood dreams.

"Where is she—your Françoise?" she asked the American.

"She was raised in North Vietnam," he said. "Her foster father was a Việt Minh cadre. She went to live in Lyon in France until she graduated from the university. I met her in Washington, D.C., where she taught Vietnamese to me and other men from U.S. government agencies."

Breathless, he paused to get his wind. Then he said, "She died"—his voice shook—"recently."

Phượng looked up at him. "As soon as my customers leave, I'll take you to my father."

"Thank you," he said. "I'm terribly sorry for disrupting your business. And one more thing." He paused. "May I ask for your name, Miss?"

She smiled. "Phượng."

—o—

She walked fast, shouldering two oversize copper pots bobbing on a shoulder pole. When Jonathan offered to help she told him she was used to the weight, that she left home at six-thirty every morning with two fully loaded pots. He asked how she could shoulder such a load back and forth every day. He didn't know that nothing is hard once it becomes routine. He asked her how far she lived from the market. She said it was about four kilometers and the cross-village bus seldom ran her route.

At times he became lost, and she had to repeat what she had said. At times she was lost because of his accent. Sweat dripped down his face. It must be from the sun on his neck, from anxiety about the language. Though the day was hot, she wasn't tired. Her cheeks, her forehead perspired lightly. The young monk trailed behind them, looking weary and glum.

"Does your father speak French, Miss?" Jonathan asked her.

"Certainly." She looked up, dabbing her forehead with the heel of her hand. "I speak French too, if you want to speak French."

Jonathan glanced back at the monk and so did she. Sweat beaded the monk's pate and brow. It seemed every time she looked back, she saw the monk's gaze on her.

"Sure," Jonathan said in French. "I wish I could explain how much it'd mean to me to discover the truth of Françoise's birth."

Their shadows moved ahead of them.

In his silence she imagined his lover standing before her just like the little girl of her dreams.

The road curved around a field, a world of green sugarcane leaves. Low thatch-roofed houses sat back from the road; the doors propped open with sticks. After a long while on many dirt paths, she turned a corner. They entered a cobbled courtyard, the stones churning loosely under their feet. A masonry screen fronted the house. At the base of the screen lay a basin of rockwork, and in it a still pond.

She entered the house and stopped momentarily outside the pleated curtain to her father's sleeping quarters. She parted the fabric just as her father opened his eyes, closed and opened them again. Though he could no longer see because of cataracts, he knew the sound of her clogs.

"Why are you back so early, Phượng?" he asked hoarsely.

"Father," she said, sitting down on the cot, "I bring you a guest. An American wanted to see you."

Her father winced.

"What happened, father? Why're you sleeping now? Don't you feel well?"

"No, I haven't felt well since last night. I have a recurring pain in my stomach." He raised himself up with an effort. The cot creaked. "What does he need from me?"

"He wants to find the origins of a baby girl. He believes that she was born in our old house in Upper Đinh-Xuân." She stopped when she looked at the paleness of her father's face. Then she went on, "What is this all about, father?"

With a wave of hand, he rose from the cot. "That's what I want to find out. Would you show him in?"

She seated the guests at a wooden table facing the pleated curtain. Her father emerged, a giant shuffling one step at a time to the center of the room. Out of respect for his guests, her father had put on his eunuch's robe. His lime-white hair was thin on top, rolled and tucked into a chignon at the nape of his neck. He stared in front of him as his hand felt the rounded corner of the divan.

Jonathan and Minh Tánh rose to greet him.

"Comment allez-vous, Monsieur?" Jonathan asked, gazing up at the host.

Her father tipped his head. "May I ask who this is?"

"My name is Jonathan Edward."

The monk did not speak. Her father set his eyes toward him. "And who is it there?"

"My name is Minh Tánh. I'm a novice at the Temple of Guanyin."

Her father gestured formally toward the chairs. "Please be seated."

He stood until they were seated and then sat gingerly on the corner of the divan, sweeping the long rear-panel green silk under him, letting it drape the divan. Then he turned to the guests, resting his hands on his thighs. His fingernails curved like hooked claws. In a soft voice he asked her to serve the guests. She turned and went to the other end of the room, through a doorway hung with a pale blue curtain. She returned with a tray and two glasses and set them down on the table.

"Please have some sugarcane juice, gentlemen," she said.

The monk drank the frothy yellow juice in one swig, set the glass down and burped. Jonathan sipped it and then leaned to the monk.

"I wish to speak to him privately."

Her father whispered to her. She rose and Minh Tánh, almost tumbling over his own feet, followed her outside.

—o—

Alone with the guest, Bộ sat erect like an old upright tree.

"Sir," Jonathan said, "do you mind if I speak to you in French?"

"Certainly, Jonathan." Bộ pronounced the guest's name with the French *oh*.

"Sir, I hope my sudden appearance at your door doesn't violate your privacy. I'm thankful to your daughter, who closed her business at midday to bring me here to see you. I come here today on a mission for a girl I love. It has to do with her mysterious birth. She was lost as a baby, and someone rescued her from a river in the hamlet of Upper Đinh-Xuân."

Bộ, blind, couldn't tell his guest's age from his voice. Though deep, a softness around its edge made the speaker sound innocent and youthful. His French was accent-free. Bộ felt he was being transported back to colonial days, when he was the grand eunuch of the Imperial Court of Huế, routinely entertaining French guests.

"I gather that this friend of yours is Vietnamese?" Bộ said.

"She came from France, but I believe she was born in Vietnam. There're some facts about her birth from the photographs and I'd like to show them to you." A silence. Then Jonathan continued. "I said that, but you must pardon me for having said that."

"Tell me about them then."

Jonathan described the photographs. "There're handwritten words on the back," he said. "*Hamlet of Upper Đinh-Xuân, 1942.*"

Bộ said nothing, sitting like an oracle who spoke only when asked.

"I couldn't find any house that had a pond in the hamlet of Upper Đinh-Xuân," Jonathan said. "But I was told there was a house with a pond like that back in the 1940s." He paused. "I learned that the original owner was a eunuch himself. This is as far as I could get in my search."

Bộ's lips parted but no words were spoken. In the silence he could hear voices talking outside. He unlaced his hands and placed one on top of the other.

"How old is this lady friend of yours?"

"She was my age. Maybe a year or two younger."

"Did you say she *was*?"

Jonathan coughed. "She died, sir."

Bộ's brow furrowed. "There was a question I asked you. I'm going to ask you again. Is she Vietnamese?"

"She's half Vietnamese."

"Half?"

"Yes, half. Do you care to know about her mixed blood?"

Bộ tipped his face and set his sightless eyes on the guest. "Yes, I would like to know."

"She's half Vietnamese, half French. And another thing I haven't told you . . ."

"Yes?"

"She could pass for your daughter."

Bộ pursed his lips. "Do you mean she looked like my daughter?"

"She looked exactly like your daughter."

Bộ shook his head. "How could it be?"

"I don't know, sir."

"Does she have a name, Jonathan?"

"Françoise," he said. "Her name is Françoise."

Bộ groaned, and only he could hear it. Years before, when he had to travel to Lower Đinh-Xuân he would ride a ferry, even after the main bridge was rebuilt in Upper Đinh-Xuân. Each time he ferried downriver, he saw the image of the bridge in the rain, and at night he would dream that he stood on the bridge while a little girl stood on the rain-washed riverbank watching him intently. She always stood in the same spot as if waiting for him to claim her, but each time he was cemented to the bridge, unable to reach her.

He lowered his head and placed his hands on his thighs. Jonathan broke the silence. "There's something that belonged to her that I wish to give to her family."

Bộ didn't lift his head. "Go on," he said finally.

"There's a ruby phoenix that she used to wear around her neck. She said it'd been with her since her birth. My job is to find her family and give it back to them."

"Didn't she have any relative in France?"

"She had her foster parents. They both died."

"Who were they?"

"They were North Vietnamese. I mean to say they were from North Vietnam and worked for the North Vietnamese government."

Bộ nodded and said nothing.

"She then lived with another family," Jonathan said, "that became her second foster family."

"Yes?"

"They're French missionaries. They were close friends of her Vietnamese foster parents."

"You said you had a . . ."

"A ruby phoenix. A pendant."

"Do you have it with you?"

"Yes."

Bộ received a leather pouch, then slipped his bony fingers inside. His fingers felt the pendant, his lips parted slightly, and after a while he pulled the drawstring shut and extended his hand toward Jonathan. His palm remained open for a moment as if it didn't feel the pouch being lifted, and then its fingers curled in slowly, his hand shaking.

"This is where I am, sir," Jonathan said.

Bộ looked down into his lap. "When did she pass away?"

"About eight months ago."

"What did she die of?"

"In a car accident, sir."

"Please tell me about the car accident."

"What is it that you wish to know, sir?"

"I wish to know how it happened."

"She was driving my car with me as a passenger, and it crashed into the rear end of a lumber truck."

Bộ heard a clink in the quiet. Jonathan must have set his glass down.

"How is she related to you, sir?"

Bộ lowered his head. "She's not related to me."

"Sir?"

Bộ didn't answer.

"How can this be?" Jonathan said.

"Strange as it may seem, I don't know her."

"Despite all the facts—"

"I realize the facts."

"And the evidence that she could be your daughter's twin sister—pardon me for my unwanted supposition—how could she not be related to you, sir?"

"She's not related to me, Jonathan. That's one more thing you must realize."

"Please help me," Jonathan said, his voice strained.

Bộ, staring at him, sightless, said nothing.

"It wasn't her wish to trace her origins," Jonathan said. "It wasn't her wish at all."

"Why wasn't it?"

"She didn't want to face some reality she could live without."

"I speculate that she'd been reared in a respectable family."

"Since she was a baby."

"Since she was a baby," Bộ said.

"They found her floating down a river in a basket. She was just an infant."

"Who were they?"

"The people who later became her foster parents."

"Whereabouts did they find her?"

"I don't know. Somewhere in this province."

Bộ muffled a sigh. "Do you believe in fate? Jonathan?"

"Only if it means something I must accept because I can't change its outcome."

Bộ listened, clasping his hands in front of his chest. Then he turned his opaque eyes toward Jonathan and said, "You and I both believe in fate, for it means exactly what you said—there are things we must accept because we can't change their outcome."

eight

Miss Phượng's memories were fragile. At times they were like the blue in the sky, throbbing blue that you could touch, feel. Other times they were fleeting shadows. Chase them and they flit like fish in a creek's bottom.

On this hot afternoon the taxi we rode in bounced on the rutted road, the red dust hazing the air. We were coming back from the Citadel where her father had lived for sixty some years. I asked the driver to take us to Upper Đinh-Xuân, where Phượng had lived for most of her life. She asked why, and I said, "I want to see it through your eyes."

"Through my eyes?" She touched her sunglasses, smiling. "Do you trust me?"

"Absolutely."

I felt warm deep down. Now she looked blank, her hands folded in her lap, gazing out and I realized she must be tired.

When we had passed the cane field, she looked back and asked, "Do you have a childhood friend—not just any childhood friend, you know what I mean?" I said, "No," and she said, "Mine died in that cane field." The name of Jonathan Edward came to my lips when she spoke again, "If one day they take away the cane field, perhaps turning it into a giant shrimp farm, I'm afraid I might lose my memories forever."

The taxi was going down a winding road paved with cobbles in coral pink; shade trees made it cool. We passed an open-air market, the cab moving slowly now, and there were people gathering at the entrance, the sun shining on their ivory conical hats. She pointed toward the market. "That's Well Market," she said. "There used to be a public well nearby that gave the market its name. My old noodle shop is still in there. I sold it."

"After twenty-some years?" I asked.

"Yes. My father bought me a stall at Well Market when I turned sixteen. It was empty, so I had to furnish it with the tables and chairs. Six tables, twelve people would be a full house. He warned me that I would have to stay up late every night making rice noodles for the next day and get up at five in the morning to make the broth and then shoulder two copper pots to Well Market. From a tiny stall it grew into a large beef noodle shop. Twenty tables, small and big, which seat up to fifty people."

"Why selling noodles, Auntie?"

"My father asked the same question. I told him I wanted to learn a trade I could be proud of and get rich with it. He said, 'You'll forfeit your schooling? You know you can continue your schooling and be carefree. When you go into business, you'll no longer be carefree. You'll deal with profit and loss, with an eye toward growth and gain.' I said, 'I've been thinking of what you told me would happen if you died while I was still young. I want to do the right thing.' He finally consented. He said at sixteen I had blossomed into a girl who would attract men, so he hoped I wouldn't become a peddler wandering the streets. He'd rather not see me going on foot from place to place, which could be dangerous. I said to him, 'The concubine you served, Ân-Phi, if she had been born poor like me, with an old father like you, what would she have done?'"

She paused. I glanced at her. Wasn't the concubine's eminence the sum of her pedigree and beauty? What would have become of her had she been born poor?

Then, after a long silence, Miss Phượng spoke. "My father said, 'Ân-Phi would have done what was best for her family. Now if you live in Gia-Linh, the most respectable trade is rice noodles. The Gia-Linh clan has owned that for over a century, and they supply noodles to all the beef noodle soup vendors in the Thừa Thiên province. The recipe can never be copied. The Gia-Linh clan keeps its formula a family secret. They never hire labor from outside. Do you want to learn such an art?' I thought for a moment, then said, 'Would they teach me if that means competition? Why don't I go into the beef noodle soup business instead of making noodles?'"

Before I could ask if she had a talent for it, Miss Phượng smiled and touched her brow with the palm of her hand. "I remember now," she said, "there was a street vendor who passed through our alley every day selling hot beef noodle soup around the time I'd come home from school. She made the best broth. Just to hear her old scratchy voice crying *Beef noodle soup!* made my mouth water. I asked her how she made the broth, and she just looked at me. I wrote down her recipe while she stared at my scribbles. I was fourteen when I made beef noodle soup the first time, and my father said, 'Dear, someday you'd make the best of all.' I remembered those words."

Miss Phượng looked toward the market, the din hammering our ears. I followed her gaze and saw an old woman sitting at a lamppost with another woman whose shirt was pulled up to her shoulder blades, revealing pale white skin. The old medicine woman dropped some liquid into a glass cup and lit a match. A flame spurted inside the cup. She stuck its mouth against the woman's back. As she let go, the cup stayed in place, sucked onto woman's flesh. Three other women waiting their turn squatted in front of the patient.

Turning away from the window she said, "My father told me then I could make rice noodles for my beef noodle soup business. That'd help avoid direct competition with the Gia-Linh clan. He said, 'Let's agree on one thing. You dedicate yourself to the soup trade, and I will stand behind you in good and bad times.'"

"Your father must've dealt with many people," I said. "The powers that be."

"Yes, if you were referring to the Gia-Linh matriarch. Blinded by cataracts, she was an unbent hag just as my father was a stubborn old mule. You see, he begged the favor to have his daughter trained. The matriarch listened but didn't answer, so he told her of his life-long career, of his service to Ân-Phi, who had come from Gia-Linh. He spoke of his admiration for her and how he hoped she would become the queen mother when the emperor died. The matriarch said, 'Bộ, sir, you are so old now that you have outlived all of our beloved emperors and queens. I am eighty-four. You make me feel young.' Then, opening a lacquered wooden box, she took a hand-rolled cigarette and the servant stopped fanning, leaned forward to light it. She puffed, said, 'The wish I had thirty-seven years ago remained a wish to the day Ân-Phi passed away. Our village would have been mentioned in history books if she had been the last queen mother.' My father said he shared her dream. The coronation ceremony, the matriarch said, was something she would have traded half her fortune to see. Eager to gain her, my father told her the details of the grandiose enthronement. I think Ân-Phi would not have minded him bargaining with the matriarch."

"Why did she lose her mind, sir?" the matriarch asked.

My father said he wished he knew. He sipped the strong black tea in silence.

"My heart broke the day the queen mother was crowned," the matriarch said. "Everyone in Gia-Linh was sad. How close to Ân-Phi were you, sir?"

My father said he attended Ân-Phi for most of her life at the palace.

The matriarch cut in. "But wasn't there a new eunuch as young as she was assigned to her? I asked because he came from Gia-Linh. I knew his family. He was the only son to continue their lineage."

The servant refilled my father's cup at a gesture of her hand. He wondered how she knew his cup was empty. She said, "I have often wondered all these years how Canh passed the physical examination. According to his father, he wasn't castrated."

My father shifted in the armchair, which was made perhaps for brief use. "I'm not sure if I could tell you that," he said.

"I want to know."

"Anything that took place inside the Purple Forbidden City is confidential, Madam."

The matriarch's hand felt for a round betel box. "Do you care for a betel chew?"

"Thank you, Madam, but allow me to pass."

"I am eighty-four years old, and I attribute the fine state of my teeth to chewing betel since I was a girl." She brushed a betel leaf in her palm with pink lime. My father asked about the color, and she said it was made from burnt oyster shells then dyed coral. She wrapped the leaf around an areca nut. "Do you believe that chewing betel reduces tooth decay?" she asked my father.

"Why do you ask for my opinion, Madam?"

"Because you know how civilization has progressed, from the day we never brushed our teeth to the day the French taught us to use toothbrushes and toothpaste. Did you lacquer your teeth?"

"Yes, Madam."

"So did I. Have you had any serious tooth problems?"

"Yes, I have, a few."

Slowly the matriarch raised the cud to her mouth and her jaws started to rotate. She tried to speak, mumbling, and worked the quid into the pouch of her cheek. She said, "You and I both know that betel leaves and nuts are antiseptic. The Chinese chewed them a thousand years ago to help digestion and do away with bad breath and sour taste on the tongue. But alone they are not strong enough to guard against tooth decay. There is a secret to it."

My father reached for his cup and sipped. The matriarch said, "Lime is the strongest antiseptic, and lime made from burnt oyster shells, besides its finer flavor, is more antiseptic than lime made from burnt coral." She chewed, paused, and then said, "I wanted to share that secret with you."

My father said nothing. The matriarch chewed her cud, her ivory face self-absorbed. She said, "There are secrets we must share sometimes, not because we are careless or break a code of ethics, but because we have something to gain in return."

She spat the juice into a brass cup and the servant quickly wiped the red stains off the rim. She said, "The secret to making rice noodles has been with my family a century and a half. It is still a secret. Yes?"

"If that is what you say, Madam."

"After all, a secret shared is a secret earned."

The matriarch opened the box of cigarettes and held it out. "Would you care for a puff of our best tobacco?"

"Thank you, Madam, but I must decline."

"I can only admire the clean life you live, and I sincerely hope you do not find my passion for tobacco and betel to be uncivilized addictions."

"I don't judge people for what they do or don't."

The matriarch discreetly wiped a thread of betel juice from the corner of her mouth with a handkerchief. "Our Gia-Linh is rich with tradition, yet cursed at the same time."

"Madam?"

"Our Ân-Phi's ill fate, her insanity. And then young Canh." The matriarch spat the betel juice into the brass cup again. "He did not die a natural death," she said. "But why? An impotent young man admitted into the palace eunuch ranks, only to return home later to be castrated. Why, sir?"

The memory again came to my father too quickly.

"If I made you feel ill at ease, please say so," the matriarch said, "and I shall stop this conversation."

My father breathed in the smell of aloeswood, its scent tinged with the piquant odor of the betel. He knew he could leave, come away empty-handed, and his daughter's future would be in doubt. He had come this far, and it was up to him to stay or walk away.

"Why does his death interest you, Madam?"

"Why *wouldn't* it interest me? Imagine the century-old court procedures. Imagine the flaws in them. Sometimes such flaws cost a life. What happened? Someone tried to correct the flaws and it resulted in his death. Do you know how much damage it did his father?"

"Did he work for you?"

"He did save my son-in-law. But he never worked for me. I presume you knew him."

"Yes, I knew him. How did he save your son-in-law?"

"My son-in-law was a French lieutenant." The matriarch took the red cud out of her mouth and gestured for the servant to refill my father's cup and then said, "That was in the nineteen-thirties, and Master Đinh was in his eighties and no longer performed exorcisms. But when our son-in-law fell ill and nothing could cure him, I turned to Đinh." She motioned for tea. She blew and then drank.

My father waited. The matriarch put the dark red cud back in her mouth and chewed leisurely.

"My son-in-law's illness," she said, "developed after he returned from a military expedition against the rebellious mountaineers near the Lạng Sơn border. He came back a victor but suffered an abnormality growing in his belly. He could not breathe. His abdomen grew to the size of a melon and kept growing. People familiar with that sort of abnormality said the mountain people had cast an evil spell on him. I did not know what it was and neither did my family nor the French doctors. When Jean-Claude could no longer eat without vomiting, I went to Đinh. He looked at Jean-Claude and confirmed the rumor about the evil spell. He set up an altar and chanted the *dharani* and then made Jean-Claude drink a glass of water. After he drank it, he threw up a great deal of water, and then something else came out. It was an iron hatchet blade the size of two fingers pressed together. Jean-Claude convalesced and recovered. After he regained his health, he petitioned the French government to grant Đinh an annuity, and his request was granted. Đinh received a small annuity until he died."

The matriarch took out the cud and held it between her fingers. "Đinh was devastated when his son lost his manhood in the tiger hunt," she said. "That meant the end to his lineage. But his son's unexpected death saddened him beyond words, for he believed his son had not died naturally. And he could do nothing about it."

My father coughed. "I take the blame for his death, Madam."

"In what sense, sir?"

"I gave in to his father's plea to save his sexual organs from castration. But word got out in the end, and he was sent back home to be castrated."

"Đinh believed that his son's death was prearranged."

My father held his breath, wary of her blind eyes seeing too deeply into him. "Madam, it could've happened to him regardless, before or after he was castrated. Death was common in those days for the castrated."

"But Đinh didn't see it that way. His son must have told him something we do not know about before he died."

"I have no way of knowing that, Madam. That would be between father and son. I'm sorry I couldn't be of much help."

"You were indeed helpful."

My father sighed, uncertain of her tone. The matriarch clucked her tongue. "I understand the complications of such a tragedy, she said, but I do not understand its implications."

My father knew she was still after the truth. The matriarch dropped the cud into the brass cup. She said, "As for your request, sir, I would like to help you and your daughter, but I can't promise you anything until I have time to consider the matter. If I disappoint you, be mindful that it's nothing personal. I have received similar requests from distant kin and reputable citizens, and I consider each request on its own merit. But, alas, the result is the same."

My father felt cold in his gut. All his joints felt stiff. The matriarch raised her opaque eyes to him as he rose from the chair.

"What do you remember most about Đinh's son, sir?"

"A very single-minded boy. Nothing in the world could stand in his way."

—o—

Three days later in a heavy morning rain, Bộ went back to see the matriarch. Bundled in his palm-leaf raincoat, he sloshed through the red mud pockmarked with water buffalo hoof prints on the long-winding dirt road that linked East and West Gia-Linh. The stiff blades of the raincoat rubbed against his calves. He wanted to get to the matriarch's early, but wading through the mud, he didn't feel like going. What if she turned him down?

Tired and drenched from the knees down, Bộ waited for the matriarch in the antechamber. She emerged, led by her butler, from the main room. Rain pelted the veranda and the matriarch, sitting down once again on the blackwood divan, commented on the torrential rain, lamenting the lack of drainage on back roads, which often led to flooding. From her tone Bộ sensed bad news coming, but the matriarch only asked him to excuse her from the visit, because she hadn't yet made up her mind. Bộ politely took leave.

A week went by. Sultry heat returned the day Bộ went to see the matriarch again, the day so hot that the blacktop melted on the walkway from the gate. Before he realized the tar was melting, his feet were stuck. On the shimmering blacktop a few sparrows shared his lot. He watched them beating their wings tirelessly to get free. Their frantic chirping attracted their kind, which hovered in midair in twos and threes, looking down on the show. He shouted for help, but his voice was lost in the quiet. At length he could no longer stand and sat down on his haunches and covered his bare head with his hands. In the end, a male servant came out and rescued him with a plank. Bộ went barefoot, leaving his clogs behind on the blacktop. Dizzy and weak, he was led around a gazebo of red gum, under the shade of tall rose apple trees, and through the courtyard into the cool antechamber. As he slumped in a chair, the servant brought him a hand fan and a glass of water.

In a daze Bộ saw the matriarch materialize in front of him as if through a haze. With her was the butler, who carried a pair of rubber sandals and asked Bộ to try them on. They were too small. The matriarch sent the butler off in search of another pair and told Bộ she had made her decision.

She said, "Because you had such a long association with Ân-Phi, the least I can do is make an exception and train your daughter. Outsiders are spies, Mr. Bộ, but I'll have your daughter trained in good faith. If she proves herself worthy of our trust, she can stay until she completes her internship—short or long, depending on her smarts. There are legal terms and conditions to be met. They are in fact honorary conditions: stay a small business in Gia-Linh after she learns the trade or move out of Gia-Linh and our business territory. I will not accept direct competition."

Bộ's head suddenly cleared. He didn't need the water and instead thanked the matriarch. He said his daughter would enter not the noodle trade but the beef noodle soup business instead and added that her intention was to make rice noodles herself for that business. The matriarch seemed pleased to hear it. Bộ stood just as the butler returned with another pair of rubber thongs. He tried them on and shook his head. The matriarch dispatched the butler to retrieve Bộ's own clogs stuck in the asphalt. When he saw his clogs waiting for him on the cobblestones, he bid the matriarch goodbye.

"Mr. Bộ," she said, "you must love your daughter very much. As a woman, I find myself personally impressed by single-minded men. They always leave a mark."

Bộ carried his tarred clogs in his hand as he left the matriarch's estate. Once outside he scrubbed their soles on dirt and sand until they were coated with grime. *Single-minded men.* As he put on the clogs, he thought of his own stubbornness and Canh's obsession—how he had willed himself to take the most gruesome path chasing his dream. Humbled by the comparison, Bộ walked home in the white heat without stopping to rest.

—o—

"I had a childhood friend," Miss Phượng had said, putting her empty teacup on the rail of the veranda. "We were very close. His name is Long," she said. "We met when we were both children. I was eight, he was eleven."

"You mentioned him, Auntie. But you didn't say his name."

"I met him at Well Market. That day my father took me there and we saw people gather at the entrance. There were sounds of music and singing."

Her father, she said, took her hand and walked up to the crowd. His imposing figure commanded respect and the crowd parted to make room for him. He cleared a space in front of him for her. She peered through gaps between hips and legs and saw a white-haired old man and a boy standing inside the circle of people. The old man's eyes looked opaque, and she saw that he was blind. He plucked the string of his monochord, rolling his head, singing. His voice was hoarse. But it gripped her with its melancholy when he suddenly raised his head with a shout and the boy mimed to the singing, stepping forward, glaring angrily at the audience, then retreating, hands raised to heaven, his face drawn with sadness. She didn't understand the fancy words the old man sang or why the people gawked. She looked up at her father, but he stood still, both hands on her shoulders, gazing at the old man and the boy. *The Ballad of the Fall of the Capital*, he later told her, brought back his memories of that fateful day on July 5, 1885. He had been an eighteen-year-old palace eunuch then, fleeing the Citadel at dawn when French soldiers raised the tricolor flag over the Zenith Gate. The royal court and families, a thousand people strong, fled on foot, in litters, on horse-back—the emperor and his queen, concubines and courtiers, mandarins, princes and princesses. To that day, her father remembered seeing a prince ride away on horseback, fleeing so fast that gold coins flew from his robe along the trail.

Painfully, her father recollected how the French had looted the Purple Forbidden City. Tons of gold and silver were pillaged from the imperial trea-sury, melted into bullion and shipped to France.

Meanwhile she watched the boy playing out a scene of a lost child cry-ing over his dead parents by the roadside. Sadness welled up in her. She looked up at her father and asked if she could go comfort the boy. He put his arms around her and shook his head. Around them, older women sniffled. The stench of fish blew in on the swirling wind. The wind gusts broke up the old man's voice and the sound of his monochord. Dust flew, people clutched their conical hats. The old man finally stopped. The boy rubbed the flying dust from his eyes and the spectators came up and dropped money into a wooden box the old man held open.

From the cloth belt under his brocade robe, her father took some money and gave it to the old man. The boy looked at her curiously. She looked at him with the same interest, then at her father who was chatting with the old man. Mr. Lục, as he introduced himself, addressed her father as Mr. Bộ, perhaps out of his respect for her father's former stature at the court. Lục called the boy, Long, over to greet her father.

Long was lanky, his skin sunburned to a dark rust. He bowed to her father, who rubbed his head and complimented his acting. Lục told her father they came from a remote village north of Huế to find work.

"I'm his grandfather," Lục told her father.

"What happened to his parents?" her father asked.

"His mother died after she gave birth to him," Lục said, groping for Long's hand. "He never knew her. The Việt Minh killed his father when he was five. He's eleven now."

"Why did they kill his father?"

"They killed everyone they didn't like." Lục wiped mucus from his nose. "His father did nothing wrong. Was just a silversmith. But that day the French came into our village on a search-and-destroy mission, so we ran to the countryside. We passed a Việt Minh checkpoint. A Việt Minh agent pulled Long's father away and shouted to his comrades, 'Spy! Spy!' They rounded up fifteen people for execution. The boy's father was one. Spy, traitor. Seen selling things to the French, giving them directions, talking to them. They shot everyone except his father. They chopped his head off with a machete. But they didn't cut it clean with the first stroke. Not even with the next stroke. Long's father had a thick neck."

Long was staring at her quietly as if the story were somebody else's. She crossed her father's large hands on her chest as he asked Lục, "Why did they call the man a spy?"

"He had a pocket watch he was supposed to fix for a French priest from our village. The priest gave him a cloth bag to keep it in. It was three colors: red, white, blue. The colors of the French flag."

"What is a spy, father?" she asked him.

"A spy is someone who tells secrets he shouldn't."

Her father asked Lục what kind of work he was looking for. "Anything," Lục said, as long as they had shelter. Blinded from smallpox shortly after Long's father had been killed, Lục had roamed the streets and now he wanted to rest his old bones. Her father told him there was a silkworm breeder in his neighborhood who might need a hand.

—o—

Upon her father's recommendation, the silkworm breeder hired Lục and Long as day laborers. That summer they lived in a shack on his estate.

Summer ended and the rainy season came. For days a cold, dry norther blew. People said a norther could parch mud, wither leaves, stunt the young and age the old. Rain came and went. The bruised sky became a murmur of rain. Gone were the chittering of birds at sunrise, the *ah-oh* of mourning doves. At night there were no sounds of peepers, frogs, nor the hooting of owls—only the sound of rain.

During the night she awoke and saw her father lighting the hearth. She asked him what he was doing.

"There's a flood coming," he said.

"I heard thunder in the ground."

"Go back to sleep. I'm going to cook before the water gets into the house."

But she stayed by the hearth while he cooked sweet rice in a large crock. He showed her how to wrap rice balls in banana leaves and store them in a wooden drum.

By the third day water reached the steps going up to the house. Rafts of auburn leaves and shoals of broken twigs swirled in the red water. At night oil lamps flickered through window gaps. She slept, wrapped in a blanket, hugging a rubber sac filled with hot water to keep warm. She dreamed of a river whirling with trees uprooted, spun free with the current. On a giant log she saw a girl standing with water dripping from her hair. Though nearly two years had passed since she last saw her, Phượng recognized the girl and wanted to go to her. A shattering noise jolted her awake. She saw a dark hole in the roof. The wind had ripped out the tiles. Rain slanted down, sizzling on the smoke-stained glass of the oil lamp.

Morning came. Her father chalked marks on the wall to gauge the speed of the rising water. By noon all three marks, chalked an hour apart, were under the clouded water. He dragged the bamboo cot from his bedroom and, old as he was at eighty-six, lifted it from the floor and stacked it on the mahogany divan. He tied the freshwater vat to a leg of the cot. "This will last us for a few days," he said to her.

Father and daughter squatted on the cot, hugging their knees, a blanket draped over their backs. Gazing at the water, she thought of the girl. She remembered her face, the same face several years earlier—she hadn't aged.

"Father?"

"Are you hungry?"

"No. I meant to tell you I saw the girl from the day of the locust again. She was waiting for me on a log in the river."

"Did she speak to you?"

"No."

"You weren't awake, so you were just having a dream. But if she does speak to you in dreams or waves for you to come, do not go to her."

"But father, she seems sad and lost."

He said nothing.

At noon a cat, wet and sick and shivering, rode the floodwater into the house. Phượng wrapped it in a gunny sack while her father fed it liquor mixed with crushed garlic.

A thatch house swept by with people huddled on its tattered roof, gripping its bamboo beams to stay above the water—husband and wife and children all flattened against the truss of what used to be the roof of their house. The wind buffeted their cries as the thatch house spun away into mist and sheeting rain.

Phượng cried. Her father stroked the back of her head. "Heaven will watch out for them, my dear," he said. "It always does." Between them sat the sick cat, rheumy-eyed, purring.

"Are you hungry?" She looked into his runny eyes. "I'm going to cook. You lie down and rest."

He didn't object. She had learned how to cook rice when she was seven. The coals smoked on the tripod. After they ate, she fell asleep in his arms, clinging tightly. He had told her children drowned in floods when they fell off their cots in their sleep. But he too soon dozed.

Sometime in the afternoon they woke to cold water lapping at their feet. They were ankle-deep in water red as rust. He held her in one arm, the wooden drum in the other. "We must go," he said. "Take the cat with you."

He wrapped the blanket around her, asked her to climb onto his back and tied his own blanket around them.

He sawed through the two window bars in Phượng's bedroom, and they climbed onto a branch of the flame tree under a canopy of dense branches trickling water. The cat snuggled against her chest, its warmth a small glow. The air smelled like wet leaves. The wind brought the smell of mud, of rotten things. She watched the floodwater flow through the house.

"How long are we going to stay out here?" she asked her father.

"Until the water goes back down. It's slacking off now."

"Will we sleep out here tonight?"

"Yes." Her father straddled the limb, his feet skimming the water. "Will you be able to sleep?"

"I'll be safe with you, father."

Shrill voices burst across the water. A great round vat bobbed on the current, drifting toward them. As it came near, Phượng saw Long's head peeking over the edge of the earthen vat. Lực floated behind the vat. It was leaking.

Lực shouted, "Where are we?"

"I don't know," Long shouted back. "Mr. Bộ's backyard, I guess."

Her father called out, "Here, over here! We're on the flame tree."

"Left, left," Long shouted, "Grandpa, left!"

Her father leaned down. Vapor curled in plumes from his nose. He grabbed the boy's hand, pulled him up. Quickly her father stopped the sinking vat with his foot, grabbed Lực by the arm and hoisted him out of the water.

Late in the afternoon the rain stopped. A mist whitened the landscape. Soon dusk fell. They sat on the flame tree, listening to the wind rush over the flat water and the ebbing floodwater gurgle. Her father gave Lực his blanket to share with his grandson. Phượng sat in her father's lap, hugging the cat and they wrapped her blanket around the three of them. She felt the dampness on her father's blouse slowly drying as his body warmed under the blanket. They ate sweet rice balls in the dark and each sucked on a piece of brown sugar. Somewhere a baby cried.

On her father's advice Lực sought a limb above them, where he could sit with his back against the trunk and rest.

"Don't fall off in your sleep," her father warned.

"We won't, Mr. Bộ," Lục said. "And you'd better watch out for yourself too."

Phượng leaned her head against her father's chest and closed her eyes to the purring of his breath. She heard Long's voice, "Grandpa?"

"Yes?"

"Can I pee?"

"Hmm. I don't think so. That's disrespectful in front of Mr. Bộ."

"But I can't hold it anymore, Grandpa."

Silence. Then Lục said, "Mr. Bộ is sleeping, I think. Phượng, are you sleeping too?"

Phượng poked her head through the blanket. "No, I'm not."

"Is your father sleeping?"

"Yes."

Lục said nothing for a while. Long groaned. Phượng heard him and she too had a bloated bladder. She tried not to relieve herself from embarrassment. Then Lục said, "Do it quick."

The branches trembled as the boy inched toward the end of the limb in the dark. Then Phượng heard a gurgle so steady she felt as gratified as if she herself were emptying her swollen bladder. The boy took a long time. Then stillness. Lục coughed. He seemed to hold the phlegm in his mouth without spitting. Then she heard it hit the water below with a tiny plop. He moaned. "O cigarettes! O my craving!"

Phượng parted the blanket. "Mr. Lục?"

"Yes, Phượng."

"What happened to your house?"

"My hut? Swept away. Clean." Lục blew his nose. "I stacked up two cots and we sat on them all morning till we could sit there no more." He coughed. Then his voice rose.

> O rain, rain!
> O all the ducklings and ducks,
> Swim around in the Milky Way.
> O soon all the fish big and small
> Rise up to the sky and snatch the stars away.

Phượng listened. For a moment she forgot the discomfort of her bladder. She pictured the Milky Way brimming with floodwater, the sky turned into a vast river swollen with fish that jumped up and gobbled the stars one by one. Dreamily she asked, "Can the fish go up to the sky and eat the stars, Mr. Lục?"

"Oh yeah, little one," Lục said. "Oh yeah."

"When will that happen?"

"When the Big Flood comes and the seas claim all the lands, then the fish will ride the water to the sky."

"Then what will happen to us? Can we go up to the sky and eat the stars too?"

"No."

"Where will we go?"

"We all die."

"It's terrible to drown in the flood."

"Grandpa once faked his death, so people thought he died in a flood," Long said.

"What happened to you, Mr. Lục? Why did you have to do that?"

Her father had woken up.

"Sorry to disturb you, Mr. Bộ," Lục said.

"Might as well tell her," her father said. "Keep the young ones entertained."

Lục laughed a purring laugh. "Little one," he said, "I faked my death so the emperor wouldn't have me executed. That was before you were born. I'd done nothing wrong except shaking my silly head while I played the opera drum. I played good, so the emperor summoned me to the imperial palace to exhibit my skills in front of him and the royal family. When he rewarded me with a handful of silver coins, he said, 'You certainly deserve the reputation given you. But I shall challenge that. What flaws your performance is your lack of body control. If you can stop shaking your head while you play, you deserve to keep your reputation. I shall see you here again in three months. If your head still shakes by then, I shall have it.'"

For three months Lục practiced every day and still the only way he could play the drum was to jiggle his head. He became ill. A few days before the command performance, a flood came in the middle of the night and wiped out many hamlets, killed scores of people. Lục was never seen again.

Later in the night as the flood withdrew, Phượng drifted in and out of sleep to the moan of wind blowing across the flat land. Lục's words left a gray feeling in her. How meaningless one's life could be.

nine

Twilight. On the lee side of the foredunes, sheltered by tall hedgerows of vetiver grass, the sandpipers rested. A flock of curlews was coming over the dunes' ridges, then another flock and another, pouring in now in a steady roar of wings, their calls throbbing, to seek a nesting place for the night. An early mist hung pale over the wharf and the waves broke in empty booms against the rocks, the wharf's pilings, and the buoys clanged.

She wasn't alone by her daddy's boat. A man was coming at her, and she backed away, jabbing the mending needle at him. I ran across the sand. She turned around to pull on the net and he lunged for her from behind and pulled down her pants. I stumbled and regained my footing and saw her swing around, her arm flying across the man's face. She saw me and quickly pulled up her pants.

He was an old man. Dropping down on the sand, he cupped the side of his face with his hand. I stood over him. A small, sharp-cheekboned, gaunt-looking man. His sweat-stained brown shirt had holes on the front like cigarette burns. The wind blew sand in my face. I could smell his unwashed body tinged with alcohol.

"You leave her alone," I said to him. "Or I'll break every bone in your body."

"Yeah? Aint done nothin to her, aint I?" he slurred in his viscous twang. "And look at what she done to me. Look." He moved his hand off the side of his face. There was a dark red gash from the tip of her mending needle.

I picked up her lantern and brought it close to his face. "You're lucky," I said. "You could've been blind in one eye. Now get lost."

He scrabbled around as if he had lost something. Then his hand came up with a squat-looking bottle. He shook it, then twisted open the cork and sniffed, muttering into the empty bottle as he staggered away. I watched him lick the bottle's neck as he bobbed across the sand then disappeared between the dark hulks of docked boats.

She looked calm as she adjusted her headscarf. "How'd you know I'm out here, *chú?*"

"I didn't see you at your house. Auntie Phượng said you didn't come today."

"I was at Auntie's today. Cooked supper and washed dishes."

"She said you weren't there. Said you'd probably be out in the pumpkin patch. Were you?"

"I were yesterday. But not today."

She got paid to help load up the trucks with pumpkins just harvested. Those ripe pumpkins weren't light, their rinds now hard in deep orange, hollow sounding when thumped. She said she worked the whole day until her back gave. Then she said, "Auntie has moments like that. Got today mixed up with yesterday."

I brushed the sand off my face.

"Don't you have a handkerchief, *chú?*" she said. "It's very windy tonight."

"I'll bring one next time. Who's that guy? A hobo?"

"You can say that, *chú.* He's drunk most of the time." She knotted a corner of a mesh with a twine and snipped it with her scissors. "One time when I was younger, eleven, twelve, he almost got me good. That evening I was coming down the dune over there to look for Daddy, and he jumped out on me from behind a filao tree. Drunk as a skunk. That good-for-nothing old buzzard."

"Then?" I squinted my eyes at her.

"He got my legs locked with his so I couldn't crawl away, and, and . . ."

"Pulled your pants down?"

"Yes, *chú.* I threw sand in his face and then I felt something hard in my hand and it was a horseshoe crab shell. It got sharp spines. And then as he bent to try to, to . . . I hit his face with the crab shell, and he fell off me."

"Did you tell your daddy?"

"Daddy knew he was crazy ever since Daddy was a boy. Said next time just outrun him. That old drunkard."

I shook my head, told her that if it'd happened in America, he'd have been locked up for good. She said, "Because America is rich." Then asked, "Did you see anything, *chú?*"

"See what thing?"

"What he did to me."

"Yes. He pulled down your pants." I paused. "And your panties."

"*Chú!* You saw?"

"Well, you asked me."

"No, you didn't see. Okay?"

"Okay. I didn't."

"Can you help me hold the net down?"

"Certainly."

There was a large rip toward the center of the net, still damp, heavy from seawater and smelling of fish. She'd cut out a patch from some throwaway net and the patch was draped over the gunwale. As she put the patch in place, I said, "Such a big hole. What happened?"

"It was rough out there today," she said. "Daddy didn't go out far. He set the net closer to shore. Lots of sharp rocks near the shore."

I watched her weave. There was a dry sound of wing beats overhead and looking up I saw a lone gull flying out into the darkening ocean now misted over. Straggling fishing boats were coming home, bobbing past the buoys toward the wharf where several gulls were already perched on the pilings, waiting. In a moment I knew they would shriek with pleasure when the fishermen hauled up their seines heavy with fish.

It was dark when she finished mending the net. The waves swelled and the wind blew out her lantern. She lit it again, her face suddenly awash in the orange illumination, her eyes a wet brown. I asked her if she had had dinner. She said, nodding, "Yes, I ate at Auntie's before I left." Then she opened her canvas bag, rummaging around with her hand, and came up with two packs of cigarettes.

"They finally had them today at the market," she said. "The kind you smoke, *chú.*"

I took the packs from her bony hand and said, "Thank you." Then, as I put the money in her bag, she refusing to take the cash, I said, "I still don't know your name."

"Didn't you ask Auntie?"

"Why can't I ask you?"

"You'll laugh."

"Well. I promise I won't."

She slung the bag over her shoulder and briskly footed across the sand. We moved toward the boat rows, the windblown sand gritty on my face, and I stopped until she turned around.

"Look," I said, raising my voice, "if you don't tell me your name, I'll make up a name for you."

She stood in one place like a statue, lantern in hand, the sand aglow at her feet. As she turned to head up the beach, she said, "Cam."

Cam. Orange. "Why d'you think I'd laugh?" I asked her.

"It's a weird name."

I thought so myself but said nothing. She looked down at her feet, then bent, hovering the lantern over the sand. A ghost crab, tan-colored, was coming out of a burrow, its eyestalks trembling like two black peppercorns as it froze momentarily in the lantern light. Off-white, you couldn't tell it from the sand until it sprinted down the slope.

"Where's he going?" I asked her.

"Follow him, *chú*," she said, smiling for the first time.

I couldn't see the ghost crab very well, as if it had blended with the sand. I watched her pacing in a straight line, the lantern raised high, and soon we stepped onto the damp sand now as dark as the color of water. Three feet away was the pale crab just barely above the tide line where waves washed in, died and trailed back. Before I could think, the crab sped backward, farther and farther up the sand flat, turned a sharp angle and stopped in front of a drenched-looking heap of perforated, round-leafed sea lettuce.

"Don't come near him," she said, looking back at me. "He can see you."

"Can he?" I looked again at its round eyestalks. I turned to her and laughed. "I think he is going for a bath."

"Daddy said he needs water to breathe. I mean, the, the . . ."

"Air, oxygen?"

"Yes. In the water."

I took a step up and she grabbed my arm. "Don't scare him, *chú*. Let him get his meal."

"Eating sea lettuce?"

"No. He eats beach fleas, mole crabs. They hide in those seaweeds."

Then she turned, and said, "I'm going to check on Auntie. Poor Auntie."

"I'm going with you."

As we cut across the sand, the crosswind blew out her lantern. She fumbled for the matchbox. In the blackness the sea came heavily on the wind with a wet, briny tang, the hollow booms of waves, and then suddenly the sea glowed in a long swath of light, pulsing like stars. I called out to her. Beyond the wharf, veiled in a white mist, the ocean was burning with an electric light of ghostly cold blue and glittering red and frosty green. She said those were sea lamps. At my exclaimed ignorance she laughed and told me that those were luminescent plankton. I said I wished I could capture the magical sea lamps with a camera.

"You ever seen sea lamps back in America?"

"No. I'm sure they're there. At the right time. I wish I were there."

"With her?"

"My girlfriend?"

"Yes."

"Would be lovely."

"When are you going back, *chú*?"

I thought then shrugged. "I don't have a date. Soon though."

"Are you going to marry her soon?"

I glanced at her. "Why are you interested?"

"I hope you'll marry her. If you don't, you'll break her heart."

"What if she doesn't want to marry me?"

"You're a man, *chú*. You can take it."

"Like your dad?"

"Yes. Except he gets drunk to forget her."

"So men aren't tougher than women."

"They are but women have more to lose."

I grinned in the dark as I walked by her side.

We walked in silence. After a while, she said, "What's her name?"

"Her name? April."

She said the name to herself. "Do American names have meaning?"

"Some do. Her name does. *Tháng tư*, the month. And it means spring for new life."

"What's she doing in America?"

"She studies, a senior in college." Then I shook my head. "She's a student."

"I know she's a student. And what d'you do, *chú*?"

"I'm working on my master's degree. Well, forget that. I'm a student, too."

"So you have to go back to school after summer."

"Yes."

"You met her in school?"

"Yes. Well, no. We go to the same school, though, but we met by chance out of school."

She turned to look at me, the lower part of her face aglow from the lantern's light, her lips slightly parted.

"We met at a Christmas party," I said, taken in by the look in her eyes. "I was twenty-two, a college senior. Her name is April McGillis, a freshman from a small town in Virginia. That evening she played the piano to the applause of the crowd. Then she sang 'The Twelve Days of Christmas,' and the crowd hummed along. Every time she sang the word "love", her eyes would meet mine. I had butterflies in my stomach. . . ."

But now, as we walked on, I felt insensitive talking about myself.

She was quiet as we left the dunes. I could smell a strong, musky smell, when I asked her what it was, she said nothing. We walked past the pond's shimmering liquid edge, which wrinkled when fish and frogs plopped into it. In the lull I heard peepers and crickets and bullfrogs in the undergrowth.

"You want to hear a funny story?" I asked her.

"What is it, *chú*?"

"About a Frenchman who trained his house cats to jump through the burning hoops."

"So they jump through the hoops like circus tigers?"

"Just like them," I said. "He lured them with a fish he dipped in gasoline and lit it up and held it behind the burning hoops. One by one, the cats jumped through the hoops. If a cat failed, he'd hold it up by the tail and shout obscenity into its anus. That cat made the jump the next time."

"Why?"

"It just did. Maybe those cats understood French."

She shook her head, but I could see that she smiled. Then the musky smell came back. I sniffled. She said that was a fox's smell and that he must be somewhere on the dune. She said sometimes if he is near and if you keep still, you could hear the soft padding of his feet on the filao needles. She knew it was him, a cross fox, his fur smoke-colored, slate-gray down his back and across his shoulders. Whenever he saw her crossing the dunes, he'd bound away and then sit down and watch her from afar. Sometimes in the evening, when she was out on the beach fixing the net, she'd see him hunting for fish washed up on the shore or beach rats, which he loved. He ruled the dunes at night. In the early morning you could see his tracks in the sand and, if you follow them, you could tell about his habitual itinerary. I asked her how she could tell his tracks from the tracks made by other carnivorous animals. She said, "I'll tell you next time. Just come out at first light."

We made it around the marsh, dense now with a heavy fog. Blurred, motionless figures on stilts stirred among the grasses that fringed the pond. The lamplight had spooked the night herons and I could smell their stench in the wind as we walked into the dense fog.

There was no light behind the window shutters of Miss Phượng's house. We went up on the veranda and stood listening. "Auntie must be in bed now," I said. We stood apart, like two strangers.

ten

I once asked Miss Phượng, "Do you ever feel French in your soul?"

"I never do," she said.

One morning on revisiting Gia-Linh we were walking down an old, paved road. Dogs yapped behind the hedgerows. Two mutts came through a hole in a hedge and sniffed at our legs. Miss Phượng shooed them with her hand, and they slunk away. In the morning stillness, she said peace was shattered in the summer of 1953 the day war came to Gia-Linh. "Right here on this road," she said.

By that year, Miss Phượng said, the fighting between the French and the Viet Minh hadn't affected her village or the vicinity. But it was bad for those hamlets where salt marshes and sand dunes stretched for miles along Route One, the north-south road the French convoys used. The Viet Minh ambushed French convoys and retreated into the hamlets surrounded by swamps and quicksand bogs. The French went after them and bombarded the hamlets or burned them down.

When the Viet Minh began to use Gia-Linh as a strategic base, Miss Phượng said, it came under French attack.

"Our house had a dugout," she said. "Many times my father and I hid in the shelter when French Hellcats came strafing and bombing." He told her that if she got caught in a bombing attack on the road to hide in a bamboo grove.

One morning she went to school just as the mist was lifting. She walked under the shade of Indian almond and poon trees, hearing the crows caw-ing in the trees and in the air. On the roadside stood a small shrine, solemn looking with its grandiose ceramic tile roof gleaming red, green and white. A group of women fish vendors overtook her, striding up in tandem, carry-ing rattan baskets in their arms. As they passed, edging her off the road, the stench of dead fish pickled the air.

Then the frantic sounds of drums and gongs swelled. Bombing alert. The roar of airplanes came so quickly, she barely managed to jump into the roadside ditch before explosions shook the earth. The air flamed. The Hellcats swooped, strafing the bamboo groves along the road, leaving a burnt smell behind them.

She dusted herself off, the front of her floral blouse hanging open where a button was missing. "Father!" She ran until her chest ached. Smoke and dust stung her eyes. Corpses lay strewn in the groves. Shreds of flesh and clothing were skewered on branches. She saw her father striding up the road in his gray pajamas, his wrinkled face etched so deep with fright it looked like a mask. His hands shook when he bent to hug her. Cries came from up the road. He took her by the hand and half-walked, half-dragged her in that direction. Past the shrine they saw a haze of dust, the tile roof gone, only the jagged front wall standing. In the smoldering ruins of houses lay the charred bodies of men and women and children. Remnants of fish baskets littered the ground among the sprawled bodies of women who sold fish for a living. She thought of the heat and shuddered.

"Why . . . did they kill them?" She gasped between sobs.

"They were in the wrong place at the wrong time," her father said tonelessly.

She wiped her tears. "This was their way to the market every day."

Her father squinted at the sun, searching for the long-gone planes that brought death. When he looked down at her, his face was pinched painfully, and his voice dropped. "In wartime a lot of innocent people die. When I said wrong place and wrong time, well, what I meant is fate brought them here where they shouldn't have been."

"But we're not the enemy. Why can't they see that?"

Her father paused to collect himself. "They hate the Viet Minh, and the Viet Minh look like us. When the French can't find the Viet Minh, they'll kill those who share the Viet Minh's skin."

—o—

Miss Phượng told me that after the bombing, she felt, for the first time, her French heritage—an indelible mark she wished to erase.

The morning after the bombing her father paid Miss Lai, one of their neighbors, to carry well water to his cistern. The public well was near the ground where corpses covered with plastic sheets awaited burial after the bombing. Miss Lai and her daughter made several trips to the well to fill the tub.

Miss Lai fanned herself with her hat. "You should see those crows, Mr. Bộ," she said. "They're all over the place."

"Surely all the corpses are buried by now."

"Oh, yeah. The crows just go for what's left on tree limbs and bushes." Miss Lai put the money in her blouse pocket. "Anything else you need, Mr. Bộ?"

"One of these days I might need you to read tea leaves for me."

"You said you don't believe in such things."

"You don't worry about your fortune until your life is disturbed."

Phượng followed the woman outside and caught up with her at the rock basin. "Miss Lai!"

Miss Lai and her daughter stopped, the empty buckets dangling on their shoulder poles.

"Miss Lai, can you read tea leaves about dreams?"

Smiling, Miss Lai shook her head. "I can't read dreams with tea leaves, Phượng. Tea leaves can tell you something about your immediate future. Why? Are you interested in something like that?"

"I want to ask you about my dreams."

"How old are you, Phượng?"

"Eleven."

"Dreams, huh? Let me see your hands."

"You don't need tea leaves, Miss Lai?"

"Don't have them with me. But I'll read your palms for you."

The woman sat down on the rim of the rock basin and Phượng sat beside her. After telling her daughter to take well water to another family in the alley, Miss Lai asked Phượng to rest her hands on her thighs, palms up, and looked at one palm, then the other. After a while she looked at Phượng curiously and said she always wondered how Phượng came to be her father's adopted daughter. After Phượng told her, she nodded repeatedly and looked back down at Phượng's left hand. "If you came from an orphanage, you must be blessed. Your father is a good man." Miss Lai traced the lifeline. "You'll have a long life, and happiness will come to you late in life. Now, what do you want to ask me about your dreams?"

Phượng told Miss Lai about the girl who came to her now and then in her dreams, and Miss Lai, looking at Phượng's hands again, bent each finger and examined the tiny lines at the base of each finger. "Hmm," she said, nodding to herself. "If you have a sibling, I don't know if yours is already dead or not."

Phượng gazed at the lines in her hands. "Do you see anything about my parents?"

Miss Lai squinted closely at my hands. "They are dead—from what I see."

"But I have my father. He'll care for me."

"Of course, Phượng, but he's an old man."

—o—

Bombs leveled Phượng's school. While it was being rebuilt, classes met in the communal house. To avoid French bombs, children went to school after sunset and came home before midnight. Even the market convened after midnight and broke up before dawn.

The communal house that became her temporary school was two kilometers from home, and her father, too old to escort her to and from, went to Lục for help. "It's no burden for me or my grandson, Mr. Bộ," Lục said, adding that Long also worked for hire at night, laying fish traps in ponds along the road to the communal house. To guard the traps, he slept near them until dawn. Long began to chaperone Phượng every night.

Phượng's sleeping habits changed because of the night classes. Instead of going to bed at night, she sat in a classroom lit by two kerosene lamps just bright enough to illuminate the chalkboard. Sometimes she dozed off like most other students, then awoke sharply to the sound of the teacher's rod hitting the blackboard. More than a week passed before she could last the class through and became familiar with the strange and eerie sounds along the winding road between home and the communal house.

Every night as they left the communal house and headed home, her classmates and she carried lanterns and walked in twos and threes until each went off her own way and the quiet road swallowed up the chattering voices and laughter. In the lull, Phượng heard crickets and peepers and bull-frogs in the paddies and the undergrowth, and her eyes scanned the dark road beyond the glimmer of her lantern, hoping to see Long. He'd come out of darkness like a ghost, emerging sometimes from the paddy and sometimes out of the underbrush, and she jumped when he called her name. He was always on time, because every time she rounded a sharp curve where trees and bushes made the night as dark as ink, where the paddies came flush to the shoulder of the road so she could see water gleaming under a full moon, she heard his voice. He knew by instinct—he didn't have a watch—when she'd be heading home. He said the body has a clock of its own, and if you ask it to wake you up it never fails.

Each night when they met, Long would take her lantern and walk be-side her with the yellow sphere dancing between them. Some nights when the moon was full, Long blew out the lantern to save the candle, and they walked along the paddies' shimmering liquid edge which wrinkled when fish and frogs plopped into it. He showed her where he laid traps to catch crabs and fish and shrimp, and he showed her the knife strapped to his calf which he used to cut the traps loose if they got tangled in water plants. He said he used it sometimes against thieves who came after his catch.

"You don't look like your grandfather at all, Long," she said one night.

"He doesn't look like me or anyone in our family, he told me."

"You know what your parents look like?"

"I knew my father until the Viet Minh killed him. But he didn't look much like me." Long shrugged. "I don't think much about my mother. I never knew her."

"Do you miss your father?"

"I don't know. I never felt close to him." Long switched hands on the lan-tern and took her hand and led her into the paddies along the earthen dikes.

He told her that was the shortest route home. She asked how he found his way home in a full moon when the paddies were under water, and no earthen dikes, no shaped plots, no dividing lines guided him. He said he knew the landscape by heart and told her a story of a strange encounter the night he got lost in the sugarcane field beyond the paddies several months earlier. One night, after hauling in a heavy catch, he lugged a tin barrel home, stopping now and then to rest. When he came to the cane field, his feet and arms were tired from carrying the barrel. He figured that if he cut through the canebrake, he would get home much sooner. If he went straight through, he believed, he'd come out at the main road again. But once inside the field he began to stumble around in the darkness, tripping over stumps and rough ground and soon lost his sense of direction.

Exhausted, he squatted on the ground, stubbly with spiky stalks, and closed his eyes. He wasn't afraid of being lost, but he thought of his grandfather waking up in the middle of the night and finding him missing. The thought made his heart ache. Then he heard a rustle coming toward him. In the blackness he saw a figure wearing a palm-leaf raincoat, though the night was clear and dry. The figure walked past him, weaving between the cane stalks. Startled, Long jumped up. "Sir!" he called out, not knowing who the figure was. The figure kept moving, hunched and pale under the yellow raincoat. "Sir, where're you going?" He staggered after the figure, his tin barrel clanking behind him, the only sound in the still night. Something told him he was being led out of the field, yet the distance between him and the figure grew greater and greater as he maneuvered the barrel around the stalks. The moment he saw the road, a swirling wind blew across the field, and dust flew. He closed his eyes, and when he opened them, he no longer saw the figure. *Where did he go?* Long wondered, looking at the only road along the field. Not a soul in sight.

Long said he believed the field genie rescued him that night. Phượng confided that she believed that good people like him were always protected, for a good heart wards off evil.

—o—

Phượng was fourteen when she played hide-and-seek for the last time. There were banana trees in her backyard where children found places to hide at night. They broke fronds at the stems and covered themselves with the leaves.

One night with a full moon, Phượng hid in the banana grove with Long, their bodies pressed against a trunk behind the drooping fronds. The sap smelled sharp where the stems broke. Something crawled under her blouse. She squirmed in fright.

"Shh," Long said.

"I've got something under my blouse."

"Where?"

"Here."

Long looked down at her chest, then pulled away a frond to see better. "Nothing," he said in a hushed voice.

"Under my blouse."

His hands came up to unbutton her blouse. She grew still. He parted the front of her blouse and looking down she saw his hand snatch a black thing from her chest. A caterpillar. Quickly she covered herself, Long's eyes never leaving her.

That night she dreamt she was alone in the tight cove while Long's voice called for her. She opened her mouth to tell him where she was, and then closed it without saying a word.

A few days later Long asked her what she wanted to be. Though having no idea what she wanted for her future, she feared becoming like Miss Lai's daughter—a maid for the owner of a large fleet of sampans in Gia-Linh.

"Do you want to learn a trade?" Long asked.

"I thought that'd be best. My father worries about what'll happen to me if he dies. He says he'll leave me an inheritance, but if I had a trade, I could support myself."

"What about breeding silkworms?"

"Silkworms? Why silkworms?"

"You could earn a living at it. Besides, if you learned the trade, we could work together. Think about it."

Phượng went to see the silkworm operation. The first few days she watched from a distance. Plump white larvae were spread out on round wicker sieves. Long chopped mulberry leaves constantly and Lục sprinkled them on the sieves. Quickly the green disappeared beneath the teeming white larvae. After a few days she came near the sieves to watch the larvae eat. She could hear them munching. Long asked her to change out a sieve.

The moment she lifted the lid she saw the sieve crawling with silkworms as plump as toes. She jumped back while Long laughed. "You're squeamish, are you, Phượng?"

"I don't like silkworms."

The following day Phượng came back and saw each bamboo twig covered completely with golden cocoons. Long removed cocoons from the twigs and dropped a handful of them into a copper pot of boiling water. Nearby, Lục sat at a loom, stirring the cocoons in the pot with a pair of long chopsticks until the silk wound around them. Then he fed the yellow silk into the loom. Even without his sight, Lục operated the loom smoothly and made several yarns of silk from the cocoons on a single sieve.

One afternoon Long came to her house and gave her a silk scarf the color of golden wheat. "I had this made for you," he said and draped it around her neck.

It must have taken many silkworm cocoons to make the scarf, which dangled to her knees. She smoothed the coarse, strong fabric with her hand. From his trousers pocket Long took a handful of yellow sage flowers, sprinkled them on her hair and tossed the rest in the air. Yellow, red, pink, mauve fell like confetti over her. She blushed and thanked him for the scarf.

"Join me and take up the silkworm trade," he said.

"If I take up a trade, it must be something I'd love to do, Long. I don't love the silkworms."

Long pulled his hand from his pants pocket and dropped his gaze to the petals in his hand. "Then what d'you want to do? You have something else in mind?"

"I haven't decided. But not a silkworm breeder."

Long's eyes filled with a brooding. He looked at her with longing as if he wanted to reach out to her. "Why didn't you wear a phượng flower?"

"I forgot."

—o—

Southern monsoons came in late summer, bringing respite from the drought. When the heat returned, the village council issued a warning of a rabies epidemic. Phượng's father told her that rabid dogs were scared of water and made her carry a bottle of water in her knapsack. He also made her carry a bamboo stick.

One night after school, she walked home with Long in the dark along the paddies. Their lantern cast a yellowish sphere in front of them. She was not thinking of rabid dogs but of a girl from school, whom a rabid dog bit. With no anti-rabies vaccine, she became rabid. Her family tied her to a bed-post. Phượng came with other children from her class to visit the victim, keeping a safe distance while she foamed at the mouth and beat her head against the chain. Two days later she died.

Wind swung the lantern to and fro, its flame sputtering, and then everything went dim. When the flame righted itself again, they saw a scraggly black dog, its sagging jaws slavering.

Phượng called, "Long!" and ran behind him. Long jabbed the lantern at the dog. That drew it closer, and it bared its teeth in the glow.

"Give me the stick!" Long said and grabbed it from her. "Get down to the paddy!"

Just as she started to run, the dog sprang. Long swung the stick, missed and fell. The dog bit him on the back. She rushed toward them and splashed water on the dog. The snorting dog tore away and stood beyond the toppled lantern, its eyes gleaming red. Long staggered to his feet and ran screaming toward the dog, which turned abruptly and dashed into the night.

The next day her father and she came to visit Long. He was listless. Phượng sat by his cot, cupping her chin in her hands, thinking of the girl bitten by the rabid dog. Then she took a red guava from her blouse pocket. "I saved this for you," she said. "When you get well, you can climb our tree and get as many as you want."

"I'm going mad soon, they tell me."

"No, you won't."

"You'll stay away from me. Everyone will."

"Don't talk nonsense." Phượng winced. "You'll get well soon."

Long's eyes were dull.

"You've been good to me and my father," she said, closing Long's fingers around the guava. "The Buddha will save you."

Her father examined Long's back. Lục had salved the wounds with salt and some crushed leaves. Her father told Lục that the boy had to have the anti-rabies vaccine. The hospital in Huế might have it, and her father offered to take Long there. At Lục's objection, he said, "Your grandson got hurt because of my daughter. Besides, I know the way."

In the morning her father took her and Long on a ferry into Huế. The trip took half a day, since the ferry docked several times when French fighter-bombers came searching for targets. In Huế they found that the hospital had been relocated to the countryside to avoid the bombing. Only an infirmary was left behind in the city. The infirmary didn't have the vaccine, and the hospital was fifteen kilometers away.

Empty-handed they boarded a ferry to return home. On the ferry someone told her father the boy would get scared of water within seven days, and by then he should not be allowed to ride the ferry. Phượng looked into the water, imagined how it would be when Long saw his own reflection and became crazed. A woman on the ferry told her father of a physician who practiced eastern medicine. She told him the man's name and the hamlet he lived in. She said if Heaven still looked down on the boy, there might be a cure for him.

The ferry arrived at their village at dusk. A solitary figure waited on the landing. At the bad news, Lục sighed deeply. Her father wanted to take Long to the relocated hospital the next day, but Lục asked him to see the medicine man. "It isn't far," he said.

They set out at first light. They had to change ferries several times to get to the hamlet where the eastern medicine man lived. He looked the boy over casually and said, "The medicine I'm going to give you might work, depending on the kind of dog that bit him. A pure breed or a mongrel."

Her father took the medicine in a pouch of faded yellow paper. He inspected it. "What is this yellow powder?"

"It's yellow dirt mixed with finely ground bones."

"What sort of bones?"

"Human bones. People killed by lightning."

Her father said he recognized the yellow dirt, because he once used it with lime to paint walls and firm up the ground around Ân-Phi's tomb. The man added that yellow dirt was used also in burying the dead. Her father re-wrapped the pouch and asked, "Has it cured anybody who got bitten by a rabid dog?"

"Very effective. But the last boy I gave it to died."

"How do I know what type of dog bit him?"

"I have only one concoction."

"What type of dogs is it good against?"

"It wouldn't matter, since you don't know what type of dog bit him."

That evening they came back to their hamlet. Lục was a lone silhouette against the setting sun on the landing. They walked home in the dark, Long leading his blind grandfather. Phượng couldn't wait to see if the medicine worked, and Lục was bent on using it, rather than searching for a vaccine that might never be available.

"No," her father said. "I don't trust that medicine. Let me take him to the hospital tomorrow. If nothing comes of it, then . . . "

At dawn she, once again, left with her father and Long on the ferry. On their way she saw French Hellcats bomb a village up the riverbank, and smoke plumed the horizon long after the planes were gone. Long tired quickly and dozed off whenever he had a chance to sit down, and then woke with his eyes rheumy. They found a ferry pilot who agreed to give them overnight lodging for a fee. Evening came, and they ate rice balls her father cooked the night before. She slept hearing the gentle waves lap the hull. Once she woke and glimpsed Long in his sleep.

She drifted back into sleep rich with the silty smell of the river. She saw the little girl, soaked and shivering, in her dream. The face of the girl hadn't aged.

In the morning they rose early and walked to the village in the mountains. Long was feverish. Her father gave him water, but he refused to drink, turning his face away. That frightened her. She tried to soothe him by holding his hands in hers, talking to him, but Long looked flushed, shaking his head from side to side as though keeping it still hurt him. She dabbed his cracked lips with water and made him drink sip by sip from the cap of the water bottle.

A doctor finally looked at Long and told her father the boy was indeed infected with rabies but that it wasn't too late for vaccination. Her father put his hands together on his chest and bowed to the doctor. Phượng felt grateful. Young as she was, she already felt empty to think of Long dying, a feeling far more chilling than seeing death itself.

On the fourth day of his sickness, Long was vaccinated at the hospital, and they returned home. Lục waited on the ferry landing. The blind old man's faith touched Phượng deeply. His love sought nothing in return. She guessed he must have waited there in the darkness the night before, waiting for the sound of the oars coming up the river.

eleven

In the clamor of the market Miss Phượng and I picked our way over its packed ground, looking down at the peddlers who squatted. A girl tugged at my trousers and handed me a shiny purple eggplant. I weighed it in my palm and shook my head. Ms. Phượng pointed toward a row of stalls at the end of the market.

"The noodle shop is over that way."

Her old noodle shop had a rush mat rolled up over the entrance. I inhaled deeply. A rich, spicy smell hung in the air.

At the back of the stall, a stove puffed wisps of steam into sooty shadows. A woman stood, her back toward us, stirring a large pot with a wooden ladle. She wore a scarlet blouse and satiny black pantaloons, and her hair was balled up into a grapefruit.

Miss Phượng just looked. Something gave her a pause.

"I trained her," she said. "I wasn't supposed to before I sold her the shop. But she came to me, heart in hand, and her sincerity won me over."

"You must've seen yourself in her," I said. "Wasn't that how you were trained by the Gia-Linh matriarch, Auntie? Way before you started this business?"

In the glaring sun she stood as if on a seam of past and present, belonging to neither. She shielded her eyes with her hand as we walked down the narrow macadamed path that went past the noodle shop and all the stalls, stepping on yellow coins of light the dappled leaves made on the ground.

Then Miss Phượng told me that the day before she began interning with the Gia-Linh clan, her father took her to the estate to show her the way. Coming back, he told her which way to go home at the fork in the road and explained she could also cut through the canebrake to save considerable time. They crossed the cane field under the strong afternoon sun. She followed her father, watching his back as they wove their way between tall stalks dotted with pale purple flowers.

That night Long came to her house as she was washing dishes in the kitchen. In one hand he had a bundle of young bamboo sticks and in the other a bamboo knife.

Phượng turned around. "Where're you going with those?"

"I'm going to make chopsticks for your beef noodle stand."

"Why?" She transferred a clean bowl to a fresh-water pail. "I can buy them."

"You don't have to, Phượng." He found a cutting board and sat down across from her. "These bamboo chopsticks will last forever."

"I thought you'd be helping your grandfather feed the silkworms tonight."

"Not tonight or the next couple nights. Those larvae already turned into caterpillars. They stop feeding." Long scratched his back with a bamboo stick. "How many pairs do you want?"

Phượng told him the eatery had six tables to seat twelve customers. Long said he'd make twenty-four pairs.

"On second thought, can you make thirty-six pairs in case I can't wash the dirty dishes and chopsticks quick enough for new customers?"

Grinning, Long said the remark was auspicious for her business. Between soaping the greasy dishes and bowls, she watched him fit a bamboo stick through a hole on the handle of the knife. He said it was the standard diameter for chopsticks, but it didn't go in. He held it upright on the board, shaved it with the blade. With the handy tool he made himself, Long said he could chop bamboo, cut it, cleave it, shave it, and shape it, and all the chopsticks came out identical in diameter, each pair a perfect match. Phượng watched him, the only sound was the sharp, dry scrape of the knife on bamboo.

Long stood a pair of chopsticks on the cutting board, checking their length and thickness. "Did your father mention anything about what he and my grandfather talked about?"

"What have they talked about?"

"About the two families. Our families."

Phượng sensed his nervousness and understood that the old men must have been talking about the two of them.

"Are you going to ask your father about it?"

"He'll tell me." She picked up a tapered chopstick and ran her fingers along it.

"Go ask him now." Long gathered the chopsticks off the cutting board. "I'm going home to see if my grandfather is feeling any better."

"What's wrong with your grandfather?"

"He has fever and a sore throat." Long rose from the dirt floor. "I'll make some more chopsticks tomorrow night and polish them for you when I'm done."

Phượng was surprised. "I thought they were done. They look nice enough."

"After they're polished, you won't be able to tell that they're handmade." Long stuck the knife under his belt. "I want your customers to know they'll get the best of everything from you."

"Thank you, Long."

Alone, Phượng went to a bin in the corner of the kitchen and brought out a small bundle of lotus seeds wrapped in a lotus leaf. After removing the husks, she trimmed both ends of the ivory-colored seeds and soaked them in water. While they soaked, she realized that she had forgotten to tell Long that she would start the internship with the Gia-Linh clan the next day.

Phượng found her father still up, reading by a kerosene lamp. When she asked him about what Long had told her, he rubbed his eyes and scratched the side of his face with his bird's-claw fingernails. "That's something I want to talk to you about, Phượng."

"Is it something Long asked Mr. Lục to ask you?" She sat down on a chair.

"You seem to know, huh?" Her father closed the antique-looking book's faded yellow pages. "Lục came to ask for your hand on his grandson's behalf."

Fingering the plait over her shoulder, she looked down at her feet. Marriage evolved not only from a long courtship but from intimacy. That special feeling she had had for Long had yet to evolve into love. Was he the type of man who could make her heart tremble with tenderness when she thought of him? He was her most steadfast friend, so steady, like the flame tree outside her bedroom window. Would love for him come from camaraderie?

"What did you tell Mr. Lục, father?"

"I told him you have your own mind, and the decision will be yours."

"But are you for it?"

"I am for it because where you put your heart is important. I think Long would take care with your heart."

"Have you ever been in love, father?"

"In love?" Her father rearranged his book. "I have never been in love with anyone in my life."

Phượng remembered what he used to tell her, borrowing his father's words: "A boy born without the burden of sex, his thoughts are clean." Maybe his thoughts were clean, most times, but his heart was empty of love, romantic love. In spite of that, he must have known what love was like when he relived his feelings for Ân-Phi. The sublime sentiment washed his being clean and filled him with tenderness and soothed him.

Her father dropped his voice. "You don't love Long?"

"You know I like him. No one else could take his place—as a friend. But for anything else, I want to wait and see what happens."

"So you think you're still too young to consider marriage?"

Phượng chewed her lower lip, collecting her thoughts. "Father, age isn't the question. Didn't you tell me Ân-Phi married the emperor when she was only fifteen? I feel special because of what Long has done for me and our family. But I can't say I'm in love."

Phượng couldn't help thinking of Canh's blind love for Ân-Phi. *Why does fate hurt us with unrequited love?* She mentioned the thirty-six pairs of bamboo chopsticks Long was making. Her father shook his head in pity. "Poor boy," he muttered. He told her how Canh used to graft gorgeous roses just for a chance to see Ân-Phi and how he taught the myna baby talk so Ân-Phi's affection for the bird might trickle to him.

Her father suppressed a sigh when she told him she was going back to the kitchen to cook sweet lotus *chè* for Mr. Lục to help his sore throat. He opened the book, closed it and then opened it again.

—o—

Miss Phượng said her first day at the Gia-Linh's noodle factory was tedious.

"First I watched," she said. "Then I took a long time to get into the rhythm of kneading and slabbing the dough."

She said she watched the women and asked questions—when to stop and add water, how to tell if the dough was ready for machine-pressing.

She worked willingly but had to rest often because of the heat under the tin roof. In a corner of the shack, clouds of steam rose from a row of giant copper pots. Above each pot hung a machine with a winch. Women stood and cranked pasty rice dough that wormed through a wire mesh, the dangling strands oozing and dropping into the boiling water. In the center of the shack, three men took turns pounding rice grains with a long wooden pestle in a huge, squat rock mortar. White dust hung like smoke around them.

While she learned the dough recipe, noting each measurement of flour and water, the ratio of rice flour and other ingredients, she noticed a boy a few years older than herself. He was the matriarch's nephew, and his name was Phát. Shirtless, he pestled rice grains with his muscular arms and looked at her through the haze of rice powder. Twice he bumped into her when he walked through the cloud. Twice she felt his hand brush her crotch. She avoided him throughout the day, but he cornered her when they stopped for snacks.

"Where d'you live?" he asked. His brow and arms were sweaty. His forehead had a red birthmark that looked like a tapeworm. "I'll walk you home tonight, okay?"

"I like to walk home by myself," she said.

"No girls like to walk home late at night by themselves," Phát sneered. "I have a bicycle if you don't want to walk. Or you already have a boyfriend to walk you?"

She said nothing.

"Aren't you afraid of the cane field? It's haunted at night."

"I'm afraid of nothing," she said, looking him in the eye before resuming her work.

That night Phượng left the Gia-Linh estate in a drizzle. She had forgotten a lantern and could barely see ten feet ahead of her. She stopped often, trying to make out the road. Slowly, she made her way to the sugarcane field. Her hair wet and her face damp, she heard the wind rustle the cane. At the fork of the road, she hesitated. Left or right? She forgot what her father told her. She could cross the cane field and pick up the road again. No. The sight of the cane field at night made her stomach churn. She thought of her father, now ninety-three, and how he had walked on foot in the harsh sun to show her the way to work and back. She thought of the trips he made to see the Gia-Linh matriarch on her behalf. Each time he walked by himself.

She entered the cane field. The ground was rough. Puddles of water collected around stumps, and she splashed and groped through them. The stalks pricked her fingers. She felt the sting. They must be bleeding, she thought, then pressed them against the front of her blouse. Rustling sounds filled the darkness. She tripped over a cane stump. A sharp pain shot up. She stumbled along for what seemed an eternity and then she stopped, her ankle hurting, her legs too tired to go on. She wanted to back out and take the long road, but her father would worry if she came home late. Worse, he'd venture out into the night to look for her. She had heard stories of people who lost their way in the cane field, the infamous cane field, and were found among the stalks in the daytime, choked with dried mud. Then she thought of Long's field genie and prayed that she too would be led out of the labyrinth of cane.

"Be good and nothing can harm you," her father had said. She repeated the words aloud to herself, then started again. Where was the moon? Suddenly she saw a sickle moon in the sky to her right, far away and thin. She was moving in the wrong direction. A toad croaked. Lightning whitened a corner of the field. Each time it came, she took her bearings and forged ahead reassured.

Beyond the field a yellow light danced, then steadied. A lantern. Her foot caught a stump and she fell, sprawling on the ground; she scrambled back up, but the light was gone.

"Who's out there?" she shouted.

"Who called?"

Phượng knew the voice. Long? "It's me!" Then she saw the light flickering ahead of her.

"Where are you, Phượng?"

"In the field."

"Wait there. I'm coming in."

She sat, eyeing the ghostly light wavering from side to side. She took a step toward it.

"Where are you?" Long called.

"Here. Stay there!"

The light stood still. She dashed out and stumbled into Long where he stood like a scarecrow. He grabbed her shoulder and she fell.

He didn't move. The lantern sizzled as raindrops hit it.

"Are you hurt?" Long said. "Where did all the blood come from?"

She saw red stains on her blouse. He winced when she said the stalks cut her.

"Why didn't you tell me you were going today?"

"I'm grown, Long. I can handle myself." Yet she saw his distress and quickly said, "Thank Heaven you came."

Long lowered the lantern, his face went dark. "You could've told me so your father wouldn't have to ask." Long held the lantern in front of her and led them back to the road. Phượng strode past him, but a sharp pain in her ankle stopped her.

"Can you walk?" Long asked.

"Yes." Long told her to climb on his back. She hesitated, but when the pain shot up her leg after she gingerly took one more step, she did what he asked. His shoulders felt bony against her chest, his torso thin. He smelled of acrid sweat, his familiar odor.

"How did they treat you?" he asked.

"Everyone was nice."

"Are they women?"

"Well, there're a few men. They grind the flour. I guess the women don't want to do that. It's hard work."

"How old are the men?"

"They're older, except one."

"What about him? From the Gia-Linh clan?"

"Of course. He's the matriarch's nephew."

Long was quiet for a while, then said, "If they treat you nice, that's good to hear."

Phượng didn't say anything. Long half turned his head toward her. "Well?"

"Well, I didn't feel at ease with him. I didn't like the way he kept looking at me."

"Because you're pretty, Phượng. Is that all?"

Phượng said nothing. She didn't want to lie.

"What did he do?" Long asked.

"He touched me."

"Where?"

She told him. "He made it look casual."

"Damn." Long panted as he topped an incline.

She tapped his shoulder. "I can walk. You're tired."

They walked side by side. She told Long how she used the moon to find her way in the cane field. He said she was lucky, for tonight was the last night she could see the moon before its new cycle. She smiled; said she was luckier that he had found her.

"My grandfather," Long said, "ate two bowls of your lotus *chè* and I ate one. It was so tasty. Grandpa suggested you offer it as dessert at your eatery."

She thanked him for the compliment and said cooking sweet *chè* was hard work. You have to push out the green wick in the center of each seed, so it won't taste bitter, she said, adding that the seeds had to be sugarcoated in a frying pan and then dusted with white sugar and wrapped inside the meat of a *longan* fruit. Afterward they were boiled in water and alum and stored in a ceramic casserole. She told him she laid a lotus leaf on top for fragrance and covered the casserole with a lid. Left out on the rim of the rock basin overnight, the chill and moisture kept it cold.

Long cleared his throat. "Phượng, I want to ask you . . ."

Had her father told Mr. Lục that she turned down Long's proposal to marry her?

"I know you'll own a business," Long said as he kept on walking and spoke with his face canted toward her. "I plan to enlist in the armed forces. That's why I want to ask you if we can marry someday. That was what my grandfather talked to your father about."

"My father told me."

"I know you're only sixteen and I'm nineteen, but I can wait. Do you want to marry me?"

"That's something I can't just say yes or no to." Phượng heard her tone of voice and feared she might hurt him. "What does marriage mean to you?"

"To settle down with a girl for the rest of my life."

"Even though you might not know how she feels about you?"

"How do you feel about me, Phượng?" He switched the lantern in his hands.

Phượng spoke clearly, drawing out each word. "I am sure of what I want in life, and I am sure of the difference between friendship and love. What we have is friendship, the best friendship I could hope for. I understand you want to take it further, but it's a kilometer, not a step, to get there."

His head jerked as if with a nervous tic. She couldn't help but look away. She wanted to say something to him, but she could not. She felt thick in her throat and couldn't tell what it was. Pity or sympathy.

When she looked at Long again, she saw the brooding cloud in his eyes.

—o—

For many nights after that Long met her near the cane field. Sometimes as she crossed the field, he called her name and she shouted back. She told him not to worry, but he seldom failed to meet her. The few nights he over-slept were when he stayed up late feeding silkworms. Then, in the morning, before she set out, he rushed to her house to apologize.

A month went by. Phượng felt confident making noodles and asked the matriarch's permission to end the internship. The matriarch agreed and that night she left an hour early. She said goodbye to everyone in the fac-tory, and some of the older women packed homemade sweets in small bags for her to take home.

Phượng went up the road, a lantern in her hand. The air hung thick, and the grass smelled dry. Insects trilled in the grass along the road and gnats and flying bugs circled the lantern, then popped when they flew into the flame.

Walking sprightly, she hummed a nameless tune. Only a few people in the Gia-Linh clan knew the noodle recipe, and she now knew it too. She was proud that the noodles being made this night and the next day from the Gia-Linh factory were from her mix, approved by one of her mentors. She felt older and wiser. Her apprenticeship had opened a door and the prospect of her independence made her giddy.

She wondered how the Gia-Linh clan had started the noodle business. One day at a time, maybe. One happy customer at a time. Keep the highest quality at all costs and keep improving. Did the first one sell noodles from a stall, or did she go from street to street? How long did it take her to establish her name? A flash of lightning broke her train of thought. When darkness returned, she thought of the day she would be established. Would her father still be around to see his sacrifice rewarded?

Phượng heard an owl high in a tree. From the underbrush came a rustle. She was familiar with the night sounds of rodents hunting for food. Before her lay the dark cane field. She held the lantern low to see her way over clumps of sedge, tiger grass, and black stumps.

She heard shuffling footsteps and turned her head just as someone flung her to the ground, knocking away her bag and lantern. His cigarette breath on her face, the attacker yanked at her clothes.

Out of the corner of her eye she saw a light far up the road. "Long! Help!" The attacker's hand covered her mouth and she bit him. His hand clamped her jaw. He tried to push himself into her. Long was calling her name from far off. She struggled and Long's voice came closer. "Phượng! Phượng!"

The assaulter sprang into the darkness. Phượng pulled her clothes around her as Long stumbled up. "Phượng! What happened?"

"Someone tried to rape me," she said breathlessly, pointing to the field.

Long dropped the lantern and ran after the attacker. The lantern glowed yellow at her feet. Soon there were shouts and she felt like crying. *Don't cry. Fear not. For a good heart could ward off evil.*

Long came back into the lantern's light, pushing the matriarch's nephew ahead of him. Phát's shirt was torn at the shoulder.

"He said he knew you," Long said, pressing his bamboo-handled knife on Phát's shoulder. There was blood on Long's shirt.

Phượng told Long who he was. Long poked at Phát from behind. "Kneel!" he said. Phát hesitated. Long kicked the back of Phát's legs and he buckled. Long pressed the knife against his neck. "What did you do to her?"

Phát didn't answer.

"If she says you lie," Long said, "I'll cut you. Now answer!"

Phát looked up at Phượng. Then he said he'd waited for her in the cane field.

"Did you rape her?"

Phát said nothing. Long nicked his neck. The man groaned as blood streaked down the side of his neck.

"Let him go, Long."

Long raised the tip of his knife. Phát got up, grabbing the side of his neck. When he was gone, they left the cane field and walked side by side on the road.

"Heaven knows how glad I was to see you," Phượng said. "I was going to drop by your place when I got home. I didn't want you to miss me on the road. Thank you, Long, for coming for me."

She said good-night to him at her house. Before she had reached the door, he called her name. She turned. "Yes, Long."

"I've thought about what you said, Phượng. I'm leaving for Saigon next week, so I want to ask you again: Have you changed your mind about us?"

She said softly yet clearly, "I have not, Long." She held her lantern low and looked down into its glow. "I'm not ready."

"Do you feel anything for me?"

"I do. Much as you feel for me—as one dear friend to another."

"When will it be right for you?"

"When I feel ready."

Long looked at her as the candle burned out in his lantern. The smell of melted wax lingered in the air. "I'm sorry, Phượng. I shouldn't have asked that question on a night like this. But I love you. We grew up together. Think about it."

He disappeared into the night. She wanted to call him, but despite her affection for him, she could not mistake it for romantic love. Would she ever be ready for his love?

—o—

A week later, Long enlisted in the army in the South. He was shipped to Saigon for training.

A month after his departure, her father bought her a stall in Well Market, and she became a businesswoman. Her day began at five-thirty in the morning and ended when she got home at sunset. By the end of the rainy season, she had a steady flow of customers and she remembered every face that came and went. People came from nearby villages to eat her *bún bò Huế*. Those who shopped at Well Market began their day with a bowl of her beef noodles, simmering red, and those who left the market without one if she had already sold out felt upset.

The first day of winter Long came home on furlough. He came to Phượng's house in the evening, dressed in combat fatigues and thudding black boots. He was darker, thinner, and his cheekbones jutted. A crew cut made him look older; there was a manliness about him.

He stood in the kitchen, wringing his maroon beret gently in his hands while he watched her cook. "You can eat with us," she said, feeling lively in his presence.

Long smiled. "I want to eat your *bún bò Huế*."

She turned the rice pot on the hearth and told him to come to Well Market the next day. She'd make a bowl just for him.

He looked surprised. "What d'you mean? Aren't all the bowls coming from the same big pot?"

"Yes, but not yours. Remember how that lady who used to come by here tenderized her beef in pineapple? You liked it. Do you still like it?"

"I do. You have such a good memory. Is that because you've been thinking of me?"

"Because your chopsticks brought me good luck." She thought of the thirty-six pairs he'd made for her in case she couldn't wash the dirty dishes and chopsticks quick enough for new customers.

Long hesitated. "You're seventeen now . . ."

"You'll like what I serve you, Long."

His eyes turned moody. She knew what he wanted to ask but hoped he wouldn't. His love for her was growing, while hers showed no sign of taking root.

That night, with her father's permission, Long stayed and ate dinner with them. Afterward he and Phượng sat on the floor in the kitchen while she ground rice grains into flour for the next day's *bún bò Huế*. The night was chilly, but the fire in the hearth was warm. Long fetched coals from a gunnysack in a corner. He stoked the fire and smoked a cigarette.

"You never smoked before," she said.

"Never needed it," Long said, glancing at the cigarette. "It keeps me company."

She noticed his new wristwatch. He never had one before. Suddenly, she felt close to him again. It came softly, like the crackling of embers.

"Do you ever wish for something very personal?" she asked him.

Long nodded. "I wish to have a family. A home."

He chain-smoked, watching her knead the rice dough. The flames shone on his copper-toned face and his eyes when looking at her seemed lost. She felt their closeness again, like the warmth of an old sweater. But seeing him smoke she felt his isolation.

They stayed up until midnight. He talked. She listened. Long smoked until he was out of cigarettes. She waited for him to ask the question he wanted to ask, but he never did. He left, saying he'd come to Well Market before she closed, and they'd walk home together like old times.

The next day Phượng waited at her stall until dark, but Long didn't come. She put away all the utensils, wrapped up the beef tenderized in pineapple and covered it with ice. He must have forgotten. No, she thought, impossible. Perhaps Mr. Lục was sick.

She headed home, her two empty pots swinging on her shoulder pole, the lantern in her hand shining about her feet. She had the silk scarf Long had made for her around her neck. It fluttered as she trotted up the empty road. Near the cane field she heard a sound like a shriek borne eerily in the wind. Farther on she came to a large puddle in the otherwise dry road. The damp dirt glistened in the lantern light and the dark stain trailed into the field. She lowered the lantern to the ground and saw the dusky color of blood. She hurried on, thinking how a good heart could ward off evil.

When she got home, she asked her father if Long had come by.

"No."

She went to Long's place and found Lục in his white pajamas, smoking a cigarette in the silkworm shack.

"Where's Long, Mr. Lục?"

Lục's blind eyes turned in her direction. "Didn't he come back with you, Phượng?"

"He never came. Do you know where he might've gone?"

"He's been out all day looking up his old buddies. He came back late in the afternoon and told me he was going to see you at the market. Where else could he be?"

She told Lục what she saw on the road. He rose from his stool, snuffed out his cigarette against the heel of his sandal. "Take me there."

The silkworm breeder's son and a male servant went with them to the cane field. The bloodstains had dried in the dirt. The search party stood on the edge of the road, swinging their lanterns in front of them and peering into the dark field.

Phượng and the men left Lục on the road and went three abreast into the field. A night bird shot up among the stalks, its shrill cry startling them. She looked to the ground and saw Long, facedown, his beret buttoned neatly in one of the epaulettes of his tunic. The side of his neck was slashed.

Her vision clouded; the lanterns seemed to sway. She heard the male servant shout "Mr. Lục!" and Lục's voice calling back from the road. She felt chilled and the cold came not from the air but from within her. When she couldn't make out Long's face anymore, she realized she was crying, and regaining her senses she asked the other two to carry Long to Lục.

They left Long's body with his grandfather and waited in his shack for daylight to report the murder to the authorities. They laid Long on his own cot under a blanket. Men and women crowded the shack. Her father sat on a stool beside Long, his hands on his knees. He saw the wound on the boy's neck and closed his eyes each time someone turned the blanket back. Men smoked and women cursed a faceless villain. Lục squatted in a corner, chain-smoking. Phượng sat on the floor by her father, wondering how the law would find the miscreant. She hadn't told anyone about the attempted rape, not even her father. Hiding it from him, she thought, would stop him from worrying about her coming home every night from her noodle shop.

When everyone had gone except her father, Lục, and herself, she rested her forehead on her knees and fell asleep. She woke in the stillness. The men snored; an owl hooted somewhere in a tree. Had it come for the soul of the dead? Phượng rubbed her eyes, smelling pineapple on her fingers. She couldn't sleep anymore and dawn seemed an eternity in coming.

twelve

When the rain stopped, I walked Miss Phượng back to her house. She gave me a hand towel to dry myself and went to change her clothes. When she came out again, sprightly and radiant in a carmine blouse and white cotton pants, she handed me a plaid flannel shirt; it smelled fresh, like linen just washed.

Behind the house the landscape was a patched quilt in glowing reds and greens. Raindrops glistened on the boughs of filaos. She gazed into her tea. I saw her and put my hand on top of hers.

"Auntie," I said, "has your father ever told you about that young eunuch?"

"Canh?"

"His death seemed to have stirred the Gia-Linh matriarch's imagination."

"I've been thinking about that," she said without looking up. "Tell you or not to tell you."

"You don't have to tell me." My voice dropped.

"Minh," she said, clasping her teacup, "after my father died—and with his influence long gone—I looked at everything with a fresh eye. What I found out did not fit what I wanted to believe." She looked up at me, her jaw set. "My father molested Canh, the young eunuch."

"Sexually molested him?" my voice raised. "Who's this Canh, Auntie?"

"He was my father's protégé and Ân-Phi's childhood friend. The best tiger catcher from Gia-Linh. That's what my father told me...."

thirteen

The tiger catcher lay bleeding on the forest floor near a wooded trail to the village of Gia-Linh. The young man's head swam with sounds. He remembered gongs, drums, cymbals, and men shouting, then the hounds barking all night. Two days, two nights. At dawn the men moved in, hacking away branches with their machetes and knives. As planned, they spread out their net and converged. But the moment the men opened an escape route to bait the tiger, it charged and knocked Canh backward as it ran into the trap.

Semiconscious now, the tiger catcher heard a deep rasping call and thought of the crow that had led him to this moment when it flew over the village communal house and perched on the roof with a bone in its beak. Preening and stretching her black feathers, she cawed until sunset: a singsong monologue that ended with the drop of a wrist bone belonging to the best tiger catcher from Gia-Linh, who had been killed during his last hunt. Villagers had built a shrine to house his spirit, and Canh spoke to the master tiger catcher through a medium to learn the ancient art.

Half a kilometer up the trail, village men carried the live man-eating tiger strung upside down from a bamboo pole. Spectators fought for a place in line to catch a look at the huge animal frothing at the mouth. Hounds bounded among the throng, barking. A gong boomed in the forest. In its lingering echo, lancers in scarlet tunics rode out of the forest in a single column, their spurs gleaming in the sun. Four military mandarins on horseback, long scabbarded swords slung from their hips, flanked the red palanquin draped with yellow silk curtains and shouldered on lacquered poles by six porters. A column of litters followed the palanquin, trailed by imperial guards who carried rifles in the crooks of their arms. The emperor and his retinue, after watching the spectacle, were returning to the Purple Forbidden City in the capital of Huế.

The grand eunuch of the Huế Imperial Court strode toward his horse in the clearing near where Canh remained still. The tiger-catcher gazed at the huge man who wore the official black hat with a figure of a cicada sewn on the front. So small a creature adorning such a giant.

The sun shimmered on his green brocade robe, illuminating the ivory tablet on the eunuch's chest. His horse saw him, pulled on its tether and stamped its feet. The eunuch appeared hot and tired.

The villagers crouched around Canh, who lay on his back, his head propped against the sculpted roots of a flame tree. The scarlet blooms mirrored the heat of Canh's body. The tiger's claws had torn his flesh from his left nipple to his waist so deeply that pellets of white fat showed. He reached for his penis, tenuously attached, and squinted at the physician.

The court physician, white haired and pink skinned, wrapped a white cloth around Canh's naked torso. "We will try to save you, save your manhood."

A village man raced across the clearing just before the grand eunuch mounted his horse. The man said, "The court physician would like to see you, sir."

The eunuch peered down at the man. "What does he want?"

"He needs to talk with you about the tiger catcher. The boy may lose his manhood."

The grand eunuch put back on his hat and followed the messenger to the group of villagers gathered around Canh.

The court physician squinted at the grand eunuch. "He asked whether, if he loses his manhood, he can become a palace eunuch?"

The grand eunuch squatted and laid his large hand on Canh's abdomen. "My name is Bộ. I'm sorry for your injuries, son. Why did you ask to become a palace eunuch?"

"I wish to serve at the palace."

Bộ glanced at Canh's penis. Flies buzzed in the heat, settling on the white cloth. "Can it be saved?" Bộ addressed the physician.

The physician shrugged. "I don't know. I can try sewing it back."

"Do it now." Bộ turned to Canh. "You won't lose it, you hear?"

Canh shook his head in protest. Bộ bent closer to his face. He listened to Canh's words, then turned to the physician. "He doesn't want his manhood saved."

When the physician asked him if he felt clear-headed, Canh nodded.

"The boy must be hallucinating. Save it," Bộ told the physician.

Canh mumbled in pain. The crow had led him to seek the wisdom of the tiger catcher, had sealed his fate with this hunt.

Canh whispered again to the physician, who then turned to Bộ. "He asked if you could help him get his wish."

"We haven't recruited eunuchs for years. You know the decree from our last emperor. No more new eunuchs."

The law passed nineteen years earlier in 1914 abolished the recruitment of new eunuchs and penalized anyone who asked monetary compensation for castration.

Bộ rose to his feet.

"What am I going to do with him?" The physician winced. "Save him? Not save him?"

"Save him." Bộ turned to leave.

Canh called out a muffled, "Please."

"What's your name?" Bộ said.

"Canh."

"Why palace eunuch? This seems fanatical if given the choice."

"I want . . . to serve. I did my civic duties . . . I got hurt. This is my choice."

"How old are you?"

"Twenty-two, sir."

"You know that we could save you."

Canh mumbled a yes.

Bộ lowered his voice, "But you don't want to be normal again. Very well. I'll write a report to the Ministry of Rites about your case. But for now, we'll try to keep you intact." He turned once again to take leave of Canh then said, "If you are accepted, the law says that a palace eunuch may have no penis and no testicles. You will need to submit to castration. Are you truly prepared for this, Canh?"

Canh nodded in affirmation. He was prepared to do anything if it meant honoring his vow to Quỳnh Hương.

—o—

The gate of Quỳnh Hương's residence had never been closed except at night, but when the neighborhood learned she would become a concubine, the gate was shut permanently. Canh and Quỳnh Hương were fifteen at the time of her induction. By then he knew every square foot of Quỳnh Hương's estate, since he spent most of his childhood trailing after her, hoping to see her, speak to her, serve her every wish.

Quỳnh Hương was everything beautiful, more exquisite than the sea of lotus flowers or the hundreds of rose species adorning her estate. She was his neighbor, and despite the class difference, she always treated him as an equal.

When they were children, Canh invited her to his house to witness his father's magic, hoping it would enchant her into loving him. Canh's father, Đinh, was a known exorcist who healed the living by calling up the dead.

Đinh smoked opium every day and always craved sweets. He told Quỳnh Hương that if she had money, she could watch a game called "Mouse, Go, Mouse." She loved the game so much she'd run to Canh's house whenever her mother gave her money. Đinh took the money and gave it to Canh, who bought candy drops shaped like areca nuts, powdered white. The sweet drops came in a paper bag. Đinh told Canh to put the bag of candies on the ancestral altar. As Canh climbed up the short ladder, Đinh kneaded a wax ball into a mouse and patted it affectionately. He lay down on his side, drawing in smoke through a copper pipe capped with a bowl, then reached behind his back for the little wax mouse. "Go!"

A paper rustle came from the altar. Dreamily Đinh exhaled the smoke through his mouth and reached behind himself. When he opened his hand for Quỳnh Hương, there was a sweet drop on his palm. "Please have an are-ca-nut drop."

Wide-eyed, Quỳnh Hương took the drop from Đinh's hand. Again, the host curled on his side, drawing deeply on the pipe. "Go!" Smoke wafted from his mouth. Another rustle of paper on the altar. He swept his hand behind his back and fed a drop into his own mouth.

Quỳnh Hương sat through these afternoons until Đinh said "Go!" and no more sound came from the altar. He asked Canh to go up to the altar and fetch the paper bag. All the drops in the bag were gone.

Quỳnh Hương's eyes danced with pleasure and Canh looked on with undying devotion.

Her family often hired him for small jobs around the estate, but Canh preferred to care for Quỳnh Hương. He made it his mission to kill the colony of red ants that formed every summer at the base of the gazebo and stung Quỳnh Hương's bare feet. Though in pain for days, she told him not to kill them. She could not bear to see anyone, or anything suffer, and she made Canh promise not to do them harm.

One summer morning her family hired Canh to pick mangoes from the tall trees surrounding the gazebo. During the day, the ants attacked and by day's end had stung him mercilessly on his legs and crotch. He sat beneath a tree, shirt off, scratching himself. When Quỳnh Hương came out, she sent the maid for some ointment and then climbed up on a limb.

"Please, Miss," the maid said. "You know you're not allowed to climb."

"Canh is here," Quỳnh Hương said. "I'm not alone."

Canh climbed into the tree with her and told her how to plant her feet to balance herself. He watched her carefully and forgot about his itches. In her presence, nothing else mattered.

The last day before the gate was closed, she wore a white dress and stood by the lotus pond under the yellow ochna tree. When Canh's gaze met hers, her eyelids drooped in a gentle curve, pensive and serene, and he smiled with absolute fullness.

—o—

After she was chosen to become an imperial concubine, Quỳnh Hương trained for palace life and was no longer allowed outside. Canh walked around the estate daily until his legs tired, hoping for one glimpse. One day, hearing the sound of her piano playing that lilted like willows in the wind, he sat on the ground outside her home and leaned against the massive ironwood gate, eyes shut.

When he got home, Canh mustered his courage and approached his father, who was cleaning his opium pipe with a rag. "May I marry Quỳnh Hương?"

Đinh scowled, then laughed. "Are you dreaming?" He turned his son around and pointed him toward Quỳnh Hương's home. "Her father is the number one mandarin of the Court of Huế. Her family is upper class. You're only qualified to work in her family's kitchen." A scowl pinched Đinh's face. "Go on with your life. She's going to be a concubine—and soon."

Canh dragged himself outdoors, stopping just as his father called after him, "One more word about marriage, and our heads will be on the chopping block." Đinh tapped the pipe against his palm. "What makes you think she would love you anyway?"

"Can you help me? Can you make a love potion to bewitch Quỳnh Hương?"

Đinh sniffed at the bowl of the pipe, his stare fixed on Canh. "You're my son," he said, shaking the pipe at Canh, "but you seem to forget I help people possessed by evil spirits. I work to heal the possessed, not possess people with the wishes of another." He jabbed a finger at Canh's chest. "Anyway, I told you to get on with your life. You're still moping around after her when there's no chance!"

Canh looked down at his feet. If he possessed his father's witchcraft power, would he bewitch the girl of his dreams? He would.

Đinh softened his voice. "Son, you know something? When I was your age, I fell in love with a girl in Gia-Linh, but her father wanted to marry her to a rich landlord. Would I cast a spell on her? No, I went on with my life. Then my good fortune came when one day her father was taken ill. He'd been in some sort of a squabble with someone. The man held a grudge against him and put an evil spell on him. The girl's father became like an earthworm—all day long he tried to eat dirt.

"I could've left him in that state to get even with him, but instead I cured him and won his daughter on my merit."

"But you said there's no chance for me to marry Quỳnh Hương, even if I could do something extraordinary for her family."

"That's the truth. So forget her."

—o—

But Canh could not forget. Every day he visited the estate hoping to glimpse her. One day he waited outside the gate until a maid came out on her way to the market. "Sister," he said, "is there any work in there for me?"

She shook her head and switched the empty basket to her other arm.

"Need to grow any ear mushrooms?"

"We still have plenty."

"How about cleaning out the lotus pond?"

"It's clean."

"Did she like the dove I gave her?" He had found a rare white dove with a wounded leg. He knew she would tend to it.

"Miss Quỳnh Hương set it free after she had its leg fixed."

"So she didn't want to keep it?"

The maid gave him a hard look. He turned and walked away. When the maid called to him from way up the road, he hurried back to meet her.

"You know where I can find a red ochna?" she asked.

"Is that what the Master's llooking for? It'd pair up nicely with the yellow ochna."

"Yes, that's what our Master is looking for."

"What's the occasion for the tree?" he asked.

"Miss Quỳnh Hương's wedding day. Master said they'll bring her double fortune."

Canh thought of the yellow ochna by their lotus pond. The graceful simplicity of their five-petaled flowers and their boughs reminded Canh of Quỳnh Hương.

The maid told Canh that Quỳnh Hương's wedding was three months away and after that she would remain forever in the Purple Forbidden City, as mandated by imperial law. The maid paused, then said, "Can you find us that red ochna?"

Canh didn't know where to find one, but that didn't concern him. All that mattered was seeing Quỳnh Hương. "I'll get it before the wedding." He walked home so deep in reverie he tripped over his own feet twice.

—o—

"I want to help Quỳnh Hương's family get a red ochna," Canh told his father.

Đinh fixed him a stare. "After that, get her off your mind. Quỳnh Hương will never come back out. She'll spend the rest of her life in the Purple Forbidden City until the emperor dies."

"Then she'll leave the Purple Forbidden City?"

Đinh hung the pipe on the wooden rack and folded the rag. "She won't ever become a civilian again. She'll live on to tend the dead emperor's tomb." Đinh told him that the Purple Forbidden City was in the capital of Huế, which Canh had never seen. The Imperial City, a walled enclosure within the citadel, was the seat of government, with palaces, gardens, halls and imperial temples. Inside the Imperial City was the Purple Forbidden City, residence of the emperor and the royal household. The Forbidden City's walls were painted purple, and ordinary people were forbidden to enter.

Đinh wiped his hands on his trousers and put one hand on Canh's shoulder. "You'll never see her again once she enters the city. Don't confuse your life with hers."

"I'll never lose sight of her, father. Before she leaves, I'll give her the red ochna. Then I'll find a way to stay near her."

"You can ask any woodcutter where to find the tree you want, son. But think of the flowering tree as your farewell."

—o—

Every morning Canh followed a woodcutter into the forest. Within days he spotted several wild yellow ochnas and among them, to his delight, a tall, wild red ochna. Canh wanted to uproot the tree and take it home, but the woodcutter told him to dig up a half-circle around the roots instead and gave him an axe to hack away at the roots.

"Why're we digging halfway like this?" Canh asked.

"To take it home later."

"Why?"

"The roots you cut now will grow back at the end of the rainy season. While they heal themselves, the tree will live by the roots on the other half. If you cut all the roots now, it'll die." The woodcutter pointed at the mesh of pale roots. "Come back in three months and dig the other half-circle and cut the roots to the other half."

Canh left the red ochna in the forest, went home and waited. He marked time as the rainy season drew to an end, notching each day the bamboo trunk used for hanging utensils. He lost sleep, haunted by Quỳnh Hương's serene look and the long swath of her black hair.

One morning he sat in the kitchen whetting his bamboo-cutting knife until it gleamed in the sunlight. He had seventy-five notches on the trunk. Fifteen days until Quỳnh Hương's wedding sealed her fate—and his. He counted the cuts again. Yes, fifteen days more. Her wedding day would be the last day he'd ever see her face. That is what they told him. He must get her the tree so he could take in her image once more.

His father called him, asking for a glass of fresh lemonade. Canh plucked a lemon from a tree in the yard, and then sliced the knife through the lemon clean to his finger. He dropped the knife and balled his hand as he ran dripping blood behind him to his father. He hissed and hissed while his father packed the wound with tobacco shreds.

"Keep your mind on what you're doing, Canh, or you'll wind up in trouble."

—o—

When the heat set in, the woodcutter let Canh use his oxcart to haul the tree back. He planted it with all its roots and leaves next to the yellow ochna by the lotus pond. He couldn't wait to see the expression on Quỳnh Hương's face. The maid was so happy she gave him a bowl of lotus-seed chè when she paid him. "From Miss Quỳnh Hương," she said. "She appreciates what you've done for her."

The juice spilled from Canh's mouth. "Can't I see her?"

"She's not available to see anyone. She's busy studying for life in the palace."

Canh gulped the cool fragrant juice of the lotus *chè* down. The sound of a piano floated from Quỳnh Hương's room. Canh stood transfixed, lost in the melody, until the maid took the bowl from him and gestured for him to follow her out to the gate. The air was vibrant with music, and the melody followed him home. Though very sad, the tune was his favorite: a summer farewell of friends parting when school is out. The song reminded him of the long absences of friendship. He would conjure it daily when she left the village.

The week before Quỳnh Hương's departure for the imperial palace, messengers marched up and down the main road of Gia-Linh East, banging gongs, shouting for everyone to clean up the road, trim hedges and tidy gardens.

Canh watched everyone scurry about but refused to help beautify the day he most dreaded.

The day Quỳnh Hương left, Canh stood outside her house with the other villagers to watch the procession. A military mandarin in a red tunic and a blue sash rode in on a black horse. Two foot soldiers followed him, and behind them came a carriage pulled by four white horses. Clad in a vermilion robe, Quỳnh Hương waited under the spreading crowns of the red and the yellow ochna. But the beauty of the flowers was no rival for hers. Canh felt an urge to run to her and give her the silver bracelet his father made him wear as protection against evil. Perhaps that cherished belonging would keep her safe, keep him close to her. But he could not move as she walked toward the gate between the narrow hedges of Madagascar periwinkles, their rosy flowers hanging like lanterns above her, and disappeared into the carriage.

—o—

After many days Canh's father dragged him out of bed. "You're not possessed," Đinh said, "but you need a cure." He took Canh to the wash trough, filled a pail with water and said, "Dunk your head in." Canh submerged his head; the water was cold. Then he felt a hand force his head down, and he began to choke. Water rushed into his nose and throat, and his lungs burned.

Đinh yanked his head up, slapped his face hard. Later, a bruise showed on Canh's cheek.

The bruise went away, but the memory of Quỳnh Hương waiting under the shade of ochnas, red and yellow, never did.

—o—

Bộ spent his day walking through the gardens with Ân-Phi. She knew the name and nature of each bird that flocked to the imperial gardens. She could identify every flower by its scent and distinguish one tree from another at a glance, and there were many kinds of trees in the Purple Forbidden City—pine, spruce, fir, cedar, Indian lilac, Chinese parasol.

When Bộ came home in the evening to the Palace Eunuch Hall at the northwest end of the Citadel, he stopped by the small shrine outside the hall. Its pitched roof of red tile glowed in the setting sun, and deep cracks in the tiles had caused them to slide, revealing the wooden beam. Like the hall itself, the shrine was built in the mid-nineteenth century. When Bộ was ten years old, having been just inducted into the ranks of palace eunuchs, the hall had been his home.

He smelled food cooking as he walked past the east wing to his room. Hungry, he also craved a cup of hot tea. He opened the window shutters. Beyond the garden the setting sun cast an orange glow on the citadel's northern rampart. The wall, baked by the summer day's heat, was shrouded in haze. Water boiled on an iron tripod. He was ready to brew tea when a eunuch in a blue brocade robe entered.

"You have visitors, sir," the eunuch said.

"I'm not expecting anyone."

"A Master Đinh and his son are here to see you. He says he's the father of the fellow who caught the tiger."

A month had passed since the youth was wounded, and earlier in the day Bộ learned of his admission to the rank of palace eunuch. "Show them in."

They greeted each other, palms pressed together on their chests. Bộ offered Đinh a chair. Canh took a seat next to his father.

Bộ lifted the lid of the small clay teapot, which sat on a red lacquered tray. "Would you like some tea?" Bộ addressed his guests.

Đinh nodded. Bộ pulled up the loose sleeves of his robe and poured tea into three cups.

The white porcelain teacups, their rims banded with gold, had no handles or saucers. Bộ raised his cup, small as a plum, between thumb and forefinger. He sipped, peering over the cup at his guests. They were looking down and didn't touch the tea. The old man's hair was gray, wrapped in a turban. The young man's shirt was white against his bronze skin. His sinewy arms were crossed on his chest. He wore a silver bracelet on his wrist. So he was here at last to introduce himself. Bộ liked such gestures.

"Mr. Grand Eunuch . . ." Đinh started.

"Please, call me Bộ."

"Sir, first, I thank you for giving my son the opportunity to serve the imperial family." Đinh raised his cup, then set it down nervously. "But I must ask you if you could exempt him from being castrated."

Bộ looked from Đinh to his son, chuckling. "How am I going to do that?"

Đinh turned to his son. "He's already sexually useless, sir. Why does he still need to be castrated?"

Bộ smiled at the guest's bluntness. "It's not so simple. There are rules."

Đinh took a first sip of tea. "He was normal, sir. Now he's half a man, and you're going to have him castrated. He's my only son."

Bộ glanced at Canh. The young man had not touched his cup. "I won't be the only one who examines him. The court physician will examine him as well."

"I'm worried he might not survive, if they castrate him. Half the men who are neutered die. I'm sure you know that, sir."

Bộ thought of the last man he saw castrated. The knifers gave him two quick strokes, and Bộ walked out soon after.

He studied Canh who kept his eyes on the table. His hair was cropped close to his head. Chiseled face, cleft chin. Dark eyes. Under the masculinity he looked vulnerable. Bộ tapped his index finger against the side of the cup.

"If you don't want to put him through this," Bộ said coldly, "why don't you take him back, sir?"

Đinh bowed his head and Bộ realized how rigid he had been. Calmly he asked Canh, "Why did you wish to become a palace eunuch?"

"Sir," Canh said, peering up at him, "all my life I've been a village boy. But I always dreamed of living in the emperor's palace, away from water buffalo and fish hucksters."

Bộ smiled. "Do you mean it's just a fancy?"

"No, sir. No fancy."

Bộ recalled what the young man said the day the tiger mauled him—that he wanted to serve. Bộ tipped his head. "What exactly is the motive behind your wish?"

"I want to turn my mishap into something positive."

Đinh's eyes opened wide. "Bộ, sir," Đinh said, "He's not as opportunistic as he sounds. He means well, sir."

Bộ shrugged. "You know what, sir?" he said to Đinh. "He's not destitute, so if we went by the old laws, he wouldn't qualify for a position among the palace eunuchs. Are you ashamed that his misfortune might bring you mockery from the village? Do you hope to quiet all the tongue-in-cheek by sending him off?"

Đinh put his hands together on his chest the way one prays. "I'm aware of that, sir. It crossed my mind. But my son has been a dedicated boy all his life. Always makes himself useful inside and outside his family. Ask anyone in Gia-Linh, sir. Of course, if he chooses to stay in Gia-Linh, there'll be snickers in the air, but that's life, sir. He's been hurt worse before." Đinh drank his tea, wiped his lips with his sleeve and shook Canh's shoulder. "Son, tell Mr. Bộ how much it means to you that because he put in a word for you, you're on your way to being a palace servant. I want to hear you say it, then we take leave of Mr. Bộ. We have bothered him long enough."

Canh blinked. Bộ met his gaze, smiled and leaned toward him. "How do you feel about what your father said? I mean the possibility of losing your body parts?"

Canh's voice was timid. "I'm scared, sir. I'm scared I might not be reborn a man if I lose my body parts."

Bộ turned to Đinh. "I need to examine him before I consult with the court physician."

Đinh nodded.

"You can wait in the anteroom." Bộ smiled. "In my days, it was more complex. The Ministry of Rites would have examined him, then the court physician, then the grand eunuch. They say that only a few died from the crude surgery, but I agree it is beastly."

Đinh bowed slightly, retreated toward the door, turned and walked out. When the door was shut, Bộ beckoned for Canh to approach. He stopped in front of Bộ and lowered his gaze to the grand eunuch's chest, where the embroidered blue-on-red flower glimmered.

The oil lamp brightened as Bộ turned the knob. He motioned towards Canh's trousers. Without them, Canh looked all the more vulnerable in the bright light. Bộ flicked his hand and Canh moved forward until Bộ's hands grasped him by the waist. The young man's hip bones were strong, his skin cool. A tear was visible above the root of his penis, and the skin, still healing, was sleek.

Bộ weighed Canh's testicles in his large hands. Bộ watched his hand sliding the prepuce back and forth: nothing changed. He rested his hands on Canh's hips and heard the young man breathe deeply, as if he were glad it was over. Bộ released his grip. Canh dressed himself quickly while Bộ sipped his tea.

—o—

Bộ decided this was the day to brief Ân-Phi on his decision to make Canh her attendant. The court physician's remark still dinged in his head: "He'll be all right, sir. As long as he's not a walking erection, he can't do any harm."

Bộ set his mind on Canh's future.

Ân-Phi reclined in a hammock carried by four men flanked by four tall women holding the accessories for her visit to a neighboring concubine—a pair of slippers, a box of betel and lime. Bộ walked beside her.

Passing under a portico, Bộ broke the silence. "Ân-Phi," he said, "I have a new boy who wishes to serve you."

"What of you, Bộ?"

Caught off guard, Bộ realized that he had been an old shade tree whose sight brought ease and trust to her daily life. "I am always available to you,

Ân-Phi," he said, bowing slightly. "He is from your village, says he used to help on your estate. He would like to be your attendant. Would this please you?"

Ân-Phi smiled. "It would be a wonder to meet a childhood acquaintance again. I haven't seen anyone for so many years." She inclined her head to peer up at him. "Who is this person?"

"His name is Canh." Bộ told her that Canh's injury had led him to seek palace life as a eunuch. "He is a novice, Ân-Phi, but willing to learn."

Ân-Phi's eyes gleamed as she smiled with a slight inclination of the head. "He was a neighbor—always helpful and kind to me and my family." She crossed her ankles. "You can bring him here, Bộ. I will meet him."

—o—

When Ân-Phi returned to her chamber, Bộ brought Canh in. He was dressed in a blue brocade robe and white satin pants. The black hat made him look stiff. He hadn't stopped feeling self-conscious about its mouse-tail back, which brought to mind what Bộ told him about the symbols: the cicada sang throughout its short life just to entertain, and the mouse found every nook and cranny in the house. Was he of equal status with those creatures?

Ân-Phi sat on a low mahogany divan; her red silk garment folded in layers around her feet. She watched Bộ while he served her tea, then half-looked at Canh.

"How's your father's health?" she asked.

"He's fine, Ân-Phi," Canh stuttered. Seven years since he heard her voice last. His ears felt hot, and his arms tingled as if stung by a nettle.

"You haven't changed much, Canh. Though you look thinner."

Canh kept a soft smile on his face, avoiding eye contact. He knew Bộ was watching him. Fists balled, he dug his thumbs into his palms. He wanted to speak to her. Do not speak unless you are spoken to. Do not look royalty in the eye. Speak softly, and do not make noise when you serve tea or meals. Rules. Protocol.

Canh gazed straight ahead. He saw Bộ pour the tea and stop with a twist of the wrist. Canh glanced at Ân-Phi's face. Her hair was parted in the middle. The scent of lotus drifted across the room, the rich scent bringing back memories of Ân-Phi standing by the lotus pond on her gated estate, the lotus blossoms fragrant in the intensely hot summer. In that moment his heart felt so tender that he took a step forward as if to pick up the teacup himself and offer it to her. Bộ's sidelong glance froze him.

Ân-Phi sipped her tea, drew a breath and tilted her head.

"Canh," she said, "you will receive my daily schedule from Bộ. He is very busy, and I thank him for providing me with your service when he is away. There is a lot of work to be done, especially in the imperial gardens."

Canh listened to her melodious voice. She no longer spoke with a pure Huế accent. She had honed it to a cross between the Huế intonation and the southern inflection the court required.

"Yes, Ân-Phi." Canh nodded solemnly.

"Are you homesick, Canh?" she asked softly.

Canh stood in the airy, sunlit room and felt light pass through him, lifting from him the deep weight he had carried for so many years. For a moment he was disconnected from his past, his memory of her, because in that moment she was most present. Before him she was as beautiful as ever with kind, knowing eyes, a voice that spoke sweetness and wisdom, a heart open, though it could never be his. Despite the occasional tingling in the middle of the night when he thought of her, he knew his bondage.

"No, Ân-Phi," he said, regaining his composure. "I'm happy to serve you again. This is the future I want."

—o—

Bộ often checked on Canh during the day, and he spent the early part of his evenings with Canh in his small room. He would chat about Canh's day with Ân-Phi, which always made Canh animated. Listening, prodding Canh to go through the events of his attendance, while he held the young eunuch, fondling him, seeing the shadow of his hand, which looked like a struggling bat on the wall. Some evenings he caressed Canh until his hands grew tired; others, he cradled the boy in his lap, rocking back and forth until a fullness welled up inside.

Canh knew what Bộ wanted with him each night, so he slept fully clothed, hoping Bộ would somehow forget to make his nightly rounds. Once Canh asked for a table and chairs like Bộ's where he could sit to receive him.

"Since there're just the two of us," Bộ said. "I don't think it's necessary. Are you enjoying your assignment? If not, we can find something else for you."

—o—

The rose apple trees in the imperial gardens attracted birds when their fruit ripened. The birds fed on the apples, and sparrows and forktails and yellow bulbuls nested. One day a pair of mynas circled over a corner of the garden with straw in their beaks.

"Do you know anything about them?" Canh asked Bộ.

Bộ shook his head. "Noisy bird," he said.

"They can make any sound you teach them. Flutes, church bells, people's voices. I used to have one when I was a buffalo boy for hire." His myna perched on his shoulder while he lay on the buffalo's back. "That bird was my pet."

After the mynas built their nest in an areca tree, Canh kept watch. An intelligent bird like a myna would be the perfect present for Ân-Phi. He could teach the bird to tell her what he was forbidden to say, so Ân-Phi's affection for the bird might trickle to him.

One morning he climbed the tree when the mynas were away foraging. He came back down and told Bộ there were four eggs in the nest. Canh said if the mynas sensed that their nest was disturbed, they would peck the eggs open and leave the nest.

Within days the eggs hatched. Canh stole one baby myna from the nest. The birds abandoned the nest, taking the remaining three young with them.

Canh built a round cage from bamboo slats, painted it red and lacquered the cone-shaped dome bright gold. Every day he gave the bird leftover rice mixed with hot pepper. Sometimes he fed it live grasshoppers, and he always let it drink his own saliva so it remembered the one who cared for it and would never leave.

Canh named the bird Zee, for the constant *zee* sound the myna made when Canh fed it. After he had trained Zee to talk, he offered the myna to Ân-Phi. He did not tell her that he stole it from its parents. Instead, he said he found Zee abandoned on the ground.

Ân-Phi looked at the caged bird, and her eyes turned pensive. "Any animal you kill or capture leaves its mate or its parents behind," she said. "Animals feel sorrow when they are separated, just as we do. Can we set it free?"

Canh thought of the white dove he gave her years earlier only to learn later that she set it free. He said that if he set the myna free, it would be on its own without a family. "Zee is attached to humans," he told her. "I have been caring for him since I found him. It would be difficult for him to survive on his own now. Will you love him . . . Ân-Phi?" It was always hard for him to remember to call her by that name and not the one that lingered on his tongue from childhood.

"I will keep it, Canh, if you will help me care for it."

—o—

In the evening after dinner, Canh asked Bộ if they could sit down so he could discuss his future. On the dining table the oil lamp burned out and shapes blurred. Bộ lit a match and turned the knob to raise the wick. The room glowed yellow. He sat motionless, his face set toward Canh, waiting. Canh hunched forward, clasping his hands on the table.

"Sir," he said, "I'm asking for your permission to go through the castration. I'm resolved to do what the law said."

"Why drastic measures so suddenly?" Bộ frowned.

"Sir, you and I aren't the only ones who know my secret."

"Unless you have told it to someone else."

"I have, sir. A slip of the tongue."

"Who might it be?"

"Mr. Tham, your deputy."

Bộ stared at the young eunuch. Tham, a senior eunuch, was to train Canh during his early days in the Eunuch Hall while Bộ and his staff went off to work in the Purple Forbidden City. Canh was to read rule books, hone his speech, practice walking with an imagined patron—when to lead, when to trail. He also learned how to bow: half bow, full bow.

"Tell me what happened?" Bộ finally spoke, fixing his stare on Canh.

Canh glanced down at his chest, and for the first time Bộ noticed brownish spots on Canh's tablet. They could be tea stains, but they caught Bộ's eyes. He would normally have admonished the young eunuch about a clean tablet, but he simply said nothing.

"We were chatting while I was helping him with dinner," Canh said. "He told me his wife died young, so he raised his daughter himself. She grew up a beautiful girl, he said. One day when she was seventeen, she passed a military mandarin on a village road. He was riding through on horseback. A month later, Mr. Tham's village council received a writ from the Court of Huế. It said Mr. Tham must get his daughter ready for her induction into the imperial palace. After she left, he visited her twice a year. He was allowed to stand in the courtyard, she remained in her room. She could see him through a screen, but he couldn't see her while they talked. . . ."

Bộ let out an exasperated sigh. He knew Tham's life story and every eunuch's under him. He read Canh's face and kept his patience by saying nothing.

"Mr. Tham said to me, 'You know how hard it was for me to make those visiting trips? Took three days to get to Huế, and even then, I couldn't see her face.'" Canh paused, glancing up at Bộ. "Mr. Tham said one day he let himself be castrated, so he could become a palace eunuch and be near his daughter again."

Bộ was about to tell Canh to get to the point when Canh shook his head, said, "I asked him, 'Must've hurt bad, sir?' and Mr. Tham narrowed his eyes. 'Did it hurt bad when you had it?' It was then I became nervous. I said nothing. Then he said, 'When you pee, do you stand or squat?' I said, 'Stand.' 'You use a quill?' he said. 'A what, sir?' I asked him. Then Mr. Tham pulled something out of his shirt pocket. I watched him unfold the paper roll. Inside was the hollow shaft of a bird's feather. He held it up between his fingers. 'You have something like this?' I just frowned and said, 'What does that have to do with peeing?' Then his eyes widened. He said, 'When you don't have a penis, you squat to relieve yourself. Everyone here does, except me. Everyone here was born with congenital defects. I'm the only castrated eunuch, but I still relieve myself like a man, with this.' He wrapped his quill up, said, 'Do you still have your penis?'"

Canh stopped and glanced up at Bộ. Bộ had told him to reveal his secret to no one, but what Tham said touched him. It must have been agony for him to lose his daughter and then to give up his manhood so he could see her again.

"Please, sir," he said to Bộ, "I told Mr. Tham my story. I said to him, 'Mr. Bộ asked me not to tell my secret to anyone. It'll cause great problems if anyone knows. They would send me away from the palace.' Mr. Tham said, 'Don't worry. It's between us.'"

Bộ mused. He knew about gossip. How long could he hide the secret? The young man couldn't keep a secret for his own good. Shall Bộ stand to be ruined by his foolhardiness? But to send him back to the knifers?

Bộ drew a deep breath. "Tham is a decent man. I trust him. He won't gossip about it."

Canh clasped his hands tight, his knuckles made a cracking sound. "That would change if Ân-Phi knows."

"You wouldn't tell her about it, would you?"

"Not that, sir. But it was me who leaked the secret to Tham. He even joked about it. Said, 'Many of the concubines will ask for you. You aren't one of us.' It shall be damaging to your reputation, sir."

Bộ held the young man in his gaze. He hadn't been with Canh for two weeks. Canh had locked the door of his room at night. Such a defiance. He was thwarting Bộ. His previous nightly visits to Canh, though short, brought him a sense of completion. Together with the young man, the smell of dripping wax documented the passing time, the lazy heat of summer warmed them, voices murmured softly, lively. Without Canh, he had only solitude in an old room with his old self. Every night and day in that void, Bộ felt estranged not only from Canh but from himself, by the constant yearning that stole his ability to be in the moment and attend to the needs of others.

Bộ let everything sink in, then pointed his long forefinger at Canh. "Do you understand the implications of this?"

Canh's eyes were still. He hid his bitterness. He was prepared to do what the law said. Otherwise the continual molestation by Bộ would never end.

"I know I was at fault for leaking my secret, sir," Canh said. "I did not intend to harm your reputation, put you at risk for saving me from the procedure." He paused. "I shall go through it, sir."

"It could be dangerous," Bộ stressed. "You understand?"

"I understand the risks, sir."

"You might not come back."

"But I must do what the law says to remain here."

"You might die."

"If that is my fate, sir, then I must accept it. I cannot expect you to protect my secret any longer."

"I am willing to help you as I always have. You are my responsibility. I brought you here and will take care of you. I guarantee that nothing shall leak out. You wouldn't have to do it."

A look of mistrust came over Canh's face when Bộ turned up the lamp and looked at him.

"I want to, sir," Canh said. "It's for my own good."

fourteen

Canh had heard that Qui, the knifer, was a laborer for hire. He worked odd jobs, digging wells, harvesting crops and castrating animals. He had castrated a man once before, a field worker brought in by a wealthy landlord for sleeping with the landlord's wife. The landlord had his wife tied to a banana trunk and sent her floating down a river. Pinned to her chest was a sign saying "Adulterer." No one dared fish her out because of her husband's power. Qui severed her lover's testes and penis, and afterward the man left the village.

Qui told Canh he had hired two men to help castrate him. At noontime, the three readied Canh for the operation. Đinh smoked a hand-rolled cigarette, puffed and coughed. Canh had told his father of his predicament. Đinh did not hide his disgust of his son being at Bộ's mercy, and so he accepted Canh's decision. He tried to convince Canh that he was so blinded by his resolve he did not understand what he was about to do. But Canh refused to be talked out of it—there was no other choice. Đinh asked Qui to pickle Canh's penis and testes in an ornate jar that sat on the plank bed by his son.

Qui had told Canh not to drink much water before coming to his house. Now Qui told him to undress and took him to a wooden trough at the back of the house. Canh sat naked on his haunches, waiting. Đinh stood behind him in the noon heat.

"Do you have any regrets about being castrated, Canh?"

Canh shook his head.

The two helpers brought a brass pail filled with water, opened a bag of crushed hot peppers and dropped them into the water. Canh was positioned at one end of the uptilted trough, and they poured the hot pepper water on his crotch. The liquid sluiced down the trough and collected in another pail at the other end. They recycled the water and continued washing Canh's genitals until he grimaced from the stinging heat. They gave him a towel to dry himself and motioned him back into the house.

Đinh returned to the table and smoked another cigarette. At the plank bed, the two helpers wrapped Canh's crotch and thighs in white cloth. Canh sat on the edge of the bed, looking down at his penis and his testicles, showing through an opening in the swaths. His crotch felt numb with a dull, dry heat. He saw his father at one end of the room in a cloud of bluish smoke, smelled the smoke of the hand-rolled cigarette. Qui approached with a small knife, its curved blade thin. Canh's stomach knotted.

The men grabbed Canh and locked their arms around his waist. They spread his thighs, bending their legs at the knees to brace themselves. Qui stepped up and pushed a pan with his foot. He took Canh's sex organs in one hand, squeezed them and sliced the knife through at their root. Blood spattered into the pan on the floor, and Canh screamed. The two men squared their feet, holding him still. Deftly Qui dropped the knife and jammed a metal plug into the hole in the Canh's crotch. The pain shot through Canh's groin. Qui splashed water on his crotch. Canh's eyes screwed shut. His temples throbbed. Thick, wet papers were pasted on his crotch.

The two men hoisted Canh by the arms, one man on each side, and walked him around the room. He took one step at a time, his feet splayed. The men propped him up. His head fell forward, and tears slipped down his cheeks. Through his blurry vision he saw the severed organs dropped into the jar. On his crotch, the papers streaked red, slowly dried up and fell. He looked down, shocked. His pubic hair was dark red from the blood, his V-shaped crotch curved in like a girl's. Was it worth it? With his lessons still unlearned, was he still at Bộ's mercy?

After several hours they let Canh lie down. He asked for water. "No water," one man said. "No water for three days."

Đinh coughed nervously.

Qui came over and patted him on the shoulder. "Sir, see the rod in his hole? That stays in there till things heal up. I'll remove it after three days. If he drinks now, his bladder will burst."

Đinh lit another cigarette and dragged on it until his eyes bulged. He blew out the smoke. Now Qui coughed.

"What's he going to do for three days?" Đinh said.

"Rest."

"Can he eat?"

"No food, no water."

Đinh cursed under his breath.

Qui handed Đinh the air-tight jar. Resting on the bottom in an amber liquid were Canh's testes and his penis. "You might as well go home," Qui said. "He should walk around some more. Good for blood circulation. Walk, rest. Three days."

—o—

For three days, save in the evenings, Đinh spent his time at Qui's helping his son walk. When Canh rested, Đinh sat on the edge of his bed. Canh moaned when he walked and writhed in discomfort when he lay down. At times he wept—the pain wasn't from the wound but from his bloated bladder. Unable to urinate, he was in agony from thirst and extreme pain. He understood that at the end of three days, the plug would be pulled out and that if he was able to urinate, he was out of danger. If the passages closed, he was doomed to a painful death.

Đinh read to him from the Chinese classic *Journey to the West*, something Canh used to do for him when Đinh smoked opium. Canh cared for his father when Đinh was ill, but Đinh told his son he felt useless to help him. A person possessed, a house haunted, he could rid them of evil spirits. But now he could only pray.

—o—

On the third day, Qui would pull the tin rod from Canh's hole. Qui and his men waited for Đinh. As soon as Đinh sat down and rolled himself a cigarette, Qui asked Canh to take off his shorts and stand. Qui knelt in front of him; a pan sat at his feet. When Qui pulled out the rod, Canh yelped and doubled over. Đinh stopped rolling the cigarette. Where Canh's penis and testes used to be was a round hole, crusted with dried blood. They watched for his urine to spurt out from the hole. Nothing came out. Qui pressed his hand on Canh's groin. He pressed harder. Canh cried in agony. Đinh groaned. One man made Canh raise his arms and take two deep breaths, while the other man massaged his abdomen.   Finally, Canh lay down. The men scowled. What in the name of Heaven had gone wrong?

"What're you going to do?" Đinh asked Qui.

"We'll try again."

They brought out a pail of water. Qui said the sound of water would help Canh relieve himself. He asked Canh to try to force himself, and one man dipped a bowl into the pail, scooped up water and poured it back into the pail. Canh pushed hard, his hands braced on his knees. After several tries, sweat broke out in beads on his cheeks, and he lay back down.

On the fourth day Canh's throat felt like sandpaper. He heard rain drumming on the roof and imagined himself standing naked in the rain, mouth open to catch raindrops. He saw his father through his blurred eyes, holding a cigarette in his hand.

"Take a drag, son."

Canh's head was raised, the cigarette plugged into his mouth, and he puffed on it. It made him gag. Pain stabbed his bladder. In a while his head numbed, and he lay down on his back. Qui asked him to try to urinate again. Canh stooped, bowlegged, forced himself in vain until his rectum hurt. He collapsed on the plank bed.

Evening came, the helpers went home, and Qui cooked dinner. He and Đinh sat at the table, eating boiled chicken. They shredded the meat with their fingers, sprinkled it with salt and pepper and sipped rice liquor. Canh inhaled the smell of food. He shivered and his skin felt clammy.

Canh groaned. His father came to him. He touched Canh's limbs and his brow. They were hot under his hand. Qui brought out a blanket and draped it over Canh. He slept. Đinh told Qui he would sit up with his son all night, and Qui left the oil lamp burning and went to bed.

When Canh woke, he was feverish. He pressed the cool silver bracelet his father gave him against his cheek. Pain stabbed through his groin. He shook and heard fluid slosh in his bladder. The oil lamp burned low, washing the walls a pale yellow. His father, a blurred shape, nodded off in a chair by the bed. A red cloud glowed like a fire ball, swelling until it enveloped the room. Canh imagined himself hurled into it. He screamed.

"Son?" his father called.

Canh moaned. "Can . . . you cure me, father?"

"No, son. Demons, evil spirits are afraid of me. But they're not inside you."

"Call on them . . . make the pain go. Have them help me."

"They wreak havoc, not peace, Canh."

"Then . . . what're you good for? I need a real doctor."

Đinh fished the worn-out copy of *Journey to the Western Pureland* from his trousers. "You want me to read you a chapter? When the monkey goes up against the Buddha?"

"Put the book away!"

Đinh sighed and put the book away.

"Why did you become a witch doctor?" Canh asked.

"I was thirteen in 1870 when my father took a government post up north, near the Chinese border. He was chief of a sub-prefecture. One morning in his study, my father noticed that all the guards were gone. Furious, he waited. Mid-morning the guards came back. He confronted them. 'Gone without my permission, eh?'

"The guards' faces went pale. 'Sir,' one of them said, 'we were afraid you wouldn't let us go to town this morning. But we must. The two ladies are in town this week.'

"'Who?'

"'The Buddhist nuns, sir. They can cure everything. If you're sick, you're possessed, go see them.'

"The guards said the ladies passed through town every six months. My father made a mental note. A few days later, he moved his office to a different room in the house; then he hired out-of-town laborers to dig a cave under the desk in his old study. He had the opening covered with a wooden board, and the board was covered with a rug. Then his desk was moved back on top."

Canh lay still, his mouth open. "What's . . . the cave for?" he whispered.

"My father sent for the two ladies when they came back to town six months later. He received them in his old study. He had a string tied around one foot, and one guard held the other end in the cave, sitting down there with other guards who carried instruments—a drum, cymbals and trumpets.

"The nuns asked why he wanted to see them. He said, 'To be honest with you, my residence has been haunted. They used to bother us at night, but now they have become a problem during the day, especially around this time.'

"'Shall we wait?' one of the nuns asked.

"My father jerked his foot. Cymbals clanged, the drum pounded, trumpets whined. The nuns smiled and said, 'Sir, with your permission, we'd like to get rid of them.'

"'By all means, do it.'

"One nun took out a handkerchief and asked for a glass of water. She took a sip, blew water onto the hanky and slapped it down on the ground. Instantly, all the noise stopped.

"My father just about froze. He listened and waited. Dead quiet. He jerked the string with his foot until it snapped. Panicked, he confessed to the nuns his intention to test them. Pointing to the cave under him, he pled with them to undo whatever they had done. The nuns asked him to take them down to the cave. He held an oil lamp and climbed down the ladder. All the guards were frozen in the motion of playing their instruments. The nuns mumbled the *dharani*, slapped each guard in the face, and suddenly they all woke.

"'What happened?' my father asked the guards.

"They said they heard a loud thunder, and then the cave was flooded with white light. They didn't remember anything after that."

"So . . . what happened to the nuns? Is that how you learned?" Canh's voice came as if from sleep.

"I ran away from home the next day and begged the nuns to take me with them. From that day on, I traveled on foot with them from town to town, through forests, over mountains. They healed sick people and exorcised demons that haunted people and places. They told me they would teach me whatever I wanted to learn. I said exorcism. I didn't know why. I thought maybe it would give me the power of a demigod to communicate with spirits in this world and the next.

"It took several years to learn it. By then I was itching to return to Gia-Linh. When I bade them farewell, my teachers said, 'Before you go back into worldly life, you must understand that you have a choice: You can get rich practicing exorcism, but never have a family—no wife, no offspring. Or you can remain poor from your skill for the rest of your life but be a husband and father. Make your choice, and vow to honor it.'"

Canh understood that he was born as the result of his father's vow. They both had made binding vows. The light tinged red, its heat swept through Canh's body, and he convulsed. Đinh held him down. Canh cursed his father. "Why didn't you learn how to cure sick people? Those nuns did! Why didn't you?"

"It wasn't my choice, son. The spirits caught my attention, and now they doom me to helplessness."

A decay seeped into Canh as if he were a spirit doomed to hell. Would he inhabit another or wander the earth in bitterness because his life ended too soon, after only a few months in Ân-Phi's company?

He heard his father still talking and felt burning heat and a stab of pain cutting through his groin. Without opening his eyes, he saw his father sitting in the dark, a head full of white hair, his lips moving. Now he was once more alone, and the room was neither dark nor light, but a cool shade of misty gray.

Through the mist, Canh saw a thatch roof wet with dew and mourning doves roosting with one eye open on the limb of a chinaberry tree. He felt himself rising—the eastern horizon blushed rosy, a rooster crowed—and he spiraled into the cool mist. He wanted to return to his father sitting beside him, but he whirled farther and farther away. Though he felt no pain, an intense longing came over him. He saw the myna circling over Ân-Phi. In the pale light of dawn, she was watering orchids on rocks facing the sun.

fifteen

"What made you change your mind to tell me about your father's secret? Auntie?" I asked her.

"My father," she said. "The truth he finally laid on me made him feel complete. So I hope that if I accept it, I will feel complete." She looked down at my cup. "Your tea is getting cold."

—o—

Miss Phượng said that the day after Canh was buried, Ân-Phi summoned Bộ to her chamber. Waiting, she sat on the cane-bottomed chair, sipping tea. A few nights before Canh's death, she dreamed the myna died and she had it buried at dawn in a corner of the imperial garden. She put an orchid pot by the little mound of dirt and watered it before the sun got warm. At the graveside she thought of the effort Canh had put into training the bird and the care and affection he had always shown her.

When she woke, sadness lingered. She heard the myna moving around in its cage and was glad it was a dream. Later in the day she learned of Canh's death and felt a deeper sadness.

Bộ's voice echoed in the hall. He came in and bowed to her. She dismissed the lady-in-waiting with a wave of the hand. Alone with Bộ she told him she had heard of Canh's death. He adjusted his black hat nervously. She stopped twice to compose herself and said, "Bộ, you will tell me the cause of his death."

"He died from the complications of castration, Ân-Phi."

Ân-Phi spoke slowly. "So he wasn't emasculated when he was admitted into the palace?"

"No, he wasn't, Ân-Phi. I take the blame for that."

"Why wasn't he, Bộ?"

"His father pled with me to save his son from mutilation."

"He was already in my service. Why make such a promise to break the rules, then not keep your word?"

"I tried, Ân-Phi. But we couldn't keep the secret any longer." Bộ kept his gaze on the ground. "He was no longer sexually capable by the time he set foot inside the Purple Forbidden City, and so I convinced the physician to help me spare him. Then Canh let the secret out, and I feared it was only a short time before we were all discovered. Canh wanted to serve you, Ân-Phi. The only way he could was to become a true eunuch. Unfortunately, the operation was fatal. As the grand eunuch, I take full responsibility for what happened."

She rose and stood at the door. On the veranda the myna was busy feeding in the cage. Canh used to stand behind her like a shadow. Whenever she turned, he would be there with his gaze on the ground. His quiet attentiveness and adulation filled her life from morning to dusk. She turned and looked at Bộ. She wished to tell him her true feeling about palace protocols and court rules, that Canh's death was but a by-product of protocols designed to subjugate the less fortunate.

Instead, she listened to Bộ praise Canh for his determination to make it through apprenticeship. Then the dream came back to her. Maybe nobody wept for the young man who hadn't been with them long. When she let her memory of Canh come alive, she missed him as a childhood friend, a devoted attendant, much more than a mere shadow.

The following day it rained and leaves fell. They lay soaked, ankle-high and brown. When they dried, they leapt and danced in the wind.

Ân-Phi waded through the bed of leaves in the garden to get to the bird feeder. Her myna flitted in front of her, and the garden came to life with bird sounds. The myna sat before her, mirroring her gaze, mimicking the sounds of Ân-Phi's lips cooing.

Ân-Phi smiled, motioned with her hand to the bird. "Come," she said, extending her hand. The bird landed on her palm, touched its beak to her finger and gazed at her steadily.

Ân-Phi left the bird feeder and came to a deep well in the clearing, the rope coiled into a spiral heap that reached her knees. She leaned over the brick rim and looked down to the dark bottom, where light glinted, far and white. She didn't know Bộ stood six feet behind her, waiting until the myna lifted into the air from her shoulder, crying, "Hello!"

Canh always covered the well with a lid at the end of the day to keep it clean. The lid stayed on during the day unless someone from the royal staff needed water. Someone had forgotten to cover it. She knew that such carelessness irked Bộ. He cleared his throat. The myna coughed after him, a tiny, dry cough, while Ân-Phi gazed into the well, her fingers tracing her green gown that rippled and changed hues in the breeze.

Bộ stepped up to the rim of the well, several feet from her. Below, the water was midnight blue, flashing silver as the sun broke through clouds.

"Ân-Phi," Bộ said. "Please allow me to put the lid back on."

Ân-Phi lifted her head. Bộ quickly set the lid down.

"I thought I could see myself in the water."

"It's too deep to see yourself in it, Ân-Phi."

"I saw my robe, the sky."

Bộ said nothing.

Ân-Phi put her hand on the lid. "Bộ, please remove it for me."

Bộ obeyed. The myna perched calmly on her shoulder as Ân-Phi leaned over the brick rim against her abdomen, gazing into the deep. The dark water was still.

For days Bộ observed Ân-Phi's behavior. She seemed unwell, dreamy. Canh's death had affected her as much as it had affected him. Sometimes Bộ still expected to see Canh trailing her. It was just the two of them again, with Bộ devoted solely to Ân-Phi.

One morning Bộ walked into Ân-Phi's chamber and saw three lower-ranking concubines and their attendants. Ân-Phi was coloring her lips. Did he have a visitation set up for her? He motioned for the lady-in-waiting to come to the door.

"I don't have a visitation in my record book," he said. "Why are visitors here?"

The lady-in-waiting dropped her voice to a whisper. "Ân-Phi wanted to see who is the most beautiful concubine in the palace. She has been in front of the mirror all morning."

Bộ scowled. When Ân-Phi and her guests strolled along the flagstone walkway in the garden, Bộ trailed them. The scent of frangipani flowers was in the air. She stopped under a tree to pick up a white petal, pressed it against her cheek and smelled it. She carried the white petal to a fir tree and picked up a cone while the myna hopped around on the grass shadowed by patches of drifting clouds.

Ân-Phi looked up at a tree. "What kind of tree is this?"

Her question jolted Bộ. The other concubines looked at one another. The fourth-ranking concubine said, "It's a rose apple tree, Ân-Phi."

She walked on. The paved path curved, shaded by fruit trees. Fallen leaves had been raked away and the ground was pale green. Ân-Phi pointed at a tree she passed under. "What is its name?"

"It's a longan tree, Ân-Phi," the same concubine said.

"And that tree?" Ân-Phi stretched her arm toward a lychee tree.

The concubine told her, knowing they were trees Ân-Phi had selected and planted herself.

Although it was the end of season, one tree still had fruit dangling. Ân-Phi motioned for Bộ to pluck a piece ripened to a pale red. With his pocket-knife Bộ cut it open, gently cupped it in his hands and offered it to her. "This is your favorite fruit, Ân-Phi."

Ân-Phi nibbled its small seeds, looking at their clear pink color. "I have never eaten this before."

"Yes, you have, Ân-Phi," Bộ said. "It's a pomegranate."

Ân-Phi picked the seeds with her fingers and fed them to the myna one by one. A smile spread on her face as she resumed her walk, clutching the pomegranate. She stopped in front of a tree, took a leaf in her hand and caressed it. She asked the concubines what kind of tree it was.

Bộ hung his head in dismay. Before anyone could answer, the myna cried, "*Cây ngô đồng.*" It was the Chinese parasol, one of her pet trees.

—o—

Bộ couldn't say when it began, but days had passed since Ân-Phi had greeted and addressed him as Bộ. Often she did not greet him at all. Bộ felt she was ignoring him completely. Only the myna still called his name.

When Bộ saw Ân-Phi wandering her quarters and the grounds, turning familiar objects over in her hands, he hoped their feel or their shape might coax her out of the fog, but nothing held her attention other than the myna and her own image.

One afternoon Ân-Phi passed a poon tree and looked at the ground littered with its marble-size fruit. After considering them, she chose a well-rounded one, gazed at it and said to herself, "The kernel of this fruit is poisonous. Yes, birds shy away from it." She turned around to find Bộ. "You know, Bộ, if you burn this to ash, you can use it to cure boils. You add a few drops of poon oil, then rub the ash on the infected areas. The pimples break out faster."

Bộ's face beamed with joy to hear his name on her lips. In that moment she seemed herself again. Maybe her grief for Canh had lifted. While Ân-Phi stood contemplating the poon fruit in her hand, Bộ walked to the Chinese parasol tree, plucked a leaf from a branch. He walked back, stooped and offered it to her in his cupped hands.

"Ân-Phi," he said, "this is one of your favorite leaves. You remember that now, don't you?"

She twirled it on its stem, mesmerized by its large shape mottled white. After a while she said, "Bộ, do you know what the Chinese used to do with its seeds?"

He thought a moment, and said he had a notion.

"Did they use the seeds to cure premature gray hair?" she asked.

He nodded as she smiled. He recalled happy moments shared with her when she was barely fifteen, vibrant, carefree, and so beautiful he felt humble in her presence.

She was a third-ranking concubine in those days, still learning royal decorum and protocols. As a concubine, her dressing codes were limited to two colors, red and green. When she put on a headband, her parted hair had to fall over the headband and down the sides. Those days she always wore a smile and mingled easily with other concubines. She remained a prominent figure among concubines of her rank and those below. She visited them more often than they did her. Every morning, clad in loose gowns and wearing headbands with their hair flowing down their sides in shimmering black, the concubines walked together in a procession into the Palace of Cận Thành to wish the emperor well. One could hear them talk in a whisper and giggle along the walk-in bell-like notes.

Bộ was grateful to have her back.

One cool morning Bộ came into Ân-Phi's chamber but didn't see her. He went into the garden, walking the length of a flagstone path lined with pomelo trees while magpies chased one another in the boughs. He heard voices, then screams. Under a poon tree the ground littered with its marble-size fruit, several concubines knelt around a prone figure. Bộ tripped as he rushed forward.

One of the concubines grabbed his arm. "Ân-Phi passed out!"

Bộ squatted. Ân-Phi's eyes were shut.

"She ate a poon fruit," the weeping concubine said, giving him a well-rounded fruit.

"This thing?" he said, staring at the split in the middle.

"She tasted only the inside."

Bộ shook his head in disbelief. "This fruit's kernel is poisonous. Ân-Phi knows that."

"Call the physician!" several concubines cried out.

Bộ felt her pulse, her breathing, and nodded to those looking on. His feigned confidence in her condition calmed them. "We must somehow force her to vomit," he said.

He asked a lady-in-waiting to gag Ân-Phi with her finger. He forced her jaws open, and the girl poked her index finger as deep as she could into Ân-Phi's mouth. He watched her eyelids for signs while the concubines looked on. One of Ân-Phi's attendants dabbed the wetness on Ân-Phi's chin with a silk handkerchief.

Mercy, Bộ prayed silently. A fleeting shadow caught his eye. The myna hovered above her, chirping frantically. A spasm shook Ân-Phi. She clutched her stomach and, eyes half open, retched. She vomited until her face turned pale. Her attendants cleaned her face and offered her a cup of water.

Relieved, everyone huddled around her. Holding Ân-Phi's hand, the fourth-ranking concubine said, "Ân-Phi, didn't you know that fruit was poisonous?"

Ân-Phi said nothing, her eyes focused in front of her. Then she turned around to find Bộ. "You know, Bộ, isn't its fruit burned to ashes to cure boils?"

Bộ feared what had taken hold of her was more than grief.

Several weeks after Ân-Phi's incident, Bộ came upon her and the myna on the veranda. She had the bird perched on her index finger and was letting it drink her saliva from her fingertip. Bộ watched. He remembered Canh used to do that so the bird would stay with him until it died.

The next day Bộ hired a ferryboat and went to Gia-Linh. He sat in the bow, looking into the water, recalling how Ân-Phi had gazed into the well. There were mirrors all over the palace. Only poor folks had to use rivers and wells as looking glasses. Ân-Phi never had.

As he made his way to Đinh's doorstep, he sensed defeat. How could Bộ ask him to do what was needed?

Canh's father was chopping tobacco leaves on a wooden board. Bộ coughed to announce his arrival. Đinh looked up, surprised at the large man filling the doorway.

"What brings you here, Mr. Bộ?"

"I need your help, sir."

"What kind of help?"

Bộ stepped into the house, sensing he wasn't welcome. "I want you to exorcise a spirit."

"Whose spirit?"

"The spirit that possesses Ân-Phi."

Đinh smiled grimly as he spread chopped tobacco out on the block with a knife and then used it to scratch himself on the back. "You know who haunts her, sir?"

The name came to Bộ's lips, but Đinh said it first. "The spirit is my son. I knew he would take root in her—it was his dream left unfulfilled."

Bộ said calmly, "For the sake of Ân-Phi, you must expel Canh."

"I can't do that." Đinh tapped the knife blade against his palm. "He was a lost soul when he died. You know what that means, sir?"

Bộ said nothing.

"To die a tragic death like my son's," Đinh said, "the soul is often held in the netherworld of darkness. Fortunately, his soul found a refuge in the living world. How can I live with myself if I drive him back into darkness? My goal all along was to help him realize his vow. Now he will be closer to her than he ever dreamed."

Patiently Đinh resumed chopping tobacco leaves and then spoke again without looking up. "He does not want to leave this world. I will go and communicate with him as my son, but I will not tell him to go to the other world. I will not, sir. He is rightly attached to this world. He has suffered, sir. You of all people should pray for him, help his spirit attain what he was looking for all along—his place secured with her."

"Take his soul to the other world. He is dead. You must save her," Bộ's voice shook. "Ân-Phi is an innocent soul."

"So is my son."

"In the name of our emperor, please do it."

"Even if it means the emperor would have my head," Đinh said sternly and raised a finger in warning, "I will not help you. And don't try to exorcise him with any witch doctor out there. Save yourself from public embarrassment."

Bộ knew it would be a disgrace if he declared Ân-Phi's irrational behavior curable by an exorcist. He also knew that Đinh had no intention of helping her. As he walked out Đinh called to him. "What made my son fixed on castration?"

Bộ left without another word.

sixteen

By the pond behind the dune people came to wash clothes. When it didn't rain for days on end, they fetched water from the pond for cooking and drinking. The helping girl washed her clothes there when she worked at Miss Phượng's. I knew clean water was at a premium and told her politely not to use the pond water except to wash clothes. I said that stagnant water gave people pink eye and diarrhea.

At the pond, without soap, she had to wash her soiled laundry twice. She rolled her pantaloons up to her knees before stepping into the cloudy water churned up by women beating and wringing their wash. She kept checking her rolled-up pants for wetness, carefully wiping her hands with a washcloth, only to soak them again as she scrubbed woolen blankets until her fingertips wrinkled. I'd noticed that a hanging thread on a blouse, a loose shirt button, made her fret. I watched her and shook my head.

"Are you afraid to get wet?" I said.

"*Chú*," she said, "you do this when you don't have washers like in America."

She went to the other side of the pond where the water was still and filled the pail with water there. I watched her carry the pail back, plodding along in her new wooden clogs. Most women at the pond walked barefoot. She winced at their cracked heels, at the black lines filled with dirt—her fastidious nature.

"I'll go look for bull nuts, *chú*."

"What for?"

She puckered her pretty lips, thought for a moment, then turned and walked to one end of the pond where water caltrop grew in abundance. Glossy and black, they looked like a leering goat-horned devil. Folks made necklaces from the already dried, oiled nuts and sold them to tourists.

With a basket of washed clothes under her arm, she walked to the fringe of the pond and carefully left her sabots and the basket on the rim and waded the shallows with her pant legs rolled around her thighs. A small boy paddled into the pond and his sudden motion sent a moss-colored frog leaping onto a half-submerged log. She jumped. She didn't want her blouse wet. Now she moved slowly toward a rosette of water caltrop, glistening with dark-gray bull nuts. Ahead of her the surface rippled and something knifed through, heading into the leafy tangles on the pond's edge. "Snake!" I called out to her, "Be careful." Both the boy and she saw the snake raise its head. She called to me, "Don't worry, *chú*, they're water snakes." She went ahead, plucking the pods in a hurry and tossing them into a paper bag. The feathery leaves trembled as the black snake slithered out and cocked its head, watching. She stared at the snake. The boy hurled a bull nut at it. The snake dipped its head and retreated into the dark mass of diamond-shaped leaves.

"You make necklaces with these? And sell them?" the boy asked her.

"Necklaces?" She said shrilly. "No, for my mom to cook."

Before she waded back with a paper bag full of bull nuts, she gave the boy a quick glance. "You one of those rich city kids, eh?"

seventeen

I brought Miss Phượng a grapefruit blossom. "Auntie," I said, "for you."
She smelled the flower, closed her eyes and held still. I watched her twirling
the flower on its stem, her eyes gazing at the stamens, mesmerizing dots of
bottle green afloat in a wash of white petals. She brought the flower to her
nostrils. Inhaling deeply. "What is this flower," she said?

I shook my head in dismay.

Yet she could remember what her father once told her on the day we
went to visit the Palace Eunuch Hall.

We entered the Citadel through the An Hoà Gate, riding past lagoons
whose tranquil waters mirrored the blue sky along the northern wall. The
ocher paint had peeled completely from the gate of the Palace Eunuch Hall
and its name in red on the gate had faded. The defaced stucco walls of the
shrine held up the caved-in tile roof. Weeds sprouted in the courtyard. The
door to her father's old room was unhinged and a musty odor and cobwebs
hung in spectral gloom. She took me to Canh's room in the east wing, a room
vacated by an aged eunuch who had died. The wing housed a water closet
and a washroom, and the rest was living quarters with several rooms then
vacant, following the abolition of boy eunuchs. As we stood in its emptiness,
trying to relive a moment of past companionship, we could hear termites
gnawing in the truss. Twelve eunuchs used to live in the hall. A few eunuchs
her father's age shared physical characteristics. Their breasts looked like
old women's, sagging with dark nipples, and their voices were shrill, unlike
her father's, which was resonant. There were a few castrated eunuchs in the
palace. When they relieved themselves, they squatted. Her father said they
carried with them a quill, paper wrapped. When they urinated they pushed
the quill into their urethras and relieved themselves like a man. Like her father, most of them didn't retire at sixty-five. Since they no longer had families, they chose to serve the royal family until they died.

From there we went to the Purple Forbidden City. As she led me under the moss-covered porticos arching over the passageway, she told me that the passageway is covered overhead against the rain and the harsh sun, because the emperor walked this way every morning to visit his mother.

She described to me the layout of the three palaces and six halls, the pathways that connected them, and, through memory, directed me to places with uncanny accuracy.

"Auntie," I said, "have you forgotten anything at all?"

"I asked my father the same question." Miss Phượng smiled. "He told me, 'I worked my whole life for sixty-three years. I knew every stone, every crack. I knew every smell that changed with the sun's coming and going.'"

In a hall, airy and empty, we stood surrounded by paneled-wood walls painted vermilion, bright with gilt ornaments.

"Where are we, Auntie?"

"Do you see those fan-shaped windows?"

"Yes."

"Trinh Minh Palace, Ân-Phi's former home."

I was struck by the unreality of the vision. This is where the concubine lived. Now we walked these floors, looked out those windows. I turned around slowly, absorbing the scene. I imagined the concubine's soft footsteps and her attendants shuffling across the hardwood floor, their low, whispered conversations. Long, undulating robes in red and green and white swept the gleaming floor. I pictured her father, wrinkled and old, and envisioned him in his eternal green brocade robe and black hat. She'd told me she loved the hat, which he kept in his clothing trunk. It looked odd with a cicada sewn in yellow thread on the front and with a mouse-tail on the back.

Down a sunlit hallway I could glimpse blue sky through the round openings on the wall. She stopped and felt along the wall with her hand until she touched a door. A clinking chime when she rang a pear-shaped bell.

"This was Ân-Phi's chamber," she said.

We stepped into the softly lit room; the harsh sunlight diffused through a stained-glass window. She set her face toward the window.

"Ân-Phi's piano used to be under the window in this antechamber," she said. "My father told me when you wandered on the walkways and heard the piano, you knew you were near Trinh Minh Palace."

All the adjoining rooms were airy and empty, including Ân-Phi's bedroom. "It's so bare, Auntie," I said. "I wish we could've seen it in the glory days."

The Purple Forbidden City was conceived and built to obey feng shui laws of perfect harmony between man and the cosmos. Her father said every morning Ân-Phi mingled with other concubines as they walked to the Cận Thành Palace to wish the emperor well. She often visited other concubines, he said, and on such visits her father led the retinue as Ân-Phi reclined on a hammock carried by four men, flanked by ladies-in-waiting holding the accessories for the visit—a pair of slippers, a box of betel and lime, a case of hand-rolled cigarettes. Though Ân-Phi did not smoke, the cigarettes were a courtesy for the host. Some visits lasted into the evening, and on returning to her chamber he walked behind her flanked by two female attendants. Mist hung low on the ground in the dark visitation passageway. Ahead of them flickered the lights of the lanterns the ladies-in-waiting carried chest high. In the trembling light, the mist around the globes of light was yellow and the only sound was the rustling of her father's robe.

Outside, emptiness and decay seeped through mossy cracks in brick walls, in weedy courtyards where peepers and hares and cuckoos made their homes. I knew we were standing among the ruins of a bygone civilization. She said the only time the palaces looked unkempt in the Nguyễn dynasty was in 1849, eighteen years before her father was born. That year a smallpox epidemic killed six hundred thousand people, claiming several lives in the palaces. The emperor fell victim, and though he survived, his face was pockmarked, and he became sexually impotent.

She led me into a garden with a lidded well. As she leaned against its brick rim, she told me again about the morning Ân-Phi tried to see herself in the well.

"Canh's spirit had possessed Ân-Phi," Miss Phượng said, "and he wanted to see her in the well."

As she led me through the garden, she said, "The government has let them fall to ruin after the war. But I can imagine what they looked like. My father said Ân-Phi planted many trees still standing in these gardens. Fruit trees, shade trees, ornamental trees." She paused then said, "Do trees remember who planted them?"

—o—

On the day I brought Miss Phượng the grapefruit blossom, I asked her what she had found out from Jonathan Edward's first visit with her father. She did not remember having told me about their meeting. But then she told me on that day her father had been sick with a stomach pain. A pain that nauseated like no pain before.

She brought her father's tea tray. Next to the teapot she put a bar of brown sugar on a saucer. With her help he pushed himself up, crossed his legs under him and groped for the lid. He opened it with a crack and inhaled the steam. She sat, watching him sip the tea. She asked if he wanted the hot-water bottle to ease the pain, but he shook his head with a dismissive wave of the hand. He looked tired and the glimmer of the oil lamp didn't hide the ghastly white of his face. She said, "I'll get Dr. Sung in as soon as first light. Are you sure you don't want to eat something, father?"

"I might throw up if I eat."

At the first glimpse of daylight, she put on her raincoat and set out into the drizzle to see Dr. Sung who lived in Gia-Linh West.

The sun came out. A woman washed clothes in a culvert, cupping water full of sunlight in her hands. A pale blue returned to the sky. In the paddies mist began to lift, exposing thatched houses huddled tiny and brown among the green rice stalks.

A man came out of a hut with a hoe slung across his shoulder. He walked along an earthen dike and then went off into the lush green. Near where the man defecated, another man was riding a plough behind a water buffalo. Phượng saw a bicyclist pedaling down the road toward her, his yellow raincoat bright in the sun. Over the tree line a Chinook helicopter came clapping.

Suddenly the Chinook swooped in above the huts, nose down, then lifted up. Bits of the junk the huts were made of—straw and C-ration cans—flew in a swirling wind. The Chinook roared away. The buffalo bawled, then took off, dragging farmer and plow. The plow bucked over a dike and the man flew through the air.

She ran into the paddy. Running toward the victim were the other man and the cyclist. She knelt, put a hand on the farmer's back and heard a voice. "Phượng!"

She looked up. Jonathan. He held the farmer's head and gently rolled him over on his back. Blood trickled down the side of his head. The other man, squatting by him, shook his shoulder. *Anh Hai! Anh Hai!*

Despite the pleading, brother number two didn't move. Jonathan put his head to the man's chest, listening. "Still breathing," he said in French and pulled out a canteen. She pried the man's lips apart. Jonathan tipped the water in. She watched the man's face, her shoulders tensed. After several tries, Jonathan stopped. The man lay still.

The brother slapped the man's cheek. "*Anh Hai*, wake up!" Then the man smacked his lips. His brother shook him in frenzy. "*Anh Hai*, come back!"

The man's eyelids moved spastically. Jonathan examined the gash on the side of the farmer's head where the plough had caught him. Phượng bent over the man as he regained consciousness and the softness in her eyes brought him relief. Still dazed, the farmer tried to sit up. Jonathan gave him the canteen. He drank as though hypnotized, spilling water down his chest. She told him to find a doctor and he looked up at her, nodding like a child.

She walked with Jonathan back to the road. He looked back at the brothers, at the buffalo standing alone among the green stalks, twitching its wet nostrils. "That was so horibble," he said to her.

"You mean accidents? Things like this happened. Like, one time in Gia-Linh when farmers were piling rice on the roadside after a harvest, a Chinook blew the farmers and the rice all over the road and the fields."

"Do you trust your government? And the Americans as your allies?"

"We never had it to begin with," she said evenly. "Everything's the same as it was when I was a child, with the colonial government and the Việt Minh. Why do you ask?"

He stopped when they got to the shoulder of the road. "Because some day," he said, "I'll be back here working with your government to help restore the faith you have lost in your leaders." He took a sip from the canteen and told her about his role in the U.S. pacification program. "That's why I learned Vietnamese, so I could talk to the South Vietnamese officials. That's how I met Françoise."

"What brought you here?" she said, squinting her eyes in the sun.

"I'm . . ." He swept his hand across the landscape while he searched for words.

"You go sightseeing?"

"Yes, sightseeing." He nodded; his gaze never left her face. A childlike gaze.

The strange feeling came back in her. "Were you out here sightseeing?" she said, half laughing.

"Yes . . . well, no." He shook his head.

"Is there anyone from our village that can help you besides my father?"

"No." His gaze left her face, reluctantly. Now he was looking at her feet, which were clad in black rubber sandals. She let him look. "Your father is the only one who could help me," he said, softly.

"He said he knew nothing."

"I wanted to ask you a very personal question."

"Ask me."

"How did Mr. Bộ adopt you?"

"I came from an orphanage. He raised me from a baby after he left the imperial palace."

"There's something I want to tell you," Jonathan said, taking off his raincoat, "but I'm not sure if I should."

Momentarily she forgot her rush to fetch Dr. Sung.

"I want to help you," she said.

"I appreciate it." He smiled, looked up to the sky, shielding his eyes with his hand, then looked back down at her. "Are you going somewhere?"

She told him where she was headed before the helicopter flew over.

"How far is the doctor's?"

"About an hour on foot."

"I'll go with you," Jonathan said. "We can ride my bike."

"Tell me first what you were about to say."

He rolled up the raincoat and draped it over the handlebars. He took out his wallet. "Please look at these." He gave her the photographs.

Her childhood home. She lived there until she was four. She remembered the pond. She almost drowned in it one day. Phượng broke her gaze, turned the photographs over and read: *Hamlet of Upper Đinh-Xuân, 1942.* Her father's handwriting in smeared purple ink. "Did she give you these?"

"Her godparents, after I told them I intended to look for her real parents." Jonathan shook his head. "There wasn't a soul in Huế who knew about this place."

"Did you see the house?"

"No. But I met an old woman in that hamlet. She remembered this house. I guess that was the same house your father used to live in." He cleared his throat. "Françoise looked just like you. If the two of you were dressed alike, stood next to each other, I wouldn't want to guess who is who. Even your voice sounds like hers."

Phượng gazed at the photographs, feeling like dust scattered from her father's hand. They came from someone thousands of miles away, someone dead, who bore a perfect resemblance to her. But her father had told her nothing. She gave Jonathan the photographs. "That was our house in Upper Đinh-Xuân before we moved to Gia-Linh. But I'll ask my father for you. And for myself." She tried to smile. "I never knew anyone else in my life except my father. Did you tell my father what you told me?"

He nodded, pulled out a leather pouch from his trousers pocket and placed it in her hand. "This is what I want to give to her family."

She pulled the drawstring. A pendant carved after a phoenix lay in the palm of her hand. Deep red in the sun. She drew the string shut, handed him the pouch. "I have a pendant like that." Then she raised her clenched fist to her lips and looked off into the bright rice field until the mist cleared from her eyes. "What was Françoise like?"

"It's hard for me to answer that question," Jonathan said. "Anything I say about her can never match how I feel for her. She was the girl I built my dreams on, because being in love with her made me feel pure. She would've laughed at the way I'm praising her. When I think of her, I remember the first scent of autumn, and I loved her for being a wayfarer who tried to find her way home."

His deep voice soothed her.

"I saw her time and time again in my dreams when I was a child," Phượng said, her throat tight. "I believe it was her."

"But clearly it wasn't just a dream," Jonathan said. "Wouldn't it have been a joy if you and Françoise met?"

Phượng felt like a child the night before the first day of the Lunar New Year festival, when the world was full of wonder.

"Let me dream," she said.

eighteen

I couldn't help thinking of Ân-Phi's mental state when I thought of Miss Phượng. She told me, back then, when her father had been sick with the recurrent stomach pain, a woman named Xinh, a well-known trader in Gia-Linh, had courted her to invest in Xinh's business. In their banters when Xinh talked about Miss Phượng's youthful look, Xinh said, "A long time ago, before you were born, there was a girl so beautiful I thought she was a fairy living among us."

"Are you telling me a fairytale?" Phượng said to Xinh.

"No fairytale. She lived sure as you and me and came from our Gia-Linh."

"Who was she?"

"She was Ân-Phi. Second-ranking concubine."

"My father told me much about her. Did you ever meet her?"

"When I was a little girl, I saw her twice. First time I saw her she was leaving home for the imperial palace. On the day she left, we children stood outside her house and watched the family ritual in her residence. Then a military mandarin in a red tunic and a blue sash rode in on a black horse followed by two foot soldiers and behind them came a carriage pulled by four white horses. She came out in a red robe and waited under the red and the yellow ochna trees. She was the prettiest sight."

"My father said the same when he first saw her at the palace," Phượng said with a nod.

"I saw her again," Xinh said, "many years later at our village ferry landing in the year before she died. I was getting off a ferry with my little niece. Ân-Phi saw my niece staring at her, so she rubbed her little head and took out some paper money and put it in her hand. I remember she said to my niece, 'Take this. I'm very poor now. They took everything from me.' She was still the most beautiful girl I'd ever seen."

Miss Phượng told me the scene at the ferry landing must have taken place several years after the last emperor had decreed the abrogation of the concubine system, which set free all concubines from the court.

The evening of the announcement, she said, the queen summoned the concubines and told them that times had changed in the face of democracy and modernization. The French-educated emperor had recently ordered the Ministry of Rites to abolish the century-old tradition of prostration and kowtowing in the imperial court. He found such acts humiliating. He valued the freedom of each human being and decreed the emancipation of all the concubines, leaving each the right either to return to her family or to stay on to tend the previous emperor's necropolis.

Ân-Phi gazed at the queen and at each concubine. She remembered they had all been together like this the night of Winter Solstice, when at midnight the watchman announced the hour and all the concubines emerged from the three palaces and six halls and filed into the Palace of Cận Thành, each holding a foot warmer in her hands, to receive the emperor's gift: a small fire for her foot warmer on one cold night.

The queen wished them well. Each concubine took a turn offering the queen her own good wishes. Candles cast shadows on the concubines' faces and a soft sheen on their colorful gowns.

Ân-Phi held the queen's hands and said, "I wish to say a few words to our sisters here."

The queen inclined her head and nodded approval.

Ân-Phi looked at the shadowed faces around her. "Dear sisters," she said, "we've been together for so many years it's hard to imagine a time like this. Remember when we were still learning the royal decorum and protocol? We were carefree and mingled easily with one another. Each morning we put on our loose gowns and wore headbands with our hair streaming beautifully, and we walked in procession into the Palace of Cận Thành to wish our emperor well. Remember our whispers and giggles. Do you remember, sisters?"

There were murmurs of *yes* and heads nodded. Ân-Phi smiled. "Dear sisters," she said, "when you leave the palace, take those memories with you. They shall last a lifetime. As the queen mother, I shall remain in the silence of the palace, remembering you. The echo of the past shall come in my solitary footsteps along the visitation passageways."

The concubines glanced at the queen. The queen nodded to them. "Eloquently said." She patted Ân-Phi's hand and spoke soothingly, "Ân-Phi, may the Buddha cast his benevolent eyes on your well-being."

Ân-Phi replied, "Be strong as you leave this home. My thoughts shall forever be with you."

That night the grand eunuch wished Ân-Phi a good night's sleep and left to return to his quarters. In the far corners of the garden foxfire glowed on dead wood. He stopped at a magnolia tree where Ân-Phi had hung a pot of dawn orchids on a branch. The tree was only her height the day she was inducted into the imperial palace and now it stood like a giant umbrella. She was going home. What would become of her?

From her chamber drifted the sound of piano, a melody he had never heard before. Every note clear, strung together like a garland of sorrow tossed out into the blackness of night.

—o—

Six years after Ân-Phi left the imperial palace, the last emperor of the Nguyễn dynasty abolished the age-old eunuch system. Her father became a civilian following sixty-three years of serving the royal families. In that time he moved up in rank from fifth to first and received an annual salary of 540 đồng.

With money he saved, her father built a house in the hamlet of Upper Đinh-Xuân, fifteen kilometers southwest of Huế. He didn't want to return to his birthplace in the South—treasured memories of the court manifested themselves everywhere he went in Huế.

He was seventy-three years old when he settled in Upper Đinh-Xuân. Occasionally he visited his former fellows. One eunuch married a lady-in-waiting, and their wedding became the village joke. Tham, his deputy, upon leaving the palace, married another eunuch. Bộ presided over their ceremony, blessed them and wished them many happy years together. He understood the urge to have a companion, man or woman, but seeing what had come of succumbing to his urge with Canh made him choose loneliness rather than the persistent throb of longing.

Mornings, before the sun rose, he woke to the grand bell of the Temple of Guanyin, drank tea and then waded through the lotus pond in the back of his house to gather the dewdrops from each lotus leaf. He still treasured the taste of tea brewed with dewdrops.

Three months after he settled in Upper Đinh-Xuân, he came face-to-face with an aching void in himself—he missed his many years with Ân-Phi.

At her parents' estate in Gia-Linh, he announced his visit by knocking on the ironwood gate and kept knocking until his knuckles hurt. He listened and heard the doleful *ah-oh* of turtledoves in the morning stillness. He left and came back a few weeks later. He waited at the gate for a long time and left. Luckily, he ran into a maid on her way back from the market. Bộ introduced himself and the maid made him wait outside the gate. Soon she came back out and, to his dismay, said that her master declined his visit because of Ân-Phi's unstable mental condition.

Bộ thought of revisiting Ân-Phi many times but kept postponing his visit until he felt the time was right. Often, he wondered if she knew of his desire for Canh, since she shared her body with his spirit. After three more months he decided he had waited long enough.

Bộ did not have to wait long at Sir Đông Các's residence. Ân-Phi's father was in his early sixties, the only one left of the four supreme mandarins of the court—the French had ousted the rest. The house was warm. A brazier crackled under the mahogany divan. Bộ admired the ironwood pillars and crossbeams, held together by mortise and tenon, that gleamed, dustless.

Bộ immediately inquired about Ân-Phi. An uneasy silence fell.

"My daughter no longer lives here with our family," Đông Các said.

"Where does she live now, sir?"

"Let me consult with my wife. Please wait."

Bộ drew a deep breath and leaned back in his chair. Đông Các returned. A corner of his mouth jerked as he said, "My daughter stays at the Thiên Lăng mausoleum."

The deceased emperor's concubines and some eunuchs had tended the sixty-year-old mausoleum of Emperor Tự Đức, nested among pine hills south of the capital, for many years. Originally there were 103 concubines, most of them long dead.

Bộ's voice dropped. "May I ask why she stays there?"

"She was pregnant."

"Sir? How?" Bộ's voice suddenly rose. "Forgive me."

The corner of Đông Các's mouth twitched again. "It's a mystery to us."

Bộ arrived at Thiên Lăng at noon. He got off the ferry under the shade of a banyan tree. Distracted, he tripped over a huge serpentine root and lost his shoe—who had Ân-Phi let into her life? He trod across the Congregation Court between rows of stone elephants, horses, and life-size military and civil mandarins.

As he emerged from the Worship Hall, he shaded his eyes against the sun. A row of wooden shacks stood in the rear. By an earthen vat an old concubine squatted, washing clothes. She beat and wrung a garment on gray flagstone. He cleared his throat. The old concubine blinked her rheumy eyes and flashed a toothless smile.

"Aren't you the grand eunuch? You came here some years ago."

"Yes, Madam." He remembered her too. She was in her nineties, having tended her emperor's tomb for seventy-five years. He stooped and raised his voice slightly so she could hear. "I was told that Ân-Phi stays here."

The concubine hung her head. Bộ thought she hadn't heard him, but then she nodded.

"May I see her?"

The concubine rose with difficulty. "What is the purpose of your visit?"

"I used to serve her, Madam. I came because I'm concerned about her welfare."

"That she's expecting a baby?"

"Yes." Bộ dabbed at his brow.

The concubine asked him to wait and went into the last shack on the row. When she returned, she brought a eunuch with her.

"Bộ," the eunuch said, "it's a surprise to see you here." He beckoned for the older man to follow him to the last shack and ducked his head to enter. There was a bamboo cot in a corner with white mosquito netting around it. An old woman sat on a low stool by the cot, hunched over a pot of boiling water. She was the midwife. The old concubine shuffled to the cot and whispered into the mosquito net. Bộ heard a voice from inside and the concubine shuffled to the door, waving for the eunuchs to approach the cot. Then Bộ heard Ân-Phi's voice clearly.

"Bộ!"

He came closer and she asked him to roll up the mosquito net. In the dim light her face was pale. Her hair was knotted above her nape, and she lay under a woolen blanket, her belly huge. She hadn't aged—she was as graceful as he remembered.

"Ân-Phi," Bộ said, bowing, "it's such a joy to see you again."

Ân-Phi gestured for him to sit, so he lowered himself onto the stool, which was too small for him. The skin under her eyes was moist. "Tell me what you have done since I left."

Bộ told her, eyes half downcast, and she nodded. "How are you, Ân-Phi?" He paused. "I mean in your mind. You were unwell at the end. I always worried about you after you left, wondered . . . if you were quite yourself."

"I don't remember much of those final months. But I remember you, Bộ. How could I ever forget you?"

He leaned toward her.

"And I know who I am now," Ân-Phi said.

He wasn't convinced. "Who are you, Ân-Phi?"

"I was the second-ranking concubine until our emperor abolished the concubine system."

Bộ peered up at her. "Who served you then, Ân-Phi?"

"You. Then Canh. I was so sad when he died." She paused. "Then I felt as if he were with me somehow. Everything was foggy to me. Later I found letters I wrote with my own hand, but they were from him. They said he wanted me to know he wished for nothing other than to be with me and for me to be happy."

"Did the letters ever mention me and Canh?" Bộ asked, his voice strained.

"They said you helped Canh come to me. That was all they said."

"Did you know he possessed you, Ân-Phi?"

"I never knew anything for certain, Bộ."

Bộ clasped his hands on his knees, thought for a moment and cleared his throat. "Ân-Phi, do you recall how much Canh adored you?"

Ân-Phi's eyes narrowed in reflection. Her serenity made Bộ's heart well with affection. How many years of her youth had been wasted?

With a sigh Ân-Phi said, "I was sad when he died." She paused. "I've thought of you and him lately. I dreamed last night that you would visit today."

"What else do you remember, Ân-Phi? You used to have a talking myna."

"He died, Bộ." She tried to push herself up and coughed into her cupped hand. "But before he died, he never left my side. I believe Canh was with the bird. In the bird, maybe. Please, pardon my irrationality."

"How long has it been, Ân-Phi, since the bird died?"

"Several months." She looked at him calmly, sitting beside her in his eternal deep green brocade, as if he had never left duty with the royal family. She tilted her head to one side. "Bộ, do you think Canh took leave of my body completely?"

Sitting with his head down, Bộ wondered if Đinh had anything to do with her sanity, then realized it was Canh all along, wanting her happiness. "Ân-Phi," he said, "I believe he left you when he understood you could be free and that he could accompany you as your treasured friend, the myna. Do you forgive him, Ân-Phi?"

Ân-Phi gazed at him without speaking. Finally, she said, "Bộ, I'm lucid today, and more so I'm carrying life inside myself. Therefore, you can see how fortunate I still am compared to Canh and his father. Have you talked with his father since Canh's death?"

Bộ told her of his final meeting with Đinh and his failed attempt to get Đinh to exorcise the spirit of Canh in her. "He would not see his son go," Bộ said. "He did not like my asking."

He glanced at Ân-Phi's belly and for a while neither of them spoke. She told him she would take an herbal medicine to induce labor, because her water had broken. Still numbed by her impending maternity, Bộ asked, "How did your pregnancy come about, Ân-Phi?"

She laced her fingers on her chest. Sadness filled her face.

"Do you know what happened to you, Ân-Phi?"

She nodded.

"Were you clear-minded, Ân-Phi?" He kept his voice even.

Again, she nodded.

"Someone who won your heart, Ân-Phi?"

She shook her head. Bộ didn't dare ask anything further.

"My father sold me to a French general. He drugged me and took me."

Bộ suddenly leaned back, lost his balance on the small chair.

"My father kept his position with the court."

After Ân-Phi took the herbal medicine, she went into labor. From outside Bộ could hear the midwife coaxing her to push, then her moans, then screams. Bộ felt shrunk. He sat down on his heels. With each of her cries he felt a pain cut deep into his bowels. *Stubborn pain.* He heard the midwife, "This can sap your strength quickly and make all your bones ache." He rose slowly to his feet, thinking of all the suffering it took to create life.

An hour later Ân-Phi delivered twin girls. Then she began to bleed.

Inside the shack three candles burned brightly. A wicker basket sat on the cot beside Ân-Phi. In it were two tiny babies wrapped in blankets. The infants' cries pierced the quiet. The midwife held a white towel, blotched crimson. Ân-Phi lay still, sweat glistening on her brow, her eyes half closed, gazing down on her babies. Her lips bled. She must have bitten down on them hard.

Bộ bent over the women, his voice shaking. "What can we do to stop the bleeding?"

The midwife folded the towel in half and slipped it under Ân-Phi's blanket. "Give her some spinach."

The old concubine ground spinach in a mortar, added water and made Ân-Phi drink. She sipped, one hand holding the basket in which the infants mewled, stopped, then began again.

"Did you feed them?" Bộ asked.

The midwife said, "They cry, but not because they're hungry."

"Bộ." At her weak voice, Bộ knelt by the cot. "Ân-Phi," he said softly.

Ân-Phi opened her eyes. "Bộ," came her whisper, "in my life as a concubine . . ." She paused, wet her lips. "I counted on you, you served me since I was fifteen, I always turned to you for advice, you had my unspoken trust . . ."

Bộ bowed in silence. Ân-Phi drew her breath in. "Bộ." She half opened her eyes to look at him. "Can I count on you now?"

"I am at your service, Ân-Phi."

"If I die, will you take care of my daughters?"

The yes was in his heart before his mind could acknowledge it. Ân-Phi stopped talking when the midwife changed the towels and the old concubine dunked two blood-soaked towels in a pail of water. It reddened quickly. Ân-Phi drank another cup of spinach water. Her voice was hoarse.

"I'm grateful to you, Bộ. Can you promise me—" she paused and Bộ leaned toward her "—that you will never tell my daughters who I am, how they came into the world?"

"Ân-Phi," Bộ said. "They will want to know you."

"Bộ." Ân-Phi tried to focus on him. "I had a pair of ruby phoenixes. The emperor gave them to my father as a gift. And in one of my spells of insanity I gave one ruby to a beggar on the street. I want my daughters to have the one I have left." She stopped, her breathing shallow.

The midwife made her drink another cup of water and her hands shook as she held the cup. The midwife replaced the third towel with a fresh one. A brass pan sat on the fire. The old concubine dropped the blood-sodden towels into the boiling water and stirred them.

Ân-Phi closed her eyes to rest. She felt Bộ wait beside her cot. Steam warmed the room as the soiled towels were boiled, washed, and wrung. Sometime in the evening the old concubine began to feed the infants. Ân-Phi asked to see them. Her eyes runny, she blinked to see the tiny humans stir with busy movements, and when she could not see them anymore without straining her eyes, she touched them. Their soft skin warmed her heart.

The midwife changed towels, then felt Ân-Phi's feet. "Getting cold," she said and started to rub the insteps. Ân-Phi shivered. She asked to hold her babies. Bộ took another blanket from the midwife and gently covered the babies with it and then the old concubine gave Ân-Phi a quilted one. He stood by her bed, praying silently. Cradling the babies on her chest, Ân-Phi's teeth chattered even after they covered her with two blankets. The old concubine found a coal brazier, built a fire and put it under her cot.

The babies cried and then fell asleep on Ân-Phi's chest. The three candles burned down, dripping wax onto the hollow dish. In the quiet the coals popped with a warm glow. Bộ sat on the small chair, keeping vigil.

As he looked on, Ân-Phi left.

—o—

In August 1945 the last emperor—the son of Ân-Phi's late husband—abdicated supreme power to the Việt Minh. All the court mandarins were stripped of their ranks and dismissed. Sir Đông Các moved his family to Quảng Trị, his birthplace. Out of shame, he didn't acknowledge his grand-daughters. Ân-Phi's tomb in Gia-Linh went uncared for after their departure, so Bộ hired a laborer to look after it year-round.

Bộ didn't know what to call the baby girls. He wished he had asked Ân-Phi before she died. They were so perfectly alike, to name them differently seemed a sacrilege, so he did not name them that first year.

Already they made him miss their mother. He tended them as lovingly as he had tended Ân-Phi, spending all his time with them.

One morning at sunrise Bộ waded through the pond. Folding each lotus leaf along its midrib, he carefully tilted the leaf toward its tip. The dew-drops shook like silvery beads, broke free, and rolled into the jar. When the sun felt warm on his back, he had a jarful. Inside, the babies cried. He hurried back in, not bothering to dry his legs.

The water in the kettle was warm when he tested it with his fingers. He opened a can of French powdered milk and shook the bottles vigorously until the yellow powder dissolved. He made two portions and sat between the baskets, watching the girls feed. They were identical, their curly hair a dark chocolate, their eyelashes long. They always finished their bottles at the same time. He had bought a bamboo cot, set it alongside his own and kept the two wicker baskets on it. At night, he made sure there were no mosquitoes inside the net before he went to bed.

A year old now, both girls were healthy, save on one occasion a week before when one had diarrhea. Bộ took his neighbor's instructions, ground some Ganidan pills and mixed them with liquid extracted from brown rice. When the diarrhea slowed, he fed her rice gruel blended with crushed ginger. On the second day the diarrhea stopped. She smiled and he held her in the crook of his arm, red-eyed from lack of sleep.

At the start of the flood season in 1945, news came of French troops massing in Huế. The local Việt Minh feared imminent raids, so their troops began to move out of the hamlets.

Bộ dreaded the French descending on Gia-Linh. The year before they had come hunting the Việt Minh in both Upper and Lower Đinh-Xuân. The Việt Minh agents demanded that each house give up two hundred bamboo trunks. Bộ's house had a handsome thorny-branch bamboo hedge. Their culms were used for furniture. The Việt Minh fighters cut down all his bamboo, took thousands of bamboo trunks from both hamlets, and drove them into the riverbed. The spikes slowed the French barges down, but the French still managed to swarm Đinh-Xuân, where they captured and shot the Việt Minh leader.

The French burned down the whole village so the Việt Minh couldn't use it as a base. And Bộ knew that in some other villages, the Việt Minh did precisely the same thing to uproot a French harbor. Both were destroying the land and the people.

Upon waking one morning, Bộ parted the mosquito net and groped for his sandals with his feet. The cold of water shocked him. He had slept while a foot of floodwater crept in. A toad *glunked* somewhere in the house and the water lapped at the legs of his cot. He couldn't find the tin can of powdered milk he always left by the bed. He waded around the house, pantaloons rolled up to his thighs, looking for it. The floodwater must have swept it away. The girls woke, talking to themselves. He stacked up wooden containers and chairs on the divan and boiled rice to make gruel.

A quick motion at the altar had him looking up to see a black snake with green-yellow flecks around its neck. He wasn't afraid; snakes often took shelter in his house during floods. He peered at the girls through the mosquito net. Their large eyes looked up at him and their arms flailed with excitement.

He made the gruel, chipped off a chunk of hard brown sugar and let it melt in the bowl. He sat on the cot, blew on the spoon and fed the girls. A dry scraping sound came from the altar. *That's his tail. He wants me to feed him.*

A *glunk* sounded in the stillness. A toad leapt out of a shadow and plopped into the standing water. Upon the altar the snake uncoiled and slithered. The toad jumped against the door. The snake shot its head out, shaking it in a frenzy, as it lifted the toad into the air.

A neighbor's voice called from outside, asking Bộ what he wanted from the market. He waded to the door, where the snake lay still, as if drugged. Outside the wind howled and the sky was gray. Two women sat on a make-shift raft made of banana trunks tied together, floating along what used to be a dirt path.

He called out to them. "Mrs. Hy, can you get me some powdered baby milk?"

"I'll get it for you, Mr. Bộ," came the answer on the wind, as another woman joined them, hoisting herself onto the raft.

The women had rattan baskets on their forearms and sat with their legs drawn up to their chins. All wore conical hats the color of pale wheat and the raft carried them away into the morning grayness of sky and water.

—o—

Though the flood had begun to recede, water still ran high in the creeks and along the dirt roads. Bộ fed the girls, this time putting the can of powdered milk high on the altar. As the girls ate, he sat on the cot between their baskets, letting each hold his fingers. The fire crackled low. A cold draft came across the cement floor from an opening along the base of the wall near his bed. It wasn't sealed, a brick plugged the opening. Every house in the village had such an opening to let floodwater drain out. He dreaded spending days afterward scrubbing the walls and floor.

Bộ lifted the teapot. He heard shouts. A man and his wife came running in, drenched from head to toe.

"Mr. Bộ!" the man cried out. "Leave, now!"

Cold air blew through the open door. "What is it, Brother Hy?"

"The French are coming," Hy said, wiping rainwater from his eyes.

"You must leave now," Mrs. Hy said. "The girls too. Can you carry both of them?"

"I think so. Where're we supposed to go?"

"Everyone's going to Lower Đinh-Xuân." They turned and hurried out the door. "Quick, sir. We'll meet you at the bridge."

"The French are going to blow it up," Mrs. Hy cried. "We need to cross soon."

Bộ looked around anxiously. The floodwater had drained, leaving red mud everywhere. He didn't know what to take. He scooped floodwater from a small dugout under his cot and shoved the clothing trunk and his antique tea set, secured inside a wooden box, in. He grabbed the milk bottles, two cans of powdered milk, some baby clothes and his own and stuffed them into a jute bag.

When the girls woke and began to cry, he strode over and patted them until they calmed down. He remembered their inheritance and went to the altar, fumbled around and took down a cloth bundle. In it were the two halves of the ruby phoenix, each wrapped in a handkerchief. He had found a master cutter to cut the gem. He tried to think, his palms tingling with nervousness. People's shouts erupted outside.

On the dirt road people scrambled through muddy water, rain blowing in gray sheets. Then car horns blared. Through the partly opened door Bộ saw two armored trucks roll in on the dirt path with French foot soldiers following behind. He slipped the ruby halves under the quilts that lined the babies' baskets.

Heavy footfalls at the door startled him. A French Moroccan stood in the doorway. He shouted at Bộ, "*Pourquoi êtes-vous encore ici? Allez! Allez!*"

"I'm leaving. I'm leaving," Bộ repeated.

"Don't you ever come back!" the Moroccan shouted. "We'll kill you."

Bộ said, "Yes, sir." The Moroccan stared at him and then walked off abruptly. Bộ slung the jute bag around his shoulder, then remembered rice. It pained him that he had nothing to store rice in. He picked up the two wicker baskets and headed out. At the altar he stopped to pray and collect the pictures of his ancestors. He looked them over and slipped them under one of the basket quilts, along with some black-and-white photographs of his house.

He donned his palm-leaf raincoat, draped the wicker baskets with blankets and sloshed through the floodwater to the main road. People streamed out from every dirt path, babbling and screaming, household goods strapped to their backs, slung across their shoulders. Children clung to their parents. Armored trucks blocked some paths and French soldiers ran into every house, rousing people. Shots cracked like thunderclaps, then died out on the wind. The French were spraying the houses with gasoline and setting them on fire. Soon the hamlet roared like a giant torch. The mass of people and animals arrived at the bridge over the river that divided the upper and lower village.

French soldiers stood around their armored trucks along the bank, pointing rifles at the crowd. Others rolled metal drums of explosives off the trucks and up the bridge. People packed the bridge trying to cross, while beneath it soldiers strung wire to wrap around its pillars. Bộ's head was above the crowd. He looked for the Hys but couldn't find them.

He hooked the two baskets on his forearms, hoisted them chest high and got in front of an oxcart. The crowd pushed. He raised both of his arms above the human mass and the crazed mass moved him out and out toward the railing and he tried to get his footing forward, holding down his exasperation. The river was swollen with dark water and the wind hissed, blowing rain in clumps of wet pins. The human mass pushed on, cries scattering in the swirling winds. The oxcart moved up, the angry crowd surged to get ahead of it and Bộ felt himself pressed against the railing. Bộ stopped and turned his body as the oxcart rammed into him from behind. The ox's horns caught him in the back. His body pitched forward and the basket on his right arm flew off and dropped into the roiling water.

He screamed, but the sound was lost in the clamor. The basket bobbed on the current, spun several times and then became an olive-colored patch downstream.

When the explosion splintered the bridge and dropped it into the turbulent river, Bộ sat by the roadside in the rain and wept.

nineteen

The helping girl hadn't been at Miss Phượng's for three days.

It was midmorning when I came to her hut and found her lying wrapped in a blanket on her cot. She said she had bouts of diarrhea followed by a fever. She'd thrown up in bed. Her father had ground beefsteak leaves with garlic, mixed them with rice liquor and made her drink. The fever didn't come down, the diarrhea didn't stop.

I looked at her tongue. Blackened. I took off her shawl and dabbed her perspiring forehead.

"It's some fish I ate three days ago," she said in a thin voice. "Daddy caught them. I said they were probably polluted by chemicals from the shrimp farms."

"Your dad won't be back until late today," I said, looking down at her blistered lips. "You need to go to the hospital."

"Am I going to die?"

"No, silly."

Her teeth chattered. "I'm cold, *chú*."

I stood up. "Okay, I'll be back shortly."

—o—

The doctor at the town hospital diagnosed typhoid and treated her with antibiotics. He injected syringe after syringe of sodium solution. I came back the next day while she convalesced. She looked thinner. I held her hand. I knew how close to death she had been.

"I brought you soymilk Auntie made for you," I said.

"How was Auntie doing?"

"She said when you get well, you can eat spring rolls she made with anchovy. Is that your favorite food?"

She nodded then said she loved steamed anchovy wrapped in rice paper with lettuce. You dip them in a shrimp sauce flavored with minced pineapple and garlic, a pinch of sugar, and a dash of lemon.

I removed the brown bag and gave her a glass jar of fresh soymilk. She palmed it, her cheeks flushed from the heat inside the small room. "Can I drink it, *chú?*" she said and wet her dry lips.

"Sure. It's good for you."

She sat up. I handed her a glass and watched her drain it down, not wasting a drop of the clear soymilk Auntie had made from the beans and left in a jug out in the yard to chill. Still holding the empty glass in her hand, she looked at me, then at the unlit cigarette between my fingers. "Why don't you light it, c*hú?*"

"I'd rather not," I said and put it back in my shirt pocket. "The smoke will make you cough."

"Am I going home today?"

Home. Her father was like a ghost coming and going in their house. Before I could answer, someone paused at the door momentarily, then came into the room. I shook hands with the doctor and said I was grateful. The doctor glanced at the chart hung on the bedpost and said the girl was improving enough to leave the hospital the next day. I thanked him and he left. She said her abdomen still hurt as she turned on her side to put the glass back on the table and the burn scar on her cheek, salmon-colored, shone in the table lamplight.

"Did you burn yourself?" I asked, pointing at my own cheek.

She squinted her eyes at me. I leaned back in the chair under her gaze and shrugged.

"I didn't burn myself," she said finally. "Mom did."

"By accident?"

"She didn't like the fish soup I cooked, said *why don't you and your dad eat this* and she threw the bowl in my face."

"Hell." I shook my head.

"*Chú,*" she said, leaning forward to hand me the jar, "don't you want a sip of Auntie's soymilk?"

"I'm not thirsty. It's for you."

She sat back. "Who brought you cigarettes now?"

"I did. I went to town. Auntie asked me to pick up a few things for her."

"I'll be back to take care of her tomorrow."

"Take another day's rest. You said your tummy still hurts."

"It's tolerable now, not like a couple days ago. It hurt bad then and I had tears in my eyes." She was stopped by a sudden cough. "But I'm feeling much better now. I want to go home and check on Daddy. Does he know where I am, *chú?*"

"Certainly. Did he drop by while I wasn't here?"

"I don't know. He might. Before sunrise. He goes to sea very early. I must be sleeping when he came."

I looked away hearing her wishful voice. Then she said, "I could've died, the doctor told me."

"Well." I tried to smile. "You're a good girl. You can't die."

"I almost died last summer."

"How?"

"I got bit by a rabid dog one night when I left Auntie's house. Auntie came to visit me. She sat by my cot, holding my hand. I asked Auntie, 'Would they have to chain me down?' Auntie said, 'The Buddha will save you. Be good and nothing will harm you.' This hospital didn't have vaccine. Said it was on back order. Daddy took me back. At dawn Daddy took me on a bus to Huế. I was feverish. The city doctor vaccinated me. We arrived at our hamlet at dusk. Someone was waiting at the bus stop. It wasn't Mom. It was Auntie."

twenty

The helping girl said, "Auntie shouldn't come to visit me because she can't find her way around anymore."

That day I took the girl home from the hospital. I went back out on the main road. In the August heat I stopped often because my sandals kept getting stuck in the blistering blacktop. The heat stirred like a white sheet of gauze hazy and yellow with dust. As a habit, I closed my eyes and then opened them with my head bowed. That way I would not feel dizzy in the sun glare. Yet my skin felt tingly under my shirt and my underarms felt damp. I nodded at a priest who wore a salako and held a large white umbrella over his head. He nodded back and walked on with his helper, a local boy, trailing behind, cradling a cloth bundle in his arm. Someone was playing music. Across the street a blind old man squatted in front of a hut, plucking a monochord. Next to him sat a little boy tapping a drum. I dropped three coins in a tin can between the man and the boy. The clinking of the coins was lost in the sound of the instruments. I was surprised at the unusual quiet on this side of the street where feet scurried about at high noon and the sun glared on conical hats bobbing up and down the narrow sidewalk.

Past the white church by the roadside, its red-tiled steeple topped by a wooden cross, I saw Miss Phượng in the distance, as if she was waiting for a bus except there was nothing around but a barren plot next to an elementary school. She moved across the lot.

"Auntie," I called out to her.

She was sitting on a chair inside an empty classroom. The wall next to the much-faded blackboard displayed an old map of Vietnam. On the chalk rail were wooden compasses, a metal triangle, a square, and a protractor.

"Where were you going, Auntie?" I pulled up a chair and sat down.

"I'm on my way to see Cam. She's back from the hospital today, isn't she?"

"Yes, Auntie. She's fine now. And why are you in here?"

"The heat out there really took my mind away."

"How's that, Auntie?"

"It seemed to blank my mind for a moment. I didn't know where I was."

"Do you know where you are now, Auntie?"

"In a while."

"Do you remember how to get to her place, Auntie?"

She nodded. "Where am I?" she said.

—o—

In the evening the eunuch felt better. Dr. Sung gave her some Ganidan tablets for diarrhea. He wanted her father to drink fluid extracted from boiling brown rice with a few ginger slivers and to eat brown rice gruel.

After the doctor left, her father stayed in bed. He packed the leftover tea in tissue paper and put it on his eyelids to help relax his eyes. When he woke, she had latched the entrance door and lit the oil lamp. She put away the dishes and walked up to his quarters. In the quiet she could hear her wooden sabots clacking. She parted the curtain, the loops jangled.

"Father?"

He rumbled in his throat.

"There's something I'd like to ask you."

"What is it, dear?"

She felt the cot give under her as she sat down. The tea bags from his eyelids were still wet and warm when he placed them in her hands. "You didn't pick me up from an orphanage, did you, father?"

He opened his lips but said nothing. She touched his hand. "Father. Please."

His long fingers found her hand. "You are who you are," he said hoarsely. "I am your father, and there's no one else."

"But you're my foster father. Who is my real father? Who is my real mother?"

"I don't know."

"How can you say that, father?"

"I don't know, my dear daughter. I don't know."

Her hand squeezed his. "I had a twin sister, father. Do you remember the dreams I used to have? The little girl I saw? That was her."

He gasped. His hand was cold in hers. Slowly she sank to her knees and wept.

"Dear," he said, "Your mother died shortly after she gave birth to both of you. From your birth until you were a year old I took care of you both. Then I lost your sister."

She raised her head, looked at him. "Who was our mother?"

He tried to say her name and could not. "You asked me about her the other day."

She bent her head. "Ân-Phi is my mother," she said.

Phượng had walked the concubine's home ground since childhood, hearing her name as if she were another notable in a history book. Phượng had gone with her father to her mother's tomb to observe her death anniversary every year since she was a child.

Her father's voice was barely clear. "Forgive me, my dear."

"How did she die?"

"She died from a hemorrhage no one could stop. It has been years, my dear, but I can never get rid of the sight of blood in my mind. Just one towel after another." He bit his lips and his fingers clenched hers.

"Who is my father?"

"I don't know."

"Father, please."

"It is not a story I want you to hear."

"I must know, father."

He groaned. "A French general. My dear child, your mother was insane in those days after her release from the palace. Your grandfather sold her, so he could keep his supreme post with the imperial court. After the Frenchman used her, your grandfather banished your pregnant mother to an imperial mausoleum to avoid the disgrace."

She asked why her mother had gone insane.

"Canh, the eunuch I trained to serve your mother, died of urine blockage after castration. He loved your mother more than anything in the world, and his spirit haunted your mother after he died. Only by leaving this world could he possess her completely. At times I saw glimpses of her old self like the sun behind passing clouds, but Canh would not let her return to herself. You must've heard of Master Đinh, the great exorcist in Gia-Linh. That's Canh's father. I went to him and pled with him to save your mother by exorcising his son's spirit. He refused. He must've held me responsible for making Canh undergo castration. Eventually Canh left her body, but it was too late for her to recover completely."

She pulled her hand away to wipe her eyes. "Why did you keep all this from me all these years, father?"

"Your mother didn't want you to think that you were born of violence. She wanted you to be proud of who you are."

"I am proud of her. What she suffered was beyond her control. It's nothing shameful."

"My child, in the old days one did anything to protect the honor of his pedigree. She despised herself because of the disgrace she suffered at the hands of the Frenchman, the shame her father brought on her. She feared it would taint your perception of her as a mother."

A dog barked in the alley. A street vendor cried, "Poached duck eggs!"

"Father, how was my sister lost?"

He told her, then stopped to catch his breath. "I can't tell you how I felt that day, watching the basket swept away by the floodwater. It'd have driven me mad to dwell on it. I thought she had drowned because I was careless." He cleared his throat. "That guilt has never left me. It haunted me for a long time and showed up in my dreams. I saw a little girl too. She always stood on the riverbank in the rain, and I could never reach her. So I believed she was dead. Then you told me about the girl you saw in your dreams, and I thought your twin sister came back to haunt you the way Canh did your mother. But Heaven watched over her. The magic bond between you two stayed alive for many years. You helped each other through difficult times. Was it a miracle that she was saved and brought up somewhere else? Or was it a curse that she died horribly when she was still full of life? Why all this? Forgive me, my dear daughter. I only meant to love you the best I could and honor your mother's wishes."

Tears welled in her father's eyes and ran down his cheeks. She gripped his hand, sobbing.

"Where's my mother's family now?" She spoke, her voice thick.

"Your grandfather moved his family to Quảng Trị, his birthplace. He was long gone from Gia-Linh when I came. You were five then."

"Did he know about me and my sister?"

"He disavowed both of you."

"Why?"

"He thought half-castes dishonored him."

Her mouth tasted bitter. The wetness on her face had dried. She caressed his fingernails. "We all come into this life as equals. I'm disturbed that he disavowed us because of our mixed blood. I want to rectify that—and clear my mother's name. I want to meet my grandfather."

Her father shook his head vehemently. Years had passed, but it seemed that he could never bring himself to forgive the man who happened to be her grandfather.

"Is he still alive, father?"

"I don't know." His voice was angry. "It's been more than twenty years."

Her father said his blood boiled every time he recalled Đông Các's words in the formal letter that said, *It is my gratitude that you take on the burden of rearing my daughter's illegitimate children. I am saddened by the loss of my beloved daughter and at the same time troubled by the nature of her children's birth. I do not see how their bloodline can be part of our pedigree.*

Her father thought Đông Các was a coward, but then why didn't he confront the man? Was he afraid of Đông Các's social stature? His affluence and power?

After Phượng worded her questions politely, her father admitted that there is a coward in each person's soul. His own had slept for decades since Đông Các had left Gia-Linh. Her decision to see her grandfather woke it. But she was determined to do what her father should have done years before. After all, didn't he once tell her a good heart could ward off evil?

She put the lukewarm tea bags back on his eyelids. "Father, what made you honor your pledge to my mother to this day?"

"Because I love her."

"Can I tell Jonathan what you told me?"

She watched his face. After all, Jonathan came a long way to find the truth for her sister. That burden should be lifted off his heart.

"Well," her father said, "We should be grateful that he came into our lives."

She rose and kissed his forehead. "Do you regret all this?"

He said softly that he repented having her grow up thinking she was an orphan. But he raised her to have a loving soul. Ân-Phi would be proud of her—a virtuous girl with a magnanimous soul.

Then he raised his hand and touched her face, her eyes. He smiled. His rare smile warmed her. In his mind, she imagined, he saw Ân-Phi.

twenty-one

Three days later, Miss Phượng said, she left Gia-Linh for Huế with Jonathan, where they would board a train to Quảng Trị where her grandfather lived.

They arrived at the Huế train station at mid-afternoon. Jonathan followed her, pushing, elbowing through crowds of people who never formed lines or apologized for being rude. He shielded her to get her safely up the steps to the coach. He looked agitated, and said he admired how calm and easy she was among strangers. *It's a matter of culture.* Sooner or later, he would have to learn more about the people of the country so he could accept them for who they were.

The train idled on the track for a long time, puffing gray smoke. People got off and then came back on, bringing news that a segment of track just outside Huế was being repaired. At nightfall the stationmaster waved a flag, and the train woke with a shudder and was on its way through town, edging a river. The train stopped often between way stations, sometimes waiting a long while for the signal to move on. From their bench Phượng looked at the people climbing onto the train. Women in torn, unbuttoned blouses nursed babies. Swollen nipples filmed white. Children cried. Watching them, she believed it must dawn on Jonathan in such a moment that the pacification program training had never taught him what poverty was like, how tenuous life was in the grip of war and shortage of food.

She dozed, lying on her side on the bench. Outside just blackness, sometimes the yellow dot of an oil lamp. Jonathan went to the latrine, stepping over bodies curled up on the floor. The air smelled sour. When he came back, he complained that he couldn't stand upright in the latrine. It wasn't built for Westerners.

The train stopped at the red dirt platform of a small station. The sudden glare of neon lights on the platform woke her. She rubbed her eyes looking at a profile cut against the lighted platform. Jonathan was already up, standing at the window.

"Do you want to go down for fresh air?" she asked.

"Don't I want fresh air!" Jonathan glanced at his watch.

The air was warm, misty. Food smells hung thick. Surprised, Jonathan looked around: Food vendors up at this past midnight hour! The conductor said the stop would be long. Viet Cong saboteurs had blown up the tracks ahead. "No bypass," the conductor said. "The bastards blew up the junction."

There were no buses, no ferries. The platform was rank with cigarette smoke. Men wore visor caps, long sideburns. The hill mists hung blue, fogging the neon globe lamps. Wind swirled the red dust, and vendors quickly put the lids back on their steaming pots. Phượng sat down with Jonathan on the dirt platform waiting while the tracks were repaired. She bought them two bowls of noodle soup with crabmeat. Jonathan mentioned that the rice noodles were thicker than the noodles in her *bún bò Huế*.

"You're very observant, Jonathan. This is *bánh canh*."

He repeated the name.

A woman peddler walked by with a basket of marble-sized berries which she sold by the measuring can. She told Jonathan that the fruit was tasty, so Jonathan bought a canfull. "*Sim*," she said. Jonathan said they looked like downy myrtle.

In the humid air Phượng could smell a mellow scent from the flowers she wore in her hair.

"That's a nice perfume you wear," Jonathan said.

"I don't wear perfume."

Jonathan rolled his eyes. "I must be imagining things."

"Must be the grapefruit flowers."

Men noticed the same things. Didn't Long once notice the missing *phượng* flower in her hair one day when she forgot to wear it? But when Jonathan said it, she flushed inside and smiled, touching her hair. She believed that, to him, the twin sisters were all but inseparable, no matter how hard he tried not to confuse them. The feelings, too. Phượng felt certain that he wasn't even sure if he was reliving his love for Françoise through her or feeling something new and different for her.

Phượng stretched her legs, looking at her white ankles. Her heels, clad in black rubber sandals, were chapped with black lines. She couldn't help but imagine Françoise's. Were they smooth, pink heels? Yes, they must be, compared to the hard life Phượng lived, evidenced by the worn-out feet that traveled the long road between home and the market every day. She dropped the berries in Jonathan's hand and peeled off the black, velvety skin and ate the fruit. After a while they looked at each other's lips smeared blue and started giggling.

"Tell me about the day you met Françoise," Phượng said, wiping her lips with her fingers.

"I was a student in her Vietnamese language class. On the very first day I knew I'd never be the same if I walked out of that class without knowing her. Everything about her was lovely. Her demeanor was so precise, her dress so fastidious. But I fell in love with her soul. She had a noble soul."

"I've never seen identical twins before. Are we exactly identical?"

"Yes. Even your voice is exactly like hers. The only difference is that she had a charming eyetooth."

Phượng thought of their parting when they returned to Huế. Would he carry her image from that day forward the way he did her sister's? Did he see her simply as Françoise without an eyetooth? She brushed those questions away when she recalled her father. *Is he well?*

The morning before she left with Jonathan, a neighbor came to drink tea with her father. The neighbor would look after him while she was gone. He still had recurring stomach pain and nausea but said he would be fine, that it would soon pass.

A young girl came, selling peanuts. Jonathan bought a bag. He cracked the shells, and the toasty smell burst fresh between them. He spat a piece of shell. "Is this your first trip away from home?"

"I'm homesick already."

"That makes two of us."

"Would you like to head back?"

"Yes, if you want to."

He helped her to her feet, and they climbed back onto the train. She lay down on the wooden bench and tried to sleep. Across from her Jonathan dozed. His white shirt gleamed in the dimness.

After a while she turned on her side, cushioning her cheek with her hands. What if something happens to her father tonight? Last night, he had stomach pain again. His moans woke her. She brought him a hot water bottle, and he slept with it. If she had the money, she would take him to the best doctor in Huế. The day before she left, she gave Mrs. Xinh two hundred thousand *dồng*—most of her savings—money she could not get to for the next three months. It had to pay off.

The train idled, coughing rings of smoke. Its trembling became a rhythm for her sleep.

When she woke, anxiety had softened in her. Jonathan came over and knelt at her bench.

"Aren't you thirsty?"

She nodded. "Are you?"

When he came back with a cup of lukewarm water, she was up, tucking stray hair into her chignon. "Where did you go to get water, Jonathan?"

He sat down and handed her the cup. "I wandered around."

The sleepers droned. The train lurched, and water spilled onto her blouse. He held her wrist to steady her hand.

twenty-two

Đông Các's old male servant told Phượng that his sire was visiting his wife at the back of their land. Every morning, rain or shine, he served her tea at her tomb. In the main hall Phượng and Jonathan waited in the cool breeze coming from the mountains. The morning light gleamed on ironwood black pillars and rosewood furniture.

When Đông Các finally came through the door, he studied them through bleary eyes with some reservation. White-haired, he leaned on his cane, but despite his stoop he was tall. He wore a crew cut, unlike the chignon old-fashioned men like her father wore.

When Đông Các sat down, the old butler served him tea and stood in the shadow of the ironwood pillars, hands clasped. Everything about Đông Các was neat and orderly—from the immaculate white trousers and white shirt that hung loosely across his broad shoulders to his manicured hands whose mottled skin looked like overripe banana peel. Clean-shaven, square-faced, and thin-lipped, he must have been good-looking in his prime. If her mother were still alive, she'd be in her fifties. What did her mother look like?

"Sir," Phượng said, "please pardon our sudden intrusion. I have come from Gia-Linh to see you."

Đông Các regarded her warily. He spoke in a cautious tone. "You're from Gia-Linh, you said? A visitor?" He paused, then smiled. "Or born there?"

"I was raised in Upper Đinh-Xuân and moved to Gia-Linh with my foster father when I was five. You were gone from Gia-Linh by then." She leaned forward. "Grandfather, I'm your granddaughter."

She watched his face. Slowly he set his cup on the saucer. He peered across at her.

"You are my granddaughter?"

"My mother died after she gave birth to me and my twin sister."

"How extraordinary," he said. "I am shocked, but it's not an unpleasant shock. You know, I have lived a quiet life since I left the court, and I have forgotten so much about it."

He had ignored his granddaughters' existence by choice and his superficial remark raised her ire. *Can he be that callous?* "You mean you don't remember that you have two granddaughters?"

"I do remember."

"I'm Phượng, and this is Jonathan, my friend from America." She turned slightly toward Jonathan, who nodded.

"Phượng," Đông Các said, half tilting his head toward Jonathan, "tell your friend he's as welcome in my home as you are. It's uncouth of me to let him feel ignored."

"He understands us, Grandfather."

Jonathan smiled but said not a word.

"He understands Vietnamese?" Đông Các turned to Jonathan. "Do you speak Vietnamese?"

"Yes, sir. But please don't let me distract you and your granddaughter."

"I heard Grandmother died." She held Đông Các's gaze. "When did you lose her?"

"Five years ago."

"You haven't been back to Gia-Linh to visit my mother's tomb, have you, Grandfather?"

"I have not."

"So I assume you commemorate the anniversary of her death at the altar?"

"Hers and your grandmother's."

"I wish I could see Grandmother. But I'm happy to meet you, Grandfather, after all these years."

"The pleasure is also mine. Where is your sister now?"

"She's dead, Grandfather. In a car accident."

Đông Các appeared to muse on the news. "You live in Gia-Linh with Bộ, don't you?"

Does he regret that he would never meet his other granddaughter? Noticing Đông Các's empty look, she said, "Yes, my foster father raised me."

Đông Các tapped his forehead with his finger. "He is much older than I am. How old?"

"A hundred years old, Grandfather. He can't see now."

"Cataracts?"

"Happens to lots of old people," she said. "You don't have them, do you, Grandfather?"

Đông Các smiled. "I am blessed. How long will you stay in town?"

"We're going back today. My father is sick."

"Will you stay for lunch?"

"If it isn't too much trouble for you, Grandfather."

Đông Các motioned and the butler bowed to receive his orders.

After the servant withdrew, she asked, "How many people in your household, Grandfather?"

"Four. I, the butler and his wife, who cooks, and their son, who drives our car." He rose from his chair. "Would you like to see the land?"

"Yes, thank you, Grandfather. May I pay my respects to my mother and Grandmother first?"

Đông Các leaned on his cane. "If you think it is appropriate to do so," he said, shifting his gaze from her to Jonathan.

"This is why I came, Grandfather," she said.

Đông Các nodded repeatedly to his cane as if it were a depository for his scattered thoughts. She asked Jonathan to wait. He bowed to Đông Các and said he'd wander around outside. She followed her grandfather down a corridor, walking under bronze lanterns dripping rainwater from the previous night's rain. The veranda outside the worship hall overlooked the lotus pond and its clear tint of green soothed her eyes. Inside the hall was dim and sunlight gleamed across the blue tiles. The smell of incense and tuberoses hung sweetly.

Đông Các's cane clacked on the tile floor. She stood by the tall red pillars, touching figures of dragons twining around them. When she commented on them, her grandfather noted that only imperial dragons had five claws. Plebeian dragons like his had four. He took her to the two-tiered altar, leaned his cane against the wall, and lit incense sticks in a ceramic holder. She stood like a shadow in front of the burnished flamewood altar that swept upward grandly. On the wall hung a bronze cross and her gaze lingered on the figure of Christ crucified. The figure looked solemn and sad, its head lolling to one side, long black hair covering half the face and blood staining the palms nailed to the cross.

On the highest tier was a framed picture of a woman wearing a yellow robe, her hair done in a chignon. She was a small woman with a serene face and a straight, elegant nose. Then Đông Các told her that she was his wife, Phượng's grandmother.

She studied the woman in the picture, searching the sunny, sympathetic face for something linked to her mother. Did her grandfather keep a picture of her mother as well? Before her grandmother, she bowed her head in silence. When she raised her head, she was looking at a black-and-white framed photograph on the lowest tier. Next to it was a gilded tablet inscribed with Chinese characters in black brushstrokes. Seated on a chair, the woman in the picture wore a shiny robe draping her feet, which were clad in curl-tipped slippers. Her headdress was studded with jewels in a geometric pattern resembling a constellation of sparkling silver on black. On her chest danced a phoenix spreading its wings in gleaming threads and the black headdress framed her oval face.

Phượng recognized her mother not only by her comeliness but also by the soulfulness pooled in her eyes. Serenity. Years of hearing her mother's name and of her grace had created an image in her mind, which bore an amazing resemblance to the woman in the portrait. Calmed by her mother's peaceful mien, Phượng gazed at the picture.

"How old was my mother when that was taken?"

"When she was made the second-ranking concubine at eighteen."

Phượng pointed to the Chinese characters on the tablet. "What do they mean?"

"Quỳnh Hương."

She had seen the name in Vietnamese on the headstone. Phượng closed her eyes and sank slowly to her knees, clasping her hands on her chest, and then raised her face to the picture like a devout Christian praying to the Virgin Mary. *Mother, may you and my sister forever be in eternal peace. My heart is with you.* Đông Các waited. He was a cautious man, a miser perhaps, but he was a good judge of character. Distant kin, very distant, had come to befriend him, only to be shown the door. He realized Phượng hadn't come for his wealth.

When Phượng turned to him, he was dozing off. Her voice woke him with a start.

"Grandfather?"

Phượng rose to her feet and put her hands on his. He peered at her.

"Do you have another photograph of my mother?"

"No."

"Grandfather."

He nodded.

"Can I have it? There's nothing else in the world I want."

Đông Các looked at the picture of his daughter. He touched the frame, the glass that covered the girl's face. Slowly it came back to him that it had been in his possession since the day she became the second-ranking concubine. The photograph reminded him of his decision to offer her to the emperor for his own aggrandizement. He told Phượng she could have the original, but he'd have the servant take it to a studio to be copied before she left town.

"You and your family are Catholic, aren't you, Grandfather?"

"For over a century. I was five when the massacre happened in our village."

"What massacre?"

"The massacre of the Catholics. When the capital fell to the French in 1885, the Regent of the Court ordered an uprising against the French, and he wanted all Vietnamese Catholics killed because those Catholics had been converted by the French with the help of the French missionaries. They sent soldiers and convicts to our village, because it was the largest Catholic community in northern Central Vietnam. They surrounded us and locked us inside our village church and burned it down. Over two thousand died. Our family got away by a miracle but when we came back days after, the corpses hadn't been buried and they stank to high heaven."

They walked back out into the main hall. "What was my mother like?" she asked him.

"In those days," Đông Các said, his head bobbing as if on a string, "I was seldom home from my duties at the court to spend time with her. After she was inducted, I visited her several times, but it was like talking to a stranger. She and I were separated by a screen during those visits, not even a glimpse of her face. But she was close to her mother. My daughter was bright and very charismatic. She had a commanding presence that, in my humble opinion, reminded me of myself. On the other hand, her unfailing humanity could be attributed to my beloved wife. I certainly had high expectations for her when I married her to our emperor. I was greatly disappointed when she was denied the opportunity to become the last queen mother of the Nguyễn dynasty."

Phượng thought her grandmother must have influenced her mother much the same way Bộ had shaped her. They were shade trees in their lifetime.

"What else do you remember about her?"

"Her musical talent. A gifted pianist. She played for her mother twice a day. My daughter had that marvelous touch and an ear for melody, which, to my understanding, came from neither of her parents."

In the empty hall Phượng stood face-to-face with Đông Các. Up close she recognized with a start the similarity of his eyes to her mother's and her own. Pooled in their depths was the serene expression that gazed beyond, beyond everything, where things were yet to form.

"What do you have to say, Grandfather, about my mother's disgrace by becoming pregnant while she was out of her mind? She was completely helpless. I do not want to delve into the details. I think I know them. I only wonder why you didn't protect her."

"We knew how she got pregnant." Đông Các leaned his weight with both hands on the cane. He saw his granddaughter knew the truth, which he had believed only he and his wife knew. "For her honor and mine," he now said, "I put her in the custody of an old concubine who lived in the Thiên Lăng mausoleum, where your mother carried her pregnancy to term. But unfortunately, God only saw her halfway on the road to becoming a mother, and we mortals must abide his decision and therein find our own souls' salvation."

Phượng decided not to press him for a confession. A man of his tact would certainly have the eloquence to make his own sin look like someone else's. She looked into his eyes. He blinked slowly the way a rooster does to summon sleep.

"Grandfather, you've had time to look back on my mother's pregnancy and death. Will you in the name of God admit that she was no disgrace but rather a victim of circumstances, singled out to benefit somebody's ambition and condemned unjustly at the same time?"

Đông Các kept nodding. "Twenty years give a long hindsight," he said finally, "beneficial to wake up an obtuse mind that time and again willed the feet to repeated missteps."

"I suspect Grandmother did not think so. Did she follow your missteps of her own free will?"

"My beloved wife was also a victim of circumstances."

"So were your granddaughters, who were condemned to disgrace just like their mother."

"They too. God forbid. But there is a time and place for certain things to happen. And God passes judgment at the end of everyone's road."

From the troubled look in his runny eyes, she wondered if he had ever confessed his sins to God. Still, he had volunteered his thoughts, which, she assumed, he must have shared only with God.

"Lunch will be ready shortly," Đông Các said, slightly turning his head toward her. "My butler will be on his way to town to make a duplicate of your mother's photograph." They saw Jonathan coming in through the pomelo orchard and walking with him was the butler. Đông Các squinted. "A fine young man. I certainly hope to see you or hear from you again, Phượng."

twenty-three

They were in the middle of nowhere when they stepped down from the train that afternoon. Ten miles outside of Quảng Trị and the train was about to turn back to town. Somewhere south the Việt Cọng had seized a town and the South Vietnamese army was coming to take it back. Most people were willing to go back to Quảng Trị. Jonathan asked Phượng what she planned to do. She asked some women merchants and learned that they could follow the track on foot until they got to a river and then catch a boat. They might take two days or so to reach Huế, but that was better than being stuck in Quảng Trị, since no one knew how soon the line would be reopened. He asked if they could take a bus from Quảng Trị and was told that the highway ran through the contested town.

They stood among a small gathering of men and women on the red earth that changed to yellow beyond glistening sand dunes. Jonathan surveyed the landscape.

"Phượng, are you sure you want to do this?"

"I'm more than sure." She shielded her eyes. "I'm only worried about you."

"Me?"

"Can you make it?"

Jonathan nodded firmly.

They walked along the track behind women hoisting wicker baskets on shoulder poles. Ahead of them walked a woman carrying a little girl in one arm. With her other hand she clutched a cloth bag and pulled a small boy along.

The train was long gone when they crossed the sand dunes through groves of stunted pines and wild azaleas. Phượng said that she wished she could let her father know they would be a day or two late.

They reached a river before sunset. As they came upon a jetty, Jonathan listened to men and women on the pier talking with the boatmen, sun-browned and naked to the waist.

He followed Phượng onto a wide-bottomed boat. The woman with her children got on just as the long boat nosed out. They went downriver in the shadow of kapok trees glowing red with tiny blossoms in the twilight. Winds brought the sound of church bells. Before dark the sky flushed red, the setting sun incandescent on Phượng's face. With his handkerchief Jonathan dabbed her perspiring cheeks and she bit her lower lip, holding her face still. People looked at them.

They talked in low voices, putting their heads together to hear better. He sat with his hands between his knees, smiling at strange faces. The air smelled of fried fish and gray smoke blew from moored boats at dinnertime. The boat kept close to the bank. The wind spun the petals of kapok blossoms in the blue light of dusk.

He dozed and woke and saw a huge shape over the river. When it came near, he made out a bridge. The boat pulled to a landing. Phượng woke and asked around. They would have to continue on foot until they found another boat going south. Those who knew the way led, stumbling in the darkness flickering with fireflies through a swale of stunted fir and up a hill of jack pine, then down into a fern-covered flat. The leaves, crushed underfoot, sent a dark aroma aloft.

The sound of a locomotive came in the wind. Ahead of them was a train blinking red lights. People broke and ran toward it. Jonathan caught the little boy in his arms and carried him. The woman said something to him as she ran with her daughter bouncing on her hip. The train was idling, the cars full of salt, gleaming white. The engineer told them he would go only as far as the next town, but he would take them.

They climbed onto the open cars and sat atop a thick bed of salt, hard and dry like white pebbles. The engineer told them to lie flat. Jonathan held Phượng's hand. Nearby lay the woman and her children. The train chugged into the night. He saw Phượng looking at him, tiny lights in her eyes the salt-white glimmer. Braided, her long hair was flung over her shoulder. Darkness let him gaze into her eyes and darkness blanketed them both when sleep came.

When he woke, her hand was still in his and the train was standing still. Across the woodland the day blushed with dawn, and they began trudging along the track. The little girl in the woman's arms moaned about thirst. Jonathan's throat was seared dry. As hawks called overhead, they crossed the woodland thick with the smell of fallen pine needles, soft as brown velour. The little girl cried, "Snake!" pointing to a brown woody vine creeping around a eucalyptus tree.

From deep in the woodland came the sound of water, a stream as clear and shallow as it was cold. They drank from their cupped hands. Jonathan splashed water on his face, letting it run down the front of his shirt. Next to him, the woman washed her children with a handkerchief. The boy said he was hungry.

The silvery railroad track flashed in the distance. Sweat dripped down Jonathan's face and the sun's glare on the conical hats hurt his eyes. He asked Phượng if she wanted to rest. She wet her lips and said they must press on.

"Do you want to rest, Jonathan? We'll catch up with them."

"Don't worry about me," he said.

Soon the little boy fell behind, hopping in pain. His mother held his torn rubber thongs and pulled him along. He tried to walk on the ties and cried when the sharp gravel cut his feet. The woman wrapped them with a sleeve she tore from a shirt. When Jonathan looked back, the boy was limping along behind his mother who carried the little girl on her hip.

Phượng tugged his arm. "Can you carry him?"

"Of course."

The mother thanked him profusely when he let the boy climb onto his back. Jonathan smiled at the little girl, who smiled back and yawned. He walked beside Phượng, the mother trailing behind.

Then the little girl asked, "Mom, can Mr. American see like us? His eyes are blue. How do you make them blue?"

The boy cut in. "You don't. They're just blue."

The girl giggled. "His hair, Mommy, it looks like duck down."

Phượng smiled. "Why don't you ask him something?"

"What's your name, Mister?" the girl said in Vietnamese.

Jonathan turned to look at her. "Jonathan. And what's yours?"

The girl hid her face on her mother's shoulder. The woman looked embarrassed and smiled nervously. "Tell Mr. Jonathan your name."

"My name is Châu."

Jonathan patted the boy's leg. "And what's your name?"

"Cung."

"Good. Are you afraid, Cung?"

"No. Mommy said it's only scary if you have to walk through the jungle."

"Why?"

"Because the orangutans will get you. Mommy said if you have to walk through the jungle, you put your arms in two bamboo tubes."

"Why?"

"Because when they grab you, they grab your arms, so you slip them out of the bamboo tubes and run for your life."

Jonathan laughed. "Is that for real?"

"It's for real, Mr. Jon-a-than," Cung said.

"The little girl piped up. "If you go through the jungle, you have to bring an old bicycle tire tube and cut it up into rubber bands."

"Why can't you just bring rubber bands? Why do you need rubber bands in the jungle?"

"They don't sell them around here. Only in the city. And you need them because the jungle leeches come down from the trees after a rain. They get into your pants and suck your blood."

"I'm glad we're not going through the jungle."

"If we do," Cung said, "you think the orangutans would be scared?"

"Why?"

"There are a lot of us. And the orangutans are smaller than you."

"Thanks, Cung. I feel important now."

Phượng looked back at Jonathan. His face was sweaty and red from the sun, and he walked stooped, the boy draped on his back, his skinny arms locked around Jonathan's neck. She stopped and waited for him. He smiled. She forgot her own thirst when she saw his lips dry from dehydration.

That afternoon they came to a hut where an old woman sold refreshments. Gone quickly were a few bundles of bananas, then rice waffles. Phượng asked the old woman if she had something else for the children and the woman began to grate cassava. She sprinkled brown sugar on shredded white cassava, wrapped a good portion of it in a green banana leaf. Before she tied it up, she slit the middle of the cassava mound and filled it with mung bean. She filled a rack with cassava rolls and lowered it into a boiling crock. The children sniffed the fragrant steam. She gave each a chipped clay plate and dropped on it a steaming cassava roll. They blew and ate with their fingers and wanted more before they cleaned their plates. Their mother said she had to save money for boat fare, and their dejected faces moved Jonathan to buy them. While Phượng talked to people outside he watched the children eat, feeling their hunger in his stomach.

The woman said they could wait until night to catch a boat, then dropped her voice and warned them that they were in a war zone controlled by Mr. Việt Cộng.

Toward the road, saddleback pigs milled around a child sitting naked in the red dirt. Soon men and women filed down the road, shoulder poles bent with swinging buckets full of salt. The lilac sky and their silhouettes slowly darkened to indigo.

At night the river was black, and the bank gleamed with the ivory skins of conical hats. People held onto one another on the clay slope, waiting. Boats came and went. Hushed. They said each boat traveled downriver in blackness, in silence, to slip through the Việt Cộng checkpoint. The crowd got smaller, quieter, only the sound of the river lapping the bank.

Jonathan, Phượng, and the mother said they'd go together, so when a boat had room only for two more passengers, they decided to wait for the next one. It came much later, carrying bundles of bananas piled to the rim of its rattan shelter. The boatwoman said she would take them to the next village. Phượng asked her about the town the Việt Cộng had captured and was told they would bypass it on the river, but the fighting was fierce.

Late at night the river came alive with unlit boats going up- and down-river without lights. Sitting on the floor, Jonathan leaned against the wall of green bananas. Starlight fell on the river, bobbing like silver sequins.

He sat with his knees against his chin, while the children lay across their mother's thighs, looking up at the stars, at the yellow and green specks of fireflies blinking in the bushes.

Phượng rested her head on his shoulder, her eyes shut, breathing quietly. He pressed his cheek against the top of her head, touching her braid with his fingers. Curls of clouds veined the dark blue sky. Where's the Southern Cross tonight? The Dipper and Orion? When he closed his eyes he smelled the river, and its muddy odor stirred his pity for the barren earth, its poverty, its people struggling for mere subsistence. His shoulder ached. He moved, then held still for fear of waking her. But she woke.

"I'm sorry," he said.

"Did you sleep?"

"*Không.*"

Phượng smiled. "I love to hear the northern accent my sister taught you."

"And she'd love to hear your Huế accent."

"Oh, it'd be nice if you had a picture of her, wouldn't it?"

He nodded, pressing her braid to his cheek.

"She never knew she had a sister," he said, "but she had longed for one."

Phượng sat up. "I stopped seeing her in my dreams when I got older. I thought I'd lost her."

"I see both her and you in your mother's photograph. She was a beautiful woman. You both have her eyes."

"Someday I'll visit my sister's grave in Lyon."

"That would be wonderful."

"How much of her do you see in me?"

"I don't know, Phượng." Jonathan smiled. "I guess I'm still not over the shock of finding she had a twin."

An upriver boat passed them in the dark. The boatman, leaning over the gunwale, blurted out staccato words, all muffled. The boatwoman signaled for Phượng to come to the stern. When she came back, Phượng told them that the Việt Cộng was setting up a checkpoint farther downriver. She said the boatwoman believed they'd take the American prisoner if they saw him.

"We can't drop you off here," Phượng said to Jonathan. "This is Việt Cộng country."

Jonathan's throat suddenly felt dry. "How about if I hide?"

"Where? We have to pass through the checkpoint. We can't stop here. It's not even safe in daytime."

He pointed at the wall of bananas. "I'll hide under there."

"What?" the mother said.

"There's no other choice. Do it quick," Phượng said, then cupped her hand and whispered a message to the boatwoman.

They hurried to move bananas to the bow. Phượng told the mother to wake her children. "Tell them what we're doing. He doesn't exist if the Việt Cộng ask them."

Jonathan lay on his side on the wet deck of the boat. The children squatted and touched his feet.

"Don't be scared, Mr. Jon-a-than," Cung said.

Jonathan raised his hand to thank him but quickly brought it back down as they piled bundles of bananas on top of him. Then blackness. He heard the river by his ear, sloshing and gurgling. He could smell the old tar that coated the floor, the stink of betel and tobacco spit. The river flowed under him, carrying him to the cadence of the oar.

The boat slid to a stop. Beneath him, gravel grinding. A flashlight beam broke into glinting needles between the banana bundles. Voices.

"How many people?"

"Three women, two children."

"You carry rice?"

"No, sir, just bananas."

The boat rocked as someone stepped onto it. The voice rose. "You don't carry rice under these bananas?"

"No, sir, I don't sell rice."

The voice grunted. "You people are sneaky."

Nobody said anything. The flashlight wavered, then the sound of water splashing and water all over Jonathan, collecting under him. Water dripped into his ear, and he couldn't move his arm. He felt the boat shake as someone walked sideways. Then water splashed again, bucket after bucket. Please stop, he pled in his head. His legs were soaked, his nose stung. He shook and sneezed just as the voice rang out again.

"How many bundles of bananas?"

"I don't know, sir. I didn't count."

Jonathan froze in terror. Out of the corner of his eye he saw the light brighter as someone brought the flashlight near an opening in the heap. The light moved from one opening to another. Someone grunted, very close, above him. Jonathan prayed. Someone dropped a bucket onto the bottom of the boat. Then the testy voice.

"Tax: two hundred *đồng*."

Jonathan swallowed a sneeze, felt the boat sway and then gravel churned under him as the boat moved out.

A short distance downriver he felt the pile of bananas lift off his body. He pushed himself up, dripping wet.

"Jonathan!" Phượng said, grabbing his arm.

The boy shook her arm. "I told you, Auntie, he'll be okay."

Still shaken, Jonathan sat down, feeling tiny and insignificant.

—o—

The sun was above the bamboo grove when they reached a jetty. The day was humid. They paid the boatwoman, climbed up the bank and walked toward a thatched hut with pots and pans hanging on its earthen wall. The owner was a middle-aged woman whose dimpled smile welcomed them at the entrance. She told them they could catch a ferry later in the day to the next town, where they could board a bus to Huế.

Phượng asked how close they were to the town by the Việt Cộng. Half a day ahead, the owner said, then pointed to the other hut, also a food stand, from where the sound of radio drifted. The owner there told her the South Vietnamese troops had taken the town back before dawn. The owner said they usually sent out a mop-up when they recaptured a town.

They sat at a long wooden table while the woman served them steamed rice and fresh coconut milk. Jonathan looked at the boy's feet, still bound in cloth. Pointing to the boy's feet, he asked the woman if she had an extra pair of thongs. After the mother told her what happened, she came back with a pair of black rubber flip-flops, bigger than the boy's feet. Jonathan paid her for the meal. She looked, then clutched it against her chest and bowed to him repeatedly. Embarrassed, he stood up and bowed back.

"Phượng," he said, "I'm going to the river to wash myself." He picked up his bag and stood over the boy. "Cung, you want to go bathe in the river?"

Cung nodded eagerly. "Sure, Mr. Jon-a-than, sure."

The boy finished his bowl, swigged down his coconut milk, and slipped his bandaged feet into the thongs. They walked to the bank, the boy plodding behind. A boat docked and let off a long line of passengers. Some went into the other food stand, and some walked into the hamlet in their indigo shirts and black pantaloons. Bare-headed, canvas bundles slung on shoulders. All men. They saw Jonathan and the boy, stopped, looked, then walked on.

Jonathan took off his shoes and stepped into the water, which was warm and brown. The boy ran naked into the river and paddled like a dog in the shallows, spouting water. His laughter made Jonathan forget his fatigue. He splashed water on the boy and the boy jumped up and down, asking for more. Suddenly magpies flew out from the trees, their legs yellow in the sun. Then gongs sounded noisily deep in the hamlet and voices screamed, "Airplane! Airplane!"

Jonathan shouted, "Cung! Run! Run!" Up the bank they clambered, gongs beating, men shouting. Then they heard a steady drone. Two South Vietnamese Skyraiders came into view over the hamlet so low Jonathan could see the pilots. The planes swooped down and bombs fell on the hut where they had just eaten their meals. The first explosion knocked him and the boy to the ground. Gravel, dirt, and straw flew through the air, trees snapped noisily. The second explosion was nearer and the ground beneath him burst upward, mortar and stone and leaves blowing up in a thick cloud. He shook with the ground, felt dirt in his mouth. His ears hurt. He gripped the boy's hand. The planes roared across the river and droned away.

He stood up. Both the huts had disappeared. He saw the long wooden table shattered; its legs blown off. He saw bodies in the second hut, men in indigo shirts plastered to the ground. "No! No! No!" he screamed as he ran. The boy raced after him. "Phượng! Phượng!" His shouts were lost in the general uproar in the hamlet. Something on the ground whimpered. He saw a head above the ground, the boy's mother buried in the earth. Her face was caked with red dirt. Clods stuck in her hair. He dropped to his knees.

The boy shouted, *Má!* and scraped at the dirt around his mother's face, crying, "Are you hurt, *Má?* Are you hurt?"

Jonathan saw the top of another head barely above ground and he dug and dug, screaming to the boy to dig. He sprung up and looked around until he found a branch. *She needs air. The mother can wait.* He plunged the stick into the dirt. It snapped. *She needs air.* He scraped and scratched with his fingers until they bled. He grunted, took out his pocketknife and stabbed at the dirt around her head until he loosened some and swept it off and stabbed the ground again and again. He scooped dirt by the handful and tossed it away until her face appeared. Her eyes were shut. "Phượng!" He shook her face in his hands, calling, "Phượng! Phượng!" hearing thickness in his voice. Her eyes opened.

When her shoulders were free, he began to pull her up. She struggled for a time before she broke free. Then she joined him and the boy digging around the woman.

Just as his mother climbed out of the hole the boy asked, "Where's Châu, *Má?* Where is she?"

The woman cried, "Where's my daughter? Châu!"

"Over here!" the owner shouted to them from the other hut.

Jonathan quickly figured out that the owner let the women use her bomb pits and took the little girl to the other hut.

"Châu!" the woman screamed as she ran to the other hut.

But there was no answer. They stood in the hot sun over the wreckage of the other hut and Jonathan's knees shook. The mother's cries resounded in his head.

twenty-four

In a white blouse Miss Phượng sat, still as a limestone statue, on the veranda's step of her house. A bright red petal fluttered in the air. Late blooms before summer died.

"Auntie," I said, sitting down next to her. "I've got the newspaper."

"Today's newspaper?"

"Yesterday, Auntie." Newspapers took a day to come from Huế. Sometimes the girl who had a fifth-grade education would read to her. Miss Phượng said her father used to sit outside waiting for a neighborhood boy whom he paid to go to the communal house and bring back a newspaper. The boy would read one war story after another, then read him the entire newspaper. She never forgot the vision of him in a white blouse, white pantaloons, his white hair let down, touching the step.

That day, she said, after Jonathan and she were coming back from Quảng Trị, he asked her father to let him stay the night, because Phượng said it was too late for him to go back to the Guanyin Temple. After he washed in the bathhouse in the rear, Jonathan came back to the mahogany divan to sleep. Next to a white pillow lay a neatly folded woolen blanket. He had turned down Phượng's offer to let him use her bed for the night and said he would sleep on the divan without a mosquito net.

A kerosene lamp burned dimly on a table in a corner. His body aching, he lay under the blanket, eyes open, looking up at the ceiling. Behind the curtain in a corner, Bộ snored. A dog barked in the distance, then another. The sound of water outside the kitchen as Phượng washed her feet. A whine by his ear. He slapped the invisible mosquito then pulled the blanket over his head.

He didn't know the time when he slid down from the divan, quietly unlatched the door and walked out into the garden. The milky light of a full moon glowed in every corner and the night wasn't black but blue bluer than indigo. The trees laid a velvety shade around the house. Cobblestones churned underfoot. Moss grew on the stucco, coloring the walls green with the years.

He walked along the edge of the garden, where bamboo and screw pines grew thick, and the nightshade let no light through. Walking so close to them he heard the squeaking of bamboo trunks, the murmur of leaves. From inside the house came a groan, clear in the stillness.

In the rock basin the water seemed blacker than ever beneath the canopy of the milk apple. A paper lantern hung on a limb of the grapefruit tree. A frail scent as he passed under, the fragrance of grapefruit blossom she wore in her hair. The night lit like a yellow shawl made of something so filmy that a touch would make it disappear. In the stillness he felt transparent. No bone, no flesh, no identity. Light shone through, scented of fragrant pines, of the brown earth, acrid and old.

He walked back to the courtyard. Phượng was standing by the rock island under the dark parasol of the milk apple. Her blouse was the only white. He went to her. Her hair, let down, touched her waist, draping over one shoulder in a long, silky swath.

"How's your father?"

"He had some pain again tonight. He said he would be fine. I gave him a hot water bottle to calm it."

"Phượng, he must see a doctor tomorrow. I'll go with you."

"You don't have to."

"That's in Huế, isn't it?"

"Yes. A long way. When are you going back to America?"

"In a few days, but I can delay it." A scent trailed in the air. He breathed in deeply. "Where's that scent coming from?"

She pointed toward a thicket of shrubs in a corner. "The Chinese call it *Yeh-lai-hsiang*, night fragrance."

He thought of the eight-o'clock jasmine with its sweet night scent. He thought of her question. He knew farewell was inevitable, but seeing to her father offered more time.

She brushed her dark hair with her fingers. "Will you come back?"

"I don't want to leave at all."

"I thought you'd be sound asleep tonight."

"The mosquitoes kept me awake."

"Really? I thought it was my father's snoring."

He laughed softly. "That too."

She looked at his feet and smiled. "Comfortable?"

He chuckled. Bộ's rubber thongs were a bit too big for him.

"Have you ever loved any man?" Jonathan said, gazing down into her eyes.

"No. But someone loved me. And I wasn't ready for him."

"Did you two grow up together?"

"Since we were children."

"What happened to him? What's his name?"

"Long. He saved me one time and got in bad blood with another man. That man cut his throat." Phượng paused. "He died. Just nineteen."

Her quiet tone left Jonathan shaking his head.

"Did you love him, Phượng?"

"I felt for him. Like you feel for your best friend who dies."

"I know how it feels to lose someone like that."

"You still think of her often?"

He thought for a moment. Perhaps in love, as Françoise said, there's no coming or going.

—o—

Early in the morning they took her father to a free clinic in Huế. In the ocher-colored waiting room, Bộ could smell a musty odor but saw only a white blur of the fluorescent light. Late the night before, when Phượng emptied his chamber pot because he was too weak to go to the outhouse, she found a trace of blood in his stool.

At his age he took one day at a time. Any morning he woke up without the pain he felt blessed. Death didn't frighten him, but the prospect of heavy medical costs did. He'd have to have some sort of treatment, he was certain, and he hoped he wouldn't require private hospital care. It'd cost a great deal there and who but his daughter would have to bear it?

Tired, he leaned his head against the wall. Moments later he slept. Children stared at him because he was so big and old, then at Jonathan because he was American. Phượng smiled at a little girl who came close to look at her father's bird's-claw fingernails and his big hands mottled with brown spots. She looked at Phượng and smiled shyly.

Jonathan sat with his hands folded in his lap, his eyes closed. He said he wasn't sleeping, just resting and thinking.

While her father slept, Phượng spoke to Jonathan about his condition. "Last night my father had more blood in his stool."

"Let's hope that he doesn't have cancer."

Bộ snored. Phượng put her hand on his thigh. Cancer meant death.

"The Gia-Linh matriarch has cancer," she said, "and despite her wealth, she's dying."

"I'm having some money wired to me," Jonathan said. "Listen, money doesn't fix all, but proper treatment at a hospital is what your father might need."

"Let me talk to him about it."

They all turned their heads when two men carried a woman in like a corpse. The nurse left her table and stopped them.

"No more room inside. What's wrong with her?"

"Lockjaw," said one man, holding the victim's feet.

The nurse bent to look at the woman's face. Phượng and Jonathan rose halfway to have a better look. The woman's face looked frozen; her eyes shut. The nurse told them to wait and went into the infirmary. A middle-aged doctor came out. People craned their necks as he pried the woman's eyelids open. He told the men to lay her on the cement floor. She didn't lie flat. Her back was bent as if she were born with a hump. Someone in the room said once the spasms take over, you're as bent and stiff as a board. The doctor mixed some liquid in a cup. He tried to open the victim's mouth but could not. Finally, he gave her an injection, left her lying on the floor and went back into the sick bay.

The two men hunkered down on the floor. Phượng thought they must be brothers. They sat with their eyes downcast as though keeping vigil over the dead. In the moldy air the wretchedness of life nauseated Phượng. Did the woman have a husband or children?

Phượng saw one of two men looking at her. His eyes had the dull look of a water buffalo's. When she looked at him, he dropped his gaze.

"What happened to her?"

"Stepped on a nail in the paddy," the man said, scratching himself behind the ear. "Dead nail from ploughs. Went right into her sole."

She asked the man if the woman might live, and the man said he didn't know. Sometimes unexpected things happen. Phượng looked at the woman, wondering if she was already dead. Nausea swept her again. Phượng leaned her head on her father's shoulder and closed her eyes. After an hour or more, she heard sounds. She opened her eyes and saw the two men carrying the woman into the infirmary.

Phượng dozed as her father snored, then woke to see the same faces and new ones and smelled the same old damp smell of unwashed clothes and bodies. It was noon before her father's turn came.

The nurse led Bộ into the examination room. Phượng accompanied him. When the doctor examined her father, Phượng turned her head. She heard him moan now and again.

"There's nothing to worry about," the doctor said. "You just have hemorrhoids."

"You're wrong," Bộ said.

The doctor's face turned red. "It isn't fair to question my diagnosis when the infirmary has no X-ray technology for symptoms beyond what the naked eye can see. And in my judgment, you have hemorrhoids."

On the way home, between the ferry and the bus, Phượng thought of the woman with lockjaw and then thought of the matriarch. For them, death was just a breath away. She waited until Bộ woke up.

"Father, if you're sure the doctor is wrong, I'll have a private doctor look at you so we can make sure it isn't cancer."

Bộ listened, hiding his worry. What he feared about long-term medical expenses seemed to be coming true. Now he felt really sick—sick physically and with worry about his daughter's future.

When they got home, Phượng told her father to rest. "I'm going to see Mrs. Xinh and get back my investment, so we'll have the money for doctors."

Bộ raised his head from the bed. "Investment? What investment?"

"Just a small sum."

On the ride home she had calculated the medical expenses. She'd need every penny of her money. Though it was barely a week since she had given

Xinh the two hundred thousand *đồng*—most of her savings—money she could not get to for the next three months. She must get it back.

—o—

Jonathan had the bike from the temple, so he had time to take Phượng to Xinh's and back before catching the ferry to Upper Đinh-Xuân. In the afternoon sun they rode past the roadside shrine. Phượng asked Jonathan to stop, went in and lit joss sticks in the dark room. May your power sustain Father through his illness, she whispered a prayer to the road genie then bowed deeply to the porcelain statue of a bearded man wearing a three-cornered headdress.

When they rode on Jonathan asked her, "What's the shrine for?"

"For wayfarers on this road."

"I see them everywhere."

"My father can tell you more about the magical powers we believe in. That's why we have a shrine for the road, a shrine for the rice paddy, a shrine for the river. But the gods will help you only if you're desperate for the welfare of others, not for yourself."

She told Jonathan that when she was young, a French Hellcat bombed the shrine to rubble. She pointed out the ditch where she had hid. She told him of the mass burial that lasted several nights and the stench of the unburied dead. Mesmerized, he surveyed the countryside, imagining terror and death against which people were powerless. Maybe praying to their gods was the only way to stay sane. He thought of the terror Françoise had seen in the North during the war. He felt a tremor in his stomach for the two little girls who had matched each other in suffering.

They biked under the cool shade of giant trees. "What are those trees, Phượng?" he asked her.

"*Bàng*. We use their nuts to stuff cakes because almonds are expensive. In autumn their leaves are very red. What's the name of the Dutch artist who painted his self-portrait with an ear missing?"

"Van Gogh?"

"Yes, like the reds he used."

"And those trees with tiny white flowers like Japanese apricot flowers?"

"*Mù u*. Children use the seeds to shoot marbles."

Jonathan laughed. "Did you shoot marbles when you were a kid?"

"Yes, Long taught me. But that was years ago."

—o—

She fought back tears after they left Xinh's house. She held it in while Jonathan pedaled in silence until they came upon the shrine. Then her sobs startled him. He stopped and got off the bike.

"What happened, Phượng?"

She cupped her face in her hands and sobbed. He held her against his chest.

"I lost my investment," she said.

"What investment?"

She told him about Xinh and the cargo boat she put her money into. She told him it sank coming back from Hội An, so all was lost.

Jonathan shook his head. "You do business on a handshake?"

Phượng stared at him, her eyes still wet.

"Do you have a receipt showing how much you gave her?"

"Sure, I do. But what good is it after what she told me? She took a loss too."

"How do you know it's true? You're too trusting."

"This really hurts." Phượng told him her first investment had paid off after a couple months. "I counted on getting the money back for father's treatment."

"You have nothing left?"

"Enough to keep the business going and our daily expenses. But that's all." She bit her lower lip hard. "Can you take me home? It's getting dark and you need to get back too."

They rode on. She thought of the shrine and wondered if the road genie turned a deaf ear to her. At her house Phượng got off the bike and Jonathan turned and took her hand.

"Phượng."

She looked at him. He was tired, his blue eyes dark. He pushed the hair off his forehead.

"Can I ask you something?" he said.

"Ask me anything."

"Will you let me help you pay your father's medical expenses?"

Words of gratitude rose to her lips, but she did not speak.

"Will you?" he said.

She swallowed the knot in her throat. "You have a heart of gold, Jonathan."

"Does that mean yes?"

She shook her head and said, "Let me talk to Father. He's so proud. He may not feel comfortable taking anything from you."

"Tell him his health is important to me, just like your happiness. I can help. Let me."

They held hands for a moment before he left.

—o—

Her father took only a few slurps of vegetable soup, complaining that he had no appetite. He asked for a piece of brown sugar to get rid of the flat taste on his tongue. She gave it to him and was struck by the strength of his teeth as he cracked it. All of them still there, lacquered black and retouched over the years. When he asked for his tea, she poured him a cup and told him about the loss of her investment. He listened, rolling the chip of brown sugar in his mouth.

"How much?"

She told him.

He stopped chewing. "Was that all you had?"

"More or less."

"What kind of woman is she?"

"She knows business, knows lots of people. She has money."

"I wonder how you could've trusted her with all your money."

"I trusted her, because I did make some profit with her before."

"But your whole savings?" He clucked. "What did she buy with your money?"

"I can find out."

"You won't find out from her." Her father sipped his tea, scratching the side of the cup with his fingernail. "You'd better find out where and how her boat sank—and how much cargo was on it."

She recalled Jonathan's doubt. Could it be a sham? She felt the thickness in her throat again. She did not want to believe someone would do that to her.

"That won't get back my money, father."

"Can you think of a better way?"

She told him of Jonathan's offer to help and her father considered what she said.

"Phượng, tell me something."

She listened and waited.

"Do you like Jonathan?"

"Yes."

"Has he ever told you . . . he loves you?"

"No, father. But I know."

"In your heart you know?"

"I knew it the first time we met. Why do you ask?"

"Does he love you or Françoise through you?"

Phượng thought. "Father, if you love somebody very much, how much can you let go if you lose her?"

Her father said it took a long time to get over losing Ân-Phi.

"In time," Phượng said, "his pain will heal. But even if he loves Françoise through me, it's obvious that it's because my sister and I are so alike. What drew him to her draws him to me. And what drew her to him, draws me as well."

"Do you love him?"

"I do, father," she said softly.

"How do you feel about taking his money?"

"If it were for *me*, maybe. But it's for *you*, so it's your decision." She touched his hand. "You tell me, father."

He groped for another piece of brown sugar on the saucer next to the teapot. He raised it to his mouth.

"In my whole life," he said, "I have never begged or stooped to take a handout from anyone."

"Jonathan does not see it as a handout, father. I'm sure of that."

"Still, it will be a debt to be repaid. My debt—and yet you will be the one held accountable. What else did Xinh tell you? Is there no hope to recoup anything?"

She said nothing was left. "I told her why I needed the money and she said she was very sorry."

Bộ grunted.

"She said she'd see what she could do."

"I want you to get your money back. Don't borrow from her."

"She's had her eyes on my phoenix for some time. I don't want to part with it, father, but I will for you if it's the only way."

"You can't sell that, Phượng." His voice rose. "Think of your mother."

"I think of her every time I see it. But I know she would want me to use it to save you." Phượng paused. "I want to get a private doctor for you."

"I don't want you in debt because of me. Unfortunately, I have only a little money left, and I don't want to sell the house."

She squeezed his hand. "What are you saying, father? If you won't let me get the care you need, then you may die. Is that what you want? It's not what I want."

"It's in Heaven's hand."

"You're a hundred years old, but that doesn't mean you should give in to death so easily."

"I'm not conceding." Bộ listened to the chittering of birds roosting in the trees. "I want you to be free like those birds. I want to make sure no one will ever have a claim on your future. Are you going to reopen your noodle stall tomorrow?"

"Why are you so stubborn? If you love me, let me take care of you the way you did me."

"You need to take care not to lose your business."

twenty-five

Rain fell. I took Miss Phượng by the hand and ran past the pond for a filao tree. I hugged her and felt dampness on her blouse. A raindrop hung on my eyebrow and fell into my eyes.

I closed one eye. "Auntie, this weather is so unpredictable. Second time now we got caught in the rain."

"I'm rarely out here by myself. You've changed my routine."

"I want to ask you something."

"Yes?"

"What made you fall in love with Jonathan?"

Moments later she said, "When you meet someone and then find yourself thinking about him day and night, you say, This is love. But what is it? Is it the voice? The eyes? Or is it the smile? Or something like a sense of belonging? Or maybe it's like a flower in full bloom." She caught a raindrop in my hair. "If you analyze each part to find its beauty, you find none."

"Did you ask him why he fell in love with you?"

"No," she said. "Because we were together, because there was no coming or going."

She told me a tale about the serpent and the sutra at a pagoda, because it was where Jonathan Edward stayed during his visit.

—o—

Jonathan left the eunuch cemetery in the back of the temple and walked toward the front courtyard. He wondered if, when Phượng's father died, he would be buried in the eunuch cemetery where many of his former colleagues rested. When we leave this world, we shall share this burial ground. Here we rest in peace, in harmony, in unison. So said the weathered inscription on the stele. Maybe he should talk to Bộ directly about offering his help.

He noticed a large crowd in the main hall. Probably the service for the dead, because he heard chanting and the cadence of wooden percussion. He saw Minh Tánh at the lotus pond talking with two novices with tufts of hair on their shaved heads. Even when he wasn't alone the monk looked alone, reminding Jonathan of a heron, a solitary bird that tolerates no man's presence. When Jonathan came toward him, Minh Tánh rose. His brown robe fluttered. Black hair stubbled the top of his head. He was thin, in his twenties, with a pale, pimply face. Because his eyes were crossed, Jonathan found looking at him difficult.

"How are you?" Jonathan said.

"Where have you been these last days, Mr. Jonathan? Sightseeing?"

Jonathan nodded. "Is there some kind of service going on?"

"It is for the Gia-Linh matriarch who died with cancer at the age of ninety-one."

"I want to wire home for money," Jonathan said. "Where can I do it?"

"The post office."

"In Huế?"

"Yeah. Then you go back to the post office the next day and get your money. How long you stay?"

"I don't know."

"You found her family—her sister."

"I did," Jonathan said, wary of the monk's caustic tone.

"You like her?"

He looked into Minh Tánh's eyes. In the front courtyard children in threes and fours were jumping rope, playing hopscotch and badminton without a net.

"Yes, I like her very much," he said finally, wondering if he had done something to offend the monk, but he concluded that it was simply the monk's nature to be severe.

They crossed the courtyard. Minh Tánh's clogs clunked on the flagstones. In the nineteenth century, palanquin bearers rested there while mandarins or palace eunuchs visited the temple. In the center a white marble statue of Guanyin Bodhisattva rose ten feet tall, commanding the view of the hill. Minh Tánh was looking at the children. Jonathan studied him and a curious thought came to his mind.

"How long have you been at the temple?" He spoke without looking at Minh Tánh.

"I grow up in the temple."

"By choice?"

"Yeah."

Jonathan sensed something mordant in his curtness. "Where are your parents?"

"Died."

"I'm sorry." He glanced quickly at the monk. "What happens if you never become a *bhikshu?* Will you remain a novice for life if you're not an ordained monk?"

"No," Minh Tánh smirked. "I am tired of being overtaken by my fellow monks. They became *Ôn* and then *Chú* after *bhikshu* ordination. I am getting nowhere."

"Will you quit?"

"Maybe. Do you like it here, Mr. Jonathan?"

"Yes, I like being here."

"Because of the girl?"

"Is that a question or a comment?"

"Maybe a question." Minh Tánh shrugged. "Maybe not. Does she like you?"

Jonathan took offense. If he could read what was behind those crossed eyes!

Minh Tánh grinned at Jonathan's perturbed look and then someone called for him. Outside the antechamber, leaning against the round latticed window of the bell tower, a man stood watching them. Minh Tánh walked over, and they talked.

Both men turned to look at Jonathan. Something in his stomach twitched sharply. He went to a corner of the stonewall where two boys were playing Chinese chess. Then he noticed a shadow on the ground next to his. He said nothing to Minh Tánh, since he expected the monk would come back with a riddle or sarcasm, anything but the truth. But the man by the bell tower stayed in the back of his mind.

Minh Tánh tapped him on the back. "Are you going to Gia-Linh East tomorrow?"

"Maybe. I'm going into Huế now, to the post office."

"You seem to know the area very well now. I didn't know you went to the war zone."

Jonathan scowled. "How did you know?"

"That's not important."

Jonathan thought of the man. Something wasn't right. "Who's that man?" he asked.

"He is the matriarch's nephew, Phát. He came for the memorial service. He said you speak Vietnamese very well. I said you also speak French very well. I envy you, Mr. Jonathan."

Minh Tánh looked at him. Jonathan's eyes bore into the monk's crossed eyes but found nothing there.

—o—

That night Jonathan couldn't sleep. The feeling that something was wrong hadn't left him. Was Minh Tánh up to something? Who was that man named Phát? A civilian? A government official? He would ask Minh Tánh.

Past midnight he climbed out of the cot in the communal room and stood looking at the kerosene lamp burning low by the door. His shadow trembled on the wall while the monks droned in their sleep.

Outside the air was cool and dew wet the veranda's concrete floor. He walked past the sleeping quarters for the novices and *bhikshus* toward the chamber where the patriarch was worshipped. There was light in the chamber.

He stood in the doorway, looking at the abbot, stooped, sewing over an oak stand.

"Hello, sir," he said, bowing slightly.

"Mr. Jonathan!" The abbot smiled and bowed in return.

"Jonathan, sir," he said. "I thought I was the only one who couldn't sleep."

"Please, come in."

He dropped his gaze to the abbot's fingers holding a needle. "What're you doing, sir?"

"Mending some defects on our Diamond Sutra."

Jonathan came near and looked at the roll of silk. Chinese characters were embroidered in five-colored thread. Some of the threads had come loose. The abbot stopped and changed the red thread for yellow. He licked it and slipped it through the needle's eye. Jonathan admired the patience in such a big man whose thick hands and fingers reminded him of those of a peasant's.

"Can you read Chinese?" the abbot asked. He said the complete set of the Diamond Sutra, the temple's revered relic, was over seven thousand hand-sewn words in Chinese characters. The work was two hundred years old, older than the temple. The late-eighteenth-century emperor Quang Trung of the Tây Sơn dynasty created the preface of 248 words, followed by the preface by his son, Emperor Quang Toản, which took up 905 words. The sutra ended with an afterword of 329 words.

The abbot gently touched a frayed Chinese character needing repair, saying the handwork was done by a nun who went around collecting rolls of silk and spools of thread. She had taken several years to complete it.

"Such dedication," Jonathan said, bending down to inspect the sutra.

The abbot told Jonathan that after the Buddhist Nguyễn had wiped out the Tây Sơn, they moved the sutra from Hanoi to Huế and kept it in a shrine in the Purple Forbidden City. When the last Nguyễn emperor gave up to the Việt Minh in 1945, many valuables were looted from the palace, the Dia-mond Sutra among them.

The abbot took scissors from his trousers pocket and snipped the thread. He told Jonathan he had never given up searching for the sutra. He found it after several years in the hands of a constable. The temple paid a large sum to buy it back.

"How much is it worth?"

"Ten *taels* of gold, or seventeen ounces." The abbot slowly rolled the sutra up and, with a pilgrim's reverence, bowed and laid it in the aloeswood box. Closing the lid, he said that if Jonathan wanted to read the Diamond Sutra, the temple library had it.

"My Vietnamese isn't good enough to read it."

"No problem. You can read it in English. We also have books in French, German, Chinese, and Japanese."

The abbot put the scissors back in his trousers. "What is your plan? Your mission is complete, yes?"

"Unfortunately, not. Mr. Bộ is very ill, possibly with colon cancer. I want to help him any way I can."

The abbot scratched his stubbled chin. "You asked to stay here temporarily until your search was over. True?"

Jonathan tensed. "Yes, sir."

"And you told me you took a sabbatical leave from your job. True?"

"That's true, sir."

"But you didn't tell me who you're working for, what organization."

"I work for the United States government." Jonathan frowned. "Why do you ask?"

The abbot jingled the keys in his pocket. The local Việt Cọng had been to call. The young American. Get a background check on him, they said. The abbot knew what they were looking for.

"May I ask you a personal question?" the abbot said.

Jonathan studied the abbot, then said yes.

"Are you staying because of Mr. Bộ's daughter?"

Had Minh Tánh told the abbot that? Jonathan didn't feel he had to defend his decision, so he chose his words carefully. "There isn't enough money to pay for his treatment. That's why I want to help, sir."

"Another question, do you mind?"

"I'll try not to, sir."

"Who is your father?"

"He's a colonel in the Army of the United States."

"Here in South Vietnam?"

"No."

"And what is your job?"

Jonathan pursed his lips. The abbot gaze held him. "Eventually I'll work with a U.S. pacification program in South Vietnam."

The abbot considered what Jonathan said. "Pacification program? Like what the French did during the Indochina War?"

"Except the French failed, didn't they? We hope to do better."

He believed that, given time and resources, the program could eventually restore the people's faith and trust in the South Vietnamese regime. The key was patience. He exhaled slowly. "Why, sir? You seem worried."

"This is wartime. Every household has to show the authorities a family register when they do house searches. The temple is no exception. We must know enough about our guests to account for their coming and going." The abbot stepped toward the door, the keys jingling in his pockets. "One more thing. Don't be out late, if you must go somewhere. It is not safe."

"Yes, sir. I'll remember that."

"A foreign correspondent was killed a few months ago in Gia-Linh."

"What happened?"

"The Việt Cọng buried him alive in the sugarcane field. They believed he was CIA."

Jonathan tried to smile. "Thank you, sir."

As the abbot locked the door of the chamber, Jonathan said good-night. Behind him the abbot's sandals dragged on the cement floor, then his own door clicked shut. Out in the courtyard moonlight washed the ground a lemon-custard yellow and in the blackness of the sky the North Star glittered, distant and steady. The air smelled of jasmine. He took a few steps toward the stone gate to clear his head.

Beyond the gate the hill fell away into darkness and the rock steps' sweeping incline glimmered. Atop the stone gate two dragons reared their heads to guard the dharma wheel in the middle. He thought of time. How many sunsets and sunrises had changed hues on those stones? What did this part of the world look like in ancient times?

Her name came to him. Her name and the sound of her voice and the flame-red of her blouse. Then they were gone.

twenty-six

It had rained for two days and the sewer in Miss Phượng's neighborhood backed up into her outhouse. With the rain she came down with a cold. Coughs seized her in the middle of conversation. The afternoon the helping girl and I were at her house, she coughed badly, covering her mouth with a handkerchief. Her sputum was streaked with red.

"Minh," Miss Phượng said without looking up, "do I have consumption?"

"I hope not, Auntie." I grimaced at the sight of the blood. "You've coughed so much you must've torn something in your throat. Do you have a fever?"

She smiled weakly and shook her head. "I brewed some herbal drink that my father used to make whenever we had cough and cold."

The helping girl went through the kitchen cabinet, rattling things up, and opened a small glass jar and sniffed. "This will cure your cough, Auntie."

"What?"

"Daddy, when he had a cold or hacking cough from smoking, he'd brew a pot of black tea and then mix it with honey and a fresh tangerine peel."

"How did it help him?"

"You'll see, Auntie." The girl winced at the odor coming from the back of the house.

I held my breath and then exhaled slowly. "Auntie, you can't use the outhouse for the time being. It's clogged."

She nodded with an unconcerned smile. "Last year I had to hire a man to clean it up after the rain. A small problem, though."

"I'll be back," I said, heading to the door to the backcourt.

"Where're you going?"

"Unclog the latrine, Auntie."

Outside, I took off my shirt and walked to the outhouse in the rain. I went into the latrine and surveyed the drain. A stench emanated from the overflowing toilet. My head felt numb.

I squatted on my haunches and thrust my hand into the pit, pulling up gobs of excrement glued to mushy leaves. I went back out and turned on the faucet, filled a chamber pot with water and poured one potful after another into the pit. Then I scrubbed my slimy forearm with wet sand in the court-yard and smeared it with Indian almond leaves. My forearm turned red, then green from the vicious sanding and scraping. I smelled my arm then washed it with a bar of soap under the running water of the faucet. Then I came back inside. My hair dripped rainwater on the floor. The house was warm from the steam and smelled of steeping tea.

While the girl cooked, Miss Phượng sipped her honey tea. A peel of tangerine, its orange color now amber, floated in her cup. I looked at the phoenix-shaped pendant the color of port wine framed by the V collar of her blouse, hearing her words again in my head when she told me how desper-ately she was in need of money that she wanted to sell this very heritage. It pained me.

—o—

The next morning Xinh showed up at Phượng's noodle stall. The place was full and several customers waited outside.

"Look at what you did to them when you closed for nearly a week!" Xinh leaned in and whispered into Phượng's ear, "I have a business proposition. Can you meet me at my house after you close today?"

"Why can't we discuss it here?"

"Listen, I'm concerned about you. I'm down too, losing my boat and all, but we can make it up."

Phượng eyed the woman suspiciously. "How? A windfall?"

"Well, it's not a godsend, but it's there. I'll be waiting."

The morning passed slowly. Phượng didn't smile at her customers until Thanh, who sold sweet soybean curd outside her stall, came in to eat lunch with her.

"Why the sad face?" Thanh said.

Phượng forced a smile.

"I never knew you were a moody girl," Thanh said. "What's wrong?"

Phượng told her about her father's sickness and how she lost money in Xinh's business.

"Her boat did sink," Thanh said. "I know the guy who manned it for her. What's she in here for this morning?"

"Money talk. She knows I'm desperate."

"And what did she want?"

Phượng shrugged. "How're your sales?" Even though she was curious about Xinh's business proposition and could have used some advice, she felt it best to wait and see what was in store rather than guess.

Dusk was falling when she arrived at Xinh's house tucked behind a hibiscus hedge in Gia-Linh West. She walked along the hedge where dodders yellow as cocoons twined around pink and white blossoms. She met Xinh in the backyard, busy inspecting her packed anchovy vats.

"Well, I'm here," Phượng said.

Xinh took her by the elbow and led her into the kitchen. She lowered her voice. "You need money real quick? How about spending a night with the province chief?"

The chief had been to Phượng's noodle stall, a thickset man with a goatee who ate with two bodyguards.

Phượng stepped back from Xinh.

"C'mon," Xinh said. "Want to know how much you'll get?"

"I don't." Phượng winced, sickened.

"One hundred thousand đồng. I'll take thirty percent for my commission." Xinh watched the girl's deep-set eyes. "How's your father doing? I thought of him last night and you know why, Phượng? The Gia-Linh matriarch died yesterday. You know that?"

"From cancer?"

"Shame, isn't it?" She touched Phượng's hand. "Hard-headed woman. Pitiful."

"What?"

"You cure cancer early. Hers was late. No doctors could touch her."

Phượng sat down on the backstep of the kitchen. No, she wouldn't let that happen to her father. What choice did she have if her father refused to accept Jonathan's money?

"You want to think about it, Phượng?"

She stood up and looked Xinh in the eye. "I'll let you know."

The next day she'd take her father to the private hospital in Huế for an examination. She had money for that. But what if he needed treatment? She calculated. Seventy thousand after the commission. Bad money. Rotten money. Her father could never know. And Jonathan? No, she'd never do that. She would not be sold like her mother.

—o—

At dawn she boarded a downriver ferry with her father to Bằng Lăng, and then waited there for two hours for a bus. When the sun was over the treetops, a Huế-bound DeSoto bus came loaded with riders and bicycles and baskets and crates strapped on the roof and the rear. A boy rode standing on the running board, another on the rear doorstep. She helped her father up on the bus and people squeezed together to give him a space to sit down. She had no place to sit and finally a dark-skinned, mustachioed man let her sit on his thighs.

The bus arrived at Đông Ba Market. They got off and she hired two pedi-cabs and rode across the bridge to the hospital on the right bank of the Per-fume River. They passed a hotel, a high school behind a dark red portal gate, then the French antique shop with its iron shutters still down. Phượng saw a figure clad in a monk's brown robe standing bareheaded with his bicycle at the front door. He looked like Minh Tánh. When the pedicabs turned the corner, he was still there, his hand rubbing his shaved head.

She waited in a small lounge while her father was examined. The gleam of the tile floor spoke to her of something clean and efficient she could trust. Black-and-white square tiles echoed footfalls in the quiet, though the lounge was full of people waiting. The room didn't smell. Fluorescent ceiling lights made the white walls stark, and the ceiling fan spun unhurriedly, printing a gossamer shadow on the floor. What will it cost? Having never been to a private hospital, she could only imagine. What if he has cancer? She didn't want to think further but couldn't stop her streaming worries. Yes, what if he has cancer? How long will the treatment take? Where would she get the money? She swallowed the lump in her throat. The air felt suddenly stuffy. Father could die. Yes. A long time ago he warned her of his death and said the abbot would raise her and their house would be sold. But Heaven had watched over him. He had never been seriously ill, and she no longer needed anyone to raise her. But she needed him and could not picture her life without him. The morning after he died, would she oversleep? The box full of brown-sugar slabs she had saved for him, their darkly sweet smell would wither her heart remembering.

Would father make it? The Gia-Linh matriarch did not, wealthy as she was. Money couldn't buy miracles. Could a good heart truly ward off evil?

As she leaned her head against the wall, closing her eyes, a dark thought came like the fixed stare of a black owl perched on a limb devouring her in the bathhouse with its stare. She hissed at it. The owl didn't budge, only flickered its yellow eyes. She gave up fighting it.

Phượng opened her eyes. The doctor and a nurse were walking her father out after a long examination. She rose just as the nurse helped Bộ sit down.

"Your father has colon cancer," the doctor said. "All the tests came out positive. He has large lesions in several places in his colon. I strongly recommend radiotherapy as soon as possible. We need to see him once a week until we see improvement."

"Will he live if you treat him?"

"The sooner the treatment starts, the better the chance."

"Is there anything I can do at home to help, doctor?"

"Not a whole lot. But a healthy diet might help, like eating brown rice and tofu and less meat."

"How much does the treatment cost?"

"Our office can tell you."

She thanked him and told her father she'd be back. She paid for the visit and examination and got the estimate for the radiotherapy. Six months of treatment, 110,000 *đồng*. When she came back to her father, she felt lightheaded. She took his hand and walked him out of the hospital into the sunlight. They waited on the curb for the pedicab. She grew dizzy in the bright sun.

Bộ listened with his head half-cocked and the breeze fluttered strands of his white hair. "Can you walk me to the riverbank?"

"Aren't you tired, father?"

"Walk with me." He coughed. "Please."

"I'm bringing you back to the hospital tomorrow. You need radiotherapy. That's what the doctor said."

"I'm not going."

"Tell me, father, why not?"

"Tell me the cost."

She told him the cost and that the treatment would run for several months.

He reached for her hand and held it without speaking. Her skin felt smooth in his dry palm. Over the years he had watched her break her back to earn a living and build a business they were proud of. Long days, short nights. Dawn to dusk. Year in, year out, saving every penny. Then overnight it was all gone. He hid his distress at her misfortune, but anxiety tortured him more painfully than his stomach. Like an ant, she would have to start over to build capital up. Dawn to dusk. Year in, year out. And if that wasn't backbreaking enough, add the burden of debts and see how quickly she would age.

"I just want you to live a happy life without debts," he said.

"Father, how could I be happy—"

"That is not what I mean, Phượng. How much money do you have?"

"I have enough to cover the first radiotherapy and a few more."

"It sounds like they think it'll take many months. Don't borrow money for that. Don't ever let that Xinh woman own a piece of your life. And Jonathan is a good man, but you shouldn't accept his money. It's humiliation. I'm not looking for a handout."

Phượng felt weak. "I told you, it's not a handout."

"Handout or loan. Either way, I don't think it's a good idea." Bộ patted her hand. "Don't turn yourself into an old woman because of me."

She clenched her teeth to suppress a sigh.

"And do not even consider selling your phoenix. I forbid you."

"I shall never sell it."

Bộ shook his head. "I wish I could see it in your eyes."

Phượng closed her eyes in turn and tears seeped. The rush hour before school was over and the streets returned to quiet with an occasional passing car.

"Let's go to the riverbank for some fresh air," Bộ said.

"Of course, father."

Bộ stopped now and then to smell the air. He asked her if there were camphor trees nearby on the boulevard.

"What do they look like, father?"

"They have black berries and yellow flowers, and the bark is rough and thick."

"Yes, father, we just passed some, but how do you know?"

"I can smell them, they're old trees."

They crossed the street, then stopped when a bicyclist pedaled up, braked and greeted them. She bowed slightly to Minh Tánh. She wasn't mistaken when she saw him earlier.

"Didn't expect to see you in town, Miss," he said. "And how are you, sir?"

She told her father who the monk was. Bộ nodded. "I saw you at the shop over there," Phượng said, pointing up the boulevard.

"The antique shop? Oh yeah." Minh Tánh glanced behind him. "Where are you heading?"

She told him they had just come from the hospital. He asked why and squinted at her father when she told him about his cancer. She said her father wanted to go to the riverbank.

"May I join you?" Minh Tánh got off his bicycle and pushed it as they crossed the street.

She glanced at him, at his sweaty face and underarms. "Did you bike from the temple?"

"I rode the bus, but I don't like walking in the city."

She looked into his crossed eyes. "Do you have some business in Huế?"

Minh Tánh wet his lips. "I ran an errand."

At the riverbank the breeze came up and left the smell of seawater. Phượng commented on the driftwood floating downriver, and Minh Tánh said there must be a lot of downed trees in the mountains. Not from rains, he said, but from bombing and shelling. He said sometimes he found aloeswood bark and twigs among the driftwood and sold them at a good price. He looked away from the sun toward the mountains to the west. He was cordial and pleasant, like the last time she had talked with him outside her house. But Phượng sensed a nervousness in his gestures, in his voice.

Bộ pointed toward the bridge. "Is the Clémenceau Bridge that way?"

"Yes, father." She knew he meant the Tràng Tiền Bridge, renamed when the French left.

Bộ raised his left hand and groped before him. "And the Citadel?"

The Citadel's brown walls stood quietly beyond the sloping tile roofs of the commercial district. Bộ raised his face skyward, his complexion white in the glare.

"I want to visit it."

"Where, father?"

"Where I used to live, where your mother used to live."

"In the Purple Forbidden City?"

"She lived in the Trinh Minh Palace, home of the first- and second-ranking concubines."

"Where did you live, father?"

"I lived outside the Purple Forbidden City and the Imperial City." He gestured toward some unknown place. "The Palace Eunuch Hall is at the northwest end of the Citadel."

Minh Tánh looked at her and rubbed the back of his neck. "Your mother was a concubine, Miss?"

"Yes."

"And . . . Mr. Bộ?"

"He served my mother before she died. When she died, he raised me."

"How many years were you with the royal families, sir?"

"Sixty-three years."

Minh Tánh kept touching the top of his shaved head. "You lived there for sixty-three years, sir? I could never live anywhere that long."

"You could," Bộ said. "And you will if you want to be a monk. Do you?"

"I don't know, sir. I don't think that far ahead. Why have you never been back, sir?"

"I've been busy living my own life and raising her." Bộ took Phượng's hand in his. "She's the reason I've never been anywhere else."

"She's the reason?" Minh Tánh said, admiring the eunuch's devotion and wondering how a concubine's daughter could end up selling beef noodle soup in a marketplace. The quaint quarters of Huế housed the gated estates of former court mandarins and concubines. Had the concubine married a Westerner?

"Was your mother wealthy in those days?"

"I don't know. Was she, father?"

Bộ wiped his face with a kerchief and slowly folded it in quarters. "If she could spare us one month of her salary, we wouldn't have to worry about these petty things."

"What petty things, sir? "

"My sickness."

"Did her mother draw a salary?" Minh Tánh asked.

"Five hundred *quan*," Bộ said. "Plus, twenty-five hundred pounds of rice a year."

"That's a lot of rice." Phượng laughed lightly. "All the families in our alley could live on it for at least six months. What's a *quan*?"

"That was our currency until the French changed it." Bộ put the kerchief in his undershirt pocket. "It weighed over a kilogram."

"What happened to my mother's fortune?"

Bộ hung his head. For the moment he felt less guarded in the monk's presence. He wanted to talk to drive the gloom of sickness away. "Your grandparents were her beneficiaries," he spoke to Phượng. "In other words, what she accumulated in her lifetime went to your grandfather." Bộ grinned cynically. "He was already a very wealthy man. He used to have a granary on his estate."

"Why didn't she leave her wealth to you?" Minh Tánh said. "Why didn't your grandparents pass it on to you?"

Phượng turned to Bộ.

Minh Tánh quickly said, "I'm being nosy."

Bộ wouldn't forbid his daughter to tell the family's secret. The burden of hiding it had been nothing short of the bane of his life.

On the sunlit bank Minh Tánh listened to the story of a mad concubine, an avaricious man who had disavowed his own daughter after selling her to hold onto power, the same man who had amassed great wealth in his lifetime and left not a *xu* for his granddaughters.

Minh Tánh looked at the girl whom he secretly desired, then at the man a century old. He blurted, "What a comedy!"

Bộ thought the monk's remark was not far from truth. Born with a cautious nature, he wasn't quite convinced of what his daughter had told him about her grandfather. Đông Các a born-again Christian? Maybe he should ask her to write her grandfather for a handout. The thought made him chuckle. Well, perhaps men could change. He leaned toward her. "Phượng."

"Yes, father."

"Would you be kind enough to take me to my old place?"

"Father, it's been a long day for you. You need rest."

"I've been resting. I'm rotting from too much rest."

She knew she couldn't deny him.

The bell sounded on Minh Tánh's bicycle. He flicked his thumb back and forth on the lever as if he were testing it. "I know the way. I've been there a couple times. You want to ride with me, Miss?"

Phượng shook her head. "Thank you, but I think my father would rather have some privacy. It's his old world, you know."

She could see the monk didn't want to leave.

"I'll get you the pedicabs, Miss. What's the place called again?"

"Palace Eunuch Hall," Bộ said. "An Hòa gate at the northwest end of the Citadel."

Minh Tánh waved down two pedicabs. He told the *xích lô* drivers where to go and motioned for Bộ to get onto one *xích lô*, and then Phượng. Then he stood back holding his bicycle, watching the pedicabs ride away.

twenty-seven

Miss Phượng helped the girl cook gobies simmered with fragrant knot-weed, pumpkin soup with prawns, and fresh garden vegetables—thin slices of tomato around the platter's edge above yellow star-shaped carambola and half-moon strips of purple figs in the center. Rain had tapered off and gone from the air now was the bad odor from the outhouse. We sat barefoot on the mahogany divan under a dome-shaped lamp. In the soft yellow light, I watched both of them, then crossed my legs, struggling to rest a foot on the opposite thigh.

The gobies were hot. My eyes watered from the black peppercorns cooked with the fish. They ate slowly, as if waiting for me. She corrected the way I held the chopsticks. "Like this," she said, making me grip them higher.

"Thanks, Auntie."

"You held the chopsticks just like Jonathan did."

I noticed that she hadn't coughed as much since she took the honey tea. Chuckling, I said that folk medicine sometimes worked wonders.

"Of course, *chú*," the helping girl said. "We're not backward like you might've thought."

"Well," I shrugged, "you misunderstood me."

"They're not unorthodox," Miss Phượng said. "They're just not system-ized enough to become standard practices. When our village was bombed by French Hellcats, our public well water was soiled because the public well was near the ground where the corpses were covered with plastic sheets awaiting burial. My father paid a woman in our neighborhood to carry well water to our cistern. The next day I had diarrhea. He wasn't affected, but he suspected the well water was contaminated. He ran out of Ganidan tab-lets and when the woman refilled his tub, she told him not to worry about medicine. She went out to the backyard and got a handful of clay. 'Go bake this real good,' she said, 'then break it into chunks and mix them in boiled water. Make her drink it.' My father exclaimed, 'In the name of Heaven!' She shrugged, 'Hardly, sir.' But I drank the clay water and got well the next day. My father considered that the woman might know something the doctors did not."

That led her to tell us what her father had gone through with the identical twin girls when they were sick. He told her that they both looked so much alike he had to do everything for them at the same time to avoid mixing them up. Once one had diarrhea and he had to go to a drugstore for Ganidan. He left a neighbor in charge of the house. When he came back, the neighbor had left without telling him she had changed one girl's clothes to match the other. Her father didn't know which girl needed the medicine.

Then she said that evening when Jonathan stayed for the night, her father told him during dinner about the twin girls she'd just told us. She said there seemed to be a tie that bound the two men together because of their losses. Jonathan asked her father, "Sir, have you ever slept a deep sleep so deep that when you wake you don't know where you are?"

Her father chewed a fig and said nothing. Finally, he said, "For me, I've lived in unreality every day since their mother died, and I've lived it every day since I lost that baby." He searched for Jonathan's hand, found it and patted it. "You and I can add our sorrows together but that won't bring back what we've lost, will it, Jonathan?"

"I hope time will bring you real happiness, sir. I can say I've found happiness with your family."

Her father scratched the side of his face with a curving fingernail. "Each day I open a door and walk through a corridor of that day and feel thankful if I make it to the end. Every day since Phượng was a teenager. I've opened thousands of doors, and I've always come back to the first one. Because I was afraid, Jonathan, afraid that I'd die before she grew up. Now she's an adult and there are a few doors left unopened for me. I know one has no corridor." Then he smiled peacefully. "But I have no fear of death—it's inevitable—only the fear of leaving her uncared for."

Now Miss Phượng stopped eating. She sat, head down, gazing at her lap. I felt a well of gratitude that I found her. To be a part of her life. To be near her. To be of any help.

She put several slices of fig in my bowl and asked me to eat. Then she put the bowl and chopsticks down and said, "That evening when Jonathan stayed with us, it was for the first time and also last."

Her face tranquil, perhaps she might never forget what she'd be better off never to remember.

—o—

Jonathan rode the bicycle to Gia-Linh East in the late afternoon and stood quietly outside the door of her house. After a while he went to the back and peered into the kitchen. She wasn't home and her father must be resting, so he decided to wait on the doorsteps.

He waited until sunset. From inside the house came the sound of her father's shuffling footsteps. Jonathan knocked on the door. He heard the latch lift and Bộ appeared in his white pajamas. His wrinkled face was lined with the imprint of the rush mat.

"Hello, sir."

"Jonathan." Bộ peered blankly into space. "What brings you so late?"

"I've been waiting for Phượng out here, sir. I didn't want to disturb you. But I need to talk to you, if you'd spare me some of your time."

The house was dark when Bộ let him in. Jonathan offered to turn on the electric light but Bộ said, "I don't need it, Jonathan."

"But Phượng will be worried when she gets back." She had told him when she came home and saw the house dark, her heart thumped.

"You can turn on the light," Bộ said.

The grooves in Bộ's face were deep, like the creases in an elephant's hide. Stuck in the corner of his mouth was a piece of brown sugar. It must have been there since his last meal. Jonathan told him and Bộ nodded.

"Would you like some tea, Jonathan?"

"No, sir. I should make tea for you."

Bộ waved it off with his hand, sat down on the edge of the divan with his back straight and his hands on his thighs.

"Sir, I'm here to ask you directly: Will you let me help pay for the cancer treatment?"

"Have you ever seen anybody cured of cancer, Jonathan?"

"I don't know, sir. I'm too young to know much."

"They can treat you so you don't die right away, but you will still die, only slowly."

"But there's a chance that you'd live."

"That's an illusion."

"Maybe that's your way of thinking."

"And what is your way, Jonathan?"

"Sir," Jonathan said, sitting down on the edge of the divan, "I want her to be happy, and the way is for you to get well again."

"Very well, Jonathan."

"Will you let her accept the money? Will you accept it, sir?"

"You're very kind, Jonathan. Your offer will be on my mind."

"Phượng won't sit back and watch you suffer. I'm sure you know that."

Bộ peered into the pale opacity beyond his eyes. No one would sit back and watch a loved one suffer. When Ân-Phi went mad, he had no recourse but to turn to Đinh. He thought of what he told his daughter about his pride—never stoop for a handout. Was he more concerned about his dignity than her happiness?

Watching Bộ in silence, Jonathan began to worry. He recalled the eunuch's stubbornness at their first meeting. Outside the sky grew steadily darker. He knew he must take leave or chance riding home on unsafe roads at night.

"I'll be back in the morning, sir."

"Jonathan." Bộ turned toward him. "You have my deepest gratitude for your good heart. I'll tell Phượng when she gets home that you're our benefactor."

Jonathan smiled even though he knew Bộ couldn't see it. "I'll go to Huế first thing in the morning to get the money. I'm happy about your decision. You'll make Phượng very happy too, sir." He rose from the divan. "What keeps her so late?"

"Sometimes even later." Bộ exhaled loudly. "It depends on the day of the week. Like today, a lot of folks go to the market, and they just won't go home without eating a bowl of her *bún bò Huế*. She can't close up until they all leave."

"I'll be back tomorrow with the money. Please tell her I stopped by."

"I will, Jonathan, and be careful on the road."

On the altar behind Bộ, Jonathan saw Phượng's mother gazing from the photograph. Her eyes could be Phượng's eyes looking at him. Were they her eyes, he wished he could kiss them and say *I love you* like the moment he first kissed Françoise in a park under a sugar maple tree in the rain.

When he left it was warm and dark and the sun's last glow glimmered red among trees. He pedaled along the road, listening to the sound the chain made on the sprockets. He wondered if Phượng's prayer to the road genie would save her from mortification of watching her father succumb to an incurable disease.

He stopped at the shrine, dismounted and went inside. Dark, an incense smell imbued the air. Next to the ceramic incense holder was a matchbox and a packet of red incense sticks. He struck a match and lit three and blew the match out. In the dusky light he saw on the altar a porcelain man whose bulging eyes and black beard conveyed a ferocious mien. Jonathan dropped his gaze. He wanted to pray for love, his for her and hers for him, but the words didn't come.

Instead, he thought of her father and looked up into the genie's dark eyes. "Dear sir, I have one wish and it has nothing to do with me. It only involves me because I want to help a man named Bộ who is very sick. I offered him money to help but I doubt the outcome. If he dies, the girl he raised will be very sad, for she has no other family worth the name. I'm not asking you to save the man for the girl's sake. I'm not asking you to save him because he deserves another chance. But he's a good person. That's his only chance."

Bowing, he inhaled the scent of the joss sticks. Peace permeated his soul. He got on his bike and pedaled down the road, passing under the Indian almond and poon trees. He noticed he hadn't turned on the light, so he bent forward and turned the switch. The light dimmed and brightened with the bicycle's speed. He rang the handlebar-mounted bell.

Ahead, the cane field loomed like a dark hillock in the night. The road edged the field, and he could just make out the lavender flowers so pale they seemed more a wash of blue. A figure stepped out of the darkness in front of his bicycle. He squeezed the handbrake and the bicycle skidded with a squeal of rubber. A flashlight blinded him. He shaded his eyes and saw a man wearing brown clothes—then a .45 pistol.

"Get off!" the man said in Vietnamese.

Jonathan dismounted. The flashlight raked him up and down as he stood holding the bicycle. Footsteps behind him. He turned his head and saw another man, taller than the first, standing a few feet from him. Slung from his shoulder was an automatic rifle pointed at Jonathan. The man jerked his chin and slapped the banana-shaped clip.

"Is that him?"

The shorter man jammed his pistol into the holster on his hip and shone the flashlight at Jonathan's hind pocket. He took Jonathan's billfold and studied his ID.

"You speak Vietnamese?" he asked, throwing the light on Jonathan's face. "I know you do." He put the billfold in his shirt pocket. "Follow us. Don't talk."

They walked in single file, save the sound of sandals on the blacktop. After a while he heard a car coming up behind them. Someone pushed him from behind and sent him tumbling into the cane field. A car sped by, the road lit by its headlights. They pulled him back up on the road. A hare sat on the roadside watching them, its eyes glowing red. Suddenly it leaped into the cane field.

What if he decided to bolt into the darkness? Past the cane field they veered off the road onto a paddy yellow with stubble. The crop had just been harvested, judging by the fresh smell lingering from the cuts. Jonathan pushed his bicycle onto the earthen dike, watching the shorter man's back until a yellow light washed suddenly over the field. The full moon hung in the sky. At the edge of the paddy stood a heron so still it looked like a sculpture until it shot its neck out at the *glunk* of a frog. They walked into the woods. The silence was unbearable.

"Where are we going?" he asked.

They didn't answer, so he repeated the question.

"Quiet!" snapped the man behind him.

When they came out of the woods, they were at a foothill in a stand of tall areca palms. Ahead, a mirror of water shone. He heard a flurry from the lagoon and saw the cranes, gray and white like paper cutouts. They cried harshly as they fretted on their reedlike legs at the sight of men. There were lights on the hill. Jonathan figured they were taking him there.

They walked around a house on the slope to the kitchen at the rear. Bamboo trunks framed the entrance. The men told him to leave the bicycle against the mud wall and sit down against a wooden pole support on the packed earthen floor. They sat on either side. The shorter man smoked quietly while the taller one rested his chin on the rifle laid across his drawn-up knees. Hens stirred in their roost in a corner of the kitchen. There were voices from the house, the sound restrained. Utensils clinked.

Finally, Jonathan spoke. "Why did you stop me?"

The man with the rifle lifted his head with a grunt. "Be quiet, or you'll be punished."

Hours later, Jonathan must have dozed off because he woke with a start. Someone was coming into the kitchen from the main house. Jonathan raised his head, bleary-eyed, to find a man squatting in front of him. A flashlight glared in his face. He shut his eyes, lowered his head.

"Are you Jonathan Edward?" the man asked in Vietnamese. He had a red birthmark on his forehead—the matriarch's nephew, Phát.

"Yes."

"Who is your superior?"

"What?"

"Who is your superior?"

"I don't understand."

"Yes, you do. Who is your superior?"

"Stop!"

A sharp pain in his shoulder blade cut off his breath. The rifle butt caught him by surprise. He inhaled sharply. Phát sat on his haunches with an unlit cigarette between his fingers.

"You speak three languages; your father is a colonel in the U.S. Army. Yes, or no?"

"Yes, but..."

"Just yes or no."

"Yes."

"What is his name? What is your mother's name?"

"Why? Why are you asking me?"

"What is his name? What is your mother's name?"

"Unless you tell me what you stopped me for..."

"Answer my questions."

"No."

The blow to his other shoulder snapped his head forward. A match flared. Phát touched the match to the tip of his cigarette. "You will cooperate, or you will be in trouble." Phát held the cigarette to his own cheek.

"This is a mistake . . ."

"You tell us your parents' names, and we'll tell you if it is a mistake."

Jonathan thought for a moment. The man waited. When Jonathan said the names, Phát scribbled with a pencil on a pocket-sized notepad and looked up.

"What is your home address?"

Jonathan contemplated the question and decided to answer.

"What were you doing in the war zone near Quảng Trị?" Phát drew on the cigarette.

Jonathan listened. Phát repeated his question.

"In fact, I escorted a friend there."

"What is your business there?"

"I didn't go there on business."

"You were there at a very opportune time." Phát dragged on the cigarette and blew the smoke in Jonathan's face. "The morning our men in Phủ Ốc were bombed."

Jonathan shook his head in denial.

Phát spat, then spoke again. "You were spotted in the war zone while we occupied a town near Phủ Ốc. We took the town and we left with a moral victory, to send a message to the Americans and the puppet government that we can take any of their towns. Some of our men stopped at Phủ Ốc and were tracked down by the puppet government's fighter-bombers. They said you came up from the river after the planes bombed the village." Phát clasped his hands around his knees. "What is your role in the CIA?"

Jonathan was so flustered he couldn't find words in Vietnamese. The man repeated the question.

Jonathan shook his head again. "I work for the U.S. State Department. Yes, I was there in that village the day it was bombed, but like everybody else, I was passing through. We were stranded because there was no train going back to Huế."

"You have been seen in areas that no tourists enter. You only stayed one night in a hotel in Huế. The rest of the time you stayed at the Temple of Guanyin. We have tracked you. You better cooperate for your own good."

"I don't deny what you said, where I went, where I stayed, but I'm not CIA."

Phát told Jonathan he knew about the pacification program the United States hoped to carry out in South Vietnam. He said they would build an intelligence network to crack the Việt Cộng infrastructure, extracting information with interrogation—and liquidation. "We don't like agents and informants."

"Do you kill innocent people while you're looking for agents?"

"Some might die by mistake, but not in your case."

"Are you going to kill me?"

"If you write a confession, you will live."

"Confession of what?"

"That you are CIA sent here by the U.S. imperialist government to exploit the freedom-loving people of Vietnam for the greed of the capitalists. You will admit your wrongdoing and make a tape for us."

"A tape?"

"You will tell your family you are against the war. You will tell the American GIs, the Congress, your hometown newspapers and politicians, that it is wrong for the American government to intervene in the civil war here."

"I won't do that," Jonathan said. "You've arrested the wrong man. Besides, I don't oppose what we're doing in South Vietnam."

"You will do what we say."

"I won't."

Phát made a sudden gesture. Jonathan knew he stopped the man from hitting him again. Slowly Phát rose to his feet and looked down at Jonathan.

"When we come back, you will write the confession."

They left him with his hands tied behind his back to the wooden pole and his elbows trussed. He turned over in his mind what his captors had said to him, the information they had on him—and what he had disclosed to the abbot the other night. They must have questioned the abbot about him. Didn't the abbot warn him not to venture outside after dark? He recalled the interrogator who came to the temple during the memorial service for the matriarch. He remembered Minh Tánh huddling with the man. He heard in his head Minh Tánh asking him if he'd go to East Gia-Linh this day. He thought until his head ached. His shoulders hurt; the pain grew with both his arms bent back. He thought of his captors' demands. Would they kill him regardless of what he said?

His head lolled forward, and he closed his eyes and then opened them. A swath of moonlight brightened the entrance. Another light flickered and a figure in white appeared at the entrance, holding a kerosene lamp. Another smaller figure stood behind. A woman and a little girl came in and knelt in front of him. The woman set the lamp on the floor. Her face, framed by long black hair, went dark. He met her gaze, then the little girl's. Their eyes were black, gleaming like a doll's.

He said, "*Chào cô,*" to the woman, then shifted his gaze to the little girl. "*Chào em.*"

They peered at him. "Did they beat you?" the woman asked.

He nodded. She sighed. Some nights she had to cover her daughter's ears against the screams. The Việt Cọng warned her not to feed the prisoners but she paid them no heed.

"Thirsty," he said.

She brought a glass and tilted his chin up to help him drink. The milk was warm and sweet. He couldn't recall the last time he drank condensed milk.

"Hungry?"

"Yes," he said.

The little girl got a palm-leaf fan and fanned him while her mother peeled a banana. She fed him one bite at a time. He chewed hurriedly. Between bites he asked if any of the men lived in the house.

The woman shook her head, "*Mấy ôn mượn nhà tui,*" she said. She said they borrowed several houses like hers on the hill, where they kept people in custody. She said they would punish the household if the captives got away. She clutched the banana peel in her hand and asked, "*Nhà anh ở mô?*"

He told her where he came from. Then he said his arrest was a mistake.

She shook her head and said, "*Tội quá.*"

Mercy. He felt blessed by her tone.

—o—

On the second day without seeing Jonathan, her heart ached. Phượng told her father she'd contact the abbot about Jonathan. She asked the boy who ran errands for her father to go to Upper Đinh-Xuân and ask the abbot. Melancholy, she left the house in midmorning for Well Market. On her way out she saw a black spider in the kitchen near the hearth, spinning down from the bamboo crossbeam. She touched it and it stopped descending and balled up, feigning death.

The boy returned in the afternoon with no firm news about Jonathan. According to the abbot, his American guest was last seen two days earlier in the afternoon. Nobody knew where he went.

"Auntie," the boy said to Phượng, handing her a piece of paper with a number written on it, "the abbot wants you to go to the post office and call him from there as soon as possible."

After asking Thanh to watch the shop for her, Phượng took a bus to the post office. The monk who answered the phone said the abbot was in a canon class, so she gave him the pay phone number and waited. Where could Jonathan have gone after he left her house late that afternoon? Did he have other business to tend to somewhere else? She hoped so. But he told her father he'd be back the next day with the money. Though she was grateful for his help, she was so gnawed with anxiety she could take no comfort. His sudden disappearance had her groping for clues.

Outside, a cross-village bus stopped to unload passengers and then pulled out, coughing black smoke down the blacktop road skirting the paddies. She felt her blouse pockets, fastened now with safety pins—she had heard of pickpockets on crowded buses. A thick roll of bills bulged in each pocket. Someone came in and used the pay phone. Nervous, she looked at the man and shifted her weight on the bench.

The phone rang just as the man hung up. He lifted it, talked, and then looked around.

"It's for me," Phượng said.

The abbot's voice came. "How's your father doing, Phượng?"

"So far, he's bearing up, sir. Did you know he has colon cancer? Yes. Bleeding some. Well, it's a long way between home and the hospital. I'm taking him back tomorrow morning for the first treatment."

She listened, looking at a man lugging in a bale of newspaper. The abbot said Jonathan's suitcase was still at the temple and asked her what time he left her house.

"After dark, sir. He said he'd be back in the morning with the money from Huế. Oh, he told you about helping my father? I'll try to be patient, sir. Yes, please do that. My father and I are grateful to you, sir. If you hear anything after the police search, please send someone over to our house. Yes, thank you, sir."

She felt weak when she walked outside to wait for the bus. The sun was too bright, she had forgotten her hat.

That afternoon Xinh visited her stall. Phượng felt sick in her stomach when she saw her walk in. The two of them stood at the stove in a cloud of steam.

Phượng narrowed her eyes at the woman. "Is it about the proposition?"

"Same proposition, much more money," Xinh deadpanned. "There won't be another chance if this passes. You can say no now and save me time."

Phượng gulped and then wet her lips. *Will there be another chance?* She looked around nervously. "I'll think about it."

Afterward the sun seemed stationary, its glare steady on the front of the shop. The day stood still, and it was busy. The south wind blew in dust, and she had to let the rush mat down over the entrance to keep it out. She took a chunk of beef from the icebox and started slicing. Pink slices, lean, veined white with tendons. Then after marinating them in crushed pineapple, she checked her supply of liquid hot pepper. Each table had a jar of red pepper paste and her customers relished it so much she had to refill the jars at least once a day. Just see a red pepper jar in a noodle shop, they said, and you know how good the cook is.

She chose fresh hot peppers one by one, picking those with fewer seeds and cooked them in oil over a low fire. Too much garlic, it'd taste dry. Too much sugar, it'd thicken like molasses. Too much fish sauce, it'd taste like salt. Constantly add oil over a low fire until the mixture glows fiery red. By the time she took the copper pot off the fire, a tart, rich aroma rose through the thin smoke. By that very first pungent smell, she knew it was done just right.

Midafternoon Phượng stopped and ate a bowl of beef noodle. Thanh joined her. They each ate a small bowl of soybean curd sprinkled with lemon and sweetened with caramel. Thanh asked if she was expecting someone, but Phượng said no, though she kept glancing toward the curtained entrance. Maybe by a miracle he'd walk in. Later she sliced more beef and watched customers come in. She twitched each time the rush mat was pushed aside. She cut her finger and dripped blood onto the beef. She stuck the end of her finger in a lemon wedge. When the blood stopped, she put on a cotton ball and tied it down. It smarted when she crooked her finger and she told herself not to hurry. Still, she started dropping things as the day waned and the sunlight now darkened to bronze on the rush mat.

She closed the shop early and asked Thanh to tell her father she had to run an errand and would be home later than usual. When she stepped off the bus, dusk was falling. All the way through the alley her stomach knotted, and her throat tightened. *Turn back and head home. Yes. No. Turn back! Wait for Jonathan.* Her heart didn't believe it. *There won't be another chance.*

The light in Xinh's house was bright as the door swung open, as if she were waiting. Phượng said nothing and walked right in. The woman smiled.

"I have another offer that doubles the chief's," Xinh said before Phượng sat down.

Phượng's stared at her. Xinh leaned forward. "You want the deal or not?"

Phượng couldn't speak. She drew a sharp breath. The woman's face suddenly looked offensive up close.

"I don't think the chief will match the offer if you take it. I'll tell him you backed out, and that's it."

Phượng eyed her feet for a moment. "I don't want the deal."

Xinh leaned over from her chair and patted Phượng's cheek. "You don't? It's a tremendous amount of money."

"Not when you take a thirty percent cut."

"You forget that this kind of money don't fall into your lap easily."

"Not at thirty percent." *Make it impossible for her.*

"Look. I'm the one who put the deal together for you . . ."

"For me? You should take ten percent."

"No way."

"Well then." Phượng rose, feeling relieved and yet foul. *Dirty business.* Xinh scratched her arm. "I'll take twenty-five percent. That's that."

"Fifteen."

"Twenty." Xinh pursed her lips and said, "You know something? You wouldn't want all that money in cash, would you? Very unwise to keep it in cash. The *đồng* has fluctuated a great deal. You know how inflation goes, Phượng. You want it in gold? I won't charge you the fee for the exchange rate if I take twenty."

Phượng felt dirty but kept her composure. She turned to leave, then on second thought chose to stay. *My father needs it. There is no other way.* "Seventeen percent," she said. "Cash."

A smirk came on Xinh's face as she rose from her chair. Phượng looked at her coldly. *Say no deal and let me go home.* Xinh opened the armoire and took out a metal chest.

"Your share," Xinh said, "is 166,000 *đồng*. Sign the agreement, and then I'll pay you. The client wants to be anonymous."

"When is it going to happen?"

"Evening after tomorrow. On a houseboat in Gia-Linh East. I'll take you there."

The floating hotel belonged to a man who owned a large fleet of sampans.

The alley was dark. She thought of Jonathan and wept.

—o—

Between sleep and wake he heard the hens clucking in the dark corner and sometimes a whoosh out back when areca nuts fell. For three nights in a row the captors moved him from one house to another and then back to the first. During the day he was blindfolded, tied to a bedpost, and someone from the house spoon-fed him. The rice was cold, soaked in a darkly salty sauce that smelled bad. When he wouldn't eat the rice, they fed him bananas. The water he drank tasted clean like rainwater.

He was tied to the support pole in the center of the kitchen and his arms ached. Days and nights ran together. Fitful sleep like catnaps. His mind snapped open and shut, leaving little time for feeling. Yet in the waking moments, he ached for her. With the longing came disconnection and invisibility. No one knew where he was. If they captured him because he would represent the United States in the name of pacification, he could justify the sacrifice. But he was still a civilian and he felt like a marked man. No, the war wasn't fought out of sight as he had naively thought. Not with troops, tanks, airplanes, and artillery. The war was treacherous and spreading fast like cancer, waged by men like Phát in villages, in cities, while people slept.

When he felt movement on the earthen floor, he knew they were back, three of them and two more they pushed in from behind. They ordered them to sit down next to him. The two new men reeked. He could tell they were Vietnamese, clad in dark-colored short-sleeved shirts and trousers. Phát knelt on one knee in front of Jonathan, the other two stood guard with their guns trained on the new arrivals. Phát took a cigarette pack from his shirt and crushed it in his hand when he saw it was empty. "Do you confess?"

"No," Jonathan said.

Phát got to his feet. "Let's go."

The armed men tied their new captives to the pole, back-to-back. Before they untied Jonathan and took him out, the woman with the kerosene lamp came in and sat on a cane-bottomed chair in a corner. They took him outside and Phát ordered him to remove his shoes and socks. They walked back single file the way they came in, down the hillside strewn with boulders and scree, across the clearing of red earth covered with scrubs and withered grass, past the lagoon like a frosted mirror bearing sleeping cranes. Jonathan hobbled along, blocking out the pain. When the moon was over the cane field, they stopped on the roadside. The rustle of cane leaves sounded like the susurrus of another world where peace awaited. Phát asked for a cigarette and took one from the taller man. A spurt of flame, a wave of the hand, a wisp of smoke. Then his metallic voice.

"You will write a confession."

"I won't."

"Because of patriotism? Because you think it's right for your government to invade Vietnam?"

"Because I'm not CIA, and I'm not a serviceman. But I do support my government."

"We won't go through that again. You will write a confession."

"No."

"We will make you."

Jonathan set his jaw.

"Think about your family. You are only thinking about yourself. Do you love your family?"

Jonathan stared into the man's eyes. "Think about them," Phát said. "Think about every person you love and think about the lives we can save if the war stops. Do you have a lover, Jonathan?"

His own name sounded foreign on the man's tongue. Jonathan said nothing while his stomach churned.

"Do you have a lover?"

Something tender in Jonathan told him to say yes, to tell the man what he wanted to know. Yes, he had a lover. He had come to find out who her parents were. Yes, he had another lover who was his deceased lover's sister, for whom he would do anything. *Say yes, Jonathan. You might walk away a free man.*

But principle held him back.

Phát motioned the other two over. They tied his wrists. The shorter man held a bunch of pins between his teeth. The taller man held Jonathan's fingers out. The shorter man drove the first pin all the way into Jonathan's thumb. A cry tore from his throat. He did not cry again even when all the pins were driven in. The only sound was the heavy breathing of torturer and tortured.

His fingers curled up like a leper's, blood beaded on his fingertips and streaked onto his palms. His head hung forward, curls dangling on his forehead as if he were pleading with the earth's genie.

Phát raised his voice. "Will you write a confession?"

Jonathan clenched his teeth.

The shorter man pulled the pins out one by one, watching Jonathan quiver.

"Will you write a confession?"

Sweat dripped from his brow into his eyes.

The pin driven into the little finger extracted a moan but no more as the pins went back into the fingers. The third time the question was asked with no answer, all the pins were pulled out. He tottered to one side. Phát told his men to untie him and stand him up. He wobbled on his feet like a drunk, his hands half open as if he were afraid to close them. Phát lit another cigarette from one of his friends who was smoking.

"We'll be back tomorrow night. By then you will change your mind."

Jonathan blanked his mind. His body shook with pain. *There's no tomorrow. There's no miracle.* The morning he and Phượng rode the bicycle past the cane field was a foggy memory.

—o—

The Vietnamese prisoners were awake when the captors brought the American back in. The woman's eyes darted to assess the job they did on the barefoot prisoner and dropped her gaze when Jonathan looked at her. The men told her to leave the kerosene lamp behind. They tied the three captives together to the pole, elbows skewed back against their flanks. They took the lamp with them, leaving the prisoners in the dark.

Jonathan's head fell forward. He gritted his teeth as he closed his hands.

A voice speaking broken English came from behind him. "You American?"

"Yes, friend."

"Who are you?"

"Visitor."

"CIA?"

"Civilian."

"What's your name?"

"Jonathan."

"Bình."

"Trung," the other fellow said.

"Troong?" There was no answer. "Why are you here?" Jonathan spoke into his chest.

"South Vietnam army commandos," Bình said.

"How long have you been here?"

"Two nights."

"Anh đã khai?"

"You speak Vietnamese?" Bình said, laughing. "You are good. No CIA?"

"No."

"We never talk. Okay?" Bình hiccupped. "Our friends will die if we talk."

"Your commando friends?"

"Right."

"What happened?"

In his pidgin English the fellow told him after his commando squad split up in the forest behind the Việt Cọng lines, his group was ambushed. Two men died. The four who were captured were detained in two places. Their captors wanted to know where the rest of them were. He said no one talked, and that was why they were still being interrogated.

Jonathan felt light-headed. A foul smell hung in the air, not body odor. Bình told him that Trung, his lieutenant, had an abscess on his lower back from a grenade fragment. The wound hadn't stopped discharging pus and their captors said they'd give him penicillin if both of them talked. The lieutenant was snoring. He had a fever that wouldn't go away.

"How old are you, Bình?"

"Eighteen."

"And Troong?"

"Twenty-six."

Jonathan turned his head to look at the boy, and though they were shoulder to shoulder he could see the side of Bình's gaunt-looking face and his very black, wiry hair.

"They'll kill you, won't they?" he said to Bình.

"We're already dead, two of my best friends, so."

The boy switched to Vietnamese. He said that when they joined the squad, they drank their blood together and swore to live or die together. To betray a friend was worse than killing an innocent man. "What about you? What'd they want to know?"

Jonathan explained his situation.

The boy listened and said, "Never betray yourself like most people do." Then he laughed. "You should be CIA and fight the Việt Cọng."

Jonathan grinned. "You miss your family?"

"I don't have a family," the boy said.

"What about Trung?"

"He has a pregnant wife."

"Did you go to school?"

The boy said yes, high school, where he learned English.

"Where was your family?"

The boy told him he came from an affluent family. "My father practiced Eastern medicine. My mother left him for a French major when I was four, so Father hired a nurse to raise me while he worked. When I was sixteen, I screwed my nurse's daughter. We ran away. Then she dumped me. A year later my father died of cancer of the pancreas. The monk who conducted the funeral told me my father had blamed himself for all of my wrongdoing. He told the monk, 'He's my son. I didn't love him enough but he's still my son.' He left a fortune after he died and everyone thought I'd spend it all before long. I took all the money and gave it to places I knew about: a leper colony on the coast, a new school for the blind in a southern town, the nurse who raised me—but nothing for her daughter. I gave the rest to a Buddhist temple. I became a commando at seventeen."

Jonathan leaned back, his fingers aching all the way to his head. Bình said the body healed on its own. He said sometimes in the jungle he drank his own urine because there was no water for days. Then he stopped talking, sucking in his breath.

"Tired?" Jonathan said.

"No, hurt."

"You got a wound too?"

"No, hernia. Them bastards kicked me like a mule." Bình chuckled. "Something broke."

"Can you fix that?"

Bình laughed and hiccupped.

The smell came back, stronger. Jonathan could see Bình out the corner of his eye.

"Damn," Bình said, "He's hot like an oven."

"The woman can help. Let's call her."

"No, don't get her in trouble, friend. We deal with what we've got."

"Sure," Jonathan said. "Will he die?"

"Eventually," Bình said. "Just takes longer." Then he turned his head trying to get a good look at Jonathan. "How old are you?"

"Seven years older than you."

Bình hiccupped again. "You smoke?"

"No." Jonathan quipped. "Would you like a cigarette?"

"Light it for me. There. Whew! Ah. How many rings you want?"

"As many as you can."

Bình blew. "There, five, and one through them all. Pretty."

Jonathan closed his eyes, leaned back and touched the boy's head. They rested against each other. Bình coughed and asked, "Afraid to die?"

Bình's words went round and round in Jonathan's head like a carousel. "Sure."

"Won't betray yourself?"

"No."

"You believe in reincarnation, Jonathan?"

"Haven't given it much thought. One life is enough." He suppressed his emotion. Yet what of unfulfilled dreams? Should you cling to life if they weren't meant to come true? Should you betray your principles to save your life?

"They say after you die you just carry on," Bình said, "like you never died."

"You tell me, friend."

"So I better get as many cigarettes as I can before I join my friends." Bình paused, then said, "You know, Jonathan, they burn paper money for the dead, so they have cash to spend on the other side. Believe that?"

Jonathan sighed. "Anything else?"

"Have a girl?"

"Yeah."

"Back home?"

He thought of Françoise and Phượng at the same time. "Yeah."

"Pretty girl, blond like you?"

"No."

"Think of her before you die."

"Why?"

"Cause I don't have anyone to think of."

"Bình?"

"Hmm?"

"I'm tired."

"Sleep, Jonathan."

—o—

The boat was moored under the shade of a huge country fig. By the rattan dome's narrow entrance, curtained by a red floral cloth, a lantern burned.

Phượng sat straight-backed in the center of the bed, gazing at the flame flickering like an orange tongue. The plank bed of deep brown hardwood ran the length of the domed shelter, and at its head a pair of white satin plush pillows lay side by side. At the foot of the bed a white towel was folded into a square.

The burning incense in a glass holder smelled of tangerine. The owner said it kept out mosquitoes. He had left a red lacquered tray with cane handles on the bed. On it were a cellophane-wrapped box of a sweet delicacy, a small pot of tea, two teacups in red porcelain decorated with a gold butterfly hovering over a flower. Soon a sampan would arrive with the client.

The evening sky and water were blue, like a serape painted darker blue above and lighter below. From a fleet of sampans downriver came the clatter of cooking utensils and the shrill twang of choppy voices. The river smelled of damp wood and the odor came and went with the breeze as waves rocked the boat gently. Her head jerked at a night bird rousing in the foliage, then at a rap against the hull of the boat, perhaps a fish.

She stretched her stiff legs and looked at the sheen on her black satin pantaloons, then at her unpainted toenails. She had scrubbed her heels and put coconut oil on them. She smelled soap on her body. She touched her hair, braided into one long plait, and held the grapefruit flower in her fingers. The scent made her close her eyes. She pinned it back in her hair and drew a deep breath.

She watched the lantern because its leaf-shaped flame harnessed her mind. Her father had the first radiotherapy treatment that morning. Before she left, she asked her neighbor to check on him at dinnertime and learned that while they were in Huế, a local policeman came and asked for her. He wanted to know when Jonathan left her house and the approximate route he took going home. Hearing that, Bộ asked her to go to the police station in the morning.

She felt as if her mind had been sliced into strips, leaving a painfully throbbing nerve in each. They hurt most when she thought of Jonathan. If something happened to him, would her life come to a full stop? Already she felt desolate. Cold as a convent.

As she watched the lantern, Jonathan came into her vision, tiny as the quivering flame in suffused yellow. Then, she heard water splash and the sound of a sampan against the bow of the houseboat. The boat swayed. Footfalls. She raised her gaze from the lantern when the curtain parted. Someone stooped to enter. She stared at the monk. Surely, he stepped onto the wrong boat by mistake. Minh Tánh took off his felt cap and held it in his hands. In gray trousers and a shirt, he looked younger without the brown robe. What was he doing here? Could he have been the one to call for her?

In a cold sweat Phượng looked back at the lantern while he removed his shoes and slid onto the bed beside her. He folded his legs under him and sat facing her with the lacquered tray between them. He half looked at her, as if he was looking at something behind her. His crossed eyes were red, as if stung by dust.

Minh Tánh lifted the teapot, poured and set the pot back down. He raised one cup and handed it to her. "Miss."

Phượng took it by the rim with both hands and watched him sip. Minh Tánh smacked his lips, looking down into the cup. She looked at his dirty fingernails, then at the top of his shaved head, where the skin had a pale green luster. When did he set his eyes on her? When they first met, his gaze had lingered. But he was a monk. What were his intentions when he approached them in town? He wasn't a secret admirer but rather a predator, stalking her when she was most vulnerable. Her heart felt icy.

He turned his head toward the curtained entrance where the lantern burned.

"You can turn it out, if you wish," she said coldly.

"No," he said, "I don't want to turn it out. I was thinking it might burn out."

"You want to finish your tea first?"

Minh Tánh half nodded, then looked at her. "Have you got your fee, Miss?"

She nodded.

"That's good." He set the cup down. "I made sure the province chief disappeared, and I gave that woman a hefty sum of money on the side to lie to him."

She wanted to ask him why but decided that knowing would not make the night any less distasteful.

"How much did she pay you, Miss?"

His formality surprised her. She told him.

Minh Tánh rubbed his chin. "Good," he said, just as the light went out.

She heard her own sharp inhalation and held still. She waited for the moves that would seal her fate and saw him slide backward to the foot of the bed.

"I'll light the lantern, Miss."

Minh Tánh fumbled with the matchbox and finally lit the lantern. The warm glow washed over the curved dome and his face. Then he climbed back onto the bed and sat cross-legged. He looked at her long and steady, and she dropped her gaze. She feared the time had come.

"You're beautiful, Phượng."

His voice was soft. Revulsion filled her. Why did he want the light on? So he could see her? A cramp in her stomach made her suck in her breath.

"I'll be glad when your father gets well."

Why was he talking about her father? Did he think that would soften her toward him? Her father was the last person she wanted to think of just then.

"I only want to talk to you, Phượng."

She flicked a glance at him, and he looked back, expressionless.

"What do you mean you only want to talk to me?"

"I just wanted to see you. Then I will go."

"Go? Where? I don't understand."

"I came to make sure you got the money. And you did, so that's good."

"You paid to talk to me?"

"I could've made love to you. That's what I paid that woman for. But that was never going to happen."

"So what is going to happen?"

"You're a very respectable girl, Phượng. That's all."

"You paid all that money . . ."

"It was a lot of money. *That* was how much I wanted you, Phượng."

Shocked by his riddling talk, she wasn't sure what he'd eventually lead her to. His indirection left her uncertain, anxious. She studied him. His pimpled face was placid. He looked down at the tray, lifted the lid on the teapot to peer inside, and put the lid back down.

"If you think I'm so respectable," she said, her eyes fixed on him, "why did you expect me to go for this arrangement?"

"You did it for your father. I enjoyed the trip with you and your father. He's full of history, isn't he?"

Again, her father. What was going on?

"He's a hundred years old," Minh Tánh said. "He's seen so much of life and understands more than I can ever hope to. Our temple is one hundred and fifty years old. Something or someone very old fills me with awe."

"Tell me what is happening."

He opened the box of sweetmeat, his gaze lingering on the various confections. Finally, he extended the box to her. "You have one, then we'll talk some more."

Phượng picked a finger-sized candy of ginger-yellow and slowly unwrapped it while Minh Tánh chewed one, sucking his cheeks.

"You know, if you're a vegetarian, you always crave sweets." He sipped the tea. "I had a craving for sweets so bad once when I was a novice I stole the abbot's prize honey."

Phượng eased the candy into her mouth as he spoke.

"I was cleaning his room one day and saw a small glass jar. There was some dark liquid inside. It was next to a teacup that was the abbot's prize. An ancient cup, a hundred years old at least. The abbot warned me to be careful when I dusted the table." Minh Tánh went for another piece of candy. "I was toying with the jar when he returned. 'Put it down,' he said. 'What's in it, sir?' 'Poison, don't even smell it,' he said. After he left the room I opened the jar and sniffed. It was honey. I dipped my fingers into the jar and sucked them. Some kind of honey, I thought. Was so fragrant I had gooseflesh and didn't know how much honey I'd eaten from the jar when I heard the abbot talking with someone on the veranda. I was so jumpy I slid the jar across the table to hide it and knocked over his prize teacup. He came in, looked at the broken pieces on the floor and the half-empty jar. 'You have sinned,' he said, and I replied, 'I broke it when I cleaned the tea set.' He said, 'You also opened the jar I told you not to.' I said, 'I thought it was poison, so after I broke the teacup, I wanted to end my life.' He seemed surprised. 'End your life?' 'Yes sir,' I said, 'I've broken this cup, I knew you'd be upset, so I had no choice but to poison myself.'"

Phượng couldn't help smiling. Who was this monk? Minh Tánh sniffed a round candy brown as fudge and licked it.

"Where's your family?" she asked, the thickness in her throat dissipating.

"Have none." Minh Tánh wiped the corner of his mouth with the back of his hand. "The abbot said I came from a homeless woman. He said when she came to the temple she was about to die. I was a baby and she carried me with her. She begged the monks to take me."

"I didn't know that. Some monks come from wealthy families. I thought you did too."

Minh Tánh chuckled. "I wasn't much to begin with and never will be. All that money I gave for you came from the temple."

Phượng stared at him, and he nodded, swallowing wetly. "I stole the Diamond Sutra and sold it to a French antique shop in Huế."

"A sutra?"

"Not any sutra. A historic one."

"You stole it? Why?"

"For you. I wanted to be with you. And when I heard there was a chance. . . ."

He slid closer to her. "Phượng, I've been coming to this riverboat since I reached puberty, and that was many moons ago. I know the owner well—and that woman Xinh who works with him. When she told me about your arrangement, I *was* shocked. Then I was hurt. How could you do that to yourself for money? I wanted you, Phượng. That was my romantic fantasy. It wasn't until I met you again in Huế that I learned you needed money not for yourself but for your father. When I met you in town, I had already sold the sutra, or the provincial chief would have been here tonight. Sinful me.

But after we parted that day, I had a change of heart. I knew I could get you the money, but I couldn't win you that way. I wanted to save you, not make your life more difficult."

The thickness returned to her throat, despite his change of heart. When she was a little girl, neighbors gave her good-luck money in little red paper pouches on New Year's Day, and she kept them in her blouse pockets until her father asked her to give it all to him so he could save the money for her. She remembered the thickness in her throat then when she had to part with the money. She felt now as if the sutra had been stolen from *her*. Was this worse than prostitution? How many people would be hurt by the theft?

"How could you do such things to the temple?" she blurted.

"I couldn't think of any other way to get the money. I didn't want you with that man. I thought I was doing the best thing. I can't undo it, Phượng, and even if I could, I wouldn't. You need that money. You were willing to give yourself for it."

She couldn't undo it either. And even if she could, she didn't know how. She would ask the Buddha for forgiveness. She dropped her head and cried silently.

When she stopped, he spoke. "Forget that I told you about the sutra and take the money. I did it. I'm accountable. Take care of your father."

Phượng dabbed at her nose. Minh Tánh's hand held out the white grape-fruit blossom. She took it and pinned it back at the side of her head.

"Something else I want to ask you, Phượng."

"What now?"

"Have you heard from Jonathan?"

Hearing his name made her shudder. "I haven't heard from him." She shook her head. "The abbot contacted the local authorities yesterday. Heaven knows what happened to him. I'm very worried. Why are you asking about him?"

"He loves you, doesn't he, Phượng?"

She looked at Minh Tánh, who returned her gaze unblinking. "Yes."

"What about you?"

Her lips barely twitched a yes.

"You know, Phượng, he might be in danger."

"Danger?"

"I told those guys from the Front that he was CIA."

"You told the local Việt Cọng *that?* Why would you do that?"

"They came to the temple asking questions."

"But you knew why he was here. He's not CIA."

"I thought I didn't like him, you know. But the fact is, I was jealous of him. I don't want to see you hurt and that's why I'm telling you. Maybe it's not too late. I'll try to help him."

"How? Go tell the other side?"

"Something like that."

Would it be too late? *It can't be.* She had to see him again. Phượng sipped tea to keep calm. Minh Tánh was set to leave.

"Do this for me," she said. "Do not let him be hurt. You were misguided."

"I'll make it right, Phượng. I meant to help you. How will you get home?"

"I'll walk."

He cocked his head. "You go by the cane field?"

"Yes," she said, "I go by the cane field."

Minh Tánh worked his feet into his sandals and pulled the red curtain aside to look out into the night.

"I'll take you home," he said. "My bike is in the other boat."

The thought of her father waiting at home made her consider his offer. And she had to find a way to help Jonathan. Maybe her father would come up with a plan. The sooner she returned, the sooner she could get help. She pulled the cord once then twice, ready to leave with him. A bell clanked somewhere outside the entrance. Her father had asked her not to be on the road alone at night. Not by the cane field.

—o—

That evening the men came for him and the other prisoners after sunset.

With Phát was the shorter man who wielded the .45. Jonathan heard them talking outside the kitchen. Bình told him what happened. South Vietnamese intelligence was tracking the prisoners and the prisoners had been split up and taken to different hideouts. Before Jonathan understood, the men came into the kitchen, each carrying a spade over his shoulder. Quickly they moved the prisoners down the hill.

The full moon was rising, and the sky was a pale yellow of faded silk. They took a new route across the recently harvested rice paddies and through barren fields of red dirt where thatched houses sat among dirt graves, lonely humps with no headstones.

Though Bình said they were relocating the prisoners, the sight of his captors with spades worried Jonathan. Bound by the upper arms and elbows, the prisoners walked three abreast across the barren field like somnambulists in the pale moonlight. Jonathan finally had a good look at both Vietnamese prisoners. The lieutenant's face looked like a tribesman's from ancient times, aged and crumpled, while the boy's face was dark and handsome, his teeth very white when he grinned. Sounds of cranes came faintly over the horizon. Jonathan imagined them sleeping in the shallows of the lagoon, tucking their bills under their wings as if in shame.

When they emerged from the cane field, they stood momentarily on the blacktop road and then crossed to the graveled shoulder. The prisoners were told to sit down.

Phát squatted in front of them, smoking a cigarette, its ember dimming and glowing, and then he flicked the stub into the air and pushed on his knee to stand up. He walked up and down in his rubber sandals, hands folded behind his back, head nodding, until he stopped abruptly and turned on his heel.

"Tonight," he said, "you'll get clemency from the Front so your cooperation might pave the way to saving your life. Everything will depend on whether or not you abandon your principles, your self-proclaimed heroism, your self-centered illusion of some grand plan that benefits no one but you."

Phát gazed at the sky and then shrugged as if he disagreed with whomever he had tried to consult on high. A small light appeared on the road in the distance. They went off into the field and stood in the blackness, waiting. The field hummed with insects and rustling leaves. The light passed by on the road, the footfalls faded. Back on the gravel Phát knelt on one knee, spread a map on the ground and shone the flashlight on it. He took the map to the two Vietnamese prisoners.

"Look at the spot we circled in red."

They looked at the map.

"You know where that is?"

Both nodded.

"Our unit was attacked there last night," Phát said, "by your commando squad. Tell us how to make contact with them. Lead us to them."

The lieutenant gave Phát a quick look and said nothing. Bình looked at his captor and grinned.

"Smile for your friends?" Phát folded the map slowly.

The boy kept his grin.

"Have you got a thought on your mind?" Phát said.

"It's all mine. You won't hear it."

Jonathan took it in. He knew then their fates were sealed.

Phát looked at the lieutenant. "What about you?"

The lieutenant kept his gaze on the ground. Phát walked around and stood behind them. He knelt behind the boy and unsheathed a knife. Jonathan's eyes fixed on its glimmering blade and Phát's other hand resting on the boy's shoulder.

Phát spoke to the lieutenant. "Tell us where we can find your friends, or I'll cut his throat."

The lieutenant said nothing.

"One last time, tell us."

When the lieutenant acted as if he had gone deaf, Phát's hand went across the boy's throat. The boy gargled and his head pitched forward. The rope jerked, cutting into Jonathan's upper arms. The boy shook, his head lolled, and the front of his shirt went darkly wet. Jonathan didn't want to look but he couldn't stop staring and staring until a sick sensation filled his gut. He shut his eyes.

"Jonathan," Phát said.

He didn't answer.

"You will write the confession."

He heard the words, the meaning, the tone. But there was nothing to say.

"Will you write the confession?"

He waited for a hand on his shoulder but instead he heard the rope snap tautly, and suddenly his arms were free.

"Stand, both of you," Phát said.

They tottered to their feet. The other guard pointed to the spades on the roadside. The lieutenant walked over and picked up a spade, then Jonathan did the same. When they turned, Phát pulled a revolver from under his shirt.

"Into the field," he said.

His man stood over the boy's body and watched them disappear into the darkness.

—o—

The sampan took Minh Tánh and Phượng across the river to the jetty. As Minh Tánh pushed his bicycle up the gangplank, she looked back across the river toward the houseboat now a long, dark shape beneath the spreading country fig tree: the house of sin. As she looked at the monk's back, she felt a tinge of shame.

Minh Tánh mounted the bicycle and lit the lantern on the handlebar. "These back roads are too dark at night," he said. "You can't see a thing with just the bicycle's light."

She sat sideways on the passenger seat, both legs to one side. The wind felt cool on her back. His trousers rustled against his legs while they pumped rhythmically. Soon there was only the light of their lantern on the road.

On her way home past the cane field she usually heard the cross-village bus coming a way back from the bridge, because it had a noisy muffler. As they passed, they heard nothing but the murmur of leaves.

"What do you think happened to Jonathan?" Phượng said.

"I don't know, Phượng. I really don't know."

"Just tell me what you think."

"The local Việt Cọng must've gotten him."

"Can you help?"

"I'll try to get hold of those men. Yes, I will, Phượng."

"But you're not a Việt Cọng or a sympathizer, are you?"

"Me? A Việt Cọng? Does it matter to you now?" He chuckled.

"A renegade?"

"A nobody."

Was Jonathan still in the village? Somewhere in the night he must be thinking of her. Up in the sky the early rising full moon was bright, and the stars were out in the clear sky. Cranes flew in silhouettes across the sapphire-blue sky, pale bodies gliding silently as in a fairy tale.

"Pretty, huh?" Minh Tánh said.

The first time she saw them on her way home from night school, Long told her the birds roosted behind the cane field and slept in the lake. On nights of high tide, when he was out to lay crab traps in the streams, the water rose everywhere and the whole village seemed to float. The cranes waded off the shallows and roosted on the bank beneath the willows. From afar, row after row, they looked like Lilliputians cloaked in white.

A sudden gust of wind blew the lantern out. Minh Tánh tried to light it but the match died. Phượng sat down on the shoulder. "Put it down on the ground," she said. "I'll block the wind and you light it."

He knelt, struck a match and held it against the wick. She squatted with her back to the wind, her hands cupping the lantern. The flame wavered and then shone steadily.

"Let's go." Minh Tánh rose to his feet.

"Wait. Look at this."

Minh Tánh lowered the lantern over a dark red pool running off the edge of the road onto the ocher-colored dirt.

Her heart suddenly went gray.

He lowered his voice. "Get up! Don't look back."

"No!" She stayed on the ground, staring into the dark cane field. Then she shouted, "Jonathan!" and heard the wind blow her voice away.

Then on the wind came the sound of the bus's muffler. They both looked back and saw headlights through the gaps in the cane. Minh Tánh raised the lantern and the DeSoto bus sputtered to a stop.

Phượng went to the driver's side and looked up while Minh Tánh held the lantern in front of her. The driver was a man in his sixties, wearing an olive army jacket and a beret.

"Won't you come on up, Miss?"

"*Bác*," Phượng said, "can you help? Someone might be hurt in the cane field."

—o—

The lieutenant stumbled among the cane stalks and regained his foot-ing, his body slumped. Phát's shrill voice, "Move on!" The flashlight beam fell on a small trampled grass clearing. Phát's voice came from behind. "Right there! Dig a hole for your hero. You have until then to confess. Or the next hole will be for one of you."

After Phát cut off the light the prisoners drove their spades into the ground, digging in the dark. They had the same thought, as the grave wid-ened—the boy deserved a decent grave. They dug hard, shoveling dirt up and out. Jonathan's hands ached sharply, and he stopped. Panting, he saw a light far up the road. Phát called out to his friend to pull the body off the shoulder. The light drew near, bobbing rhythmically. Jonathan could tell it was a lantern. As he looked, a longing to live filled him.

The lieutenant coughed.

Phát hissed, "Silent!"

Suddenly the lieutenant slumped to the ground. Jonathan knelt over him and put his hand on the man's chest, feeling for the heartbeat, then the side of the man's neck: a faint pulse. He groped in the darkness for the man's face, which felt hot like a baked brick. His stomach churned with a sense of something lost forever.

"What is it?" Phát whispered from above him.

"He's lost consciousness," Jonathan answered.

"Bring him up," Phát said, gritting his teeth. "The bastard is faking."

A long, rueful rush of wind shook the leaves. On the road the light disap-peared. Jonathan stood the lieutenant up and flung him over his shoulder like a sack of rice—he didn't weigh much. He brought him out of the grave and put him down gently on his back on the ground. He caught a glimpse of the lantern again through the cane. The light was stationary for a while and then moved away.

Standing over him Phát looked down, shining the light on the lieuten-ant's face for some sign of life. Not finding any he kicked the man in the head. The heavy thud made Jonathan's stomach turn. Phát dropped to his knees and played the light on the lieutenant's face. Jonathan stared while Phát pried the lieutenant's eyelids open in the light. Phát cursed just as the blade of Jonathan's spade hit him on the side of the head. He fell backward, swinging his arms wildly.

Jonathan crouched on his hands in the darkness, breathing hard. A heavy wind rolled across the cane field carrying with it a voice: *Jon-a-than!* O dear God! He couldn't see her, but he knew she had come for him. His hands, his feet burned. *Run!* He heard her coming through the cane, calling his name. His heart beat wildly. He heard an engine sputter. Her voice called out again. The road whitened in the headlights.

From where he crouched the lighted world seemed part of a dream. He was staring ahead when a shadow materialized in front of him. The figure stood still. Jonathan flattened himself on the ground. The smell of the earth, old and dry, filled his nose. The shadow moved, tripped, then crawled across the ground, feeling with its hands where Phát lay. Jonathan held his breath as the engine rumbled up the road.

A click and a flashlight shone a lighted circle on the ground, skipped and danced around on the grass. When it hit Jonathan's face, he charged out from his crouch. He knocked the man backward and ran, stumbling. Figures moving on the road, footsteps rushing behind him. He crashed into the cane and ran, hands out front like a blind man. A shot cracked like a whip, then shouts beyond and another shot.

"Phượng!"

He shouted and ran toward the lighted world, toward the silhouettes of people crouched on the shoulder. Someone raised a lantern. He saw the figure that held it.

"Phượng!"

He called her name just as he heard the shot that lifted him off the ground. His back didn't belong to him anymore.

He fell. The lights glared beyond. He got up, fell, and got up again. He saw lights wildly searching the darkness and heard voices descending on him.

She cradled him, weeping. He woke as if to a whitewashed memory and in that moment he knew all that he had lived through. He saw her eyes and her face as if he had never left her, as if nothing had happened or changed, like the smell of the earth.

"Jonathan! Speak to me, Jonathan!"

She turned him on his side so her warmth would keep him awake.

"Hold on, Jonathan. Just hold on."

Red hot pain dimpled his back, so hot his breath seemed to flame. He felt her hands touching his back and saw they were red when she covered her mouth.

"Wrap him. Stop the bleeding," someone said, hovering over him.

A monk. He knew the face, but the name didn't come. Hands touching him. His body no longer belonged to him. He felt an energy shrouding him and a deafening commotion without sound. He saw a young girl who smiled as she walked hand-in-hand with him through a valley yellow and red with autumn. He saw cranes sleeping in the lagoon at low tide, and among their mirrored white bodies he saw himself cloaked in white.

She pressed her cheek against his. "Jonathan."

He closed his eyes. The scent of the earth came to him. He saw her eyes very close to his, then his head fell against her chest. The dimple of pain went away.

twenty-eight

Miss Phượng wasn't home when I came by at noon. I didn't see Cam either. I went back to the lodging house, picked up my notebook and made my way down the hill then through the pumpkin patch. Late in August the deep yellow of pumpkins bore a shade of fiery red, the setting-sun red, their tendrils crawling freely between the raised earthen beds, the leaves now tattered having aged with a full season, and among them thin-stemmed flowers in golden yellow completely unfurled at high noon. By dusk, upon coming back, I saw the flowers, folded in, had died.

There were black-and-white-striped skinks sunning on the ledges of rock, dry now at low tide, their long bright-blue tails curled into a U. They were dazed in the sun as my shadow suddenly fell upon them. White-daubed tips of the rocks shimmered in the heat, where below, sheltered by rock cliffs, a pool of seawater shuddered when a matchstick-thin fish darted across. The water in rock-harbored hollows was seaweed green, but it was not always green. I saw one hollow curtained heavily with rock-wall sea-weed, where water was red as blood. The helping girl once told me the pool water took on the colors of tiny plants or living things that inhabit it.

The day was humid. As I made my way up the dune, toward the spread-ing shade cast by the filaos over the slope, a flock of gray-green fruit doves shot up in the air, darkening a corner of the sky. Along the shore sand dunes shone with a white glare that hurt my eyes. Swallows darted in and out of distant limestone cliffs and higher, a peregrine falcon circled, looking for fruit doves.

I sat down under a filao and read April's letter. I forgot how many times I'd read her letter, but I read it again slowly so it wouldn't end, lying on my back, the slivers of sun in my eyes. I covered them with her handwritten let-ter. The sea-salt odor was thick in the air, waves boomed against tidal rocks, swishing as they ebbed. She asked in the letter how people made perfume from wild ginger, for I had told her a local—I didn't want to say a girl, the helping girl—had taken me out to hunt wild ginger, the two of us going deep into the marsh behind the dune, where the soil was damp, the ground cool, searching under shade trees where grass didn't grow until we came upon a patch of heart-shaped leaves like a groundcover. Crouching, we could make out little maroon jug-shaped flowers that seemed to bloom out of the earth. They bore a scent like gingerroot. While digging up the roots, the girl told me that one can made perfume from the oil in the roots. I knew that wasn't her intention, but she didn't tell me. Later back in the lodging I came upon a newspaper article written about wild ginger, which said its root was used for many things, one of which was for irregular menstruation.

In the lull between the booming surf, I could hear the sound of filao cones falling, their dry scratching against the needle-carpeted ground like a faint rustle of a rodent's feet. I slept and woke to see the sun gone from my eyes. It was past noon, and the wind was blowing misty spray off the waves. Walking back, I felt something missing. The dry sand was painfully white, and if you walk on it at sunset, depending then on the intensity of the sun, you will see a glint of gold or purple in its grains. The wind blew hard, the dune crests smoked.

Then I remembered that I hadn't written my thoughts down in my note-book, a habit I had for keeping track of things. I knew I had to go back to her house.

There was no one at the house. The next day I went back and found Miss Phượng sitting at the table, sipping morning tea. When I asked, I received a vacant look in her eyes, her face placid. The helping girl said, "*Chú*, Auntie won't remember a thing."

"What thing?" I said.

"I went with Auntie to the hospital yesterday. They kept her there until late."

"Why did you go there with her?"

"Auntie wandered out on the road the night before. Someone found her by the marsh and took her back."

I felt like sitting down. Instead, I looked at the large lacquered painting of the Imperial Throne Room on the wall. Then I went to the door, looking out past the fenced-in garden, where sand drift had strangled vegetation and most of them, save for the tops of those still fighting, had given up the ghost.

"What did the doctor say?" I asked without turning my head.

"He said she has amnesia. Hospital wouldn't be able to help."

"He's right. I don't think hospitals can help her either."

"Said they have a place in Huế where they look after people like Auntie."

"Yeah." I turned around and walked to the table. She didn't look at me but at a space behind me where the girl was standing in the shadowed nook slicing a lemon. It would be a hot day. The girl always made a fresh jug of lemonade whenever she came in the morning.

"I wish Auntie could be taken care of in her home," I said. "I wish she wouldn't have to be confined to another place. And I won't be able to help her—I'm leaving soon."

"When, chú?"

"In a couple days."

There was a silence. I glanced at Miss Phượng as she set her cup down and reached for the teapot. Her cup was still full. "Auntie," I said, putting my hand over hers. She withdrew her hand and rested it on the table. A sudden cry from the girl. I looked over. She was dropping the knife and clutching her hand.

"You cut yourself?" I asked.

She balled her hand. Blood was dripping. I grabbed an already squeezed lemon wedge and packed it around her cut finger. After a while I wrapped the cut with gauze.

She bit her lips, hard. I looked back at Miss Phượng. She was looking toward the door. "I wonder what I can do today," she said to no one.

I looked at the girl. She lifted her face but kept her gaze at something over my shoulder.

"Let's do something with Auntie," I said.

She nodded and crooked her cut finger.

"What d'you want to do?" I asked her.

"I don't know, chú. It's your idea."

I pursed my lips. "We can make something. Anything. We haven't done anything together and I'll be gone soon. Well."

"I have something at home." Suddenly she stopped with a shrug.

"What?"

"No." She shook her head emphatically.

There was a pile of old newspapers in a corner and on top of them were stacked wicker baskets and in them were balls of yarn. I saw pieces of cardboard set on their ends against the wall. "Okay," I said, "we can make something with those pieces of cardboard."

"Like what, chú?"

I was thinking of an origami bird and before I told her, she blurted out, "Ah, a treasure box."

"Treasure box?"

"Mom had a wooden box. She kept her jewelry in it."

I nodded, smiling. "Okay, that makes sense. We'll make a treasure box out of cardboard, and we'll decorate it. Auntie can watch. Okay?"

"I want to see how you do it, chú."

I told Miss Phượng what we were going to make. She listened, her gaze empty. Then she smiled and said, "Treasure? For whom?"

"She wants one." I leaned my head toward the helping girl. "Auntie, would you like to see how we do this—together?"

She nodded. "I want to get out of the house too."

I glanced quickly at the girl. She said nothing.

"I don't have glue," I said to her. "Do we have any glue?"

The girl shook her head.

I thought of going into town as I looked out the door toward the filao stand along the fence. "We can make glue," I said. "Get two cups and I'll show you out front."

She took Miss Phượng by the hand, and we went out in the bright sunlight. She said excitedly, "How do you make glue, chú?"

"You will see."

"Are you going to do some trick?"

"Purely scientific."

At a filao tree, its trunk straight and hard in dark red brown, scaled with light gray-brown, smooth furrowed bark, I stopped and pulled out my pocketknife. They watched as I cut a horizontal curved slit and then notched a deep V above it. I took a cup from the girl and fit the cup's lip into the slit as the sap began to seep down the notch. Miss Phượng's eyes were fixed on the cup, her hands clasped on her abdomen. I let the girl hold one cup and took the other cup. I cut through the bark. A red squirrel darted along the ground, holding a filao cone in its mouth.

Miss Phượng pointed at the squirrel. "What's he doing with the cone?"

"Auntie, he'll store it somewhere and eat it in the rainy season."

"Where?"

"In some hollow tree stump. Or a log. He'll pile the cones around it and cover them with leaves."

Two more squirrels, one chasing the other, streaked down the trunk of a filao. They stopped on a cone-laden bough flecked with red awl-shaped flowers. By then the amber sap had just covered the bottoms of the cups. I turned to them. "Smell it," I said, raising the cup to Miss Phượng's nose.

She sniffed it.

"We're going to heat it," I told her.

We brought the cups inside, poured the resin into a pan and heated it. The sharp odor from bubbling resin made Miss Phượng sneeze. While the resin was cooling, the girl and I sat down on the kitchen floor and Miss Phượng sat on a chair, her elbows on her knees, her hands cupping her chin, watching us. I asked the girl how big she wanted the box to be. She thought for a moment, then reached out for the pen in my shirt pocket. Her lips crimped; she began sketching on the cardboard. I watched, surprised at her accurate strokes, clean and straight without a ruler. Miss Phượng pulled her chair up until her knee brushed my shoulder. After a while the girl finished sketching and capped the pen.

"You draw like a draftswoman," I said.

"I can see things, *chú*."

I took out my pocketknife and cut the cardboard along the outline. I smoothed the rough edges with my hands. "Glue time," I said.

The girl jumped up and brought the pan from the stove.

I glanced up at Miss Phượng. She still looked down at the cutout. "What're you making?"

"Auntie," I repeated, "a treasure box."

She sat down beside me, watching me glue the flaps one at a time, giving it time for the glue to dry. The girl helped. My forehead bumped hers. She laughed a rare laugh and said the resin aroma seemed to come from my hair.

"Do we have anything like gold paint or glitter?" I asked the girl.

She went into the back room where rice grains were stored along with spare furniture and household supplies. She came back with a paper bag from which she took out a small can. I opened it. Gold paint.

"What?" I said, shaking my head.

"I did some drawings," the girl said. "Auntie said they'd look nicer with gold paint."

She shook the bag, rattling things inside it. "Here the beads, *chú*."

I started brushing the box with gold paint while she dabbed the corners with glue then fastened the beads in a geometric pattern she wanted. We worked on it until the sun was high.

When I rose to my feet, holding the treasure box in my hands, Miss Phượng gazed up at me. The girl cleaned things up. I placed the box in Miss Phượng's hands. A smile came on her face. Watching her I felt as if I had been here before and now I was just reliving it.

The house was quiet. For a long time after we put away the treasure box, the resin glue still smelled of filao.

—o—

After dinner the girl brought Miss Phượng tea and served me a cup of coffee. Evening came like a stranger cloaked in black outside the window. Fireflies around a row of potted geraniums on the ledge winked like specters.

"*Voulez-vous de la crème avec votre café?*" Miss Phượng said to me.

I stared at her. Then I said in Vietnamese, "I take it black, thank you, Auntie."

I sipped coffee. *What would become of her?*

"*Chú.*" I heard the girl as I was gazing at the blinking fireflies. She asked if I wanted a fresh cup. I shook my head.

After the girl cleaned up and said good-night, I saw that Miss Phượng went to bed and then I went into the guest room. I told the girl someone must be with Auntie all the time and asked her to stay the night, every night, after I left, with Auntie. The girl said she would try after asking her daddy.

I turned on the table lamp and sat down on the chair. On the wall above the table was a Christmas card the girl drew. Yellowed along the edges, the card showed two snow figures wearing black top hats and holding hands at the foot of a hill, one taller than the other. Green pines dotted with white flakes covered the hillside. Children in bright-colored scarves and mittens sledded down the hill. She shaded the background pale blue. I looked with much curiosity. Either she copied the scene from a book or imagined it wholly of a snow country she had never seen nor been to. The scene framed the greeting:

Dear Auntie

You are a great aunt.

Merry Christmas!

Other than the card, the walls were bare. The table too was bare except for a rectangular tin box in one corner. It could have been a box of chocolates stripped of its wrapping. I opened it. Inside were stamps of different shapes and sizes arranged neatly in layers. Some stamps had come a long way and were all there, collected, safe. I looked up at the Christmas card, at her handwriting, neat and clean.

The bed was cold when I slipped in; the pillowcase smelled fresh.

Now the wind blew the filao cones off the trees and the cones fell rolling down the roof. I listened to the wind and closed my eyes, trying not to think. The girl too had slept in this bed. *What did you dream in this bed?*

A while later the wind stopped. I got up, went to the window and sat looking out between the parted curtains. The neighborhood dirt path was dark. I lit a cigarette. A dry bark came. Beyond the window in the garden stood a long-bodied, bushy-tailed creature. No dog had that slender body or pointed muzzle. A fox. As I watched the fox, it dawned on me that it must have seen the cigarette light. Maybe animals also gravitated to light. The fox too, a solitary hunter.

I closed my eyes, holding Miss Phượng's face in them.

twenty-nine

"Auntie, look here."

I gave her a grass ball I had picked up from a hollow in the sand. She weighed it in her hand, a tennis ball made of sticks and grass and seaweed. "Who made this," she said. I shook my head, said, "I don't know where they came from." The helping girl, tightening her headscarf because of the wind, chimed in. "I've seen them before, *chú.* Daddy said the waves roll them together and the wind blows them up the shore."

While the girl stood, I knelt beside Miss Phượng by a clump of grass. The wind blew sand up the beach and you could hear the sibilance of sand. She watched the grass blades bend and dip, drawing their tips in the sand. Arcs and circles. She said arcs foretold disquiet weather, and circles fair weather. She said she hadn't been to the beach in a long time. She asked what lay in a depression between the dunes. The girl said vines, sometimes cranberry sometimes bayberry. Densely clad, they carpeted the hollows in shining green.

We came upon tracks in the wet sand. The girl said, "That fox was out here early." I said, "It could be a dog's footprints." The girl shook her head, said, "I know they're his tracks." She said his footprints were clean-looking, each with a two-toed, two-clawed impression in front. She stood back and gazed at the tracks where the fox's footmarks suddenly became erratic, gapped. "What is it," I asked. She squinted her eyes, thought, and said, "He must've been scared by something, and I wonder what that might be."

On the wet sand there were shore birds' footprints. As the girl stood back with Miss Phượng watching the sun set, I followed the birds' tracks down the beach until I saw ahead of me a flock of sandpipers, tan-colored, white-breasted, running with the waves. Twilight now. They were still hunting for food, probing every spot of sand, every ripple mark for mollusks. When they saw me, they scooted up the beach in ghostly silhouettes. I followed their tracks until they were washed over by the waves. Alone on the sand stood a sandpiper in a pool of water. Sunset was red glimmers in the pool. The bird looked out over the sea and gave a lonely cry.

—o—

Before I left the girl said, "*Chú*, wait." She ran into the guest room where she would stay for the night with Auntie, and when she came back out, she gave me something wrapped in an old newspaper. I unwrapped it. A necklace made of bull nuts. Those glossy black bull nuts she picked from the pond. I felt them. Each of them looked like a goat-horned devil.

"For your girlfriend," she said, biting her fingernail.

"Thank you, Cam."

She shook her head as if in denial of hearing her name.

I wanted to hug the girl, but she stepped back and ran into the guest room. I called out to her. As she closed the door I could hear her voice, "I hate you, *chú*."

I hugged Miss Phượng. She held my hands in hers, said, "I don't pay much attention to things around me, and they pass me by. But they come back to me—at least today. Thanks to you."

I walked with her to the veranda. Then she stood back and watched me leave. When I turned to look back, the door was closed, and the windows were lit and a blurred shadow moved behind the curtains.

I stood until the light in the windows went out.

epilogue

Dawn.

Pale light fell on her father's eyes, so familiar he once said to her he could foresee the weather. She held open the mosquito net and let him ease himself out of the cot. He walked barefoot onto the mat and sat down. He struck a match. Before his eyes a sphere lit up. It was like something bright behind a translucent screen. He ran his palm over the coals, as he always did, and a faint heat told him the coals were catching flame.

He had slept well during the night, his body benign save an occasional abdominal pain from the cancer treatment that started a month earlier. Every Monday. Like clockwork. He told her it'd be a warm Monday when he dressed for the treatment trip to Huế.

As the coals popped, she sat down on the rush mat with a tray. The smell of hot gruel warmed the air.

"I bought some sweets for you yesterday, father."

He took a finger-long candy wrapped in cellophane paper and unwrapped it. It was a chewy caramel coated with sesame seeds.

She took the candy from his hand. "You go on and eat your gruel. I'm going to make tea, and then you can enjoy the candy."

"Get me the tribute tea, Phượng. I have a craving for it with caramel candy."

He picked up the thick, glazed bowl. A small slab of brown sugar floated in it. He stirred the gruel with the ceramic spoon, round and round, until the brown sugar shrank, marbling the white gruel. Then he lifted the spoon and sipped. At the credenza where he kept tea and the tea set, she stood holding the golden canister. Neither her father nor she had touched it since Jonathan had given it to him. She looked at it and cried.

More than a month now since they sent his body back home. Her father and she prayed for him often, as her father did for Canh. He prayed when she wasn't home. One night, awaking from sleep as she often did, she listened for his moans. Pain was habit. It roused you from sleep at a certain time in the night and your body remembered it like a timetable. All was quiet. Relieved, she lay awake.

She recalled the night Jonathan had spent with them. Sweet memory! The damnation of men! The Canhs, the Longs, the Jonathans. If a stretch of river was haunted, people built a shrine to pacify the spirits. Perhaps someday they should build a shrine by the cane field. By the constant praying, the lost souls of the dead would find eternal peace. Maybe Jonathan would come home again in his own ethereal world, in peace, with no hatred. But her father believed his soul wasn't trapped in the world of darkness, like Canh's. A good soul like Jonathan reminded her of Long. All goodness, all giving. He had given her her mother and her sister. He had lived out his dreams and walked away with the girl he loved—maybe not in this life but in the next, for love is timeless.

That night she cried and heard her father stir and knew he was awake hearing her. Her crying kept him awake a long time, but he didn't comfort her. Solitude had its own moments. Bitter and sweet. It would eventually die into itself. She was destroyed when the abbot sent over a thick envelope full of money, saying it came to the post office in Huế for Jonathan Edward. The dear Jonathan Edward who had come from a faraway land on a selfless quest. He had come out of nothing and left them with everything. He had freed her father of his guilt, the bane that had plagued him, and had given him a chance for a future.

After her father drank a third cup of tea, the fire was dim but warm. Outside on the doorstep she took his hand and stood beside him. Three steps went down, and he still let her walk him after all the years.

"Father," she said softly.

"What is it?"

"Our flame tree is covered in red."

Then the cicadas began to sing.

Acknowledgments

Portions of this novel have previously appeared in somewhat different form in the following magazines: *Eastlit, Outside in Literary & Travel Magazine, Little Curfew Press, Writing Tomorrow, Poydras Review,* and *THRICE Fiction.* A short story version of this novel also appears in "The Eunuch's Daughter & Stories" (Blackwater Press, 2024).

About the Author

Award-winning author Khanh Ha is a nine-time Pushcart nominee, finalist for The Ohio State University Fiction Collection Prize, Mary McCarthy Prize, Many Voices Project, Prairie Schooner Book Prize, The University of New Orleans Press Lab Prize, Prize Americana, and The Santa Fe Writers Project. He is the recipient of the Sand Hills Prize for Best Fiction, The Robert Watson Literary Prize in Fiction, The Orison Anthology Award for Fiction, The James Knudsen Prize for Fiction, The C&R Press Fiction Prize, The EastOver Fiction Prize, The Blackwater Press Fiction Prize, The Gival Press Novel Award, and The Red Hen Press Fiction Award.

Fiction/Nonfiction from Gival Press

by Myles Weber

The Pleasuring of Men by Clifford H. Browder

Riverton Noir by Perry Glasser

Redshift, Blueshift by Jordan Silversmith

Second Acts by Tim W. Brown

Secret Memories / Recuerdos secretos by Carlos Rubio

Sexy Liberal! Of Me I Sing by Stephanie Miller

Show Up, Look Good by Mark Wisniewski

Speaking Out: Families of LGBTQ+ Advance the Dialogue edited by Esther Schwartz-McKinzie

The Smoke Week: Sept. 11-21. 2001 by Ellis Avery

That Demon Life by Lowell Mick White

Theory and Praxis: Women's and Gender Studies at Community Colleges edited by Genevieve Carminati and Heather Rellihan

Tina Springs into Summer / Tina se lanza al verano by Teresa Bevin

The Tomb on the Periphery by John Domini

Twelve Rivers of the Body by Elizabeth Oness

For a complete list of Gival Press titles, visit: *www.givalpress. com*

Books available from Ingram, Brodart, Follett, your favorite bookstore, on-line booksellers, or directly from Gival Press.

Gival Press, LLC
PO Box 3812
Arlington, VA 22203
givalpress@yahoo.com
703.351.007

Printed in the USA
CPSIA information can be obtained
at www.ICGtesting.com
JSHW021511061023
49448JS00006B/22